Brigandine

By Jack Shannon

Copyright © 2023 by Jack Shannon

United Kingdom

All rights reserved. This book or any portion thereof may not be reproduced or used in any manner whatsoever without the express written permission of the author except for the use of brief quotations in a book review.

For permission, contact jackxshannon@googlemail.com
https://twitter.com/Jack_Shannon

This book is a work of fiction. Any references to historical events, real people, or real places are used fictitiously. Other names, characters, places, and events are products of the author's imagination, and any resemblance to actual events or places or persons, living or dead, is entirely coincidental

Cover by Etheric Tales
Map illustration by Aaron Howdle
(http://www.aaronhowdle.com)

*To Dad,
For inspiring a love of Fantasty, and letting me watch Conan The Barbarian even though I was far too young for it.
So technically, this is all your fault.*

Prologue

If you see someone in full plate armour, chances are, they're a cunt.
 They might not be, but I've never met someone wearing full plate armour who wasn't.
 First of all, if they're wearing full plate, you know they're rich. And if they're rich, then you know they're a cunt. Don't get me wrong, I've known a lot of poor people who were cunts as well, but you don't get to be rich, and stay rich long enough to buy armour like that, and not be a cunt.
 Have you ever seen a set of full plate? Not in parades or watching a tournament or shit like that, but up close. Close enough to get a good look at the fucker. See how tight it is? You couldn't get a sparrow's cock between the plates. Which brings me to my second point. Do you know what happens when a cunt in full plate needs to take a shit? You've guessed it. He just shits himself. A battle can take hours. Even days sometimes if the commanders are fucking about enough. Do you think he's going to take off his fancy steel suit to take a shit only to get shot up the arse by some little bastard with a crossbow?
 And after the battle, when he goes for a nice, warm bath with rosewater and a glass of wine, do you think he cleans the shit out of the armour himself? You've guessed it again!
 Finally, the last reason why anyone wearing full plate is almost certainly a cunt is this: they kill people. And they are fucking good at it. Imagine being wrapped up in steel. Your head is covered and padded so your hot breath is steaming all around you. You can see out of a tiny slit, so you know where you're going. But you can hardly feel the clang and clash of the shitty little knives and messers the peasants are hacking at you with. You don't need to block. You don't need to worry about these poor bastards. You can sweep through them like shit through a goat. And you can't kill that many people day after day without being at least a little bit of a cunt.

Chapter 1:
Fuck off, and die in a fire

It was raining again. Everything was wet in that horrible way when it's been pouring for days and you can't even remember what warm and dry feels like. I pulled off my boots and flung them under a bush in the vain hope they would be dry by morning. My feet were cold and covered in mud where it had oozed in through the leather. I desperately needed new soles, or better yet, a new pair of boots. But boots cost money and I didn't fucking have any.

Unbuckling my sword belt, I took off my armour and leaned in a little closer to the shitty fire I built, the burning wood spluttering in the drizzle. I rubbed the balls of my feet to get some relief and possibly some warmth into them. My arse hurt from sitting on the bumpy log that I had pressganged into a seat, but it was either that or sit on the ground and let myself get soaked with mud. Well, more mud.

I sat just off the road with a dense wood to my back. The overhanging trees gave me some protection from the rain and I kept half an eye on the path in case someone nastier than me came riding along.

Scratching my good cheek, I made a mental inventory of what I had to eat. Half a loaf of bread, a few eggs I stole from a farm a few miles back, two pears, some dried up cheese and a piece of sausage

I'd been saving. I pulled my haversack close to me and rummaged around. Whetstone, spoon, plate, flint, steel…Sausage! I can't really smile - not anymore - but I did the best job I could. It's amazing how the little things can make you happy.

I reached up to the tree and snapped off a twig, then whittled away till it was just green wood, the shavings curling up and burning on the fire. I impaled the sausage and wedged the stick into the dirt. A hot meal! I felt a tiny bit of dribble roll out of the hole in my face and down my chin, so I wiped it off with the back of my hand.

Then I looked up and cursed. Two people on horseback were riding down the road towards me. Both had their hoods pulled up tight. The horses looked well-fed and so did the riders. As they got closer, I saw it was an old man and a young woman. They stopped a few yards away and he raised a hand in greeting.

"Good evening to you traveller, the night is grim indeed!" The man stepped off his horse and his high boots squelched into the mud. He was wearing a long cloak of good cloth lined with dark grey fur. "My daughter and I are weary from travel, and would be most grateful to share-"

"Fuck off, and die in a fire."

His mouth hung open for a moment. I moved my hand slowly and deliberately to the hilt of my sword. The international gesture for 'piss off and leave me alone.' "I'm sorry sir, I hope-"

"Fuck off." I said it again.

He scowled at me with a furrowed brow before remounting his horse. His cloak got tangled on the saddle horn and he threw it off angrily. "By the Virtuous Ones!" He roared. "I have never been spoken to so rudely in my entire-"

"Fuck. Off." I said it again one more time. Slowly, I pulled a hand's breadth of the blade from the sheath, and the steel glistened in the firelight.

They both rode off hard, hooves sending mud flying. The noise died away and I was left with the patter of the rain and the hiss of the droplets hitting the flames. I felt warmer now, but I instantly regretted my decision to scare them away. I clenched my teeth and glared into the fire.

I cursed myself for being stupid and driving them off. They were clearly rich. I should have robbed them.

The stick slipped and the sausage fell into the flames. "Bugger!" jumped up and used the tip of my scabbard to flick it out. It landed in a small muddy puddle and I reached down to wipe away the worst of it on my cloak. The mud was almost gone, but there were a few strands of wool to be picked off.

I looked at the sausage - mostly dried up, past its best, and splashed with mud – and considered it a metaphor for my life before thinking "Fuck it". I ate it, made myself as warm as I could and forced myself to go to sleep.

The sword is heavy and the stone is cold beneath my bare feet. My muscles burn and I feel the blade dip. I shake myself and heft the sword up again, the point towards the ceiling. I close my eyes and pray.

I woke up cold and hungry. The sun climbed into the skies and I muttered a half-hearted prayer of thanks to Oswald the Fierce for letting me survive another day. How sincere my prayer was I couldn't really say.

Crisp smelling dew covered the landscape and dripped from my skin and hair. There were still a few embers in the fire, and I managed to get one going after a fair bit of cursing. I rubbed my hands and eventually managed to drive out the cold. I took the pan from my haversack and heated it over the flames. After a few minutes, I cracked an egg and watched it sizzle on the iron. I should have probably eaten the bread before it got much worse, but fuck it. You can't fry an egg when you're walking, after all.

I broke camp and headed off. My boots were still wet and my feet rubbed painfully with every step. I ignored it and continued. It was either that, or lie under a bush and wait to die. At least the fucking rain had stopped.

After a couple of hours, I came to a fork in the road. I'd come from Ashpool in the south and had no intention of going back there in a hurry. To the east lay Little Mark, and Middle Mark to the northeast. Both of them were about a day's ride away. Well, I didn't have a horse, so call it two.

I would have flipped a coin, except I was broke, so I decided to go to Middle Mark, because Little Mark sounds like a shitty little hamlet where cousins fuck each other.

I stopped when the light faded. I ate the rest of my bread, lit a fire and slept. There wasn't as much dew next morning, but my stomach growled at me. I cooked the final egg and finished off the pears. There was a blackberry thicket at the side of the road, and I picked as many as I could before I curled up to sleep. I knew eating that many blackberries would probably give me the shits, but it was either that or starve to death.

The next day came and I alternated between blackberries and cheese until I reached Middle Mark at dusk. I saw the guards were shutting the gates so I waved my arm at them and hurried as quickly as I could. The foul smell from the piles of refuse filling the ditches outside the town walls hit me and I tried not to gag. I couldn't help but feel a small amount of pity for those miserable bastards who had to stand outside and breathe it in all day.

The guards looked at me with unmasked disgust. Even if I didn't have a gaping hole in the side of my cheek, I doubted they'd be doffing their helmets to me. The fact I was keeping them late really didn't work in my favour. There were two of them: a small fellow and an older, larger man with a hard face and a nose which looked like it had been broken a fair few times.

"What do you want?" He was missing a front tooth. The rest were crooked and yellow.

"Sell-sword." I said plainly.

He rolled his eyes. "You fuckers are nothing but trouble, you know that?"

I said nothing.

He sighed, and his companion got out a ledger. "Name?"

"Ulf."

"Where are you from then, Ulf?"

"Banrillar." No point in lying. I couldn't be arsed anyway.

He frowned and looked me in the eye. "Never heard of the place."

I shrugged. "It's a village. In the south." Which was true.

He paused, clicking his tongue. If he was going to tell me to fuck off, he would have already done it. But luckily for me, he just wanted to get home and it was clear he wasn't in the mood for a fight.

"Watch yourself, Ulf of Banrillar."

He stepped to the side and allowed me to pass. I nodded my head and stepped into the streets.

The large beam that barred the town gates thudded into place behind me, and I heard the guards exchange pleasantries with the night watch who were just starting their shift. Torches and braziers were being lit along the street as the shadows lengthened.

I left the guards far behind me and walked down a side street. One alleyway is pretty much as good as another. I looked around for some straw, an animal pen, an abandoned building –anywhere I could spend the night and preferably not get stabbed. I peeked out onto the main street. All around people were going back to their homes. The smells of hundreds of evening meals mingled in the air and my stomach growled jealously.

Then, something amazing happened. Something that altered my life forever. I met a man who, although I didn't know it at the time, set something in motion that would change the world.

I bumped into a drunk in the next street. After checking no-one was around, I balled up my fist and punched him hard in the gut. As he bent over vomiting, I smashed his teeth in and stole his purse. I left him on his back, drifting in and out of consciousness as I quickly walked away.

The small brown pouch made a rather satisfying jingle and I emptied the coins into my palm. My optimism was misplaced, however, as all I got was a fistful of copper Ecar and three silver Wyear.

I swore, more out of habit than anything else. I threw the empty pouch into a pile of horse shit and then stepped out onto the main square. The market traders were closing their stalls and rolling down the covers. A baker's apprentice packed away the unsold loaves while his master cooled the oven.

"How much?" The bread looked good. It was baked that morning, but still looked fresh.

"Errm . . ." He looked at me in confusion.

"For the bread!" I snapped. "A loaf of bread, how much boy! You do sell bread, don't you?"

His master stood up, brushing ashes from his apron.

"Sorry, friend. No buying or selling after sundown. Guild rules."

I turned away. "Oh, for fucks' . . ."

He called after me. "But, tell you what. You look like you could use a meal." He tossed me a round loaf, the top studded with sweetfruits, and I caught it awkwardly. He gave me a smile, and I offered a nod of thanks and headed off quickly, shoving the loaf into my haversack. "Virtuous Ones guide you, friend," the baker called after me.

There were two taverns nearby: The Bloody Wolf and the Wheatsheaf. I tossed a coin and went to the Wheatsheaf, a big inn with adjoining stables. My nose was pummelled with horse sweat and dander mixing with the cooking and stale beer of the inn.

I opened the door and stepped through. The locals had already started to have fun. It was early in the evening and except for the drunks, who lolled and bobbed around like apples in a barrel, no-one was the worse for wear. I pressed my way through the throng to the bar and took out a copper coin.

A middle-aged woman with a stained apron met my eye. "Evening sir. What can I get you?"

"A drink. And I need a bed for the night".

She poured me a mug of dark ale. I passed her the coin and I took a sip. It was a little sour, but still good. "We have space in the men's room. It's six Ecar a night."

"For a shared bed?"

She shrugged. "There's space in the stable if you're shy…"

I rolled my eyes. "How much for the stable?"

"Let's see. For hay, straw, water, mucking out and rubbing down…six Ecar. And I'll throw in a carrot."

I clenched my fists and bit my tongue. "I'll take the bed." I handed over the coins. My purse felt a fair bit lighter now, but it had been a long time since I had slept in a bed, even if it was with other people.

"Will you want supper?"

I thought hard about it. The stew on the hearth smelled good, but I couldn't. I needed to watch my money. "No."

She shrugged and nodded towards the stairs. "It's the first door on the right." I moved to go. "You'll need to leave your sword with us, sir."

I froze. I didn't like the idea of being without it, but I liked the idea of sleeping in the street even less. I unbuckled my sword belt, wrapped it around the scabbard, and handed it over. She passed me a wooden disk with a number four carved into it. I decided not to mention the dirk I had in a sheath on the small of my back.

"Be careful with it!" I snarled.

She nodded graciously. "Of course, good sir. There are also bowls of water and towels for your use."

I glared, but she did have a very good point. I picked a table fairly near the fire and away from the locals. I downed a big mouthful of the beer, and the drink tasted better than anything I'd had in weeks. I ripped off hunks of the fruit bread and tried to eat it as discreetly as I could. Most inns get prissy when you take in your own supper. When the bread was gone, I tipped the rest of the beer down my throat. I got a few queer looks, but I'm used to that. I wiped the spillage off my face and headed upstairs. Early for bed, but I was tired and didn't know when I'd next get a proper night's sleep.

The room was small, and most of it was taken up with a large bed covered in patched blankets. True to the woman's word, there was a bowl of water and a soft cloth on the table. I splashed my face, stripped, and washed for the first time in weeks.

The water in the bowl was filthy by the time I'd finished, but I struggled to give a shit. I threw my armour and gear into a corner and got into the bed, relishing the softness and warmth of the blankets. There was still noise and song coming from downstairs, but I felt myself drifting to sleep.

The other travellers staying in the room arrived just as I nodded off, waking me up with the punchline to some stupid joke. A pair of brothers, by the look of them. Young, with clothes of good wool and hoods cut in a rakish pointed style. I instantly knew they were a pair of cunts.

They said hello politely and I grunted a greeting to them. They got into bed and blew out the candle. Between the three of us, the bed was warm, and I swiftly fell into a deep sleep.

My wooden sword is knocked from my hand. "Keep your guard up!"
"Sorry." I stoop to pick it up and I'm struck hard on the back.
"Don't apologise to me, you're the one who just died." He clips me round the ear and smiles. I bring the sword up and square my stance. "Like this?" I bend my elbows a little, just like he showed me.
He copies my stance and thrusts at me quickly. I only just manage to turn aside the blow.
"Better."

I awoke sometime after midnight. The cold air in the room chilled the tip of my nose and the two brothers were snoring away. I groaned with the awkward realisation that I needed to piss. I swung my legs out of bed and winced as my feet touched the cold floor. No pot under the bed. Bugger.

I looked at the window and briefly considered pissing out of it, but it was too high up. I pride myself on being an accomplished pisser - my best is being able to hit a field mouse full stream - but if I tried to get it out the window, I'd just get my feet covered in piss.

I slipped on my boots and shirt and stepped out of the room, down the stairs. I moved the latch on the inn door and carefully placed it to one side. No point waking people up. I thought about seeing what I could steal from behind the bar, but decided it wasn't worth the risk.

Jack Shannon

The wind whistled through the hole in my face, and I grimaced as the night air chilled my teeth whipped at my shirt. I hitched up the hem and took a satisfyingly robust piss against the corner of the inn stables.

The wooden sheaf of wheat swung in the night wind and my breath came out in steaming clouds - as did my piss, but that's neither here nor there. I moved over to the water butt and cupped my hands, taking a long cool drink. I reached down for another mouthful and saw a dark shape ripple in the water.

I spun around as a dagger glinted in the darkness, the curved blade stabbing down into the barrel as I dove to the right.

"Did you really think we wouldn't notice you?" He stabbed at me again and I just managed to step aside, my feet skidding on the filthy cobbles.

I hurled myself into him and slammed him hard against the stable wall. We fell in a tangle of limbs and I struck him hard with my elbow, feeling his nose crumple. He screamed out and I grabbed his wrist, the knife turning and slashing me across the forearm. I ignored the pain and the spurt of blood as I forced myself on top of him, keeping the dagger away from me. He tried to knee me in the bollocks, but just kicked my hip.

"What the fuck do you want?" I yelled at him. I tried to get the dagger, but my fingers scrabbled against his grip.

He spat into my eye and I shook it out. He punched me in the side of the head, but I'm a tough old bastard and I punched him back, bouncing his skull off the street. I punched him again and shoved a finger into his eye socket, rupturing the eye. The warm jelly felt horrible, but the arsehole had it coming.

He dropped the dagger and tried to throw me off, so I snatched it up and rammed it into his mouth. I saw the blood rupturing from his jaws, and I stabbed him in the side of his neck. He flailed around a bit and reached to his belt, so I stabbed him a few times in the chest to make sure. When he stopped moving, I stood up on weak legs, panting heavily. My arm started throbbing, and I clutched at it to staunch the bleeding.

Footsteps. Fuck…

Two men – guards, by the look of them – rounded the corner with short swords drawn. They pointed them at me. "Get down on the ground!"

Normally I fancy my chances, but I didn't think I could win this fight armed only with a second-hand dagger and my cock. I dropped the dagger and slowly got down on the ground, palms spread to show I was unarmed. The assassin had shat himself and the smell filled my nostrils.

They bound my wrists with rough hemp ropes and dragged me to my feet. "Come here, you little bugger." I didn't say anything. I doubted anything I had to say could have improved his mood. The other one blew a whistle and a few more guards turned up, carrying lanterns.

They dragged me through the streets to a narrow stone building, then took me inside and threw me into a cell. "You can wait here and explain yourself in the morning." I looked up and a guard sneered at me.

I probably shouldn't have, but I glowered back. Force of habit.

"Ugly fucker, aren't you..." I didn't disagree. To be fair, he was right.

He locked the cell and left me in the darkness with a pot to piss and shit in and a scattering of straw. Looking on the bright side of things, at least the straw was fresh. I huddled myself in the straw and closed my eyes. Whatever was going to happen in the morning, being tired wouldn't help things.

Chapter 2:
What's In a Name?

The sun crept through the window of the cell. My arm throbbed, but the cut had started to scab over. I made a quick prayer of thanks to Oswald the Fierce for another day. I also mentioned that if he could find his way to making sure my arm didn't get infected, I'd be very grateful.

I heard voices and perked up. If I were to hang then at least I'll die on my feet. Or at least on my feet for a while, then dangling in the air while I choked to death and pissed myself. I've seen a fair few and hanging is a bastard of a way to die. If you've got someone with money, they can pay the executioner to do a quick job. One snap of the rope and it's over. If you haven't, then they might "accidentally" get the measurements wrong and you'll be dangling in agony for a few minutes.

Still, it makes a good day out for the family and it means the hangman might get a few tips.

The cell door swung open and two figures stepped in. The first was the nightwatchman who had arrested me, and my heart sank as I realised he was with the big bastard from the town gates last night.

He sucked the air through the gap in his front teeth. "Nothing but fucking trouble." He kicked me hard in the ribs, and I got the impression he could have kicked me a lot harder if he'd wanted. "Get up. This isn't a bloody flophouse."

I stood up and stretched.

"Care to explain what happened last night?"

I looked him in the eyes. "I went for a piss and he tried to stab me. I threw him on the ground and poked out his eye. I got the dagger off him and stabbed him."

He stared at me. My eyes darted to the door. I clenched my fists and thought about making a run for it, but they both had swords and looked like the type of people who wouldn't bother with a friendly 'Halt in the name of the law!' They'd cut me to pieces before I got more than a few paces, but I was still tempted.

"Fuck off." He said without a trace of uncertainty. I unclenched my fists and breathed out, trying to calm myself. "You should get down on your fucking knees and thank the Lady of Mercy that he was a foreign bastard."

He stepped aside to let me out and I could see the corpse laid out on a table outside the cell. I hadn't gotten a good look at his face in the dark, but in the daylight it was obvious. His skin was almost albino pale, with cruel, thin lips and long perfumed blue-black hair.

"Killing a C'targian in self-defence isn't a crime as far as I'm concerned." he said. "You might be filthy sell-sword, but at least you're an Ashenfeller."

He spat on the corpse and the glob landed square in the ruined eye socket, floating like scum on a pond. I was impressed with the aim, but had sense enough not to say anything. He opened the main door and the morning sunlight shining through mademe blink. He held something out: a leather pendant. The cord was stained dark brown from the dried- blood, but I recognised the symbol.

A black ram.

"Do you know what this is?"

I looked him in the face and tried to keep my voice steady.

"No."

He put it into his pouch. "Not everyone is as nice as me. Watch yourself, final warning. Now, as I said before: fuck off." I didn't need telling a third time. I walked quickly out the door, his voice echoing after me. "And If I see you here again, I'll tear your bollocks off, you little shit!"

Somehow, I didn't think it an empty threat. It took a bit of wandering about in just my boots and shirt, but I managed to get back to the Wheatsheaf. The pair of cunts I had shared a bed with the night before were sitting downstairs eating breakfast. The one nearest me stood up and bowed deeply.

"Good morning to you sir!" He had an annoying, squeaky voice, like a flute stuck up a dog's arse.

"We didn't see you depart," his brother added, "but we made sure your belongings were safe, so there is no need to worry. Pray, sit with us! We would be grateful for your company."

As annoying as I found them, the offer of a free meal was too good to pass up. I sat down and nodded my thanks. "The hour was late last night and we were not able to introduce ourselves. This is my brother Quentin-"

Quentin gave a little flourish and tiny bow. "-and this is my brother, Decroix."

Decroix repeated the gesture. "At your service, and that of your family!".

"And you sir?" Quentin raised his eyebrows.

"Ulf of Banrillar."

He smiled as if I had just told him his headlice were made of diamonds. "Ah! Well met, Ulf. Please, eat with us and make merry!"

I took a hunk of bread from the plate on the table and dipped it in the berry sauce.

Decroix's face went dark in exaggerated rage. "Merry? You talk of merry, sir? When the king lies mad with the Witch-Fever? While your daughter is bound in a foul dungeon? I can talk of merry no longer. No, you must die!"

He drew a wooden spoon from the table and stabbed his brother in the chest. Quentin's eyes crossed and he gave a long moan of agony. He stood up, staggered a few paces, and then tucked the spoon under his arm.

"Oh, brother! I can't believe thou just stabbed me!
Oh, I am slain by the cruel dagger of thy deception!
As well as the literal dagger which thou dost wield!

Alas, I am, I am slain. I die as I lived, a man of honour. As Sampson dies, so Sampson lives! As Sampson's name goes on a light of virtue…"

I muttered into my bread, "Bugger me, they're actors."

He slumped down at the table and his brother applauded. A few other patrons politely joined in.

Quentin miraculously came back to life and took a bow, sweeping his mantle along the floor. He drew a slender knife, cut a thin piece of bread, and dipped it into the sauce.

"We're thespians, you see."

I rolled my eyes. "No, really? But the murder? It looked so genuine."

He smiled. "You're very kind. But we both have a lot to learn."

He popped the bread into his mouth and Decroix piped up. "Father didn't approve, but in this life, you must follow your vision and be true to your own virtues."

Quentin nodded sadly. "Yes. We took our inheritance and struck out to Cassioc."

I generally don't like plays. My life is violent enough as it is, and I don't like the flouncy words. I prefer cockfighting or a good bear-bait. You know, proper entertainment.

Quentin leaned in conspiratorially. "But Ulf, tell us about yourself! You look like a fellow who has trod the roads of life. You must have a hundred thrilling tales."

I ripped off another chunk of bread and swirled it in the last of the sauce.

"No. I don't."

His smile wavered a little. "A dozen thrilling tales then!"

"No."

"A few thrilling tales?"

"No."

"One thrilling-"

I spat out a cherry stone. "Shut up."

He looked crestfallen, but he soon started smiling again. If I had cavalry who could rally that quickly, I could take over the world.

Decroix tapped the side of his nose and winked at me. "I saw your armour upstairs."

"So?" Did they want to borrow it to dress up in? I didn't know where they were going with this and my hand moved to where my sword should have been. It was still behind the bar. Bugger.

"Would you excuse us for a moment, good sir?" Quentin and his brother stood up and went to a corner. Fortunately for me, they were actors, and both had a stage whisper. I finished off the last of the bread and stuck an ear out.

"Have you seen the size of him?" Quentin asked. "He'd be perfect!"

"I don't know, he seems a little . . . rough."

"He's a mercenary! What do you expect? One look at him and any bandit would shit himself."

"We should at least ask around. Try and see who else there is to hire."

"Really? You want to spend another day in this dump? We need to get to Cassioc, that was the whole point of this trip."

Decroix sighed. "Look at his face! If he was any good then he wouldn't be missing half his cheek."

I turned in my chair and smile at him as best I could. "You should have seen what happened to the other bastard."

He wet his lips nervously. "Forgive me, I didn't-"

"Shut up."

They walked back to the table, embarrassed. After an awkward pause, Decroix spoke up. "We need a guard for the road. We know the route, but the highways can be dangerous."

I nodded. If there was any justice in the world, these two would have been robbed naked, beaten to death, and thrown in a ditch by now.

Quentin smiled at me. I meet his gaze head-on. "How much would you charge to-"

"Two Wyear a day, plus expenses."

They exchanged a quick glance. "That sounds more than fair. Shall we set off presently?"

"I need a horse. First five days' pay in advance."

"Of course! Absolutely, sir! It would take far too long to walk there." Quentin counted out ten Wyear and finally a large golden Guilder. "Don't worry, Decroix. We can sell the horse when we get to Cassioc."

He handed over the coins. "For the horse." he said. The coins felt good and heavy in my hand.

"But what shall the horse do with the money?" Decroix asked. The brothers both laughed at the joke. Insufferable twats.

"I'll need a few more Wyear. For supplies."

"Supplies?" Decroix looked at me quizzically. I bit my tongue, worried that I had fucked this up. I was really pushing it with the price and now they were going to realise I was full of shit. A good archer should earn two Wyear a day from a decent paymaster, and even then, he'd be expected to risk his life. Mind you, most archers I've known would slit your throat for a rusty Ecar, so they are probably overpaid anyway.

"Yes . . . supplies." I said. "You know . . . rope and suchlike."

"Of course! How silly of me! Will another five Wyear do?" I breathed a mental sigh of relief. Thank Aeder the Kind these two were fuckwitted.

"Five Wyear should be fine." I decided not to push my luck, seeing as I was already holding more money than I'd seen in months, even if most of it is earmarked for a horse.

At this point I remembered I was sitting in the common room in just a shirt and his boots, with my cock flopping out, so I made my excuses and headed upstairs. True to their word, my clothing and armour were where I had left them. I put the money into my purse and dressed quickly. I had been in this town less than a day and I'd already been stabbed and thrown in prison, so I figured it would be a good idea to fuck off.

I handed in the wooden token, strapped on my sword, and headed to the market. By now the traders were all set up and displaying their wares. I passed a row of butchers, some of them cutting away at great slabs of meat, flies buzzing and dogs lapping at the pooling blood. Two of them fought over something grey and slimy.

It felt good to have some coins in my purse. I didn't know what was going to happen, but I'd taken far more dangerous jobs for far less money. And unless I killed them first, the brothers would be fairly safe.

I eventually found a cobbler with some readymade boots. I found a pair I liked and managed to haggle him down to just three Wyear. He kept the old pair for scraps and we parted company.

The 'supplies' came to only two Wyear and three Ecar, so I pocketed the change. I filled up a few sacks with enough food to get us to Cassioc: a wheel of cheese, two dozen apples, some dried meat, and some nuts I got a good price on. I picked up an extra couple of links of blood sausage because I felt like I deserved it. I made sure the rope I picked up looked suitably impressive.

We needed a few loaves of bread to finish off the supplies, so I followed my nose and found the stall in the market. It took me a second to recognise the baker when he smiled at me. "Glad to see you've found your feet, lad." He reached to the oven and gave me six of the freshest loaves. "Nathaniel." He stuck out a hand and I shook it.

I tried to smile, but I stopped when I noticed a woman gawping at me. "Thank you." I managed. I handed over a couple Ecar and he clinked them into a strong box.

"Virtues guide you and keep you."

I nodded. "And to you."

I asked around and found a horse trader on the far side of the market with a pen for his wares. He was a tall man with a broad face and a strong brow.

"I need a rouncey." I said.

He scratched his jaw and looked thoughtfully at me. "You're in luck friend. I bought one this morning. The stables are getting pretty crowded, but it was a good price and I didn't want to pass it up."

And for a rare time in my life, I was indeed in luck. He pointed to a beautiful horse at the back of the pen, a palomino with good strong legs.

He led me over to take a good look. "Fair warning-" He pointed to some bite marks on the fence. "She's a chewer."

I reached out and rubbed her neck. I know much more about swords and armour than I do horses, but I could tell this one was good. "How much?"

He scratched at his jaw again. "Well, tell you what-"

"One Guilder. Including tack and saddle."

He blinked. "Done!" He spat on his palm, and I did the same. We shook, and the horse was mine.

I managed to keep the Guilder for almost an hour. That's a record for me.

"Does she have a name?"

"Reed."

"Reed? Like the water plant?"

"Yep. That's her name.

I paused. "Fucking hells . . ."

"I didn't choose it, friend."

It's bad luck to change a horse's name. Just like swords or dogs, once they're named, you're stuck with it. I once knew a man who brought a sword with "LIGHTNING" on the scabbard. He thought of a better one and called it Render instead. Good name for a sword-better than "LIGHTNING"-but it wasn't that sword's name. I tried to tell him as much. We got into a brawl with a couple of other mercenaries the next week. I can't remember why; we were all drunk and wanting for a fight. He drew his new sword and took the biggest one. Within a moment 'Render' was broken into two pieces and a poleaxe split him down the middle. He was a decent man, but a right stupid bastard.

I loaded the sacks on Reed and headed back to the Wheatsheaf. She trotted well with a good gait.

Quentin and Decroix were standing outside the tavern, dressed for travel. They were holding a pair of fine grey geldings, and I could see they were both carrying broad-bladed short swords. The wider the blade, the more pictures can be engraved on them. Dress swords, but to be fair, what did I expect?

Quentin shouted a greeting and I nodded in acknowledgement and waited for them to mount up. "Let's get going," Quentin said. "Our fortunes await!"

They both seemed relieved when I headed off, and they fell in behind me.

We left the town just before noon. Eventually, the sounds and bustle of the people washed away behind us and we had the open road to ourselves with a long journey ahead. Part of me wished I could have spent a few more nights in a proper bed, even if I did have to share it, but another part of me remembered the Brotherhood of The Back Ram, and felt fucking glad to be somewhere they were not.

We had only been riding half a day when the sun was beginning to set, and already Decroix was complaining of having a sore arse. There was no point riding in the dark, so we found a decent spot and stopped for the night. We made camp on a slightly raised bank near the roadside. The road followed the River Phon to Cassioc, and I drank my fill of the cool, fresh water. We unsaddled the horses and let them drink deeply before tying them to a nearby tree. Quentin and Decroix went to fetch wood while I got a fire going. They couldn't find much, so I had to go find more. I brought back enough fuel to last us until morning and stacked the fire high.

"Father has never approved." Quentin shook his head sadly and Decroix nodded reflectively.

"He thought it no better than common begging. Can you believe that?" Decroix asked.

I absolutely could believe that. "I absolutely can't believe that," I said, in what I hoped was a convincing manner.

For supper, we ate dried meat along with some apples and bread. Quentin yawned as the embers from the fire danced and crackled. "It's late. We should all get some rest."

"Who's taking the first watch?"

They both looked at me as if I'd just tried to shit on their toes. "Pardon?"

"The watch. Who's doing it so that we don't get surprised by anything unpleasant during the night?"

The brothers looked to each other uncomfortably.

I sighed and re-buckled the vambrace I had just removed. "I'll take the first watch. At midnight Decroix will relieve me. Decroix, wake up Quentin after four or so hours. Keep the fire burning."

The brothers got out sleeping rolls and after ten minutes of chatter, they went to sleep. I unbuckled my sword, put it across my lap, and looked into the flames. Both of them dreamed peacefully. About what I neither knew nor cared.

It would be really easy. One might wake the other, but there was no way he'd be able to get out of the sleeping roll in time to do anything. Put the blade through Quentin's stomach, hack at the other one. Bodies go in the river, I go the other way with a full purse and the certain knowledge I have improved the world of theatre.

I took my hand off my sword. I may be a bastard, but I'm not a cunt. I put another log on the fire and watched a few sparks jump up.

The hairs on my neck bristled, and I turned around. I saw some shapes moving in the darkness down the road towards us. There were four of them; mean looking bastards with more knives than teeth, dressed in dirty leathers and holding cudgels. Their pace quickened and they spread out.

I stood up and drew my sword, shoving it into the ground. Two kicks, and the brothers were groggy but awake.

"W-what?" Decroix blinked hard.

"Get up. Now." He only murmured so I kicked him harder. "Get the fuck up and draw your swords!" I dragged them out of the sleeping rolls, and shoved swords into their hands as they scrambled to their feet. I pulled my sword from the dirt and stood with my back to the fire and the woodpile by my feet.

They stopped a few yards from the fire and I noticed that the ratty looking one at the front had a falchion, which he pulled out slowly. He gave me an unpleasant smile.

"Evening friend-"

I cut him off. "Fuck off, or I'll rip your bollocks off."

He didn't like it and snarled at me. "Give us the horses and your food." He nodded to my sword. "And we'll have that from the ugly fucker as well."

"Fuck off, or I'll rip your bollocks off."

Quentin piped up. "Is there a way we can-"

I snatched up a log and hurled it into the ugly face of the closest one, and his nose smashed like an old strawberry. He dropped his cudgel and howled, so I sprang forward and hacked him down.

One of the thugs hit the armour on my leg with a crash, so I stepped to the side and parried the falchion downwards. He stumbled, so I punched him on the side of the head and he fell to the ground, but when I stepped in to cut his head off I got cracked by another cudgel.

"GET OVER HERE AND FUCKING HELP!" I shouted. I stepped back and took up a low guard as the leader scrabbled to his feet. Two of the thugs paired off and the brothers darted in with quick, fierce fencing thrusts. Quentin grabbed a wrist and wrestled his opponent to the ground while Decroix swung overhead and his sword bit into another thug's cudgel.

Their cunt leader stood in front of me, breathing raggedly. I brought my sword up slowly, point level with his face. He looked at me and wiped the mud from his eyes.

"Final chance. Fuck. Off."

He charged at me with a roar and I stepped forward, lowering the blade so it skewered him through the belly. He stumbled as I pulled it out, and I could smell the stink of his guts. The falchion fell to the earth and he said something about his mother, but I didn't care. I smashed in his teeth with my sword guard and dragged the blade across his throat.

Quentin had his foe pinned, hands forced down to the road. There was spitting and thrashing but the little man was stronger than he looked. I stepped over to the first one I put down and I stabbed him through his eye socket.

Brigandine

Decroix had his dagger to the throat of the final living bandit. "Tell me exactly what I want to know and you get to live. If you don't-"

I stabbed my sword through his neck and the last sound he made was a horrible gurgle.

The bandit, not Decroix. Just to be clear.

I wiped my sword on his tunic and began rifling their pouches. Fuck all. The falchion was the only thing of value, worth maybe a few Wyear, so I grabbed it.

"What did you do that for?" Quentin asked indignantly.

I shrugged. "Finders keepers. Besides, I killed the bastard."

"No, why did you kill him? We could have found out what they were doing, why they attacked!"

I started unbuckling my armour and getting ready for bed. I'd deal with the bodies in the morning. I felt apathetic about who took the next watch, but it wouldn't be me. "I don't know and I don't care. I'm going to sleep. Don't wake me up unless more of the fuckers come, and even then, only if we're outnumbered."

I kept my sword close by and unbound. I closed my eyes and lay in the darkness. Quentin was taking the watch and he had his short-sword to hand. Thoughts ran through my head. I probably should have found more out from that man, but I couldn't be bothered to listen to him plead when he wasn't of any more use.

The brothers had more to them than first glance would seem. Most actors just know how to stage fight, and they didn't shit themselves at the sight of blood. I drifted off into a deep slumber, with a whole lot of questions going round in my mind.

Chapter 3:
Mucky Stuff

The horse trots nicely, despite the noise. I can feel the animal under me and it's calm. The crowds are roaring and I can see hundreds of people waving and shouting. A young girl my age catches my eye and blows me a kiss. I blush and look the other way. The flag wobbles. "Keep it straight!" Taran hisses at me before waving to the crowd with a gauntleted hand. The banner snaps in the breeze and I look up. A golden cup on a dark blue field. It looks glorious, and I know nothing can stop us. I turn in the saddle and see the other squires, all holding standards beside their own masters. But none are as bright and beautiful as ours.

Our banner. My brother's heraldry.

I woke up to the smell of something frying and the sound of crackling wood. Quentin was cutting another slice from a side of bacon and laying it in the pan. The dripping fat made me dribble and I wiped away at the drops on the side of my face.

Decroix wiped his hands. "Good morning."

"Morning." I nodded back.

"I got rid of the . . ."

"Corpses?"

"Yes . . ."

"So, what did you and Quentin do with the buggers?"

Decroix looked awkward. "River."

"Good idea," I mumbled. "Did you fill up the canteens first?"

"Yes."

"Good. Thanks."

By the time I dressed and armoured myself, the bacon had cooked. I thanked Quentin, and we all ate together in awkward silence.

I got my gear together and waited for the others to do the same before we set off. I looked at Reed and patted her flank. She nuzzled at me, her nose soft as silk against my hand, and I'm taken aback. Horses don't normally like me too much. I fed her half an apple, then cut a slice from the other half and popped it into my mouth.

My sword had a deep nick where the falchion had bitten into the blade, so I swore and spent a few minutes with a whetstone to smooth out the burr. I finished just as the brothers were mounting their geldings and we set off.

The day passed slowly, and we ate lunch when we stopped to water the horses at a roadside well. I checked to make sure nothing has died down there first. When you've had a dead rat fall on your upper lip, you don't want to repeat it.

We each broke off a chunk of the bread and I hacked off some cheese for us. I swallowed and then washed it down from my flask. "You're a good fighter." I said, gesturing at Decroix with my flask before putting it away.

Decroix perked up. "Thanks."

I took a long look at him. At both of them. They were young and clean-limbed, with intelligent eyes. "Quentin, you're not too bad a wrestler, are you?"

He held out his hands and gave a little shrug. "It pays to be able to protect yourself . . ."

I gave him a stare. "Harsh, are they?"

"Hmmm?"

"Theatre critics where you come from. For you to learn stuff like that."

Decroix speared a piece of cheese and chewed it slowly. I looked him in the eyes. "Who are you?"

He put his knife down and exchanged a glance with his brother. He set his jaw and his shoulders subtly shifted. "I can tell you with absolute honesty that we are both actors. But most importantly as far as you're concerned, we're the people paying two Wyear a day." Decroix wiped his blade on the grass and tucked it into his belt. "And I think we should be making a move. We need to get to Cassioc."

"Is the theatre going anywhere?" I asked. He ignored me, and we saddled up, riding in silence until nightfall.

A few days passed. I tried to talk to them a few times but they stayed tight-lipped. I was still getting paid, though, so I didn't care too much. On the sixth day, there was still a bit of food left, but we were all happy when we came to a big coaching inn about an hour before sunset. There were a fair few people I guessed were heading towards Middle Mark. The sign above the door showed a snake with feathery white wings.

Decroix handed over the fee to the stable lad, who gave us numbered tokens for each horse. I held Reed's reins tight for a moment to get the boy's attention before handing her off. "Fresh straw and a good rub down. And don't half-arse it!"

The Winged Serpent was a busy place. An old woman shuffled around collecting the empty mugs. Decroix entered with a flourish and gestured to his brother. "Good morrow fellow travellers! It is my great pleasure and honour to make known the tyrant of the stage and the captain of the painted sea! Quentin!"

Quentin blushed and stepped into the inn. "And for your delectation please applaud the thief of hearts and the dampener of eyes, my dear brother, Decroix!" Decroix made a sweeping bow and blew a kiss to the old woman who rolled her eyes.

I heard her mutter, "Fuck me . . . actors."

I noticed there was a huge bastard of a bouncer standing in the corner. He had a set of knuckle dusters on a piece of string hanging from his wrists, which he rubbed at fondly. The jerkin he wore was covered in blood stains and I'd have bet my left ball that none of them were his own.

"And of course, our associate and dear companion, Ulf of Banrillar!" Decroix lead a round of clapping and Quentin beamed at me, clearly loving every second.

The bouncer looked over to me and I noticed he had a cleft lip and was missing a chunk of an ear, which looked like it had been torn off. I made a mental note not to fuck with him.

There was a very small bit of scattered and awkward applause as we walked over to the bar. I saw more people staring at me than usual and I'm pretty sure my face was bright red.

Decroix propped himself up on the bar and gave a wide grin. "Good morrow, stout yeofolk! My companions and I are weary from travel and have need of a room and fine, hearty fare to warm the pit of our bellies and-"

The innkeeper cut him off. "Seven Ecar each for the room, two for dinner, one for breakfast."

I frowned. "The sign there says four Ecar for a bed."

He spat on the floor. "I know what the fucking sign says."

Quentin gave a look of shock. "But, good innsman! Vigilant friend of travellers, have charity on these poor wretched souls." He grabbed me by the shoulders and my hands instantly turned to fists. "Poor Ulf here was born to a mother who left him before he was born, in the gutter to be raised by hogs! And his father was forced to sell earwax to candlemakers to support the family!" He brushed away a tear as I gritted my teeth.

"Oh, Papa! Don't be a brute."

A very pretty young woman appeared behind the bar. Bit of a flat nose, but apart from that, she was the best-looking thing I'd seen in a while. She pleaded with him, tugging on his sleeve. "You've promised to take me to the theatre for months! And look! The theatre has come to us!"

"Good lady," Quentin took her hand and kissed it slowly. "You flatter me." She giggled madly as he waggled his eyebrows.

"Please, not again." Decroix muttered under his breath.

The innkeeper held up his hands. "Fine, fine! You do a bit of the acting stuff this evening-" he jabbed his thumb at the clear space near the heath. "-an' you can stay for the night."

Quentin gasped with exaggerated excitement. "A thousand thanks, good sir! Not only have you given shelter to these poor, wayward souls, but a chance to tread the stage of this fine hostelry! Oh, what a tale we shall tell!"

The old woman stepped up and jabbed a finger into my chest like a dried-up sausage. "No mucky stuff! An' none of those rhymes which mean something dirty in secret!"

"Perish the thought . . ." I muttered.

The innkeeper looked Quentin dead in the eye. "An' you stay away from Charlotte. You hear me, boy?"

Quentin did his best to look innocent, which he failed at spectacularly.

The watery chicken stew they served wasn't great, and I'm pretty sure I ended up with a beak, though the bread wasn't bad. The brothers cleared away a few chairs and pushed two tables together to become a makeshift stage. I tried to find somewhere to sit where hopefully no-one would look at me.

Decroix made a great show of limbering up and stretching his legs and arms most obscenely, while Quentin opened and closed his mouth, loosening up his jaw for the great speeches to come.

Decroix banged a tankard for silence over the inn and, surprisingly, he got it.

"Friends! My brother Quentin-" Dramatic flourish.

"-And my talented, better-looking brother Decroix!" Quentin chipped in.

"For your moral betterment and to bring the magic of theatre into your lives-"

"We are proud to present the most lamentable tragedy and gruesome murder-"

"-of the fair duchess Bagito of Skulir."

"And of her daughter's bloody snake-filled revenge . . ."

Praise when it's due, they put on a good play. I found it a little hard to follow but I laughed along with everyone while Quentin staggered around, milking the death scene for all it was worth. Charlotte kept the drinks coming, and the fire warmed the room. I downed maybe a few more ales than I should have, and everything

Brigandine

went a little fuzzy around the edges. The innkeeper stacked the fire up high and the two brothers laughed and joked with the crowd.

I yawned, and headed up to the room to a soft bed with sheets that smelt faintly of onions. I threw my gear into the corner, and it bounced off of a big barrel that turned out to be full of onions. I fell into bed, closed my eyes, and felt myself drifting away.

There is a terrible crash and a splinter of wood lands at my feet. My brother trots towards me, panting. The cup on his tabard is stained with the dust stirred into the air by thundering hooves.

Destriers. Big, fierce horses bred for war. He raises his visor. "Water." I pass the mug up to him and he drains it. He throws it down and nods his thanks. "Lance." I run to the rack and pick a new one out. He takes it and shuts the helmet fast. The big, ornate one he uses for jousting. His armour is beautiful-I should know, I polished it. Gilded on the edges, the steel thicker towards the front and thinner at the back. This isn't a suit for war or travel. This is a harness for the glory of a tournament. And no knight looks finer than my brother.

Most of the crowd is cheering for him now, including all of his friends in the Order. There must be a thousand people who have come to watch the joust. The other knight is older and was a great fighter in his day, but my brother is quicker and no-one can ride like he can. Lances smash again and my brother knocks him from his horse.

There is a horrible sound, a clatter of metal and a man's desperate yells. The other knight's foot had caught in his stirrup as he fell from his horse, and people are screaming as he's being dragged through the dirt by his ankle. It's twisted at a weird angle and his gauntleted fingers are desperately reaching out, scrabbling at his heel to pop his boot free. The horse is panicking, white foam on its lips.

"SWORD! NOW!" I throw my brother's sword into his hand. He flings off the scabbard and rides hard towards the horse. They look like they are going to collide, but at the last moment, he swerves and slices through the stirrup. The other knight rolls to a stop, a moaning pile of filthy metal. My brother dismounts, throwing the sword down to help him to his feet. The knight pushes back his visor and leans heavily on my brother. He is clearly in agony, but he lifts Taran's arm in triumph. The Order begins chanting his name, and soon the whole crowd joins in.

Hands shook me awake. I grabbed the wrists and sat bolt upright.

"OW! Get off!" Decroix pulled himself away. "Get up, we're leaving. Now."

"What the fuck is going on?" I swung myself out of bed and threw on my clothes, limbs still stiff from sleep. I heard some shouting downstairs-the innkeeper, Charlotte, and…Quentin. How could I have guessed this would happen?

"YOU LITTLE BASTARD!" A voice raged from below. "YOU COULDN'T KEEP IT IN YOUR TIGHTS FOR ONE SHITTING NIGHT!"

"PAPA, PLEASE! I LOVE HIM, AND HE LOVES ME!"

"Well let's not jump to any hasty conclusions here . . ."

The quip was met with shattering glass and more screams. Decroix raised an eyebrow before sweeping everything into his bag and racing down the stairs. I threw on my sword belt and followed. Quentin was trying to keep a table between him and the innkeeper while his daughter was screaming. I couldn't make out the words, but judging from Quentin using one hand to keep his tights from falling down and Charlotte's tits hanging out, I could guess the context.

"I GIVE YOU FOOD AND LODGING AND THIS IS HOW YOU REPAY MY KINDNESS? BY BEING THE ONE TO STEAL MY DAUGHTER'S VIRGINITY!"

"Again, let's not jump to conclusions!"

The innkeeper made a lunge for him. Quentin dodged and stumbled towards the door. He flung it open and crashed into the bouncer, who cracked his knuckles before sending Quentin flying. Blood poured from Quentin's nose and he doubled up in agony as a calloused fist slogged him in the gut.

I moved like a crossbow bolt. Taking my sword by the sheathed blade, I swung the pommel as hard as I could in a murder-stroke, smashing the bouncer in his ugly mouth. With a vicious crack, teeth flew and he went down like sack of shit. I dragged Quentin up from the floor and kicked the door wide open.

Brigandine

The innkeeper bellowed at me. "You bastards! You utter bastards!"

I turned around and smiled. "It could be worse. If it was me who shagged her, you'd still be mopping up the mess."

I ran to the stables, fast on Decroix's heels. I stood watch, sword in hand, while the brothers readied the horses.

Decroix furiously buckled up the saddle of his gelding. "EVERY. SINGLE. INN!"

"Don't forget the outs!" Quentin chipped in, cinching his tights.

"Why do you have to do this to us, brother? Why?"

Quentin frowned. "What was I going to do! *Not* shag her senseless?"

"Go for a run! Take a cold bath! Make a list of everything in the room coloured brown! Literally anything apart from shagging the innkeeper's daughter!"

Quentin paused, grunting as he tightened his gelding's saddle girth. "Still, apart from that, I think we made an excellent impression."

To be fair, the play did go well.

We mounted up, and in a handful of heartbeats the Winged Serpent was nothing more than an angry mark on the horizon.

We carried on for a few days. The roads here are well travelled and we pass merchants, pilgrims, mercenaries and other folk looking to earn a coin.

I'd been to Cassioc a few times, but it's always impressive. You notice the smell first. The tanneries are a few miles from the city, filthy pits of slop and half-cured leather next to shanty houses filled with the poor bow-legged bastards who spend their days in the muck. The city walls stand huge, five times the height of a man, and made of smooth, white stone. A life-sized portrait adorns the wall every five paces, depicting of one of the city's aldermen, guild leaders, or whoever had enough money and power to demand their image be forever immortalised on the walls of Cassioc.

Or, at least, that was once of the idea. Over the years they have run out of space, so instead portraits jut up from each other's shoulders, faces painted over the top of each other. Some of the less popular figures have had animal heads scrawled onto them, or, in the case of one unfortunate long-forgotten head of the blacksmith's guild, a todger going into his mouth.

Mounting the gate was a painted statue of Queen Karidine, face snow white and hair clad in gold leaf. She has a blank expression and the sculptor made her breasts too pointy, like a pair of daggers under a robe. The statue had been there for years. I imagined her now, old and wrinkled up like an onion left in the sun, and chuckled a bit.

The queen was rarely seen. There were no more grand parades, no alms given. Rumours buzzed like flies, of course, but the fact remained that Queen Karidine was not well loved. I mean, people still loved her, of course, but they loved her in the way they'd love an old, rambling relative who shits himself occasionally. She was the queen, after all.

There was a small queue at the Queen's Gate to enter. A bureaucrat wearing the blue and green of the city fiddled with a wax tablet and an iron stylus, taking a tally of the goods coming into and out of Cassioc. While we waited, we bound up our swords and moved our weapons to the opposite hip.

Decroix gave our names and paid the fees: one Ecar per head, one for each weapon and one Wyear each for the horses. His purse a little lighter, we trotted the horses onto the main plaza and looked for an inn.

"Try not to fuck the innkeeper's daughter this time, Quentin."

He smiled at his brother. "I refuse to make a promise I know I can't keep."

Suddenly, we stopped. They both stared at something with misty eyes. "Can you feel it Ulf? The history! The presence!" Decroix wiped away a tear. "The Bearded Swan!"

He pointed to what looked like an overgrown hovel, and it took a moment before I realised it was an inn. The thatch was mouldy and I could smell the patrons from the plaza. The sign - a flaking painting of a boss-eyed swan with a huge shaggy beard - looked like a child's nightmare.

"Look at it, Ulf!" Quentin sighed breathlessly. "Think about how many actors have been through here! Think of how many great minds have spoken of great things between those humble walls!"

"It looks like a prostitute's shithole." Their look told me that apparently, that was the wrong answer.

Decroix rolled his eyes. "We'll get the rooms sorted and then we have a few enquiries to make." He passed me five Wyear. "In the meantime, take this and try and stay out of trouble. We'll meet back here."

I handed them Reed's reins and my gear and left them to it. As I walked away, I casually wondered how badly Decroix knows me if he thinks giving me five Wyear is any way to keep me *out* of trouble.

Chapter 4:
Three Iron Bars

The sun sat at its zenith when I got to Mary's. The sweat was running down the inside of my armour, and that bath seemed better and better by the moment. A man walked out looking pleased with himself, and I knew exactly why. As I opened the door and stepped through, the perfumed incense hit me like a gentle slap. There were a few other men relaxing on pillows and I could smell the steam from the rooms upstairs.

Mary stood behind the bar. She smiled when she saw me and clapped her hands together in exaggerated glee. "Why, Ulf! What an unexpected delight!"

I found myself smiling at the sight of her. "You remember me?"

"Of course!" She leaned over and kissed my good cheek. "I never forget a face. Especially one so handsome . . ."

"Are the outrageous lies extra, or are they complementary?"

"All part of the service, my dear." She uncorked a bottle of wine and poured out two generous measures. I gulped mine down greedily and a bit dribbled out of my face.

She coughed politely, holding her full glass raised in a toast. "To old friends." I nodded and finished off the last drop in the goblet. "So, what brings you back to Cassioc?"

I shrugged. "Pair of actors hired me."

"For what? The pleasure of your company?"

"Very funny, Mary."

"Thank you, Ulf, I do try my very best." She simpered and I could feel myself salivating a little. I swallowed it down and blinked a few times. "They said they needed protection. But both of them can handle a blade, so I don't see why they needed a wet nurse to travel with them." I put down a few Wyear, which disappeared almost instantly. "Anyway Mary, I need a tub and a tug."

"In which order?"

"I'll take the bath first; it's only fair on the poor lass. I don't suppose you'd be . . ."

She held up her hand. "Why own dogs and bark yourself? I'll send Lesharne up in a while. You'll like her, she's new."

"I'll make sure she's back in one piece."

"And still able to walk! I know what you're like, Ulf."

"I'll do my best, but I'm promising nothing. Room six?"

She rolled her eyes and nodded. I headed upstairs past a few doors filled with giggling and the unmistakable sound of young, beautiful women pretending to be interested in rich, fat men.

I entered the room, shut the door, and turned the wheel on the side of the tub. I plugged the hole in the bottom and it began to fill with hot, steaming water. I breathed in deeply and listened to the splatter of the water as I began to strip off my armour. I dropped it to the floor with a series of clangs, and my clothes shortly followed, my bare feet feeling wonderfully cool on the tiled floor. I lowered myself into the tub and the water rushed up, flooding over my skin. I took great handfuls and poured them over my head, relishing the sensation as the water washed over me, taking the grime with it.

I flexed my shoulders and I could feel the tension in them melt away. The door swung open behind me. "Lesharne, is it? You're a little early, you might want to come ba-"

A metal wire bit into my throat. I scrabbled at a pair of black-gloved hands and thrashed, water flying everywhere. I slipped out of his grasp and tumbled, skidding along the floor. He kicked me square in the bollocks and I doubled over in pain.

"Not you fuckers again." I gasped. He drew a short, serrated blade and lunged for me. I could see something blue shimmering on the edge and I darted to the side, my wet feet skidding. I grabbed for my sword and swung it at him. The sheathed blade was clumsy, and he darted backwards before swiping at me again. I blocked the blow and tried to draw my sword, swearing at the peace binding. I hurled myself at him, forcing the scabbard edge into his throat. I pressed him back and down into the bath. He dropped his dagger as he tried to fight me off and I pushed him under the water. I dropped the sword, pressing my hands into his neck to hold him under the water and I flipped him over, pressing my knee into his back for leverage. He grasped at my fingers, twisting and pulling at them frantically, but I'm a big, cruel bastard, and he had kicked me right on the cockshaft. He was going to die.

I heard shouting below and the sound of feet as the last few bubbles faded away. Mary stood in the doorway holding her dagger. She looked at the corpse and then glared at me. "Fucking hells, Ulf! *Again?*

I fell back on my arse, panting, then staggered to my feet and looked at the man who just tried to kill me, face down in my bath. I reached around his neck and yanked off a pendant, a leather disk with a black ram engraved on it.

I sighed. "Yes, Mary. Again." I took a few deep breaths to steady myself as she shut the door behind her, then started fumbling with my hose and pulling on my boots, dressing as quickly as I could manage. "So, how did he get into what is supposed to be the safest brothel in Cassioc?"

She grimaced. "Don't worry. I'm going to be asking my lookouts that same question. Loudly."

I slung my sword belt over my shoulder and glanced at the body bobbing about in the tub. "Same as before?"

She closed her eyes and sighed. "Same as before."

Mary popped out and looked over the route down to the cellar. She came back with an old sheet and we wordlessly rolled him up. I hefted him onto my shoulder and flexed a little to show off my muscles. Mary rolled her eyes and checked once more that the way was clear. The sounds of happy customers and hardworking girls slipped from each room as we snuck past. I tried to think of a funny joke about a stiff in a brothel, but reading Mary's expression, I decided to drop it.

We arrived at the cellar door and I stooped as the ceiling got lower. I dropped the body and dragged him by the ankle, and his head made a rather satisfying *thunk* on each stair we went down. The temperature was roasting, and I cursed that after a bath I'd ended up as sweaty as a hog again.

The vast furnace for heating the bathwater was roaring away merrily. Mary opened the iron grate and I flung him inside. The air smoked and hissed as the assassin's wet clothes steamed in the fire before finally giving way to the flames. She shut the grate and we stood together as strips of flesh melted and poured off his bones in gory chunks.

"Drink?"

I nodded. "Drink."

We left the brothel and walked the streets for a while, saying nothing. Mary found a little place off the corner of the plaza and we sat down with mugs of beer. She took a long draught. "So, what exactly do those thugs have against you?"

"It's a very long story, Mary."

"Try me. I've heard pretty much everything there is. You should hear what girls have told me over the years. Bored and wanted some fun. Husband beating her. Children starving and living with an innkeeper somewhere. I've listened to everything. So come on Ulf, let's sit here and you can tell me your story."

I drained what was left of my ale, wiped my mouth and slapped a handful of copper on the table. "Or we could go watch the dog fights, get pissed, and fuck each other?"

"Or that."

The dog fights were great. I spotted a savage little fucker with no ears and scars around his muzzle. He looked like a mad thing, so I stuck money on him a few times. He ended up with his throat crushed, whimpering so his master called it off. The dogs were beaten off each other with a stick and shoved into cages. He had a good run, though. I finished three Wyear up, even after a few mugs.

We staggered out into the street and ended up somewhere in the eastern quarter called the Golden Anvil. It was filled with apprentices drinking away their meagre wages, and they gave us some odd looks as we burst in singing a song about tits. I grabbed a handful of coins from my pouch and hurled them at the barman and everyone started cheering. I don't remember much.

We ended up in bed, as usual. We had a room to ourselves and I stared at the ceiling as Mary lay snoring. I mentally swore as I tallied up how much money I'd spent, but the bed was warm and soft, and so was Mary.

It is cold. Not just because it is winter, but because of the wind which whips about the church through a dozen or so drafts. I clutch my tabard around me. The rest of the Order is here, even the squires like me. We sit towards the back, struggling to see or hear the sermon. The journeymen who support the Order are in the middle, knights at the front and the manifold ranks of clergy are arrayed under the huge stained-glass window. Sellor, the Patriarch of our order stands at the lectern. His hard face is creased with a fierce expression.

"Know this!" He jabs a finger towards the roof and gazes over us all. I sense him looking right at me and I freeze still. "Know that this Order is beset with foes. Those who would divide us! Trample us! Take our holy words and burn them, scattering what we hold dear to the wind." He lets his speech sink in, the words throbbing through the stone. "You must know these foes! Mark them as your eternal enemy and give neither mercy nor succour." He's looking right at the squires now, but I'm sure he's only speaking to me. My mouth is dry as a crypt and I can't move, even if I wanted to.

His ancient finger turns a page in the book before him and a grim smile crosses his face. "There are many who hate us for our virtue. Just as many fear us for our righteous anger. But as it is in a den of serpents there is always one whose fangs are sharper; whose coils are thicker and whose venom is deadlier than all the others. The Brotherhood of the Black Ram."

His lip shakes and he points a finger towards us. "Learn their foul ways as one studies a beast before hunting. Fear them for their temptations, but above all this; hate them. Hate them with every beat of your heart, every breath that you draw! Hate those who would harm the ones we protect! Hate their malice and hate their evil with every waking hour until, at last, you die."

I'm shaking as I hear him. Every word stabs at me. I try to spot my brother among the knights. He stands perfectly still, his gaze locked on the Patriarch.

Sellor pauses and softens his voice. The whisper carries to the very back of the church. *"When the land of Ashenfell stood corrupted, rotten to the core, who fought and slew the spawn of the Black Ram? Who held up the light which turned back the darkness when all others cowered? Only one - the Order of the Cleansing Flame!"*

Sellor turns, his shrivelled hand reaching out slowly, pointing to the iron brazier which burns and crackles. Its light dances, and the perfumed smoke rises high. Its warmth is far beyond me, but I still see the fire and my eyes drink in the flames. Two acolytes stand beside it, constantly stoking and feeding the fire as they keep alight the very heart of our Order.

I woke up with a headache that felt like a blacksmith had set up shop between my ears. I forced myself out of bed and over to the washing bowl on the table. The cold water shocked me, but that was probably a good thing. I turned back to the bed, but Mary wasn't there. From the noise outside it was mid-morning, and she probably had better things to do than spend all day in bed with a stinking sellsword.

My breath could melt iron and I was famished. I checked my pouch and swore loudly as I was now pretty much broke. Still, it was a brand new morning, and at the very least that meant two more Wyear from Decroix.

I headed downstairs after throwing on my armour and turned to the innkeeper. "I don't suppose I paid for breakfast last night before I went to bed?"

"No, but your friend did. She said she had to get going. Left about half an hour ago."

He brought out a plate with boiled eggs and some dried ham, and gave me a look that told me I shouldn't outstay my welcome. After lining my belly, I went to the Bearded Swan where Quentin and Decroix were drinking in the corner.

I grabbed a stool from another table and sat down, rubbing my temples. "First of all, two Wyear. Secondly, what do you need me to do today? Preferably something quiet and still."

Quentin gave me a sly smile and Decroix slid me two silver coins.

"Wonderful news, Ulf!"
"What is it?"
"You're going to love it!" Decroix chimed in.
"What. Is. It." My head was throbbing again.
"We're going to the theatre!"
"Bugger."

The grand plaza sits in the middle of the city where the roads meet; a sprawling marketplace with a bit of everything you can imagine. Animals bellow in stalls at auction, jewellery glints in the sunlight and for the right price, anything can be bought, or at least rented for a while. And squatting in the middle is The Ouroboros, the grandest theatre in the land.

Most actors will settle for a couple of planks over some barrels, but for the fancy types, there is The Ouroboros - stories without a beginning or an end. Last time I was in Cassioc I was hired to guard some cruel bastard of a merchant who was afraid for his life after the crossed a few people he shouldn't have. He took me along to a play there and it was more than anyone could hope. They had demons rising from the ground in clouds of smoke, people twisting themselves backwards in strange shapes and clothes so beautiful they would leave your jaw hanging open. The acting was terrible, of course, but then it always is.

We left our swords at the inn and headed off to The Ouroboros. I felt naked without it, but unlike most places, The Ouroboros could be picky about who they let in, and one of the rules was no blades longer than a hand. Also, no cripples, beggars, open flames, drunks, or cheese with veins, according to the sign at the entrance. The huge wattle walls loomed up, the bright white of the daub shining in the sunlight as we were swept along with the rest of the daytime crowd.

Brigandine

We jostled and pushed through the lively crowed to get a good view of the stage. We paid three Ecar for a ground spot, so we stood with the others. There were better views above us, and for six Ecar you could get a wooden stool, but everyone sees the same play, so paying more is pointless unless you're too old or fat to stand.

They had put down fresh straw, but the oily smell of paint lingered near the stage, mingling with the stale reek of cheap beer from the cart off to the side. I probably shouldn't have spent half my day's wages on hot sausages and a mug of beer, but I did anyway.

The bear baiter came out to get the crowd excited before the show started. The bear looked a little grey around the muzzle, but he still gave a decent roar as the brightly dressed clown jabbed at him with a stick, and he made a good go of swatting away the small vicious dogs who nipped at him. I chucked the end of my sausage at him and it bopped on his nose, getting a good laugh from the crowd as he left to solid applause. They always do the funny plays in the daytime and the murder ones in the evening. Probably because it's hard to have a tense scene of bloodshed and betrayal when you can hear a fishmonger's wife in the background yelling at her husband to get off his arse and help with the cod.

The play was 'The Pair of Pairs', which turned out to be a fairly good play once it got going. Two twins are separated at birth and they are both shagging the same woman. Except here's the thing: she's also a twin and one of them is robbing the miser who owns the tailor's shop while the other one is shagging the brothers so that if she's caught, she has an alibi. Except she gets jealous that her sister never does anything but stay in bed all day shagging while she steals stuff so she nags her into swapping but she's no good at thieving and- all right, I won't ruin the ending for you, but it's a decent one.

We returned to the Bearded Swan and I knocked back a couple of ales. Quentin and Decroix were in the corner planning so I made a few Ecar on a hoop and hook game betting with a struggling lute player. Clever fingers for playing, but for the life of him, he couldn't throw a fucking wooden ring over an iron hook.

I was in a good mood when the brothers asked me over to the table. Decroix handed me a note, and suddenly I wasn't feeling so good anymore.

SHOPPING LIST

THREE LONG IRON BARS
THREE DARK CLOAKS
ONE YARD BLACK CLOTH

He handed me a Guilder along with a grin that would make a fox blush. I finished my ale, wiped my lips, and headed out.

I easily got what I needed after a short walk around the southern quarter. I haggled for some good prices, and with a few Wyear change in my pocket, I headed back to the Bearded Swan. In our room, Quentin told me the plan. It wasn't the worst thing I'd ever done, but it was definitely up there.

We waited until dark before we set off. I left my armour under the bed with my sword. I didn't want to rattle, and weapons could have made things nasty.

They were twin brothers: Andrew and Theobald. They couldn't quite afford the overpriced rates of the Bearded Swan, so they were lodging at the Golden Balls a cheap little place near the nastier end of the city. We found a small alley near the inn and I unwrapped the cloaks. Decroix cut up the black cloth and we wrapped it around our faces. Each of us took an iron bar, and we lay in wait.

They returned about an hour after the evening show had finished, singing to each other with an accent I couldn't quite place. Quentin put a finger to his lips and I gripped the bar tightly. I stepped from the shadows and smashed down hard on one of their collarbones. A sickening crunch followed as Quentin and Decroix took the other brother out at the knees, and he fell screaming into the gutter.

Mine grabbed at me, so Quentin hurled him over his hip to the ground and we beat him around the ribs till he started sobbing. His brother crawled towards him on legs that didn't look quite right, desperately trying to help. I ground my boot down hard on his hand, leaving his fingers a mangled mess. Finally, Decroix drew his dagger and made a long, thin cut down the side of one of their faces.

I heard someone coming, so we hurled ourselves down the alley, tossing the cloaks and masks away, leaving the iron bars to roll across the cobbles as their cries and moans echoed in our ears. We went to a tavern along the way back and drank in silence before heading to the Bearded Swan and up to bed.

All part of the plan. An alibi as a worst-case scenario, but there was no way they saw who we were.

"Bravery is the soil of knighthood, glory the rose."
"Excellent. Tell me of manhood."
I furrow my brow for a moment. "Battle is the test of manhood. In the majesty of war, one's true character is finally known."
"And lastly, what is the mark of a true knight?"
"A true knight . . . A true knight is always- Never! A true knight . . . is never . . . err--"
He cuts me off with a sigh. "A true knight is never rash. A true knight is always merciful. A true knight will defend those who are meek unto death, knowing in his heart that what he does is righteous."
My brother looks at me with disappointment. I can't hold his gaze so I look down at the floor instead. "You have to learn this Ulf! A knight is far more than his armour and a horse. He must be-"
"-strong of arm, stout of heart, and pure of spirit. His is the flame which burns away the wicked."
He smiles. "See! You do know it. Now you just have to remember it. Sellor can ask you anything he wants from the Book of Flame. Anything on the history of the Order, the Aphorisms of Virtue or, indeed, anything he feels like. Do you think he'll go easy on you because your brother is in the Order?" He looks at me sternly.
"No."
"Exactly. He'll be looking for any chance to show us up. And unless you want to be tending horses and polishing my armour for another year, I suggest you learn this." He raps a finger on the massive closed book in front of me.

Jack Shannon

It's a sunny day outside. The air is full of the crash of wooden waster swords against each other. The other squires are training. My brother snaps his fingers in front of my face to grab my attention and opens the book. He frowns at me and taps the page. "Book."

Chapter 5:
Fire and Stone

I felt like shit the next morning. I dragged myself out of bed and buckled my armour on as usual. I could hear a bit of commotion downstairs as people argued and whispered about what had happened the night before. News travels fast.

Quentin and Decroix weren't about, but the innkeeper passed me a sealed piece of paper.

Ulf,
We will be busy today.
Thank you for your work.
Please find enclosed seven Wyear- today's wage and a keep-out-of-trouble-stipend.

-Q&D

The coins were heavy in my hand. They clinked as I quickly dropped them into my purse, suddenly uncomfortable with their heft. I headed off to find something, anything, to do. I wandered the city for a while, heading north on a whim, and found myself surrounded by the clashing buildings of vying faiths and the heady smell of burning incense. The towering spires of the temples pierced the heavens as voices cried out their devotion to all the Virtuous Ones.

It was a small shrine, barely bigger than a shed and tucked between the much larger ones of Reginald the Vigilant and Guthrum the Wealthy. But it was still there, maintained and tended as it should be. Two mercenaries were inside. I couldn't hear much, but I gathered they were praying for protection on a journey with some merchant, who I guessed was the fat bloke at Guthrum's tacky shrine next door.

As the sellswords got up to leave, I saw it. An overly muscled man carved from dark oak, holding a cheap iron sword, painted to keep off the rust. He stared at me with empty sockets. His pupils would have once been rubies, or maybe sapphires, but the statue was blinded long ago to pay whatever tax or levy was demanded at the time.

Still, it was Oswald the Fierce. There was no mistaking the face, or the three flames carved on the plinth.

"Have you thought about what will happen when you die friend?"

A piece of paper was shoved under my nose, held by a filthy little man with bare feet. I slapped it away with a grunt. He smiled up at me with yellow teeth and fumbled around his neck for a painted wooden symbol in the shape of the sun.

"When we die, there are two choices-we can either embrace the loving arms of Kalidar the Wise or be hurled to destruction on the rocks of oblivion!"

"Oh no, not the rocks of oblivion. That sounds like a right hassle . . ." I muttered, trying to push past him.

"Don't you want eternal life, friend?"

"Not if you're there, I fucking don't."

"Kalidar is bountiful beyond all measure to the righteous!"

I shoved him backwards and he fell on his arse. "And how does he feel about cunts like you?"

As I strode past, he scrambled to his feet. "Kalidar bless you, friend!"

"Tell him to go fuck himself!" I yelled back in a cheery voice.

All around me was more of the same. Everyone was convinced that their Virtuous One was the one who was particularly virtuous.

That they, out of the dozens of heroes, sages, caregivers and bastards who have a temple dedicated to them- have lived the life everyone should emulate. After the old gods died, the people found solace in the Virtuous Ones, drawing on their example in this life and hoping to meet with them in whatever lies hereafter. I was promised damnation, redemption and everything in between before I crossed to the other side of the square.

I spent the rest of the day at the Bearded Swan. I scrubbed down my armour and sharpened my sword for want of anything better to do, then sat around nursing a few drinks. Part of me thought about going to see Mary again, but she had better things to do than spend time with a sack of shit like me.

The brothers came back in the afternoon, seemingly in good spirits. "Good evening my friend!" Decroix said, back to his usual self.

I gave the brothers a grunt of acknowledgement. "So, what did the pair of you get up to today?" We were sitting in the corner. The tavern was quiet, but they did a quick theatrical glace over their shoulders.

"Nothing much." He shrugged. "The theatre was closed. Sadly, the two lead actors have suffered an unfortunate accident." He winked at me and I gave him a long, cold stare. "But the show must go on! Auditions are tonight."

Quentin leaned in. "Tell me Ulf, how do you feel about the theatre?"

They made me leave my sword and armour in the room, but I kept my dagger under my shirt at the small of my back. We walked through the open doors of The Ouroboros as the sun set. A small bald man in a slashed doublet paced the stage, anxiously tugging at a scraggly beard.

Decroix and Quentin bowed low. "Good evening!" Decroix and Quentin bowed low.

The man turned on them, angrily throwing his hands in the air. "What do you want? Can't you see I'm busy?"

Quentin flashed his wolfish smile and bowed again. "Sir, as fairest dawn follows the bleakest night, so may opportunity follow tragedy. I am Cardel, my brother Maiken-" Decroix bowed low, scraping his knuckles on the straw. "-and this is Scalagrim, a tragic, deaf-mute idiot who is under our care." I clenched my fists and ground my teeth a little. "We heard about those poor lads."

"Terrible stuff." Decroix chipped in. "Simply dreadful!"

I watched Quentin and his brother wringing their hands and a bit of sick rose up into my throat. "And we were wondering if we could help." I stifled a groan.

The little man looked aghast for a moment, then broke out into a beaming smile. "By the Virtuous Ones! This is indeed fortuitous! I mean, you're not twins, but you're close enough. Flavius!" He snapped his fingers and a round fellow with beady eyes bounded onto the stage. "Get these two into costume right away! We've missed the day performance, but if we cancel tonight's The Feast of Ravens we can run Pair of Pairs instead."

The fat man pouted. "Oh, Revin! Say it isn't so! That Pairs nonsense is such tosh!"

"It's bringing in three times the money! Feet on straw, Flavius, feet on straw!"

He rolled his pudgy little eyes and snapped his fingers. "You two, with me. I'll need to let the costumes out of course . . ."

After being given a broom and a brief yet elaborate demonstration by Revin, I was left on my own to sweep the cellars and storerooms backstage. The honeycomb of chambers under the theatre was packed with all manner of props and scenery, flung together. Boxes of skulls, crowns, blunted swords and wooden trees lay stacked in piles atop each other. Rows upon rows of costumes stood on rails like the silent ghosts of old stories, made from thin, cheap fabric that looked good from a distance.

I would occasionally catch movement out of the corner of my eye. Each time, I would tell myself it was probably just rats, which would certainly be better than the alternative.

I watched the play from the ground spots. Quentin and Decroix lapped up the applause like a pair of dogs in a butcher's

Brigandine

alleyway. After, we headed back to The Bearded Swan and sat around, sharing a cold pie.

Decroix dabbed away a crumb from the corner of his mouth. "I think that went exceedingly well. What do you think, Ulf?"

I gave him a glare.

"Ulf?"

"I'm sorry, I can't say anything. I'm a deaf, mute idiot, remember?"

Quentin laughed uproariously and Decroix tutted. "Very funny. But the point is, no one notices an idiot pushing a broom around. You could be fucking their wives and mothers at the same time, and no one would notice!"

Quentin shrugged. "Hopefully the wives and mothers would, at least . . ."

Decroix leaned in conspiratorially. "The point is, Ulf, you're our man to observe what's going on. While we are busy accepting applause, taking bows-"

"-and sleeping with the rest of the cast-" Quentin added.

"-you'll be keeping an eye on things." said Decroix, frowning at his brother.

A week passed. The brothers were a big hit and ticket sales were booming. The Feast of Ravens was taken off in favour of a second performance each day-much to the wailing and moaning of the "proper" actors. During the day I touched up the scenery, swept the straw, threw out the drunks and did various other jobs nobody gave a crap about. Especially when I cleaned out the crapping-pots. To be fair, it was very funny when I pretended I couldn't understand Revin and poured one over his feet.

Most evenings, the brothers were out drinking with the rest of the troupe, leaving me on my own in the Bearded Swan. I tried to work on a save-half-drink-half system of money management, but it swiftly turned into a drink-most-spend-the-rest system. With the two Wyear a day from the brothers and the three Ecar from sweeping the theatre I had enough money to enjoy myself, but I became so bored that it quickly got pissed up the wall. Or vomited against the wall, in the case of one cheap, nasty pie I had.

Late one night, after the show was done and the actors had all fucked off, I took my broom and a lantern and started tidying up the storeroom. The actors always left it like a shit heap, throwing things on the floor as they rushed out to get pissed at the end of each day. While moving around a few crates of wigs, make-up, and false beards, I bumped into a box. It slumped back against the wall and made a loud rip as it tumbled through. I looked closer, and I saw that the section of the wall was just hardened paper, like they used for masks. The false wall was painted with the same white daub as the rest of the building, and in the dark storeroom, it would have been impossible for anyone to have spotted the difference. A shelf attached to the wall worked as a lever to open it. I peered into the darkness and my eyes slowly adjusted to the gloom.

I felt the rush of stale air and the smell of wet stone. Taking up my lantern, I stepped forward gingerly and my foot found a hard flagstone. I had to duck as the tunnel sloped downwards, winding deep into the earth. The air around me smelled musty and fetid. My neck cricked and my back was just starting to ache when the path opened wide into a chamber.

Holding up the lantern, I saw the sides were carved with whirls and ovals that seemed to shift and dance under my gaze. A pain started behind my eyes as I tried to focus on them, but to no avail. Rust brown dust coated the bottom of my boots and the room reeked of old blood and sickly-sweet decay. In the middle of the room squatted a huge jagged tooth of stone bound in strips of iron. It pulsed hideously, writhing at its bonds.

My head swam and my breathing came in ragged puffs as I staggered backwards, banging my head on the tunnel ceiling. I forced myself up to the surface, each step a labour as my vision swirled. I shoved stacks of boxes in front of the hole, then ran outside and dunked my head in a rainwater barrel to clear it.

I spat on the cobbles and wiped my face with my sleeve. "Oh, fuck me sideways . . ."

Luckily, I found enough daub to patch up the door, and then headed back to the Bearded Swan with a hundred questions.

I waited up in the room, sober as a gravestone for the brothers to get back. Quentin staggered into the room with Decroix close behind him. Their faces were still smeared with makeup from the performance, and wet patches of ale stained their jerkins.

"Hello, Ulf!" Decroix smiled stupidly. "I didn't realise you'd be-"

"Shut up." He fell quiet. I looked them both in the eye. "I know."

Both of them sobered up instantly.

"What did you find?" Quentin asked quietly. "Think carefully."

"A hidden door in the storeroom. Tunnel under the earth. A big stone with queer writing on it." I picked at my thumbnail. "No idea what the fuck it was." I lied. How well, I wasn't sure.

They looked at each other. "Four Wyear a day." said Decroix.

I snorted. "Ten."

"Five."

"Done."

"Good."

Decroix bit at his knuckle, then turned and shut the door. "Now listen well, Ulf of Banrillar. What we ask of you is of the utmost importance. You are to follow us. Trust us. And this is most important of all: don't kill the one we tell you not to."

"Back pay."

"What?"

"Back pay. The rate has gone up and I want back pay for all the past days it's been at the old rate."

Decroix rummaged angrily in his bags "Oh for . . . there!" He threw two Guilder at me. "Now fuck off!"

I pocketed the money and they both readied themselves for bed. Quentin turned to me, "Get a good night's sleep. Ulf. I have a feeling tomorrow will be a very busy day for you."

I rose early and headed out to the southern quarter. The southern parts of the city are the domain of merchants and traders.

The guild houses and middle-class homes are to the south-west, the craftsmen are to the southeast, and the merchants are nestled between. The grand plaza sits in the middle of the city where the roads meet, a sprawling marketplace with a bit of everything you can imagine. Animals bellow in stalls at auction, jewellery glints in the sunlight, and, for the right price, anything can be bought, or at least rented for a while.

I bought a good, solid hammer with a stout handle from a peddler and took it to a jeweller. The shop bell rang and he looked up from his work bench. His lips pursed and he gave me a thin smile.

"Good morning, fair sir." The disdain dripped from him like a cheap candle as his eye wandered to my mess of a face. "How might I serve you?"

I took out a Guilder and placed it on the countertop, then put the hammer down next to it. "I want a solid inch of silver, cast onto the head, and carved with this symbol on the face." I reached into my shirt and pulled out an old wooden disk, battered with age, bearing three flames dancing in a circle.

He looked at me like I was mad, so I looked at him like I was as well. Mad enough to bend him over the countertop and fuck him with a candlestick if he asked any stupid questions. He slowly reached out and took the money. "This should be fine. Of course, it will take a day or two. I have other orders which must take priority."

I took out the other Guilder and put it into his palm, cursing under my breath. "Now."

He gave me another thin smile. "The customer is always right." He gestured to a worn but expensive looking chair. "Please, sir, take a seat."

It took about an hour for him to cast the silver, file off around the edges and engrave the symbol. The soft metal yielded readily to the chisel, and he handed me back the hammer.

"Good day, sir." He said, in a voice that also implied "And please fuck off out of my shop, you ugly bastard."

Brigandine

I hid the hammer down my trouser leg and sprinted for The Ouroboros. I got there as the other menials were putting down straw and moving the scenery at the start of a new day.

"And just where the fuck have you been?" I nearly turned around before I remembered I was deaf, so I waited for him to grab my shoulder. Flavius wobbled his chins in fury and I tried to mime that I saw a pig in the street and I thought it looked friendly to play with. He slapped me hard across the face, and it was all I could do not to snap his neck. I looked sad and started spreading straw on the ground dejectedly. I tried not to dwell on the irony that I was the best actor in this fucking dump.

The day's performance came and went. The crowd laughed at the normal parts and they still simpered at the happy ending. While I was backstage tidying, Decroix came up to me, tossing a cloak onto the clothes rail. "End of the day. Storeroom." He walked away quickly, and I got back to work.

I waited in the storeroom for them to arrive. Quentin and Decroix entered, along with Revin, Flavius and four more of the actors-a pair of men and women. Quentin smiled at me. He gently took me by the hand and I played along. "Hello, Scalagrim. You're going to come with us now. Can you do that for me?" He mouthed the words widely and slowly. I looked puzzled for a second then grinned and nodded.

Flavius looked at me suspiciously. "Are you sure that he will be acceptable?"

Decroix pursed his lips. "We are serious about this. We want in." Revin walked into the back of the store and took out eight long dark robes. He passed two to Quentin and Decroix, who donned them eagerly. Each of them then kissed and donned a small leather disk. The wooden symbol under my shirt began to feel very heavy indeed, and I prayed to Oswald the Fierce that they didn't see it.

No-one noticed my hasty repair job as Revin pulled the shelf and the false wall opened into the tunnel. Travelling silently, I let Quentin lead me by the hand into the depths.

We arrived at the chamber, and the obelisk in the centre throbbed with an obscene appetite. My skin crawled as Quentin placed me against it, then took a length of rope and bound me to it.

I flexed my arms and subtly pushed against the bonds, keeping my face a mask of idiocy. The cold silver of the hammer against my leg was at once a comfort and a terror, as I was convinced they could see the bulge.

The dizzying musk of the room rose up again. My sight faded for a second before I snapped myself back. Six voices droned and chanted twisting, hissing words which merged into each other horribly. Smoke rose from the floor, pale and acrid.

Suddenly, the chanting stopped and one of the women stepped forward. I recognised her as one of the sisters in the play, the one who was annoyed she was robbing the miser while the other got to do all the fucking. She held a knife in her hand, the blade glinting as she held it up high.

Quentin barrelled into her, sending her flying. There was a scream, and a man next to Decroix doubled over, desperately holding his guts in.

"ULF, DON'T KILL HER!" Quentin slammed her hand against the wall before being punched square in the jaw by another. He elbowed his attacker hard in the teeth, then screamed at me, "FEEL FREE TO FUCK UP ANY OF THE OTHER ONES, THOUGH!"

I fumbled with the ropes and desperately drew my dagger. One of them lunged at me and cut me across the shoulder, nearly ripping open my neck. I stabbed down hard into his bicep, pulled it clear and tore his throat out. Blood splashed in my face as I threw him down.

Decroix danced around Revin and Flavius. The fat man was jabbing at air before Decroix sliced the back of his hand and then slashed him across the groin. He fell down, hands between his legs as blood poured over them. I rushed over and rammed my pommel into the side of Revin's head. Stumbling, he sprang upwards and slashed at me wildly.

"Help Quentin!" I shouted, then hurled myself against Revin and we tumbled into the wall. The little man was quick and deceptively strong. He grasped my dagger hand and I lunged for his, taking a nick on the forearm. We rolled on the floor, tangled in his robes, and I pulled his hood over his eyes and stabbed him twice in the neck for good measure.

Quentin pinned down the leader and Decroix withdrew his dagger from the other woman, spilling her guts. She dropped her blade with a horrified gasp and it clattered to the floor before slumping down into a pool of gore, her yellow hair smeared with blood.

I heard Flavius still moaning, so I rolled him on his back and stabbed him through the eye socket. I couldn't feel the cuts and bruises yet, but I knew they would hurt in a while.

Quentin pinned the leader's arms down and moved his hips so she couldn't kick him in the prick. Decroix tied her feet with the rope that had just scant moments ago bound me to the Waystone. "You bastards! You complete bastards!" She screamed at our betrayal and thrashed against her bonds. She laughed. "You will pay! You'll all pay with your lives and those you love! The Black Ram will rise once more and-" Quentin forced the rope into her mouth and tied her, strapping her arms to her sides.

I dragged her across the rough floor and back to the storeroom. "I need to go back," I said. "I forgot my dagger."

Decroix raised his hands in frustration. "For fuck's sake, Ulf!" he snarled. "I'll get you a new fucking dagger!"

But I was off. I ran back down the tunnel, stooped over. Back in the room, the smell of blood was overwhelming, challenged only by the stink of Flavius' voided bowels.

I took out the hammer and looked at the Waystone. The awful power coursing through it was plain to see as it writhed and pulsed. I held out the hammer and, for the second time tonight, asked Oswald the Fierce for his protection. I closed my eyes, desperately trying to remember the words.

"Flame of the mind. Flame of the body. Flame of the spirit. Oswald, grant me thy aid!" My mouth was dry as I swung the hammer with every piece of strength I had. The silver buckled and spread across the surface like rainwater, melting into the stone. The Waystone groaned, filling the air as it whined and splintered.

I snatched up the dagger I had left in Flavius' eye socket and ran as fast as I could, bursting into the storeroom. "We need to leave, now!"

Quentin looked at me puzzled. "But what about the bodies?"

I grabbed the woman and threw her over my shoulder. "I wouldn't worry about that if I were you. Now, go!"

We ran out of the theatre, followed by a terrible shrieking noise like some great beast tearing itself in two with pain. Foul-smelling flames danced across the walls of The Ouroboros as timbers buckled and cracked. Walls caved in and the thatch burned high. Sparks carried by the wind blew towards the market and people flooded from homes and taverns to grab water. The market lay in chaos as the greatest theatre in all the land collapsed into a terrible inferno.

"This way!" Quentin cried. We ran towards the city walls. Madness all around us now as word of the fire echoed out across the city.

A guard stood nervously by a wooden ladder. "And here's the other half." Decroix shoved some coins into his hands and the guard stepped aside.

"Who's the girl?" the guard asked.

"She's my niece. She's had too much to drink." I said. He glanced at the angry, thrashing woman, decided she wasn't worth the bother, and ran away into the night. A coil of rope lay on the top of the wall and we scaled down. I thought about just throwing her over, but instead, we lowered her down slowly. I nearly dropped her a few times, because it was funny, but she plonked safely onto the piles of filth at the bottom of the wall. We shimmied down and hustled off into the night.

Quentin took us about half a mile to the north-west under the cover of darkness. We moved quickly and quietly until we came to a road where a man stood, holding our horses with the gear from our room in the Bearded Swan. As we got closer, I recognized him as the stable lad.

Decroix passed him a Guilder, and I noticed his pouch didn't look quite so full as it did when I first met him. The dancing flames we could still see over the walls of Cassioc told me we shouldn't go back there for a while. I quickly grabbed my stuff, threw the girl over Reed's saddle, and slapped her hard on the rump to get her going.

The horse, not the girl.

Quentin and Decroix rode off quickly, following me.

"Wait! Don't leave me! Take me with you!" The young man ran after us, wailing desperately. Quentin looked back and thrashed his reins as hooves pounded the road. Tears were streaming on his face as he fruitlessly chased after us. "You said I was beautiful and you loved me! We were going to see the world together!"

As his cries faded away into the night Decroix turned in the saddle to fix Quentin with a cold, hard stare.

"What? I kept my promise! I can say, hand on heart, I did not seduce the innkeeper's daughter."

"For fuck's sake, Quentin . . . ." he muttered.

We rode hard until the sun rose, a bloody smear across the horizon. When we stopped, I was rather pleased to see that Quentin's beau had packed enough food for five into our saddlebags. I loosened the girl's gag and threw her a red apple.

"I'll kill all of you! You'll rue your foolishness! The Black Ram rises to once more rule over this land!" She screamed at us till she was red in the face, so I took the water skin from Reed and tipped it over her. She shrieked a bit, but she calmed down.

"You bastard!" She yelled at me. I rolled my eyes.

"For an actress, you're not very imaginative. You've already called me that about fifty times." I took out my knife, cut off a piece of apple and shoved it toward her mouth, keeping my fingers well out of biting range. She spat it out and then gobbed in my face.

"Suit yourself." I picked up the rest of the apple and Reed munched it happily.

"I'm Decroix, and this is Quentin." Quentin gave a small bow and a wolfish grin. "And this is Ulf, our associate."

She snarled at us, "Siffisante. Charmed, I'm sure. I'd curtsey, but you tied me up and threw me over a horse".

Quentin wagged a finger. "If you didn't want to have your friends all killed, and be tied up and thrown over a horse by a violent maniac and his handsome friends, then you shouldn't have been leading a cult of the Black Ram, now, should you?"

I shrugged. "He makes a good point."

Decroix took the first shift watching the prisoner, short sword laid bare across his lap. Even with the sun overhead, I was knackered. It had been a long night, my arse hurt from the ride, and I could still smell smoke in my nostrils. There was no way a blaze that size didn't send a few people screaming to their graves.

Quentin whispered to me. "Do you want to tell me what happened there? Why you really went back? What was going on with that stone?"

I shut my eyes.

"No."

Chapter 6:
A Good Child

I open my eyes. I can hear her coughing again. It's cold enough that my breath steams, and the bed is huge and empty. I look over and I see my brother. He looks exhausted, holding a bowl under our mother's mouth as once again she hacks and splutters a red mess of blood and phlegm.

I know she's dying. Neither of them will tell me, but I know my mother will die soon. That's why Taran is back in our sleepy village. Everyone stood outside their door as he rode past on a huge horse, armour gleaming in the winter sun.

I don't know who wrote the letter to tell him to come back to Banrillar, but I'm glad he's here. Taran left to become a knight. He was chosen by the Order because he was special and had to go away to live with them in their castle. That's what Mother told me.

It's been years since I saw him last and I can barely remember him from before, but he remembered me. He brought me a wooden bear, carved and painted. I am far too old for toys now, but I put it next to my bed anyway.

Mother sits back in the bed and closes her eyes. I watch as her breathing slows and she drifts to sleep. Taran takes the bowl to the door and dumps the foul mess into the weeds outside. I hear the door shut again and he slowly climbs into bed beside me.

"*Taran?*"

He smiles at me. "*Yes, Ulf?*"

"*Nothing.*"

"*Alright, then.*"

He rolls over and stares at the ceiling, and I do the same. The only sounds are my mother's shallow breathing and the snap of logs on the hearth. Normally it's stupid to burn up fuel at night. There is only so much wood, and winter is long and harsh. But Mother won't last for the whole winter, so Taran decided she should at least stay as warm as she can in the tiny house.

"*There must be something we can do.*"

We can hear the mice shuffling through the thatch, snuffling around for anything to eat. He turns towards me. His face is handsome and strong, but his eyes are heavy and red.

"*We're doing everything we can, Ulf. We have to make her comfortable, keep the house for her, and let Mother know that we love her.*"

I start crying. I know I shouldn't, but I can't help it. I sob and shake, and Taran pulls me to him.

"*There has to be something! It can't happen like this!*"

"*But it is happening. And there isn't, Ulf. You have to trust me.*"

"*Why can't it be like a story! With a potion or a charm . . . magic.*"

I feel Taran's arm tense, then slowly relax. A silence hung heavy in the air.

"*Ulf. Let me tell you something. A story. Do you want to hear a story?*"

I nod and listen to him. His eyes are wide open and he looks right into me, whispering.

"*A long time ago, so far past that no-one can remember, there were people who had that same thought. That magic could help people. That it could heal sickness, make the crops grow big and strong, let more children by born-all kinds of things. But as they used the magic, they got greedy and wanted more and more. Money, power over other men-even to live forever.*"

I strain my ears and listen in. His voice is like a feather, but it seems to fill the whole room.

"*But as the people wanted more, the price grew greater for the magic that was granted. Magic does not come from no-where, Ulf. It comes from dark things in dark places. Things blacker than shadow that live where you just can't see them. They demanded many things to make the magic work. Terrible things.*"

"*What happened? What did they do with the magic?*"

"*They got stronger and stronger, until one day they ruled over all of the land and the whole of the world was in chaos and madness. The gods left, and no prayers were answered. The land turned to salt, the crops failed, and the animals* died. Some people became little more than beasts, snarling and howling like wolves. Or they worshipped the dark things, desperate for protection. The rest all sailed in ships, off to Ashenfell. The one land that was spared the blight. Magic followed them, creeping like a snake. But then a warrior arose, who challenged their power and came to lead the people."

"Oswald the Fierce!"

He smiles. "Who's telling the story, me or you?"

"Sorry . . ." I mutter.

"Oswald found the source of their power, the things which opened up and let magic into the world: the Waystones. Rocks carved with evil symbols and bathed in blood to help them summon wicked creatures to give them magic. He cast them down and destroyed them one by one, draining away their power and leaving them helpless without magic. They fled and retreated into the corners of the earth, forever filled with hate and plotting their revenge."

My heart is pounding away and I find I can barely speak. "But . . . but what if they come back? What if they try to make more of the stones? What if-"

He grabs me close in a hug and kisses the top of my head. He feels stronger than an oak tree and I know that I'm safe if he's there.

"Now this is the clever part, Ulf. That's why there are people to stop them."

We travelled for ten days north-west up the coast. The road reached to the sea, and the ocean crashed on the cliffs below. Reed proved to be a great horse, sure-footed and untroubled by the noise of the waves. I rode right along the edge to make Siffisante nervous, because I found it funny.

"Could we toss her off the cliff?" I half-heartedly suggested to Decroix.

He shook his head. "No, not a good idea. We need her."

"Why, is Quentin getting the itch again?"

"She's not to be harmed, Ulf. That's final."

I decided not to press the plan. Besides, it wouldn't have been fair on the fish who would've had to eat her. "So, are you going to tell me why you need this useless sack of tallow?"

He turned round in the saddle to fix me with a look. "No."

"Fair enough."

The high cliffs and bare rocks gave way to plains and field land as our course turned inland, to the west. A few miles along, the road turned into a winding path into the deep forest of Wallenpel, a thick clot of wood packed with bears, bandits, and worse.

The woods were flanked by two mountains to the south-east, the Long Blade and the Short Blade. Nasty, slippery stone, hard to cut and even harder to climb. Most folks take the long way around the side of the Long Blade rather than risk passing through the Wallenpel - sensible, sane folks that don't want to have their guts ripped out by a bandits' spear, or end up having their arsehole eaten by a bear.

We made camp as the light died and Quentin took out some cheese for supper. As we ate, Decroix shared the next stage of his plan. "We're going through the woods."

I looked Decroix in the eyes as the fire crackled. "You mean around, don't you?"

"No, Ulf. I mean through. We'll be harder to track, and time is important. We wasted too much of it in Cassioc."

"It wasn't entirely wasted." Quentin said, wistfully.

Siffisante sneered at Decroix. She did a great line in sneering. I'd seen most of her sneers these last few days, and this was one of her all-time best. "Idiots! Everyone knows those woods are haunted!"

As much as it annoyed me, she was right. Something in the soil makes the trees grow densely together. The wood is phenomenally strong and their roots go down for miles. Over the years many rulers had attempted to clear the land for farming, but it never worked out. All travellers have heard the stories. Foresters arrive and make camp, singing about how rich they are going to be. Axes are sharpened, saws readied, and work starts.

The problems start to happen after a few days. Tools begin to snap, trees fall the wrong way, targets are missed. Tempers start to fray as the weather gets bad. Then it gets worse. Accidents happen. Men are injured and animals get sick. A couple of people are crippled, or worse, by falling trees.

Then, after a few weeks, folks go missing. No-one ever talks about it. Shouting and brawling among the workers gives way to violence and a few have to be hanged, bodies twitching on the boughs of trees that they planned to cut down. More leave during the night, either going back to their families or deeper into the woods.

Soon, everyone has left. The forest grows back and all that remains are a few rusted axes, which are swallowed up by the twisting roots. Even with a whole ship full of Guilders, you'd never be able to pay men enough to stay in those woods for long.

Quentin and Decroix scoffed and they each took another slice of hard cheese. "Look on the positive side, Ulf!" Quentin swallowed a mouthful. "You can forage for berries in the woods! That will be fun."

The rations were starting to wear thin. We finished off the fresh stuff for breakfast that morning, so we would soon have to start the part of the journey where we ate the crappy dry stuff to stay alive. I ignored further taunts from Siffisante and settled down to sleep, casually wondering what colour bear it would be that would tear out my arsehole and eat it.

As the sun rose, I woke up and stretched the sleep out of my limbs. Decroix had a fire going and we warmed ourselves as we ready to venture into the Wallenpel. Reed pawed the earth anxiously as we stood on the forest's edge. I tried to calm her, but she whined and stamped, pulling against me. The brother's geldings weren't doing any better, so we dismounted, and I pulled Siffisante down from Reed's back, dumping her on the ground.

"You're walking. You could do with the exercise." I tied a rope around her neck and looped it a few times around my forearm, then unbound her wrists and ankles. She rubbed the raw patches left by the coarse bindings, but I struggled to give a shit.

That's a lie. I didn't give a shit at all and kicked her hard up the backside. "Get up and get going."

She got to her feet and gave me a filthy look. I grinned back at her, letting her see the mess that is the side of my face and she quickly mellowed her demeanour.

The shabby path was overgrown, and after a few minutes the light behind us died. All that remained were shards of dusty sunlight stabbing through the canopy. I took my sword from Reed's saddle and slung it over my shoulder, the untied peace binding hanging limply at the side. We pressed deeper into the woods until the darkness started to creep and the trees came to life with the sounds of twilight. We found a clearing and I re-tied Siffisante for the night.

The fire brought me little comfort as the shadows birthed from the flame flickered and danced over the branches and twigs, casting horrible figures at the edge of the clearing. I stood guard while the others slept as best they could, watching the darkness and sharpening my ears to the sounds of the forest. I took some small reassurance from the rub of the leather on my sword's hilt and the cold steel of the crossguard against my hand.

I stirred Decroix at midnight and he shuffled awake. He held his drawn short sword, bare steel gleaming in the firelight, and I could tell we felt the same. We nodded to each other as I put on my shift and slid under my blankets and into a restless sleep.

We buried mother this morning. She was so still. It seemed so strange that she was quiet after so many months of coughing and hacking. Taran wiped the specs of blood from her mouth and wrapped her in a blanket. He bade me fetch the shovels from the woodshed and we dug wordlessly. We made the hole as deep as we could, under the apple tree I had played on. The branches were low and strong, perfect for climbing. I tried not to cry when he lay the body down into the earth, but I couldn't help it. He held me close to him and kissed the top of my head. He handed me a shovel and together we filled in the grave. He patted down the earth neatly, and together we prayed for her.

It's mid-morning and we have been riding for about two hours. I'm at the front of the horse, holding its thick grey mane in my hands. Taran helped me to mount it and he sits behind me, hands on the reins. The horse is steady and it moves with a purpose, urged on gently by my brother, his armour pressing hard against my back as we ride on.

I can see two men standing in the road ahead. Their hoods are low and brown and they each carry an axe. The big kind for chopping wood. Taran stops the horse.
"Hail friends."
They yell to him roughly. "Get off the horse."
He taps my shoulder and I turn to him, his face frowning. "Stay here." He dismounts and walks towards them.
"Horse. Armour. Sword and any coin." The first axeman holds out his palm.
"That's a hefty toll, friend."
The thug spits. "There's two of us and one of you." He holds up a finger and hefts the shaft of the axe to his shoulder.
"I know." My brother has his left hand resting on his pommel, feet set apart. "Now if you'd be so kind, I need to pass, friend."
He snarls and points the axe towards Taran. "I'm not your fucking friend!"
"That's a shame, I like having friends." Taran draws his sword faster than anything I've ever seen. A blur of shining grey and the blade hooks under the axe, sending the man stumbling. A backhanded blow cuts him on the back of the neck, and he's bleeding onto the road. There is a roar as the other man charges like a bull. My brother holds his sword high and cuts down on him, splitting him to the waist. He sheathes the blade and walks back to me swiftly, mounting the horse in one smooth movement. We ride past, and I can see the first man twitching in the dirt, his hair smothered in gore, his blood seeping into the mud.
"Ulf." he says softly, "Remember this."
And I do.

I woke up to a chilly morning. The drizzle dripped from the trees and a miserable excuse for a fire was burning. I pulled myself out from under my blanket, and wiped the sleep from my eyes.

"So, what's the plan for today?" Siffisante smirked at me, and it was all I could do not to punch her.

"Fuck off." I snarled, pulling my tunic overhead.

Decroix chewed his lip. "We keep going through the forest. It will be a hard march, but we have to press onwards."

Quentin ripped off a piece of dry tack and handed it to me. He threw the last piece to Siffisante, who caught it clumsily and took a sullen bite before wrinkling her nose. "Don't you have anything better?"

Decroix gritted his teeth at her. "I'm so sorry my lady, but sadly the breakfast menu is somewhat limited as the butcher's boy has a twisted ankle and can't deliver, the quail loft ladder is broken so we cannot collect the eggs and, oh yes, WE'RE IN THE MIDDLE OF A CUNTING FOREST! So, eat the tack or starve, your choice."

"What about those mushrooms over there?" She nodded towards a decent patch that we must have missed when making camp last evening.

I sneered at her. "Only if you don't mind shitting like a waterfall for the next few days." She shut up and we headed off. The mushrooms might have been fine, but for the reward of a pleasant side dish against the risk of having my arse hanging out like a banner in the wind, I figured to play it safe.

It was a muggy, horrible day. The path twisted and turned as we went deeper, and several times we wasted our energy heading down trails which led to nowhere. Thorns and vines choked the forest floor, and I had to hack through the dense growth. The falchion I had looted made short work of the vegetation, but I quickly dulled the blade and cursed when I saw the steel marked and stained with sap.

My arm ached after the effort, and when we finally made camp I slumped down to catch my breath. After pulling off my boots, I stripped out of my armour and scrubbed at the sweat lining the interior with a rag to keep it from rusting. The fire had just started to burn properly, and Quentin was off looking for some logs while Decroix kept an eye on Siffisante.

I took out my sword and looked down the edge, running a thumb across the blade. It couldn't hurt to sharpen it again, so I spat on the whetstone and drew it across in a long, slow motion. I repeated it on the other edge, the rasp and grind blending with the crack of the fire to fill the clearing.

Then, I noticed it: a small movement, barely a twitch in the scrub. I moved my eyes over slowly, looked up at Decroix and put my finger to my lips. He and Siffisante stared at me with confusion, and I rolled my eyes. I stood up slowly, and the bracken on the forest floor pricked into my feet as I crept forward, sword in hand.

Another small rustle in the bush. I hacked down hard and there was a spurt of blood. I reached into the bush and pulled out a brown and bloodied mess that was once a rabbit. I knelt, pulled out my dagger and started skinning it, lopping off the feet and head.

I shouted over to the pair of them. "Something hot for supper at least!". The fur came away with a wet rip and I opened the guts, tossing them to one side. Messy work, but it meant we wouldn't have to eat any more fucking tack.

"See if there's a few Y shaped sticks about we can use as a spit. There might be some wild garlic around. I thought I saw some earlier. Take our guest and see if you can find anything to go with it?"

Silence.

"Any thoughts, or are you both just going to sit there?"

They were both ignoring me. I looked up angrily and met the eyes of a massive, ugly bastard in brown standing over me. There were about a dozen more, two of which were holding knives to Decroix and Siffisante's throats. Grabbing my sword, I slashed upwards in a wild swing, scrabbling to my feet.

He parried the blow with a quarterstaff as thick as my wrist, but it let me get my footing. He slammed the staff at my head and I brought myself into a high guard. I slid the blade down to shear off his fingers, cursing as he stepped back and cracked me hard on the shin bone. I limped and brought my sword round as quick as I could and the steel bit into wood as the staff blocked it. I heard the subtle creak of yew, and I could see at least three arrows pointing right at my guts.

"Drop it. Now".

I pointed my sword at the staff. "You heard them. Drop the stick, fuck-face!"

"You! Not him! The sword, you dozy prick!" One shouted at me.

"Worth a try." I let go and the sword fell to the forest floor, hilt buried in leaves.

They tied my arms behind my back. They weren't as stupid as they looked so they kept my sword and dagger well out of reach and stuck at least two guards on each of us, leading the horses along behind with all our gear.

They smelled foul and their clothes were tatty shades of greens, grey, and brown. How anyone could live in those shitty woods was beyond my ken, but apparently these cunts did. They started tying a strip of filthy cloth over my eyes. I tried to bite the big bastard with the staff when he did it, but he backhanded me.

I laughed. "I've paid to be hit harder than that." He didn't rise to the bait, and my face did hurt quite a bit, but it was the best taunt I could think of right then. We walked in silence for a mile or so. I found it hard to tell as I blindly stumbled on the stones and roots which seemed to infest that cursed wood.

Chapter 7:
The Pale Lord

I tried to focus on my other senses as we walked: the ring of metal, distant talking, the smell of cooking fires. I got kicked hard behind the knees and I fell to the ground, the impact jarred the blindfold, loosening it a little.

We were in the middle of a camp. From what little I could see, there were shanty shelters built around a fire pit, and a portable forge where a middle-aged woman ground a blade near where we were laying.

"Charon! That is no way to treat our guests!"

Oh, fuck me. They were those type of bandits. The ones who like to pretend they are a cut above your standard murdering cunts.

The rags were pulled from our eyes and a man stood over us, next to the big bastard with the staff, who I guessed was Charon. His skin was bone white, and the blue-black hair which he'd dragged back into a foppish looking ponytail marked him as a C'targian. Looking around the camp, a lot of them were.

C'targians are a nasty bunch of thieving curs, and I like killing them.

He bowed low. "I am Azrael Bordane, leader of this honourable band!". He got a huge laugh from the assembled brigands and simultaneously managed to reassure me that I was right first time round when I thought he was a complete cunt.

I snarled. "You're either going to kill me, torture me, or fuck me. Pick one and get on with it, you pasty little bastard."

Azrael laughed uproariously, hands on his hips.

Yep. Complete cunt.

"My dear fellow, you think so little of us! Come, enjoy our hospitality." Our bonds were loosened and Charon threw a wineskin towards us. I raised the skin to my nose and took a small sniff. It smelled like cat piss, but it was free, so I drained most of it. I threw it to Decroix who glared at Azrael and then took a barely perceivable sip. Siffisante wrinkled up her face before passing it to one of the bandits.

A man walked up, dragging a body behind him. "My lord!"

Oh, so he was a fucking lord now.

"We found this little bastard snooping around. 'Collecting firewood!'" he scoffed, throwing down a bloodied and battered body which I recognised as Quentin.

He was breathing, but it was shallow.

I sprang forward and I smashed Azrael as hard as I could in the face. I felt cartilage crackle and shooting pain which meant I'd cracked a knuckle. Charon and the rest were on us in a heartbeat and he punched me in the gut, doubling me over before kicking me into the dirt. A blade was at my throat and Azrael stood over me, red blood dripping from his white nose. He looked as pissed off as a bull with its cock in a vice, but he gave me a nasty grin.

"You're loyal to your friends. I can respect that."

He wiped the blood on his sleeve. He clearly wanted to cut my throat, but he couldn't; him being the noble and generous bandit leader, and having built up a band of followers who think that he's good and kind and wouldn't do something like that. I looked him in the eyes to let him know that I knew. And that I know that he knows that I knew. And that I also know he's a cunt.

"What's your name, friend?"

"Ulf of Banrillar. And I'm not your fucking friend."

"I'm Decroix, this is Siffisante, and that is my brother Quentin." Decroix looked at his brother, concerned.

Quentin started stirring, but he was badly beaten. Azrael gave Siffisante a wolfish grin. The same grin I've seen Quentin give anything with decent tits and a pulse.

"Good day to you, madam." Azrael kissed her hand, and Siffisante, sly bitch that she was - and I swear on the Virtuous Ones this is true - blushed.

"Good day to you, my lord." she said, curtseying.

Azrael took her by the hand and they walked away together. He turned to us over his shoulder. "Charon, please make our guests comfortable. We can attend to business tomorrow morning. But tonight, we feast!"

A cheer came from the band of happy fuckwits as we were bound to a tree. We were watched during the night by a shift of men and women holding cudgels in case we tried something. The rest sat around the fire pit and laughed along to 'Lord' Azrael's stories while Siffisante made herself comfortable on his lap. The flames danced away as more skins of the foul wine got passed round in a circle.

It's a cold night. I can't remember exactly when. It was a better day though, I know that. Before she fell sick. But It's a cold and bitter winter. She tucks the blankets in tightly.

"No child ever, if they are good,
Should go to the cave in the heart of the wood.
And no child ever, no matter how brave,
Should stand and stare at the mouth of the cave.
And no child ever, no matter how bold,
Should set foot in the darkness, horrid and cold.
And no child ever, if they be wise,
Should ignore the moans and the horrible cries.
And no child ever, for their own mother's sake,
Should pass the stalactite curled like a snake.
And no child ever, not even a fool!
Would stop for a drink at the deep, dark pool.
And no child ever, again I implore!
Take a step near the pool, on the cold black shore.

And one final warning, to thee I impart,
'Ware she in the water, who dines on men's hearts.
So listen well, child, and always be good.
Stay away from the cave in the heart of the wood."

My mother kisses me and I lie still in the darkness, her words dancing around my skull. I try not to think about the cave and the horrible thing in the water from her story, but I know she's there. Waiting to catch me. Even if it takes her years, she'll be waiting for me deep in the woods.

I woke up cold as the sun rose. My arms ached and my arse was numb from a root that had been digging into me. Looking over my shoulder, I could see Quentin laying nearby. His face was purple and swollen, but the rise and fall of his chest told me he was still alive.

Two bandits untied me and dragged me through the camp. The clearing was cluttered with shoddy lean-tos and ramshackle tents, with huge vats storing cat-piss wine interspersed amongst them, sheltered under the boughs of the trees. All around, people started waking, readying for a busy day of living in the forest, like a bunch of wankers.

They took me to the largest tent, with a banner of a golden tree on a green field tied to a pole outside. I say gold, but it was more like a dirty yellow. 'Lord' Azrael Bordane seemed to be taking this far too seriously. Outside, there were a fair few armed thugs who looked like they would take exception to someone trying to kill their master. Charon was also there, fixing me with a decidedly unpleasant expression.

A scraggly looking man with a clubbed foot opened the tent and ushered us in. The snow-skinned bastard was lounging on a pile of deer hides, feeding wild cherries to Siffisante from a bowl. She wore a new dress of fine blue wool trimmed with silver fur. It was too big for her, so I could only assume he'd nicked it from some passing merchant's wife.

"Good morning, Ulf! I trust you had a pleasant night!" He flashed me a smile and popped a cherry into his mouth. However, I took some satisfaction in the purple, swollen mess I had made of his face. "Although, probably not as pleasant as we had . . ." Azrael spat out the stone and kissed her softly.

Siffisante giggled moronically. "Oh, my lord . . ." she purred, stroking his leg. She was either a far better actress than I initially thought, or those were really, really good cherries.

I wasn't in the mood for this. I snarled and my hands bunched into fists. "Did you want something from me, or can you only get your prick moving if someone's watching?"

Azrael laughed and then nodded at club-foot who poured out a mug of the horrible tasting wine. I snatched it from his hand and downed it. The sour liquid quenched my thirst, but I wondered exactly how they managed to get the cat to sit still over the jug.

"You must understand, Ulf, that as a noble I am obliged to provide hospitality to all prisoners according to their rank and station." He held out his hand and his gangly servant poured him and Siffisante yet another glass. He looked at me, his pale face stern. "However, Siffisante has informed me that you have been less than gentlemanly towards her." He raised his voice slightly, fixing me with a cold stare. "Not the actions I would expect of a knight, or indeed any man of honour."

I snorted. "I'm not a knight. And did she also tell you she's a fucking cultist of the Black Ram?" Siffisante glared at me furiously, panic darting across her face.

Azrael laughed and ran a hand over her thigh. "Ulf, you think such things would bother me? There are more things in this world than you can understand. I do not care which so-called 'Virtuous Ones', demons, or gods men bow down to, as long as they bow down to me." He took a sip of wine and smacked his lips, closing his eyes to savour it. I had no idea what he was drinking inside that mad head of his, but it was probably nicer than what was in the cup.

"It is clear to me what has happened, Ulf. The kidnapping. Your intention to ransom this innocent and beautiful woman." Siffisante looked at me and smiled, making me mentally promise to kick them both to death if given half the chance. "I am within my rights to put you to death, Ulf." He let it hang in the air. He was expecting me to look shocked, or to plead, but I'd had my fill of actors for a while, so I just stood there, bored by the theatrics.

"However, as a noble, I am inclined to be merciful. I will spare your life, but you must understand that this places you in my debt. You are to perform a task for me."

I sighed and look dejected. "All right, all right. How do you want it then?" I spat in my hand and got my cock out. "Rough and tumble or nice and fluffy?"

Siffisante screamed at me and Azrael sprang up. "Not THAT sort of task, you idiot!" he yelled. I put it away and tried my best to look like I innocently misunderstood. I failed spectacularly, but it was certainly worth a go. Azrael lowered himself back into his seat and took a long, bracing pull from his goblet.

"Roughly five leagues to the north from here there is a fearsome, lone grey wolf. It has been driven mad by something and is slaughtering all the game in my woods, leaving nothing but rotting, uneaten corpses. Several of our hunters have tried and come back with nothing but empty quivers. You are to slay it, Ulf of Banrillar, and return with its pelt."

"And if I refuse?" I had no intention of refusing, but I felt like pushing my luck to annoy him.

"Then you will die." he said with finality.

The wretch with the club foot cleared his throat diplomatically. "My lord Azrael, as I am sure you recall, it is not just the game in the forest. There is . . . the other matter, as well."

For a fleeting moment, the mad lord looked uncomfortable, shifting under his servant's glance. "Well, yes. About a fortnight ago, a woman and her daughter went missing. A Dyer. She was gathering woad to boil, or some such affair." He waved his hand, the day-to-day boiling of plants being far beneath one such as him.

Club-foot coughed politely.

"My lord, you will of course recall there have been several others as well. Children, off playing in the woods, who have not yet returned."

"Well then, in that case, it looks like you and Siffisante will have a new rug to roll around on."

Azrael's cupbearer led me out of the tent and took me to my armour. Charon handed me my sword and dirk with an ugly glare. I buckled them on around my waist and slung the baldric over my shoulder as the big man stared at me with naked contempt.

Decroix and Quentin were nowhere to be found, and I doubted Azrael would've been keen for me to bring a friend. I headed off to the north, morning sunlight creeping through the trees and my boots sinking softly into the rotting vegetation on the forest floor.

After walking for a while, my stomach growled like an angry bear. I found a wilted briar with some berries on it, and I munched them greedily. They made barely a mouthful, but were just enough to sate my hunger.

I sat on a speckled log and thought for a while. I considered just fucking off out of the woods. Azrael's band of merry morons probably wouldn't find me, and if they did, I could easily take a few of them. I thought about the brothers, about Quentin tied up and bloodied, but then I remembered what a pain in the arse they had both been in Cassioc.

In the end, Reed swung it. She was a good horse, and it made my blood boil to think of Azrael riding her. I pressed on, forcing myself through twisted branches and thorn smeared vines which whipped my face.

Hours passed before I found some marks: slashes and gouges in the tree bark at waist height. Broken twigs and the odd grey hair. My nose wrinkled up as I smelled something sickly-sweet. Out of habit, I drew my sword, taking some measure of comfort from the weight in my hand.

I approached as cautiously as I could, spreading out my weight and stepping with the toes and balls of my feet. I glanced down to avoid the twigs and dry leaves, and the smell got stronger with each cautious pace. I saw a limb stuck out at a twisted angle from behind a tree.

Moving closer, I could see a stag. The guts were burst open and the once noble face torn, tongue lolling to the side. Flies buzzed angrily around, and I held my forearm to my mouth in disgust. The deer had been ripped and sundered, with legs and flesh strewn freely around. At a casual glance, none of the flesh had been eaten, but I had no doubt this was a frenzied attack.

I almost missed it, but I took another glance at the clumps of fur. Something was off. I got down on my hands and knees, rolled it between my fingertips, and frowned. It was short and soft to the touch. Wolf fur is thick and greasy on the fingers. Good for a rug or to hang on a wall, but not pleasant for anything else.

The marks were odd as well. Similar to claws, but the distance between the lines was inconsistent. The lowest gouge was level with my navel, and looked more like a carved "V" than the semi-circular indent of an animal's claw. I'm a big bloke, and there was no way even a massive wolf could gnaw that high.

The stench was getting to me, so I walked past as quickly as I could. I spent some time circling the area around the ruined deer. Eventually, I found more marks, broken branches and trampled vegetation. Following this trail, I came to the mouth of a cave, surrounded by trees stripped of the bark on their trunks.

The ground lay littered with cracked bones, bleached yellow-white by the rain and sunlight with lances of sinew clinging to the jagged edges. That and the festering piles of shit about the place marked it as the beast's den. I looked around, desperately keen not to be ambushed.

Wolves hunt mainly at dawn or dusk, so I guessed it was probably sleeping. The cave roof hung so low, I'd have to crouch down to get inside and I didn't fancy fighting this bastard on my hands and knees. The forest was silent, apart from the caw of a distant raven.

I set myself into a wide stance and roll my wrists, readying myself for the fight. No point in wasting any more time. "OI, WANKER!" I kicked up a pile of debris and a small skull clattered against the cave. "I'M OUT HERE!" My voice echoed around and for a moment silence fell before my challenge was answered by a low, slow growl from the depths of the cave.

I stood and waited for what seemed like an age. No other sound came forth from the cave, and nothing stirred within the darkness. It was only when I focused my senses that I heard it: a subtle crack and the faint smell of smoke.

"Fuck it . . ." I muttered. Getting down on my hands and knees, I drew my dirk and held my sword out front, hoping that whatever lay within the cave might be stupid enough to impale itself on the point. But it wasn't a bad idea to keep a shorter blade handy.

I crawled through the tunnel, my armour scraping on the bare stone as the air grew moist and cold. I dragged myself forward slowly, the light behind me dying until it was only variation in the deep shadows that told me where to turn. While trying to sharpen my ears and eyes, I desperately wanted to block up my nose. With every crawl, the stench of shit and offal became more pungent, undercut by the acrid smell of smoke.

I felt the passage turn, and the cramped walls gave way to an open cavern. I blinked violently as I spied a guttering fire beneath a small iron pot. Blended with the smoke and filth, the air was dank with the fetid smell of stagnant water, which came from a pool, fed by a steady drip through the mossy stone. I scanned the shadows warily, sheathing my dagger to hold my sword two-handed, now that there was room to fight. I took up a stone and skimmed it across the water, watching it ripple across the surface before vanishing with a plop. Behind me, the iron pot bubbled, the lid shaking and vibrating as the flames licked at it from below.

Turning towards the sound, I took a pace towards the fire. Each flicker giving snatches of the cave floor. With the tip of my sword, I flicked off the lid, the silence of the carven suddenly shattered by the clattering iron.

Mercifully, I could not see much, but the stench that rolled up nearly caused me to vomit. I retched and choked, doubling up and staggering backwards. Thankfully, the darkness hid most of it, but one thing was unmistakeable. Rolling and bobbing within the putrescene mess was the bleached round shape of a child's skull.

A steady drip. The subtle pad of feet. I turned around and my head rang from the impact. And I crashed to the floor. I felt the pull of darkness, but the stink of wet fur acted as a smelling salt to drive me from my stupor.

Its slavering fangs scraped against my gorget, the points scratching deep grooves into the steel. I rolled out from underneath and scrabbled for my sword as it leapt up at me again. I slashed blindly and clipped it on the flank, but thick fur turned the blow aside. It circled me, hissing and snarling. I moved my feet slowly along with it, each of us looking for a moment to strike. As it moved closed to the fire, I could see its form more clearly: a hunched, semi-human figure clad in filthy, matted fur. The fingers were outstretched, pointed and sharpened to wicked spikes.

It sprang towards me and I rolled low, crashing to the floor. I brought my sword up and slashed into its underbelly, the blade slicing into a leg with a streak of dark blood. It snarled with rage, lunging for my throat once again, but this time I was ready and my blow bit into the skull, crumpling the bone. The thing twitched on the ground, writhing around with its jaw split in two, looking up at me with roving eyes filled with madness. Beneath the lunacy, it knew what was to happen now. I took a ragged breath and then thrust my sword between its ribs, piercing the lungs and heart.

Panting, I sheathed my sword and collapsed to the floor, head swimming with half seen horrors. After taking a moment to catch my breath and fight down the rising bile in my throat, I grasped the corpse by the ankle and pulled it out through the passageway.

In the light of day, I could see the creature more plainly. It had been a woman once, that much was for certain. Her mouth was caked with gore and the teeth were broken or filed into savage points. Shards of flint and rusted metal were wedged where there were once fingernails, crudely hammered into the bone. The patches of blue on her arms and hands clearly marked her as the woad dyer, driven mad by this awful wood, or perhaps by something else. Either way, she was dead now.

I cleaned my sword with a fistful of grass and sat down on a rotten log, turning my gaze from the horrible tableau. I put it off as long as possible, but I had a long journey back to Azrael's camp and I needed to crack on. Taking my dirk in hand, I harvested my grisly trophy.

Chapter 8:
Goods to Trade

I got back at dusk. My armour chafed and all my limbs ached, dripping sweat as I tramped through the bracken. The flayed skin trailed behind me, splattered with mud and disfigured with gaping holes and tears from our fight and my cack-handed skinning.

Decroix and Quentin were still bound to the tree at the edge of the camp, and for once I was glad to see them. I nodded and they both perked up.

"ULF! We thought you'd been killed. Or at least buggered off somewhere and left us to die."

"Nice to see you too, Decroix." I scooped up huge handfuls of water from a rain butt to my lips. After quenching my thirst, I splashed my face and neck and took a few deep breaths.

Quentin stared at the bloody mess on the ground by my feet. "What the fuck is that?"

"That thing is what will keep us all alive." I grabbed the mess and headed off. "Now if you'll excuse me, I have to see a man about a dog."

I strode through the camp to the main fire pit. The wine and singing were already out for the evening, and Azrael sat surrounded by his cronies while Siffisante reclined at his right hand, sipping from a carved wooden goblet. I barged my way through and slung the skin at his feet, the bloody pile flopping with a wet squelch. The crowd abruptly stopped talking and he wrinkled his nose in disgust. "Urrgh! What the-"

"One mad woman who murdered a bunch of children. Now decidedly less fearsome. If you wanted it to look neater, then you should have sent a tanner." Someone at the back chuckled, but then thought better of it.

He gawped at the mangled hide. To his credit, Azrael rallied well. "I congratulate you and praise you for your valour. Ulf of Banrillar, I grant you your freedom." He stood up and extended his milk-white hand for me to kiss.

I stared at it, then turned to Siffisante. "Come on, we're going."

"I think you'll find I'm staying right here." Siffisante gave me a thin smile and drained the rest of her wine, finishing with a satisfied sigh. I fixed her with a glare.

"We are going. Now."

Azrael stood up in front of me, his hand on the silvered hilt of his thin arming sword. "She is under my protection as lord of this realm. She's free to do as she wishes. You will leave this place, but she may remain here as long as she wishes, and that is my word as lord!"

I reached forward and tore the collar from his tunic, dropping it to the ground. Calmly, I shouted out my challenge for the whole camp to hear. "Lord Azrael Bordane of the Wallenpel. You have dishonoured me and I require satisfaction. I, Ulf of Banrillar, Squire to Taran of Banrillar, Master of Arms of the Order of the Cleansing Flame, challenge you to mortal combat."

A dozen men and women moved towards me, knives drawn, but Azrael held up a hand to stop them. He looked at me. I could see him for exactly what he was: a poor, mad C'targian play-pretending at being a noble. But if he let them kill me, then he'd be no different than any other bugger with a band of thugs.

As I looked at him, he could see me for exactly what I was: a dangerous, violent bastard.

He cleared his throat and proclaimed, "As a noble, I claim the right of a champion to bear my sword and fight in my name." He drew his sword, a fine piece of workmanship with a blade that looked sharp as ice. "Charon."

The big man stepped forward and grinned at me, showing a mouth full of crooked, yellowed tombstones that passed for teeth. Azrael handed him the sword and he hefted it effortlessly. "Will you bear my sword and fight in my name?" Charon nodded. I drew my own blade and stood with the point forward, lowered level with his throat.

"Then I command you, FIGHT!"

Charon's first blow came in fast and vicious. He aimed at striking away the tip of my sword, as I knew he would. I pulled my sword up quickly and lunged at him. He barely parried and I followed up with another strike to the shoulders. I drove him back as he circled around the fire. The others started cheering him on and throwing curses to me, but I blocked them out and pressed the attack.

He forced my sword backwards, his arms bulging like an oak tree as the hilts of our swords bound together. He stepped to the side and I tumbled forward. His pommel struck me hard on the small of my back, making my armour shake and rattle. I stumbled to the ground and brought my sword up two-handed to block a strike that could have split me in two. We began circling each other, Charon keeping his back to the fire. Stepping backwards, I held the blade in both hands, swinging the sword like a war hammer to crush his skull. He met my blow mid-air and our weapons bit. He threw aside my effort to pull his sword and stabbed hard at my shin. The sword point skidded across my greave, turning a crippling attack into a nasty bruise.

I forced his sword down with a hard blow and barged into him with my shoulder. He staggered back, heels perilously close to the fire. He slashed at me as I stepped forward, and I snarled through the pain as he cut open my arm. I hooked the guard of my sword behind his knee, wrenching it upwards with all my might. He tumbled backwards into the fire, screaming as the flames licked at his flesh, the stench of his burning hair foul in my nostrils.

Roaring, he flailed around, desperately smacking at the flames. Snatching up a jug of wine, I grabbed him by the ankle and pulled him hard towards me, throwing the drink into his face. The flames hissed out and he writhed around, moaning, horribly burnt. One of his eyes was a runny mess, dribbling down his cheek and the other looked at me with pleading. I lowered my sword to his throat and stared at Azrael.

"I won that." It was a statement, not a question. I picked up Azrael's sword and shoved it into my belt. Siffisante yelled something at me as I threw her over my shoulder, but I ignored her.

Reed and the brothers' two geldings were nearby. Leaving Charon and the crowd behind me, I threw her over the back over my horse and tied her hands to the saddle.

"Stop him!" Azrael's pale face was flushed with rage as he pointed a shaking finger at me. About half a dozen men took some half-hearted steps towards me, knives out.

I turned around. "Between all of you, you could probably kill me. But I'll sure as balls make sure I don't go down easy. I reckon I could put three, maybe four of you in your graves before bleeding out. Are you willing to die so that your 'lord' can get his prick wet?" They backed off slowly, sheathing their weapons. "No? I didn't think so."

I cut the animals frees and led them over to the brothers. "Get up. We're going."

Unlike Siffisante, Decroix and Quentin didn't need telling twice.

We hiked hard through the night, desperate to put as much distance between us and the mad albino as possible. I kept my exhaustion at bay by focusing on how pissed off I was at Siffisante. Her constant screeching and furious indignation helped me to stay awake until the sun loomed up in the sky. Eventually we stopped, aching and shattered from the effort, and flopped onto the ground. Reed's flanks were slick with sweat and I patted the side of her neck, grateful for her patience. She rubbed her nose against my hand and I ran her ears through my palms, clicking at her.

"Let me down!" I remembered about Siffisante. I flipped her off the horse and she landed with a satisfying thud. "Not like that you oaf!" She managed to sit up and treated me to one of her best glowers. "I could have been very happy there! The wife of a lord!"

I rolled my eyes. "Yes, listening to rambling stories around a smoky campfire, shitting into a hole in the ground, and as much cat-piss flavoured wine as you can drink. What girl could ask for more?"

"Lord Azrael knew how to treat a woman! He was a proper noble. Not some . . . squire for a bunch of nasty old men who's wasted his life drinking and fighting."

I looked at her hateful face and thought about how easy it would be just to lop off her head. "You got a shag and a new dress. What more do you want?" I took off my armour and threw it under a tree.

"Bugger."

I turned around. "What?"

Decroix clicked his tongue angrily as he held up a barren saddlebag. The robbers had rummaged through and made off with all the food. He threw down his sleeping roll and a squashed bag of dried barley flopped out, hidden from the prying hands.

Famished, we wolfed down the plain gruel. All of us were bitter at the lack of hospitality, apart from Siffisante, who was treated to the very finest morsels an insane bandit chief could offer.

Quentin pointed at Azrael 's blade. "Don't you already have enough swords?"

"No. I have a falchion for hacking back branches, a bastard sword for hacking up people, and this new arming sword to sell for a few Ecar once we get to the next town."

Quentin sighed as he mopped up the last of the sops in his bowl. "You couldn't have stolen a few sausages instead, could you?"

"Fantastic idea! I'll ride back and ask if he'll do a swap!"

Decroix looked glumly at the bare saddlebags. "To be fair, considering what the wine was like, I'm not sure I want to think about what they would put into the sausages."

We made camp in the clearing, too tired to press on, each of us taking a turn to watch and to guard Siffisante while the others rested.

It's a long way to The Hearth. Taran tells me it's the monastery and headquarters of the Order of the Cleansing Flame, a vast castle with stables, forges, training yards, and a dozen other things.

Apart from Bulton on a few market days, I've never been outside Banrillar. The road is long, and we pass through dozens of small villages. Everywhere we go they treat my brother with respect. He gets the best tables when we stay at inns, people walking in the road make way for him and everywhere they bow low when they see the shine of my brother's armour and the blue and golden cloth of his tabard.

The sun is setting, and he takes his armour off as we stop for the night. He places it carefully under the tree and starts a small fire to keep us warm. My sleeping roll is itchy but it keeps out the chill of the night.

The morning comes and I wake up to see the ashes smouldering. I look around and for a moment I panic until I see my brother looking at a piece of dirt, rolling it between his fingers. He spots I'm awake and rushes over to me.

He thrusts it under my nose. "Smell this!"

"Urrgh!" I push it away in disgust. "It smells like shit."

"Exactly!" He says with excitement. "Pig shit!"

I look at him in confusion and he sighs. "Pig shit means wild boar. Fresh pig shit means wild boar nearby. Wild boar nearby means-"

"Bacon?" I cut him off.

"Now you understand! Hurry up and get dressed." I pull on my clothes and as I do, he fishes in his saddlebags and takes out a weird looking thing of wood and metal.

"What's that?" I ask.

There is a small groan as the metal bends, and he places what looks like a tiny arrow into a groove in the wood. He grins at me, "A crossbow!"

The point of the arrow gleams in the sunshine, I frown. "Why is the arrow so small?"

"Firstly, it's called a quarrel, not an arrow. Secondly, knights aren't meant to use bows of any sort in battle. It's dishonourable. But it's all right for

Brigandine

hunting. And finally-" He throws an empty sack into my hands. "You'll need this to carry back breakfast."
    We move through the woods slowly. He stops every so often. A broken branch, some disturbed leaves. He points to a tree that looks just like any other until he shows where the boar has lefts some hair. "Scratching itself on the bark." He whispers. He licks his finger and moves to get downwind.
    Then, he puts a hand to my shoulder to stop me. I'm about to ask why when I spot it. Just a small patch of grey and brown in the berry patch ahead. Taran brings the crossbow to his shoulder, the butt flat against his pauldron. He squeezes the trigger, and there is a slap as the quarrel flies forward. There is a flash of red and a crash as the boar runs through the undergrowth.
    "Come on!" he yells, and I sprint to follow him. The boar lies dead a few yards from the berry patch. Taran reaches down and cuts out the quarrel with a small knife. The shot was perfect, straight into the heart. Taran rubs his hands. "Right!" he passes me the knife. "Time for a quick lesson in field dressing, and then let's get back for breakfast."

    The horses were fed at Azrael's camp, but after the long walk the previous night we needed to take it easy. We eventually headed off in the early afternoon and journeyed for a few hours before stopping again at dusk.
    It took us another few days to get through the forest of Wallenpel. We spent hours each day foraging for enough food to keep our bellies full. I managed to find a few patches of mushrooms that I knew wouldn't kill us, some wild garlic and even I was impressed when Decroix used a rock to bring down a squirrel. Our belts were tighter and my armour felt looser around me when we finally left the Wallenpel behind us, but once again we had proper road underfoot and a full sky overhead.
    I could see a few plumes of smoke on the horizon. "Carstock." Quentin happily remarked.
    Siffisante tilted her head. "What?"
    "It's a small but decent town. They make most of their money from ash wood and smoking fish from the coast." I added.
    "Ash wood?" Siffisante looked at me, confused. "But that stuff grows everywhere."

I couldn't decide if she was playing stupid, or was genuinely that thick. "Not like the coppices near Carstock. It's the same stuff in the earth like Wallenpel, but instead of wild wickedness, the trees grow quicker, straighter and better than anywhere else. Weapon shafts, wagons, boxes, tables, chairs-everyone needs ash wood and Carstock can get it cheaper and better than anyone else."

Quentin shrugged. "Plant some saplings, come back in a few years and they are 20 feet tall and broad as a man. Fell them, dry them, stick them on a ship down the coast and off to Cassioc, make a small fortune, plant some more and do it again until you're old and fat, then retire with a beautiful young mistress with a lovely pair of great big t-"

"I think she gets the idea, brother." snapped Decroix.

We got to the outskirts of Carstock at noon, and my nostrils were filled with the smell of burning wood. Huge, vast A-frames were set up with piles of smouldering ash to cure the trout and salt-salmon common on this part of the coast. We saw the towering ash groves nearby, trees planted in neat, tight rows. Each trunk was carved with an owner's mark, and each roped off section had a hired muscle or two to stand watch.

The town had a fine wooden barricade. The walls were the yellow-white of bleached and oiled ash, and as we rode towards the town a guard gave us a friendly wave from a watchtower at the gate. Two other guards stood dutifully at the entrance. "Hail, friend."

"Well met." Decroix smiled and I decided to let him do the talking. I'm not great at being friendly at the best of times, but with no money, covered in mud, and stinking of the woods, we didn't look like the type of people anyone sensible would let into town. The guard spotted Siffisante bound upon Reed and looked cautious, moving his hand to his sword.

"Why, exactly, is that woman tied up on your horse, sir?"

"PLEASE HELP! THEY'VE KIDNAPPED ME!" she screamed.

Decroix laughed and shook his head, raising his hand as the guard half drew his sword. "Please, don't mind my sister. She's an idiot." He let his face go limp with sadness. "She has been since she was a girl. She drank some milk after a raven flew over it and her mind has rotted."

The guard nodded sympathetically. Ravens feast on the bodies of criminals, and if they fly over your food, they can bring the evil into it. Siffisante screamed and tried to elbow me in the face. "YOU LYING BASTARDS! Look at me! I don't look anything like them! I'm an actress from Cassioc and they killed the rest of the theatre cast and burned down The Ouroboros!"

The guard didn't know whether to laugh or cry. I put one hand in front of my mouth while the other tried to keep Siffisante still. Quentin shook his head in sadness. "We are journeying west to the shrine of Aeder the Kind in Melpapier in the hopes it will cure her. Although in truth her madness is so fierce-"

"BASTARD! YOU UTTER BASTARD" she screamed.

"-that we can only pray that Aeder in her mercy will grant our sister a sliver of sanity. Please, good sir, we have items to sell and trade in the town and once we have restocked our provisions with some of your fine fish, we will be on the road again."

The guard looked at Siffisante's thrashing and screaming, and it was clear he was considering telling us to just fuck off. But he sighed and reached for a pot of ink and a brush. "Very well. But keep her under control."

"We will." I promised in what I hope is a sincere tone.

"She'll need to wear the mark, of course. So that normal folk know to be wary."

"WHAT!" she said, horrified.

"But of course!" I smiled and turned her head to the side. There is more screaming and kicking while the guard drew a large 'L' in ink on her face for lunatic, and we then rode into town.

"Virtuous Ones bless you and keep you, my friend!" Decroix yelled back.

"Don't cause any trouble, you hear me!" he shouted.

Quentin grinned at his brother. "As if I would!"

Carstock was a neat little town, ordered and laid out just like the coppices that have made it rich. We stopped by a fountain, and I sharpened and polished Azrael's sword before handing it over to Decroix so he could get the best price. "That's the only thing we have to sell, so haggle hard." He gave me a nod of thanks as he headed off. I could have told them both to go fuck themselves, sold it myself, and ridden off, but they owed me back wages, and I still needed to find out exactly what was going on here.

We hitched the horses to a post and they drank greedily from a nearby trough. Quentin and I were at a bit of a loose end while Decroix got us whatever coin he could for the sword. We could have sold the falchion too, but we'd have gotten a Wyear for it at most. I had Reed and my equipment, but a mercenary without a horse, armour, or a sword is basically a corpse, so I wasn't too keen to flog those just yet. Besides, I liked Reed.

Decroix said to meet us in an hour, so we had a wander through the street. The "L" on Siffisante's face drew some odd looks, and people tended to give us a wide berth. It wasn't a market day, so the central square lay empty.

A team of men was digging in the middle of the plaza. A broad man with a full beard wiped the sweat from his eyes and climbed up a ladder out of the hole. Another followed him, hauling a huge sack of earth. Round the corner, a youth pushed a cart, stained dark brown. They sat together by the pit and ate a meal, passing around a jug of watered beer. Quentin waved and they nodded back politely. "Come on, let's find out what they're doing!" he said.

"Let's not." I sighed, getting dragged along, with Siffisante trailing behind us.

The bearded man gave Siffisante a kindly look and broke off a chunk of bread for her. "There you go, my dear." He gave us a sympathetic smile. "My sister was like that. Kicked in the head by a donkey when she was eight."

He passed the last of his share of the bread to me and I took it. He pointed to me and nodded to Quentin. "Kind of you to look after the big fella as well. Did he get hurt in the wars or something?"

Quentin kept a straight face and I was too busy eating the bread to care that he thought I was an idiot.

"I found him like this. It's very sad." The bearded man and his workers nodded sympathetically. "Big hole you're digging!"

They snorted. "Bloody deep one! No fucking idea what they want it for, but they're paying good wages. Twelve Wyear a man! With an extra five each if we can get it done in a week. Don't get me wrong, a forty-foot-deep hole this wide is going to be a bastard to do, but for money like that I'm not going to complain."

Quentin frowned. "But what could they want something like that for?"

"No idea!" He shrugged. "If you need a hole dug, we're your men. If you need questions answered, you're better off with a philosopher, friend!" The labourers laughed and I fixed a stupid grin on my face and dribbled a little. I was getting rather good at that.

Quentin thanked him and we set off. Within the hour we'd seen everything worthwhile in Carstock, so we sat bored waiting for Decroix to come back. He returned with a few sacks of food, looking glum.

"How much did you get?" I asked.

"Not a great price." He puts down the bags and stretches. "Six Wyear."

"Six Wyear!" I yelled. The sword was easily worth a Guilder.

Decroix rolled his eyes and snapped at me. "You couldn't have done any better! The 'silver' on the hilt turned out to be tin! I'm lucky he didn't drag me in front of guild alderman and have my balls cut off for trying to cheat him!"

I pinched the bridge of my nose and sighed. "After the food, was there any left over? Is there any chance of staying in a warm bed tonight?"

Decroix gave a half-hearted smile. "No. On the plus side, I did get a good price on some sausages. But, sadly, not enough to pay for an inn."

Siffisante snorted derisively and I turned to her. "We could cut the fur trim off that new dress? Probably worth an Ecar of two?"

"DON'T YOU DARE!" She shouted, kicking me in the shin. "OW!" She yelped, pulling her foot back.

"Then don't try to kick me in the armour!"

"You could kick him in the bollocks? They're not armoured." Quentin chipped in.

"I don't think I could hit such a small target." she said, rubbing her toe.

We rode out of Carstock, gazing longingly as we passed the inns of the town. The Dancing Duke, the Bloody Lamb, the Broken Mug - all of them carrying the wonderful smell of sweaty bodies, sour ale and someone who had pissed themselves. I got a little lump in my throat and wondered if I could hire Siffisante out as a prostitute to a bloke with no sense of sight, smell, taste, or touch, who coincidently had lots of money and very low standards.

"So, about my money."

The brothers rode next to me in silence. "Let's see . . . four Wyear a day, plus interest. Plus late payment fees. Plus performance bonus."

Decroix raised his eyebrows. "Performance bonus?"

"You're alive, aren't you?"

Quentin shrugged. "Ulf makes a fair point."

Decroix looked out at the horizon and smiled. "Don't worry, Ulf. You'll get your money. We're nearly there."

I looked out onto the road ahead, the sun dipping down. "How near is nearly there?"

"About a week."

"Fuck."

Chapter 9:
The Eagle's Talon

My back was groaning at me, and it wasn't long before my knees and hips joined in the chorus. The others were already up and moving about. There were four sausages streaked with herbs and fat sizzling in a pan, and I'm not too proud to say I dribbled a little. Breakfast wasn't quite as good as it smelled, but it was better than what I had eaten the previous morning, which was nothing.

We turned from the coast to travel inland, riding slowly over the rough, hilly earth. We remained on constant vigil for stones that would lame the horses or rabbit holes that would hurl us arse over tit from the saddle. The stony soil of that region is only good for grapevines, and the twisting stands shook gently in the wind as we rode past. The grapes had been harvested months before, and the dry stone barns were filled to the brim with barrels of young wine.

We rode on for a few more days through the vine-draped hills. Little hamlets spiked the countryside, scarcely more than a handful of cottages made of the same grey stone as the vineyard walls. They were shitty little places, even smaller than Banrillar. Places where the only entertainment is when one of the mangy goats clinging to the hills does an odd-shaped shit.

There were a few villages too, but nothing worth considering. We watered the horses at roadside wells and spent our nights huddled against the hills, hiding from the biting wind.

A cart coming from one of the local farms passed us, clearly on its way to Carstock. The old woman driving it nodded at us out of politeness. Also, because she could see three armed travellers, one of which is clearly a dangerous lunatic with a bound hostage, and she didn't want me to murder her. As she passed, I spied the faded heraldry of a silver eagle painted on the side of the cart.

"So, these are Duke Colsarne's lands." I said. Quentin nodded. "Is that who we're seeing, then?"

Decroix interrupted, "That's none of your concern, Ulf. You'll get your money. I've promised you that. Any other matters are for my brother and me to worry about, not you."

Siffisante spat into the ditch at the side of the road. "And what will become of me, good sir? Pray tell!"

"Well, that depends." said Quentin.

"On what?"

"On if you're better behaved for Duke Colsarne than you are for us."

Decroix turned to him angrily. "QUENTIN! Shut up!"

"Sorry . . ." he muttered.

After a couple more days, we came to the edge of an estate. The borders were marked with grey boundary stones, each bearing a weather-beaten eagle chiselled into the rock, the features eroded by the centuries. We announced ourselves to a pair of guards at a gatehouse and huddled against the cold as a servant took our names and rode up the house to announce our arrival. After my bollocks had nearly frozen, he returned and escorted us to the stables, where boys in Colsarne livery took and brushed down our horses. I patted Reed's neck, and she rubbed her nose against my unscarred cheek. "Good girl." I scratched her ear, and we were taken into the fortified manse of the Colsarne family.

Long vines choked the stone and wrapped around the building. We were led in through huge dark oak doors bound with ancient iron into a long, narrow entrance hall lined with tattered banners claimed in battle down the centuries, hung in silent testimony to the might of Colsarne.

Long ago, before the Brotherhood of the Black Ram had risen, and before Order of the Cleansing Flame had broken them, there were far more 'noble' families. Every petty bandit like Azrael Bordane would have had a standard with his arms on it. All you needed was a loud voice, a sharp sword, and a dozen bloodthirsty soldiers, and you could call yourself a lord. The strongest families survived, and the weak ones were put to the sword or swallowed up into the stronger houses with marriage. Having scattered their enemies before them, House Colsarne now owned the land and taxed the people on it. The houses they crushed were broken and forgotten, save for a tatty scrap of faded cloth lining the walls of their old enemy.

A dozen men at arms wore coats of plate under their lord's livery. Their grey tabards matched their expression as they stood, six on each side of the hall as we waited for the seneschal. Even though we were finally at the end of our journey, both the brothers were silent and sullen. I could understand why Siffisante was dreading whatever the consequences were, but why the brothers were so hesitant to meet with Duke Colsarne, I couldn't guess.

I also wondered what the consequences would be for me. I doubted very highly that he would be happy for me to just leave, knowing what I did. Why take the risk? If I were him, I would just have my throat slit and have done with it. But then, who cared about some filthy sell-sword?

I made a silent prayer that Duke Colsarne was a kinder man than me. That wouldn't be hard, because I'm a complete cunt, but chances were, so was he. The main difference between us was that he had a dozen heavily armed men who would do exactly what he said.

An old man with an expensive-looking cloak walked towards us, the household keys jangling at his waist. It wasn't until he got a little closer that I realised he was the same bastard I met on the road from Ashpool to Middle Mark. Bugger.

"Where do I know you from?"

I shrugged. "No idea. I've just got one of those faces."

He scowled, but thankfully didn't press it. "Follow me." He snapped his fingers and two of the men at arms followed us as we climbed the broad staircase.

We found ourselves in a cramped study, the walls groaning with books. The seneschal bowed to a thin man seated at a worn oak writing desk, piles of vellum and parchment stacked before him, sporting a dark woolen robe and a neatly trimmed beard. "My lord."

"Thank you, Roderick. That will be all."

Roderick bowed again and left, taking the soldiers with him.

The duke slowly looked up from his papers, rapping a fingernail on a square of parchment. "Decroix! Quentin! How charming to see you both again." He pursed his lips and fixed the pair of them with a cold smile. "How are you both? In good health, I trust?"

The pair of them offered sweeping bows. "Well, my lord." Decroix answered. "Thank you for asking." Out of the corner of my eye, I noticed Siffisante performing a curtsey with something approaching simpering grace.

"I trust your journey was uneventful?"

I stifled a cough.

"Yes, lord." said Decroix.

"Although somewhat later than expected. Which is strange, would you say, for an uneventful journey, when you are both in good health?"

The question hung in the air for a brief moment. Quentin stood in silence, eyes darting over to his brother.

"Yes, lord." Decroix muttered.

"Not to worry, Decroix. I am sure you had an excellent reason for keeping me waiting."

Our gazes met. "Ah. Where are my manners? Duke Edmund Colsarne, of the Proud and Fearsome House of Colsarne."

"Ulf of Banrillar."

He fixed on me for a moment, head tilted and eyes flickering like a bird's before resting on the side of my face. "Be a good fellow and pop another log on the fire, would you, Ulf? I do so feel the cold."

My boots clicked on the flagstones as I crossed over to the great stone fireplace. I threw on a hefty piece of ash and sparks flew from the grate.

"Thank you, Ulf." He turned to the Siffisante. "And who is this enchanting creature I see before me?"

She fluttered her lashes shamelessly. "Siffisante, my lord."

"Most high priests of the Black Ram are blood-smeared lunatics, ranting about human sacrifice. What a pleasure it is to meet one so charming." Her mouth hung open for a moment. She started a rambling reply, but Colsarne cut her off with a raised hand. "We will be speaking shortly."

He turned to the three of us. "The rest of you may go. I look forward to seeing you at supper this evening." We bowed and exited the room, leaving Siffisante standing to face the inquisition of Duke Edmund Colsarne.

Servants led us to private chambers and provided each of us with fresh clothes and a basin of water. I stripped out of my armour, reasoning that if Colsarne wanted to kill me I would already be dead, and he might even be less likely to kill me if I made the effort to look halfway presentable for supper. Or, if he was going to kill me, then at least I could get blood all over his fancy guest clothes out of spite.

Arching my back, I stretched, rubbing my shoulders. I can run, climb, even fuck in my armour if I need to, but there is nothing like getting the weight off. You feel lighter and more agile, and your muscles can finally relax. Not that I was terribly relaxed at the moment, but theoretically it should have helped.

The cold splash of water felt good on my face after so long on the road, and the clean linen was wonderfully soft on my skin. I placed my sword and armour inside a chest along with the rest of my gear, then, aware of the soldier's adage of 'kip when you can' sprawled on the bed for a nap.

Some hours later, we were escorted to the main hall by a young page. The three of us sat uncomfortably on a raised dais at the head table. The fine scent of good beeswax candles filled my nostrils as more were lit throughout the hall. Roderick stood to the side, glowering at us. Glowering at me, specifically. I was pretty sure he'd figured out where he knew me from.

A fire was snapping in the huge hearth. A vast panel of oak hung above the mantle, engraved with the eagle badge of House Colsarne, talons unfurled. The entire household was before us at the lower tables - the servants, craftsmen, and soldiers that ran the home of a great duke of Ashenfell.

The hall doors opened and a well-dressed young woman entered with Siffisante in tow. Roderick cleared his throat and announced her with expert grandeur. "The Lady Alexia App Colsarne, of the Proud and Fearsome House of Colsarne."

The light from the fire made the fur around her neck shimmer, and the entire household stood as she entered. She moved with a practiced certainty as she stepped gracefully onto the dais and slowly sat at the centre of the table, with me to her left and Siffisante to her right. Her face seemed familiar and my head churned for a moment trying to stir the memory. Suddenly it dawned on me where I knew her from and a huge "Fuck!" rattled around in my brain as I recalled her and Roderick on that muddy road.

Oh, bugger me sideways . . .

"My father sends his deepest regrets, sweet guests. He has pressing matters to attend, and instead looks forward to speaking with you all tomorrow morning at breakfast in the gardens."

A central dish of pottage was placed before us on the top table. A large wooden bowl of it, mixed with roasted meat and drizzled with wine and honey. The rich smell floated over the table and it was all I could do to stop myself from scooping a handful into my mouth.

She held her palms outward, and the servants sat down and began to dine on their pottage. Compared to our dish, it was merger fare - peas and barley with hunks of bread - but I would much rather have been eating that than sitting next to the daughter of a Duke.

"Ulf?" I nearly jumped out of my chair when I realised Lady Alexia was talking to me. She smiled sweetly. "As my most treasured guest, I would be honoured if you would take the first bowl."

"But, as my most gracious host, I would be honoured to see you dine." I recalled the proper words, spilling them out like sour ale. She nodded to Roderick, who portioned out a delicate serving.

She ate slowly and gracefully, bringing the silver spoon to her mouth and taking the smallest of morsels. My stomach snapped at me like a chained dog, but I pressed my thumbnail into my finger to distract myself.

After what seemed like an age, she gently placed her spoon next to the empty dish, tilted slightly. The seneschal took away her bowl, other servants bringing us each a portion. The pottage was slightly colder now, but still delicious. The tang of the wine blended with the sweetness of the honey. It was a stroke of luck that I sat to her left, so she couldn't see the mess of my eating through the side of my face. I did feel sorry for Quentin, though, who looked like he might lose his appetite.

The empty dishes were taken away. Wine was poured out and I took a sip from a small silver goblet. My heart started pounding away, but I cleared my throat. Fuck it, might as well give it a go. "Lady Alexia, I must thank you for the wine. The aftertaste lingers most wonderfully and the colour is beautiful."

What the fuck was I meant to say about wine? It gets you pissed, and it's stronger than beer but weaker than mead.

"Thank you, Ulf." She touched my hand lightly. A sign of good favour.

We moved through the courses. Next came a salmon, smothered in garlic and parsley with wide dead eyes staring up at the ceiling, mouth agape. I struggled through the dinner conversation. It was my first time for a long while eating somewhere that wasn't a sleazy tavern or the side of the road.

I looked up and saw Siffisante staring at the slice of fish in front of her awkwardly. I stood up, moved to her right, and offered her my dirk. "Siffisante, it would give me great pleasure if I could present you my eating knife."

She took it gingerly, looking at a weapon that had previously been used to slash open other members of the cult. "Thank you." She took the knife and skewered a piece of pale flesh.

I bowed to her and returned to my seat. I met Roderick's gaze and placed two fingers on the top of my left wrist. His face reddened at his oversight. He nodded to me and walked swiftly away, returning in a moment with a full pitcher of wine. Alexia touched a finger to the rim of her glass and Roderick moved past her. I put my right hand to the base of my goblet and he filled it, discreetly placing a small eating knife by my plate.

I finished my fish, timing myself bite by bite so that Alexia and I finish at the same time. She continued talking to Siffisante, but though we were next to each other, the noise of the hall and the musicians who had started to play made it hard to hear a word.

Quentin tapped me on the shoulder. "How was your fish?" I turned to him and glared. He looked confused.

Siffisante met my gaze with a smile. "Ulf, I would be delighted if perhaps you would furnish our ears with some verse. Of course, if it pleases you, my Lady?"

"Indeed, it most certainly should please me. Greatly." Alexia rested her chin on her fingers and looked at me expectantly. Decroix and Quentin exchanged worried glances. My hands were shaking a little and my mouth felt dry. On the plus side, this meant I wouldn't accidentally spit on anyone.

I stood up slowly, so my chair didn't scrape. I could see everyone was looking at me, and for a moment I genuinely considered vaulting over the table and making a run for it. I could steal something valuable on the way out, get to the stable, ride off on Reed, and figure out the rest later.

I was convinced I was going to be a little sick in my mouth, but this was how the game is played. Besides, if I were sick in my mouth, it would have come out the side and hit Quentin in the face, which wouldn't have been be fair on him.

I realised someone was speaking, and that someone was me.

"On stark grey cliffs,

Brigandine

O'er sailing ships,
Two lovers, young and fair.

Hands entwined,
Hearts pure and kind,
And he with golden hair.

Yonder by Sir Konrad, the knight with golden hair.

Konrad loved his lady maid,
with voice soft as dew-swept glade,
In whose eyes he lost all care.

Her limbs were filled with fawnish grace,
And sunlight sparkled on her face,
Which made all nature for to stare.

Loved by Sir Konrad, the knight with golden hair.

As in love they dwelled,
Her mantle fell,
And tumbled through the air.

"Alack! Alake!"
Her voice did shake.
And the sorrow it was shared.

Shared by Sir Konrad, the knight with golden hair.

Down the cliff t'was swept,
Sir Konrad leapt,
As a man of valour dared.

As for his love,
From grey cliffs above,
By his honour was ensnared.

Bound by Sir Konrad, the knight with golden hair.

Dying for his love's own sake,
And now still she waits,
Atop cliffs in silent prayer.

For her lover's return,
And this kiss he has earned.
So over the cliffs she stares.

Stares and waits for Sir Konrad, the knight with golden hair."

If I had sat down any quicker, I would have shattered the chair. The room filled with polite applause and Siffisante gaped at me with astonishment, which swiftly shifted to her customary glower.

Lady Alexia smiled warmly at me. She touched my hand lightly and I forced myself not to instantly pull away. "Thank you, Ulf. That was beautifully spoken. The Ballad of Sir Konrad is one of my favourite of the old chivalric classics. Although, I do wonder why he didn't just take a path to the bottom of the cliff instead of jumping in."

I shrugged. "Or why his love didn't just carry a spare mantle, my lady?"

Alexia laughed lightly and gently patted my hand. "Ulf, I do hope we shall find each other most fair company."

The rest of the meal went well. After the fish, we dined on spatchcock with rosemary, medallions of rare venison and, finally, small pastry parcels dipped in honey and topped with crushed almonds. I don't normally have a tongue for such sweet things-they are mainly for women and children-but I have to admit they were delicious.

Having said my poem and knowing that no-one would ask to hear another from me, the wine flowed. I knew that I should have been on my guard, but fuck it. I hadn't eaten like that in years.

Brigandine

At the end of the night, I bowed deeply and thanked our host, who in turn thanked us for our company. "My father looks forward to speaking with you tomorrow in the early morn. Most pleasant dreams, Ulf." she said.

"And to you, my lady." At this point I noticed her eyes, shining in the candlelight. They brimmed with the same calculating intelligence of her father, but were tinged bright with the ambition and drive of youth.

Outside of my room, I turned to the brothers. "Decroix, a quick question."

"Yes, Ulf?"

"How scared are you both of Duke Colsarne?"

He swayed for a moment, filled with wine. "Put it this way, Ulf. Quentin hasn't tried to fuck his daughter yet."

"Sit up! You're at a banquet, not a brothel."

I straighten my back, putting my hands palm down on the little table.

Taran places a small bowl of pottage in front of me and pours us both a glass of wine. The ruby liquid shimmers by the firelight in my brother's chambers.

"It would be my greatest pleasure, Ulf, to watch you dine."

I dip a spoon into the dish, pushing gently away from me before bringing it up to my lips. Taran snatches it away.

"NO. The host offers you the honour of dinning first but you should never accept. The correct response is to say how much you'd love to watch them eat."

I crinkle my brow. "Why?"

"Because it shows restraint. It shows that you value your host's company far more than stuffing your face. Besides, it's only for the first course. Pretend I've eaten my pottage and now you've started on yours at the correct time. Ulf, how is your meal?"

"Very fine, thank you for-" Taran raises a warning finger, and I sigh. "The wine is excellent, my lord. It's very . . . nice."

"Very nice? Is that all you can say about it?"

"It's also . . . especially wet? I don't see why I can't just say that the food is good! Why do I have to talk about the wine?"

"Because the food was prepared by servants. You're not dining with servants, are you? Your host will have spent hours choosing the right wine from the cellar personally. It's the seal of a gracious host and an appreciative guest. If you compliment the food, you look like a glutton who is only thinking of his stomach."

He shoves his eating knife onto the floor and puts on a high pitched, squeaky voice. "Oh my! I, a lady, have appeared to have misplaced my knife! What an embarrassment!"

I roll my eyes and clenching my teeth I head round to my brother's side of the table, holding my knife to him, handle first.

"My lady, it would be my deepest honour if you would accept the use of my eating knife."

"OH, THANK YOU, GOOD SIR!" he pipes, taking the knife graciously. "And now what do you do?"

I tap two fingers lightly on the back of my hand.

"Excellent! Now the seneschal will bring you a new knife."

"Why can't she just ask for a new knife herself and save me the hassle?"

"Ulf, it's called etiquette. It's not meant to make sense." We sit in silence for a moment. The log crackles in the fireplace and a spark jumps up. "Ulf, this is important. You need to understand this, just as much as riding or swordsmanship."

I throw my spoon back into the bowl. "Why? It's pointless games!"

"These pointless games are what make a man into a knight and not just a heavily armoured thug. Suppose you need a favour from a lord and he invites you to dine with him? Or what about if you want to become a high-ranking member of the Order one day? Do you honestly think Sellor would be happy for you to dine with him throwing bones over your shoulder and gnawing at gristle?"

I can't help but crack a smile and my brother does the same.

"You'll get there, Ulf. It's like anything; it just needs practice. Now, let's have the ballad of Sir Konrad."

Groaning, I slump down in my chair. "Really? Oh, come on! It's the stupidest thing I ever heard! Do women really want to hear a story about how a knight jumped off a cliff to rescue a scarf?"

Taran fixes me with a hard look. "Firstly, yes they do. Secondly, it's a mantle, not a scarf. Thirdly, the ballad of Sir Konrad is a beautiful story of passion that shows how a knight must behave to his lady love. Ardent, intense,

Brigandine

and devoted until death. And finally-" He takes a draft of wine and smacks his lips. *"Do you have any idea how many beautiful women I've charmed into bed with that poem? Literally, any idea?"*

"Taran!"

"I had to buy a new bed, Ulf. The old one wore out. That's how many beautiful women." He drains his wine. *"You never volunteer to recite a poem. That would be boastful, unbecoming. You wait until someone asks you to. Then you stand up and make everyone in the room weep with beauty and fall into your arms and, consequently, your bed. Now, from the top."*

I stand up and clear my throat.

"On stark grey cliffs,
O'er sailing ships...."

Chapter 10:
Digging Deeper

I woke reluctantly in a soft bed, the warm morning sun washing over my face. After briefly considering stealing the sheets, I rose and dressed again in loaned finery. As I finished, a servant entered with a polite knock, Decroix and Quentin in tow, and escorted us into the Colsarne gardens for our morning appointment.

Duke Colsarne sat in the sunshine. The dark folds of his robes contrasted starkly to the beds of blooming flowers, dancing with colour. He bade us be seated at a small table laid with sweet breads, fruit and cheese.

"I trust you all slept well." He cracked open a small roll and smeared something red over it. He offered me the pot. "Wineberry?" he said with a thin smile.

I thanked him and spread a little onto a corner of bread. The sourness was so overwhelming that I nearly spat it out. Eventually, I choked it down as he looked on, amused. "An acquired taste." he said, reaching for the pot.

We dined in silence for a while. The birdsong in the trees was sweet and soft, but I wasn't in the mood to relax. Eventually, Decroix cleared his throat and spoke. "My lord?"

He swallowed a small mouthful of the hideous jam and looked up. "Hmmm? Yes, Decroix?"

Decroix swallowed. "My lord, what is to be the next part of the plan? We brought you the leader of the Cassioc cult, as you commanded."

"And I commend you for your competence, Decroix. I really do. I must also congratulate Roderick on his foresight in outfitting your little adventure as it seems he gave you the exact right amount of money, considering how you didn't come back with any whatsoever."

"Ah, now about that, my lord-"

"Nevertheless, here you are. Or, to be more accurate, here we are, wondering what the next step will be." He popped another piece of bread into his mouth and chewed thoughtfully.

I decided I'd had enough and poured myself out a glass of watered-down wine, draining the cup. Duke Colsarne turned to me, smiling. "Ah, Ulf! It is most wonderful to have you here. I trust you have found Decroix and his brother amicable company?"

"Yes, my Lord. I have enjoyed both their company on the journey. Except when nearly starving to death in the forest, when people were trying to kill us, or when we had to flee from a huge fire."

The smile abruptly dropped from his face, and I wondered if I had overstepped the mark. Actually, I didn't wonder at all. I damn well knew I had.

"Of course. The fire. Siffisante mentioned it last night, and I was meaning to ask you about that." Quentin started fidgeting in his chair, and I could see Decroix avoiding Colsarne's gaze like it might turn him to stone.

He looked me dead in the eyes. "Would you care to elaborate on how that started?"

"No."

"I'm sorry?"

I met his gaze, and he rapped his knuckles on the table. "No. I wouldn't care to elaborate." I could hear Decroix's teeth grind together.

"A lot of people lost their homes in that fire, Ulf of Banrillar." His cold eyes were stabbing at me, but I held my ground and kept my lips tightly shut. After what seemed like an age, he drummed his fingers lightly.

I slowly drew my dirk and reached out to cut off a hunk of cheese. I popped it into my mouth and chewed deliberately. The fact that Duke Colsarne could look at my face while I was eating was proof he was a hard bastard.

I swallowed my cheese. "So, when are we hanging Siffisante?" I tried to look like I wasn't too excited about it.

He drummed his fingers again and popped a berry into his mouth. "Siffisante? She works for me now." I couldn't help but splutter. He arched his brow. "She has provided me with vital information. Information we badly need to accomplish our goal."

"And what exactly is this goal, my lord?" I tried to keep my face as expressionless as possible, although I was certain Colsarne could read my thoughts if he wanted.

He blinked slowly. "Nothing less than the security and safety of my ancestral lands of Rusia, and all of Ashenfell."

I leaned back in the chair, choosing my next words carefully. "I see. And you are the one man who is acting altruistically, in the best interest of the realm? When everyone else is scrabbling for money or power, there is at least one person who is selflessly looking out for the interests of the common people. Someone wise, kind, and beloved by all. Someone who the Queen should trust and take into her confidence . . . my lord."

He smiled broadly and claps his hands together. "Exactly, Ulf! I'm so glad we understand one another." I nodded back in acknowledgement as he sipped his wine and continued. "Siffisante doesn't care about the Black Ram. She started a cult for the reassuringly petty reasons of money, fame, and power. Things I can easily give to her as a lady in waiting to my daughter, Alexia. She has given up all she knows. The Black Ram is waxing once again. Its agents are abroad once more, and I will not allow it to take hold over my land. Let me make it abundantly clear: I rule in Rusia, not the Black Ram."

Decroix coughed. "My lord?"

He turned to Decroix. "Yes?"

"We are willing and able to serve you in this and all matters, Lord. My brother and I are at your service."

"Decroix. I pay you to inform me of things that I don't know." Decroix smiled nervously.

"Things like what is happening in Carstock, for example." The smile fell away from Decroix's face like a whore's dress.

"Siffisante said that was where her contact with the Black Ram was travelling next. The one who helped her set up the . . . what was it again?"

"The Waystone." I interjected.

The duke looked at me quizzically. "You know a lot about this sort of thing, don't you, Ulf?"

Bugger.

"Yes, my lord. I suppose so."

Duke Colsarne dabbed at his lips with a napkin and reclined, satisfied with himself. "Anyway, Decroix, I'm sure you will want to be departing soon. It's a decent ride to Carstock. I am sure Roderick will be able to provide you with whatever you need."

Decroix rose and bowed. "Yes, my lord."

"Quentin?"

He almost jumped to his feet. "Lord?"

"Please see to it that your brother doesn't get into any trouble. I'm dreadfully fond of Decroix, and the road can be so dangerous." Quentin bowed deeply.

"And Ulf. I'd ask you to make sure Quentin doesn't get into any trouble, but no man is obliged to do the impossible, so just try to mitigate the damage."

I stood and bowed, wishing I had eaten more of the cheese.

Duke Colsarne stood, and some nearby servants appeared to clear away the dishes. He surveyed the beautiful garden, his cold eyes sparkling. "Lovely day for a ride, would you not agree, Ulf?"

"Yes, lord."

And, with that, we left.

As we passed the stables on our way back to the main house, I noticed stable hands were already fitting Reed and the brother's geldings with saddles. It was nice to know Colsarne hadn't wasted any time. I sighed and headed back to the room to gather my gear.

The bed looked so soft and inviting. I was tempted to pretend I'd caught syphilis and needed to spend a few weeks in bed recovering, but Duke Colsarne would have probably just told me I needed to get more fresh air. I've had enough fucking fresh air to last me a lifetime.

With my gear collected, I returned to the stables. I patted Reed's neck as waited on the brothers, and she nuzzled at me. "Good girl." I muttered and scratched her ear a little. We were on the road within the hour, the vine-draped seat of House Colsarne getting smaller with every hoofbeat. I bitterly regretted not stealing something valuable. Oh well, there's always next time.

"Hey, Ulf!" I turned to Quentin and just managed to catch what he threw to me. A fruit bun, freshly baked with dates and honey. I ripped off a chunk, and it was the nicest thing I'd had in my mouth since I shacked up with Mary.

Our saddlebags were filled with dried food, the normal plain fare that you'd expect a tight bastard like Roderick to provide us with. "But, how did you-"

"I'm fucking the baker."

"Ah. Should have guessed."

The journey to Carstock passed uneventfully. And, on the plus side, I had a purse full of coins, hanging fat and heavy on my belt. Roderick was none too keen about handing over the money. He gave me a cold glare as he counted out every piece into my palms. Which made it all the sweeter.

The fish on the drying racks swung in the wind as we approached the town. Annoyingly, the same guard from a week or so ago was on duty. "Hello again. Where's your sister?"

Decroix looks puzzled. "Who- Oh yes! She's with family, recovering. She took ill on the road and we had to divert."

"Where?"

Oh shit . . .

"She is with our cousin, Archibald. He's the baker at Duke Colsarne's manse."

The guard shrugged. We peace bound our weapons, dismounted, and headed into town. Decroix jingled his purse. "Luckily, there's enough for an inn this time 'round!"

"Good point!" I said. "So, you two are local. Where's half-decent to stay?"

Quentin tapped his lips thinking. "Well, I haven't tried the Old Rope."

"And by 'haven't tried', you mean-"

"You know exactly what I mean."

Decroix raised his hands. "We are not staying at an inn purely on the basis that your cock would like a change of scenery. We'll go to the Two Goats. It's cheap and discrete, and the landlord's daughter has a wooden leg and a lazy eye, so hopefully the lunatic here will stay relatively well-behaved."

"Sorry, Decroix." I said. "Two against one! The Old Rope it is." It was mainly just to annoy him.

Decroix pinched his nose and sighed. "Fine! But please, just try to stay out of trouble. Just once. That's all I ask."

Quentin held up his hands in acquiescence. "Alright! Alright! I promise to TRY. And for the record, Decroix: Bertha was a gentle and considerate lover."

The Old Rope wasn't too much of a cesspit. The sign was as unimaginative as you'd expect, with the frayed ends swaying in the breeze. Reed and the geldings were taken to a dilapidated stable clinging to the side of the inn. An old man missing his right hand led her to a stall and bent over to pick up a bale of hay. His back creaked like a broken door and I winced as he struggled with it.

"Here," I offered, bending down to pick up the bale.

He swatted me away with his stump. "Off wit' cha'!" he spat, and I noticed his mouth could certainly do with a few more teeth.

Fine, be a grumpy bastard. I left him to it as Reed tucked into the hay.

After stabling the horses, we entered the tavern. A few old men were sitting at worn-out tables on much mended chairs with patchwork legs. Behind the bar stood a sour woman with a face like a dried apple core. "What do you want?"

Decroix smiled politely. "Livery for the two geldings and the rouncey. Good hay, none of the cheap shit you give to the others. Room with meals for the three of us. One week."

I could see her lips moving as she mentally added up.

"It's five Ecar for the night in the bed. An' another five for meals." She scratched at her nose and inspected the finger. "An' it's six Ecar for a horse for the night-."

"Three hundred and thirty-six." Decroix cut her off.

She scowled at him. "'Hold on! That's . . . ten per day per man. Seven days . . . that's . . . seventy! But there are three of you . . ."

"Three hundred and thirty-six." Decroix repeated.

"I said hold on! . . . right, where was I?"

"Seventy?" Quentin chips in.

"Oh yes! Seventy per man for the week. Three men . . . that's . . ." Her brow knitted together in concentration and she tapped each of her fingers in turn, cursing when she ran out. "Two hundred an' ten! Right, and you've got horses as well?"

"Can't forget about the horses . . ." Decroix muttered.

"Let's see. So that is six for one horse for one night. But you've got three horses for six nights."

"Seven nights." I remind her. I watched with glee as Decroix turned redder by the moment.

"One hundred and twenty-six!" Decroix yells. "It's a hundred and twenty fucking six for the horses!"

"I was getting there! Right hundred an' twenty-six for the horses an' . . . what was it again for the beds an' the meals?"

An old man looked up from a table. "Two hundred an' ten it were, Aggie."

"Right! So . . . two hundred an' ten and one hundred an' twenty-six . . . that's . . ."

Decroix flung a handful of coins at her. "HERE! Keep the cunting change!"

Aggie stood with her broad mouth hanging wide open as Decroix stamped up the stairs, and it was all Quentin and I could do to not burst out laughing.

By the time we had unpacked our things and shook off the dust of the road, we were all hungry. I brought food upstairs, as I felt that having Decroix strangle Aggie probably wouldn't help us on our mission.

Now less flustered, Decroix went over the idea. I nodded along while munching on a pickled onion.

"Right, here's the plan. Siffisante said that her contact in the Black Ram was going to Carstock, and went there after sorting out the . . . Waystone, was it?"

I nodded again and Decroix continued.

"According to Siffisante, it was an old man, and he claimed to be high in the cult's ranks. He coordinated with her in setting up the cult in Cassioc. Taught her what to do to . . . make things work." He shuddered a little and scratched the back of his hand. "So, this time we aren't fucking about with a bunch of money-hungry actors looking for a life of comfort and ease. He's going to be a dangerous man."

He was right to be cautious. Even being around magic for a short while can fuck you up in the head. It gives you nightmares and twists your mind.

Quentin drummed his fingers. "Right, so let's assume he's rich. He had enough money to travel to Cassioc and back, and he would need an excuse to do that. He might be a merchant? Or with the guilds?"

Decroix nodded. "Agreed. Siffisante also mentioned he was going to come back to check up on her progress, leaving about now. Although, with the news of the fire, he might have already left." He gave me a dirty look. "So, there is no time to fuck about. I'll ask around the markets and see if anyone is planning on leaving for Cassioc. We'll be sell-swords looking for protection work. Ulf, get us some cheap armour and some impressive looking weapons. Halberds or something."

I held out my hand and he passed me three Guilder.

"I'll see if I can get in with the guilds. See what's going on."

"Good idea, Quentin. Let's meet back here later, see what the mood of the town is like."

It was late afternoon, but the shops were still open. I followed the smell of charcoal and the sound of grinding metal to find the handful of armourers in Carstock. I entered a small workshop, with the usual sign of a helmet and crossed swords hanging above the door, and blinked my eyes to adjust to the gloom. It was an old man's shop, full of tatty little boxes of rings and rivets, bottles of oils arranged just-so, and dark, worn tools made in the days when things were built to last. I coughed loudly for attention, and the owner shuffled round from the back. He was bent over double with crooked, calloused hands. He put down a riveting hammer and waggled his finger in his ear. "Good day. What can I help you with?"

"I need three halberds and two mail shirts. Coifs too, if you've got them."

After some rummaging, he took out a pair of old sacks from behind some boxes. They made a satisfying heavy clink as he put them on a bench. "You're in luck and out of it, friend. I can let you have two shirts with coifs for only two Guilder. They're a little rusty, but some sand and a bit of piss will shine them up in no time. But no weapons, I'm afraid."

"No weapons? You're an armourer, aren't you?"

He shrugged. "Sold out!" he said happily.

"Sold out? As in, nothing to buy?"

He grinned at me and rattled his money box. "Sold out, lad! Same with all the others. Even that bastard Stephanwolf and the shite he makes. Buggers brought every damn dagger, poleaxe, and falchion."

"Who?" I handed over the money for the armour and slung the sacks over my shoulders.

He shrugged again and dropped the money into a safebox. "Lots of 'em! Different people coming in and buying up all the weapons. Sold a few swords I picked up last month at a decent profit and I thought to myself, 'this has been a good morning!' and by supper, every blade was gone! The wife was pleased, to say the least. Although, with the money I made, I might sell her and buy a younger one!"

He laughed and hacked out a cough. "Going to have to whip that lazy sod of an apprentice hard. People are buying as quick as I can make! Anyway, I'm just shutting up the shop, so it will have to be good day you, young man."

I checked in at the other armourers and I got the same story, so I took a wander around Carstock. The people seemed in good spirits, and bits of coloured cloth were hanging from windows. Soft smells flowed from houses- cakes, pastries, pies. Festival foods. Mentally, I ran through the sacred days of various Virtuous Ones. There wasn't one for at least a few weeks, but the tavern doors were open and the streets were lined with tables full of happy people drinking.

I walked into the central plaza market square, and saw it filled with raised benches cobbled together from fresh timber. The pit they were digging now yawned like a massive, jagged wound in the earth. Six men with longswords clad in shining breastplates stood guard by the side of the pit.

I tried to look friendly as I approached the nearest one. "Hail, friend. Good evening to you."

He gave me a curt nod. "Good evening. What do you want?"

I looked over at the pit with interest. "I'm new in town. Mercenary." Not strictly a lie, so I think I got away with it. I certainly looked the part, at least.

"So?"

"Well, I was just wondering what that pit was for? Those are some deep foundations!"

"That's not your concern. Now, move along." Without looking I knew his hand is on his sword hilt. And he didn't look like the type to weep too much over spilling blood.

I shrugged. "Well, fair enough. Good evening."

The brothers and I met back at the Old Rope. I tossed the sacks on the floor and they looked dismayed.

"Couldn't you find anything a little lighter?" Decroix asked. "And where are the halberds?"

I stretched, glad to be rid of the weight of the armour. "Some buggers have been buying up all the weapons in Carstock. Multiple people, getting hold of everything they can."

Quentin wrinkled his nose at the rust. "If this stains my clothes, I will be furious, Ulf. I want you to know that."

"What did you expect for three Guilders? Oh, I've got the best armour, so I'll be the captain."

Decroix clicked his tongue and tried on the chainmail, shaking it loose as it fell over him. "It's a little big."

"You'll grow into it. Also, that pit is getting bigger. Lots of chairs and benches in the main square. Fuck knows what they're up to, but it seems like a party."

Quentin nodded in agreement. "That's what we were told, as well. The Carnival of Justice."

"What the fuck is that?"

"Something new. To celebrate the laws which govern Ashenfell and protect us all."

"Sounds dull as fuck."

"Well, I didn't come up with the idea, Ulf, so don't blame me. Anyway, people all seem pretty pleased about it. Every tavern is serving some fancy wine tonight, bought by the town. Everything else is half price!"

"Hmmm…" Decroix looked worried. "Well, in that case, the guilds must be behind it. You'd need some pretty strong clout to make a landlord sell his ale cheap."

"What about the weapons?" Quentin ran his hand through his hair. If he was taking something seriously, it was enough to worry me as well.

Decroix shrugged. "I don't know where they would fit into this, but we need to keep digging. On the positive side, I do have a small piece of good fortune."

"Oh?"

"Quentin and I have asked around. Food merchants, stables and all that nonsense. No one has left for Cassioc recently."

Brigandine

"Or perhaps they did and just didn't tell anybody?" I suggested.

"Maybe." Decroix conceded. "But until we know otherwise, we need to stick to Carstock and find out what is going on here. A new festival? Someone buying up enough blades for a private army?"

"A weird pit in the middle of the market place?" I chipped in.

"Exactly! Quentin, you and I are going to do some drinking in a few taverns and see if we can find anything else out. Ulf-"

"I'll stay here, get pissed, and try not to get into any trouble."

"Good man!"

Chapter 11:
A Bitter Wine

Within an hour, The Old Rope sat fit to bursting with people enjoying the cheap drinks. The air filled with a busy thrum of laughter, chatter, and speculation. Despite my best efforts to look unfriendly, people were sitting pressed together at every table. Including my own. They introduced themselves as Something and Someone-Or-Other. Carpenter's apprentices. I promptly ignored them and hoped they'd fuck off so I could get on with some serious drinking.

The door swung open and a couple of guards stood in the doorway, panting and red-faced. One, leaning on his knees, stammered out, "... delivery."

Aggie grunted and pointed to the bar. A huge cheer erupted as they wheeled in some vast barrels, grunting as they pushed them upright. The crowd gathered around with greedy interest before they were shooed back. "One Ecar a pint. No more, no less." Aggie nodded and cracked open the first barrel, slopping out a great mug of rich dark wine.

Dozens of fists thrust copper coins towards her as the innkeeper slammed mug after mug down on the bar, the wine spilling over and dribbling onto the floor. A dog lapped at the mess and rolled around to the delight of everyone. Some stupid bugger even threw the mutt half a pie. Funny, there are beggars who would pluck out their eye for a meal, but people will throw food to a dog because it's funny.

I don't know what it is about a dog in a tavern. In the street, folk will kick them in the ribs, or at home, they'll beat them to death for shitting in the wrong place, but in a tavern, a dog is a king.

After a while I drained my tankard, went to the bar, and slapped down my own Ecar, just to see what it was like. I took a sniff, and the heady mixture pulled itself into my brain. I took a small sip and spat it straight out again. I scraped my tongue and spat on the floor again to get rid of the foul taste, like a rancid vinegar laced with copper.

"Hey there! Oi!" A hand landed on my shoulder and spun me around, and I found Someone-Or-Other in my face, drunk to the hilt. "Friend. FRIEND! I've got a question for you!" His wretched breath was dank on my face.

I gripped my fists tight. Right foot went backwards, stance shifted.

"What's that hole in your face for? Huh? How'd you get that?" He laughed at me, little bits of spit flying onto my chin. He leaned forward and whispered into my ear. "Is it so you can suck two cocks at the same time?"

I smashed him in the mouth, cracking one of his teeth. He howled in anger and lashed out at me blindly. I dodged it and slammed my elbow in his nose, watching happily as it crumpled and spread to one side. He staggered back into a group of builders, who roared as their wine spilled to the floor. One of them grabbed at Someone-Or-Other, and then Something is there, cracking him in the face with a headbutt.

Suddenly, the whole tavern started fighting and the common room was filled with jagged, broken wood that used to be furniture. A fat bloke with a badgered beard tried to swing a chair at me, but I caught his wrists and kicked him in the bollocks.

The back of my neck prickled and I spun round. Someone-Or-Other stabbed downwards at me with a knife, and I thrust my forearm up under the blade against his arm. Pain rushed down my wrist as the blade opened my arm, but I ignored it and grabbed the pommel with my left hand. He clawed at me and scratched at my eyes making me lean back. His feet slipped as I pulled him forward, forcing his arm under my armpit. I felt a thud on my back as he thumped at me, but I tore the dagger from his grip. I caught a firm grip on his belt and hurled him over my hip. He sprawled on the ground moments before my foot pressed down on his neck.

I spat down at him. "If you have even a lick of sense you'll stay on the floor, you little cunt!"

He looked at his dagger, then at my face, and thought better of it.

The door slammed open and five guards rushed in, smacking and laying about with clubs to break up the fight. "For fucks' sake . . ." The sergeant cursed under his breath looking around at the chaos. "Right! Which one of you bastards started this?"

"This silly sod pulled a dagger on me!" I pointed to the empty sheaf on his leg and the blade, half-buried under filthy straw.

Two guards grabbed him by the arms and dragged him out, silencing his protests with a slog to the guts. The sergeant took the dagger and tucked it into his belt, no doubt to turn up on a market stall in a few days. He looked at me, not bothering to hide his disgust at my face. I tried not to meet his eye; I didn't fancy pushing my luck with this one.

Everyone fucked off pretty sharpish, so I helped Aggie to clear up the broken wood by hurling the shards into the fire, which soon began roaring away. Dealing with fights is part of owning an inn, but it can't be an easy life dealing with cunts like me all the time, so occasionally I try to help out. It was the early hours of the morning by the time we finished. She thanked me for the help as I headed up to bed.

It must be hard to be her. Thicker than a donkey's todger and so ugly Quentin wouldn't fuck her.

The brothers still weren't back yet. Fuck knows what they were up to.

After flinging my clothes and armour onto the floor and finally falling into bed, I reflected that, although Aggie is so ugly, Quentin would probably still fuck her, so at least she had that to look forward to.

"Ulf? ULF!"
I wake with a jolt and I spin and tumble, smacking against the floor.
"Wake up! You'll be late!" My vision swims into focus, and my brother is standing over me. He throws a set of clothes at me, good cloth and brand new.
"What are these?"
"Ulf, these are clothes. People wear them when they don't want to be naked. Now I suggest you get a fucking move on and don them!"
I drag a fresh linen shirt over my head and it feels wonderfully soft. The hose are dark blue with gold trim and they fit me perfectly. "Taran, thank you. These are-"
My brother pulls something over my head. I look down and it's a tabard, dark blue with a cup of gold. "Am I . . . am I allowed to wear this?"
"You're my squire, aren't you? Besides, I'm not letting that bastard Windor App Decare show me up." *He spits on his fingers and smooths my hair.* "Oh! One more thing." *He grabs a long package wrapped in oilcloth and quickly unrolls it.*
It's a sword! The pommel gleams, fresh from the forge and the scabbard smells of new leather. "It's only a Federschwert, I don't want you killing anyone. Wrap the belt around twice and then let the long bit dangle at the front. No! Not like that!" *He takes over as my fingers fumble with the beautiful silver buckle.*
"So, what exactly do you have against Sir Windor?"
Taran sighs. "Some people are in the Order because, like me, they are dashing horsemen and fantastic fighters. Others, like Decare, are here because of who their fathers are and how many Guilders they have. A knight should earn his place through merit, not through who they are related to."
"I'm here on merit though, aren't I?"
"Bloody . . . Come on . . ." *Taran fiddles with the new holes and cinches the belt tight.* "There!" *He steps back to admire me.* "Well, aren't you just the knight in making? Now, hurry the fuck up!" *Taran drags me by the wrist, my heart pounding.* "Here, eat this." *As we run, he shoves a hunk of bread into my hands and I wolf it down. We run across the courtyards, the bright sun nearly blinding me.*

We get to the parade ground just ahead of the last squire. "Good luck, don't fuck it up!" *Taran shoves me forward and I fall into step behind the others. I'm fifteen now, and this is my first year.*

One day a year when it's about us and not the knights: The Grand Tourney of Foot!

We march around the edge of the parade ground. The cheers of the knights, priests, and servants of the Order are pounding my ears as I try desperately to keep my feet in step to the beat of the drum. I scan the crowd for my brother and I think I see a flash of blue. I put my hand on the hilt of my sword to stop it from slapping against my leg with every step. The wood is smooth dark oak, and the pommel is curved like a fig.

We suddenly halt and I only just stop myself from bumping into the squire in front of me. With a rattle of the drum, we turn to our right to face the High Council. The most senior knights and leaders of the Order, led by Sellor. The old Patriarch sits shaded by the canopy on top of the raised stand, a full goblet by his side. A hush falls over us all as he stands to address the Order.

"*Followers of the Cleansing Flame! Sons of Oswald the Fierce! My brothers!*"

A massive cheer rises up, drumming of feet and cries of jubilation. Sellor holds up a hand for quiet.

"*Today we honour and test the next generation of our Order. We stand as a chain, from when we struck back against the darkness to this very day where we stand, strong and unbroken. Now, we look to the future of the Order. The heroes of tomorrow. Fight well, and with honour.*" *He raises his cup in salute and the crowd applauds.*

We file out and take our places by the side of the arena. Servants bring gambesons - thick suits of padding to prevent broken bones - and padded caps. Years of sweat and oil have turned some of them almost black, and the smell stings my nose, but I manage to get one of the fresher ones.

Once dressed, each of us reaches into a vast pot and draws out a stone bearing a number. My hand closes around one and pulls it out. Five.

"*Bugger.*" *I curse under my breath and slip the rock into my pouch.*

"*ONE AND TWO!*" *comes the cry from a herald. The crowd roars and the two squires bow and salute with their weapons. They each take up a stance, a drum is struck and the weapons clash. Both of them are older students who*

Brigandine

know what they are doing and the blows come fast and terrible. They break off and encircle each other, feinting and lunging to test their opponent for weakness. Suddenly, one of them strikes. He thrusts forward, past the guard and the blunt tip his sword hits home. The drum is sounded. "FIRST STRIKE, FALMORN." Falmorn bows to his opponent, who bows back, acknowledging the strike with honour. The drum sounds again to restart the bout, and there is another strike, a huge blow leading with the top of the sword. Falmorn grips the tip of his sword and brings it up, the blades ringing together. He then sweeps the sword round and cuts upwards, binding the swords together. He's too slow, and he takes a slash to the padding on his throat.

"FIRST STRIKE BARTON. FIRST STRIKE, FALMORN." Barton's bow is made and returned and the bout continues.

It ends with Falmorn victorious, three strikes to Barton's one. I can see Barton's face, red and panting in the sunshine as he pulls off the padded coif and throws it to the ground angrily.

"THREE AND FOUR!"

The next fight is over almost instantly. A twenty-year-old squire beats a boy my age with contemptuous ease, disarming him three times. He hands the blunted sword back to him and bows as the knights in the crowd whoop his name.

"FIVE AND SIX!"

My brain is pulsing in my skull. The padding sticks to my ears and blood rushes around my face. We both step forward. I don't know him, but he's taller than me. His grip tightens over the haft of a poleaxe, the burs and notches on the blunt edge glint in the light. I hold my sword up high in salute and I notice Taran at the front of the crowd, pressed up against the wooden stand. He nods to me and I smile back. We turn to face each other. He's crouching low, the point of the weapon towards the ground. I shift my guard, my left hand on the pommel, right towards the top of the hilt.

The drum sounds and he strikes upwards, just as I thought he would. My new sword vibrates with the impact as it bites into the head. He thrusts it forward and pushes me back. I quickly step to the side and jab at him, the point strikes his haft and he swings back at me savagely. With one hand I slash downwards as hard as I can, smacking the weapon to the ground. I push it away and cut him cleanly across the chest. As I do, the drum sounds loud, pounding in time to my heartbeat.

"FIRST STRIKE, ULF". I'm giddy with power and my muscles are tight with energy. We part, and I almost forget to bow. As I rise, I can see his face masked in anger, but I don't care. I'm going to win this. I'm going to be the champion and nothing can stop me!

I rush in with my hands first, like an idiot and he jabs me in the thigh after effortlessly blocking a clumsy overhead blow. "FIRST STRIKE, ULF. FIRST STRIKE, ULRIC." I can hear Taran's voice chastising me now for that stupid mistake. As I acknowledge the blow, I can see he's grinning now and I set my jaw, leading with the point of the sword like a plough.

He sweeps low and I step back to parry. But the cut is a feint and I barely bring the blade up quickly enough to intercept the strike. He pushes me back. Huge, heavy blows which rain down fast. He cuts to my shoulders, forcing me backwards with hacks from his forearms interspersing his main attacks. Pressing against the tip of my sword, he forces my blade away and then pushes the head of the poleaxe into my shoulder with a shove.

"FIRST STRIKE, ULF. SECOND STRIKE, ULRIC." Even through the padding, I feel the impact. He bows to me grandly, sweeping his knuckle across the floor, a smirk on his face. I grind my teeth. He stands up and drops his weapon to the ground and opens his arms wide. I bring my sword up quickly. Is he going to grapple me? But no. He stands there, arms open with that smirk on his face! Like he doesn't have to try! I'm still cautious, so I step towards him slowly. He makes no move. Hooking the poleaxe with my foot I kick it away. A few people in the crowd laugh as Ulric pulls a stupid face of mock concern. Although it's tempting to just snap his fucking neck with my sword, I touch him on the chest.

"SECOND STRIKE, ULF. SECOND STRIKE, ULRIC." More titters from the benches and pavilions. My face is flushed with embarrassment as well as heat. Don't let him get to you. That's what Taran would say. Don't let him get to you.

The drum sounds again and I step forward with the blow, meeting his attack. My blade slides downwards, ready to force him to drop his weapon or lose his fingers, but he anticipates the move and sidesteps. The blades connect with a clang and while the vibration still rattles in my brain, we are both bringing our arms round for another exchange. I sweep from left to right and he hooks the hilt of my sword. With all my might, I force it away, twisting the cross guard free.

He barrels into me. His body is like a slab of muscle and my face is numb with the impact. Both our weapons go flying and he grabs me by my new tabard, pulling it down over my face. My arms are wrapped around his waist and I stumble like a wounded ox trying to throw him off balance, feet kicking up great clouds of dust from the arena floor. My belt is wrenched up and he throws me over his hip, sending me tumbling face-first into the dirt. Pain as I feel the warm blood of a split lip.

"SECOND STRIKE, ULF. FINAL STRIKE, ULRIC." The crowd applauds, and I realise there is a metal tip resting on my throat. My own sword. The bastard got me with my own fucking sword.

I scrabble up to my feet, the humiliation sinking deep into me. Ulric is smiling at me as he bows to me again for the third time.

"Hard luck, but you did well. Two strikes! Maybe next year, eh?"

He politely offers up the hilt of my sword and I snatch it back. I turn, running out of the arena and biting my tongue hard to push back angry tears.

Chapter 12:
A Good View

I awoke to the sound of Quentin and Decroix chatting while getting dressed.

"Ah! Good of you to join us, Ulf."

My body still ached from last night's brawl, and my head wasn't much better from the booze. "URRRRGH." I groaned.

"How very articulate." Decroix threw my clothes at me. "Hurry up and get going. We need to be in the main square sharpish."

"What's happening in the main square?"

Decroix sighed. "That's what we're trying to find out, stupid!"

I let the insult slide and pulled on my shirt and hose. My boots were sticky and stained dark red, and I began to panic until I remembered all the wine sloshing about on the floor.

The entire town was in the streets, and most of the shops were closed. People were already drinking despite the early hour, and the air echoed with the crack of splitting wood as people hacked open the lid of yet another barrel. Everywhere people were eating, shovelling great handfuls of food into their mouths, spilling slops over their chins onto the ground. The stray notes of some song that I couldn't quite place floated over the crowd.

When we arrived at the square, we saw a man on silts breathing great gouts of flame from a torch as people cheered. Beneath him, a juggler spun five knives in the air, and a kindly old man passed wooden balls out to children to hurl at a bear, declawed and tied to a stake.

"Roll up! Roll up! Today it's all free!" He gestured to a little stand with some gaudy looking prizes: brightly coloured hats, small dolls with glass eyes, and a dagger with a staghorn handle. "Take a shot! See if you can hit the fearsome man-eating bear! Test your mettle! You, brave sir!"

He offered me one of the balls with a smile and I lobbed it at the creature, cracking it on the nose. "Well done sir!" He clapped and handed me a doll with wonky mis-matched eyes.

"Can't I have the dagger?"

"Sorry, sir. That's only if you can get in square in the bollocks."

"But that's she-bear!"

He tapped his nose. "Never said it was easy, sir!"

I tossed the doll at the nearest child and she squealed with delight, running to tell her mother.

We walked off to get a decent seat high up at the back of the viewing benches. The seats were spread wide, so even those at the back got a good view. A vast pit squatted in the centre of the square, the one they were digging two weeks before. I could see something at the bottom, but I couldn't make out what the hell it could be.

The crowd was buzzing with anticipation. I could taste it in the air, a heady mix of drunken excitement and the promise of a spectacle.

I didn't like it. Not one jot.

The man in front of me suddenly stood and cheered, blocking my view. I sprang to my feet with the rest of the crowd as a procession filed into the square. Dozens of young men and women marched forward, each bearing a tall pole mounted with the symbol of their guild: a sheaf of reeds for the thatchers, a miniature barrel for the coopers - even the prostitute's guild had a big pair of painted wooden tits. Dozens of trades were represented by an apprentice bearing their symbol.

The guards marched behind them, armour and weapons gleaming in the sunshine, surrounding a wagon pulled by two oxen draped with scarves and flowers. A middle-aged woman in the dark woollen robes of a scribe, an ink quill pinned to her breast, stood atop the wagon and waved to the crowd. Behind her, more guards dragged along a gaggle of wretches bound in chains. The crowd booed and threw whatever shit or rubbish they had to hand, much to the displeasure of the guards caught in the crossfire.

The bright sun overhead felt warm and light on my face and I could feel myself relaxing, enjoying myself and being part of the spectacle. I scratched the back of my hand, hard enough to tear the skin and shock the fuzz from my head. Decroix and Quentin seemed enraptured, cheering along so I slapped them both on the back of the head. "FUCK! What was that for?" Quentin grimaced, rubbing his scalp.

"Pay attention!" I hissed, and they both nodded their thanks. "Who's the old bitch on the cart?"

Quentin squinted. "Elivar. Alderman of the scholar's guild."

"What's she doing out front? I didn't realise fish smoking and woodcutting had much call for academic discussion?"

Decroix shrugged. "Buggered if I know, Ulf. Anyway, shut up!" He pointed and I noticed Elivar before the crowd, raising her hands for silence.

"GOOD FOLK OF CARSTOCK! WELCOME . . . TO THE CARNIVAL OF JUSTICE!" The roar was deafening and the wooden stand vibrated with the sound. A hush fell as she held up her hands again.

"The Guilds' Council of Carstock is proud to host this feast of recognition and thanks to all law-abiding and gentle folk of our fair town. However . . . what of the others? What of those who do not share our values? Who do not keep our laws? Who spit on tradition and harm us all!"

She spread her gaze across the crowd before glancing to the wretches behind her, bound up in chains. She pointed a quivering finger, shaking with rage.

"THIEVES! ADULTERERS! MURDERERS!" She threw her hands skyward, howling in pain as the mob vented their hatred. Stones flew out and struck at the prisoners. I saw a flash of red and a woman fell to the floor sobbing, a vicious gash opened in her forehead. A guard dragged her up and struck her across the face with a gauntlet, getting a laugh from the crowd as a spray of blood and teeth flew from her mouth.

"We cannot allow such people to live among us! To corrupt us!"

"NO! NO!" Came the reply.

"We cannot simply allow these foul abominations to wander free, to go unpunished for their crimes, to spew their wickedness over the earth!"

The crowd was hysterical now, pulling and tearing at their flesh, screaming to the sky. A few moments ago, this was a festival like any other. Now, the entire town bayed and snapped like a pack of hounds.

"But what punishment to administer? To hang?" She asked. "Over in a moment! Their suffering must reflect the severity of their crimes!"

Torture them. Burn them. Break them on the wheel. All around us, threats and pleas were made by the town. Desperate to see the guilty die violently. Guards levelled their spears at the crowd, keeping them back and away from their mistress.

"NO!" She yelled out, and instantly all was silence. "We cannot and we will not stoop unto their level of evil. We will not kill them. We will remain pure!" Groans of disappointment and wails of frustration cut the air, the pain of denial washing over them like a wave.

"But there is a way . . . THE PIT!" She flung her arms wide at the gaping maw in the ground before her. "We will not kill them. We will not sully our hands with their evil blood. BEHOLD!"

Two guards dragged a man forward. His eyes were swollen shut and his face a mess of ugly purple. Elivar looked down at him with theatrical contempt, wrinkling her nose and glowering.

"This man has robbed! Breaking into a house under the cover of shadows to take what was not his!" She pointed to a woman in the crowd. "What if it was your home? What if it was your children that he threatened? Your own purity he could have violated!" She spat the last word, lips quivering with emotion. The man moaned desperately, struggling against his bonds.

"PLEASE! I didn't do any of that! I was just-" he fell flat as a guard knocked him down and the crowd roared.

"TO THE PIT!" She cried, finger outstretched, pointing to the hole before us.

I watched in horror as the spectacle unfolded. A stout rope was looped around his waist and under his arms, tied firm. His hands fumbled with the knot for a moment before another punch flattened his nose.

Five more guards took the rope while two of them hurled the man down into the depths. There was a wet crunch and a howl of agony as he struck the bottom.

"PULL HIM UP!" She bellowed and they dragged his body to the ledge. He started sobbing pitifully and I could see his leg was twisted, bent back at an unnatural angle.

"AGAIN!" Her voice screamed and I saw the crazed look in her eyes. The noise became deafening as all about us people begged, threatened, and implored the guards to hurl him down to the jagged rocks on the bottom. As he was cast down, moans and groans of relief filled the air. The body lay limp and twitching as they pulled it up. Blood slathering the ledge. He was thrown for a final time before his skull cracked open and crimson gore seeped from the gaping mess that used to be a face.

They threw the body onto a cart and the next prisoner was taken forward. A woman in a rich dress, torn and stained. Her screaming pleas were drowned out by the noise of those around us. "ADULTERER!" Elivar pronounced as she was dragged to her fate. Afterwards, the mangled body was thrown onto the cart beside the first in a vile tableau. Beside me, a woman started screaming out some indecipherable ramblings, her mouth frothing as she fell down spasming. I watched as she rolled down the steps, landing in a dusty heap at the bottom, to roars and whoops of delight.

To the side of us, a man and women were fucking violently. Scratched red lines of blood streaked down his face as she moaned obscenely, slipping a thumbnail into his eye socket with a moist squelch. All around were similar scenes of depravity, like a veil had been lifted between man and beast.

Another man was dragged forward. It took me a moment, but I recognised him. It was Someone or Other from last night. He could barely stand. "MURDERER!" She exclaimed and they dragged to the edge.

I couldn't stand by and watch this. Not anymore. I gripped my amulet tight in my fist. "Oswald, grant me strength."

To the brothers' shock and horror, as well as my own surprise, I shouted above the crowd.

"LIAR! YOU'RE A FUCKING LIAR!" Heads turned to me. The miasma shuddered for just a moment, but it was all I needed. "THAT POOR BASTARD DIDN'T KILL ANYONE! HE JUST DREW A DAGGER WHEN HE WAS PISSED. SINCE WHEN IS A BLOODY DEATH A FAIR PRICE FOR WHAT SHOULD BE A PALTRY FINE?"

The frenzied crowd fell silent. Everyone started looking my way, and my heart felt like it would hammer its way out of my ribs. "DO YOU REALLY WANT THIS SADISTIC BITCH TO RULE OVER YOU ALL? WHAT HAPPENS WHEN YOU GET DRUNK? OR WHEN YOU FANCY A FUCK WITH SOMEONE YOU'RE NOT SUPPOSED TO? WHAT THEN? WILL YOU JUMP INTO THE PIT WITH A SMILE ON YOUR STUPID FACES?"

"Ulf?" Quentin tugged at my sleeve. I was red and panting. Elivar looked up at me, her face twisted with rage.

"Ulf!"

"What?" I snapped.

"About half a dozen guards are coming to kill us."

"Oh, fuck . . ."

At that moment, the crowd burst back into their violence, flailing among the guards and themselves, desperate to see blood spilled, no matter the source. Atop the stands across the square, an infant's brains were dashed against the ground, thrown by her mother to the cobbled streets. She whooped in delight before flinging herself off to join her.

The bitch turned to her captive. "HURL HIM INTO THE PIT!" Elivar screeched, and the sickening wet thump told me my protests were in vain.

"This way!" Decroix stepped onto the rear of the raised benches and leaped with the grace of an acrobat, despite the chainmail. His fingers just grasped the ledge of a house and he pulled himself up in one fluid motion. "Come on!"

Quentin followed his brother, grabbing his outreached hand. He swayed dangerously for a moment, ripping out a handful of thatch before they were both steady.

"Ulf! You've got to jump! You can do it! Trust me!" Decroix frantically gestured.

"In this fucking stuff?" I pointed to my armour. At that moment I was keenly aware of the irony that the thing that had kept me alive on numerous occasions would now cause my death.

"Behind you!" Quentin yelled. A few yards away, a guard shoved revellers aside, his naked sword gleaming. I drew my own and hacked downwards, using my height to my advantage. He blocked the cut and tried to press forwards, but I brought my blade around and cut him about the neck. His hand jumped to the wound and in an instant, I severed it at the wrist, sending him tumbling backwards with blood streaming from the stump. Two more took his place and I stepped backwards, desperately weighing my options.

I grabbed the nearest lunatic and hurled him towards them. By a stroke of luck, he was a fat bastard and one of the guards went flying. The other thrusted towards me and I narrowly made the parry. He stabbed at me again and the blow caught on my pauldron. I lunged towards him and grasped his wrist, using my strength to force his arm backwards. He tried to punch me in the cock, but he couldn't get a clear blow. I stamped down hard on his kneecap before sending him sprawling down the steps with a headbutt.

"ULF! JUMP!" I sheathed my bloody sword and hurled myself forward, reaching for Quentin's outstretched hand. Time seemed to stand still for a moment. Then I noticed the wince on Quentin's face, and I crashed to the ground.

I lay wrapped in canvas, my eyes swimming. For one horrible moment, I though it a shroud, then I realized a market stall had broken my fall. My foot shrieked out in protest, but I ignored the flashes of agony and forced myself up, limping badly.

"Decroix, you absolute cunt!" I snarled to myself through the pain and dragged myself out of the mess. "'Go on Ulf! You can do it!'"

"Ulf!" I looked up, and Decroix mimed a galloping horse before they ran off along the rooftops.

I rolled my eyes as I started to hobble after them "Really? You think we should get out of here? Are you sure? I thought I might have another go on the wooden ball bear game if I can get my hand in."

I could hear the chaos behind me and threw myself down an alley. I fell into a pile of shit behind a half-collapsed wall and forced my breath into silence. I closed my eyes for a moment when it was relatively safe. "Thanks be to Oswald . . ." I muttered and rubbed my amulet for good luck.

Thank fuck it was a clothier's stall and not a blacksmith's. I didn't fancy landing with a pair of tongs up the arse.

It took time, but I eventually got to the stable of the Old Rope. I didn't know where the brothers were, but their geldings and Reed were still there. Reed seemed nervous, pawing at the ground and snorting fiercely. "Easy now, my girl . . ." I murmured, taking her reins and opening the stall.

She twisted and turned in my hand and it was all I could do to stop her from pulling free. "Calm down, you silly bitch!" I snapped. My ankle was throbbing with pain and I needed to get out of there. I heard a noise and spun around, hand to my sword. The stable door opened and the old man with the missing hand stood before me.

"Oh. It's you. Sorry." My shoulders sagged with relief.

"Good day, sir." He walked towards me, scratching at his stump and smiling a gappy grin. "Let me help you with the saddle."

"It's fine, I just need to-"

And then there was a knife in my chest.

"Hail the Black Ram."

I twisted away and he ripped out the blade, sending agony coursing into me. I wasn't dead, so he hadn't gotten a lung, but fuck me sideways, he got it right between my armour.

He jumped into the stall and circled me, both of us frantically trying to avoid Reed's lashing hooves as she panicked wildly. I yanked my dagger free; no room for a sword. He stabbed at me and I stepped back. He avoided my clumsy riposte and he swiftly kicked up, his boot crashing into my temple. I swung my arm too late to catch his foot and my vision blurred. I staggered from the stall and held the point of my dagger out, jabbing to protect me.

He vaulted over the top of the stall and twirled his knife idly, rolling it between his fingers. "Ulf of Banrillar!" he spat. "I don't know what I've done to deserve this chance, but by the old gods I'm grateful!"

"Then go and meet them, you cunt!" I grabbed up a handful of horse shit and hurled it into his eyes. He howled in rage, and in that moment I stabbed and scored him across the chest. He punched out like a snake and blood burst from my nose. With a mad cackle he swept my legs from under me and I crashed to the ground. His left boot crushed into my right hand and the other pressed my throat.

With a flick of his knife, my dagger clattered to the floor. He giggled for a moment at some private joke and fixed me with wide, mad eyes. "Poor little Ulf . . ." he murmured. The tip of the blade pressed lightly into my forehead. Then he crashed to the ground with a feathered crossbow quarrel in his heart.

"Good shot, Quentin!"

"Why, thank you, brother dear!"

Decroix dragged me to my feet. I felt like shit, but that didn't stop me from kicking the corpse in the bollocks. Despite the shooting pain in my foot, it was worth it.

"Acting, wrestling, fucking, jumping, and now you're a crack shot with a crossbow. Anything you can't do Quentin?"

He looked sad for a moment. "Roll my tongue. But I've got a massive willy, so the girls don't mind. Now, shall we?"

I grinned, despite myself. "I didn't think I was your type."

"No, I mean SHALL WE? As in, 'shall we get the fuck out of here?'" The brothers mounted up and we galloped out through the open gate, and left the madness of Carstock behind us.

"Where did you get the crossbow?"

"Oh, this? I stole it in case it would come in handy. But if you can keep it a secret that I nicked something then I won't tell that you nearly got your arse handed to you by an old man with one hand. Deal?"

"Deal."

Chapter 13:
Implications

The blood dripped and pooled inside my armour. I was incredibly lucky; it wasn't a deep blow, as the armour slowed it down, but it still hurt like buggery. We rode until we were about a mile and a half outside of Carstock before stopping at a roadside well to look at the wound in my chest.

Decroix whistled and raised his eyebrows. "That must have hurt!" I gave him a cold stare, peeled off the rest of my armour, and washed off the dried blood. The cold water felt good against my skin. I took a few deep mouthfuls of water and started to feel better.

"Does anyone have a needle and thread?" They shook their heads and I swore.

"You need to let the air get to it so it can scab up." Quentin said, and I nodded in agreement. The sweat and musk of a shirt under armour is not a pretty thing, and I have seen far too many soldiers crying with pain as they lie dying days after a battle, their cuts all green and runny. First comes a fever, then the weakness and finally madness and death.

The wind picked up and whipped at my bare chest as we rode along. The jolting of the horse was painful, but I much preferred riding to walking on my twisted ankle. We pushed as hard as we could to get back to Colsarne's manse without laming the horses, making camp when it was too dark to ride and setting off as soon as the dawn broke.

We pushed our mounts to the limit. I could feel Reed's stress, and I knew she'd been worked hard. Each night I rubbed her down with grass and wet her flanks to cool her. She put her face to mine and I held on to her neck.

Lying awake looking up at the stars, too tired to really sleep, I found myself wishing that either Reed had a much better set of tits, or that Mary could run faster with me on her back. Why can't I find a woman with both?

We arrived at the manse at the dying of the light on the fifth day. Stones, kicked up by the horses' hooves, skittered across the cobbles as we rode into the courtyard. I dismounted and threw the reins to a nearby servant, and we rushed into the entrance hall.

Roderick sniffed as we entered. "I didn't expect you back so soon. I'm sure Duke Colsarne will wish to speak with you tomorrow-"

"Fuck off, Roderick. I'm not in the mood." I pushed him to one side and the brothers followed. Roderick bustled behind, squawking at me, but I'd be damned if I had the patience to listen.

Decroix led us up a staircase. "He'll be in the study. This way." He knocked at the door, which I immediately slammed open.

Duke Colsarne sat at a desk next to a small fire, the table covered in maps, scrolls, and an ornate writing kit. "Ulf." He said frostily. "I trust you have an extremely good reason to burst into my study in such a rude way?"

I walked over to his desk. "My lord, the Brotherhood of the Black Ram has taken over Carstock, maddened the populace. The town is controlled by someone from the Scribes Guild called Elivar, who is executing people for minor crimes in the most brutal and violent way possible to power her magic."

Duke Colsarne slowly reached out, taking a small knife and deliberately preparing a new quill before dipping it into a small inkwell. "Ulf?"

"Yes, my lord."

"I must admit, that is an extremely good reason. Roderick?"

"Yes, my lord?" He pushed past me and bowed.

"Have the kitchen bring up some ale, bread, and cheese for Decroix and his men. They look like they have had a hard ride, and I get the feeling we have a lot to discuss."

Through his study window, I saw the sun bleeding across the horizon. There were a few little huts, shepherding homes tucked between the black treetops and hills. I couldn't help wondering, just what would happen to the people who lived there if this all went to shit? Well, goes more to shit than it already has gone.

"Ulf, this is Tallow."

I look at the horse. It's massive. A vast barrel-shaped belly on four powerful legs, with a head nearly the size of my torso and eyes full of undisguised loathing.

"Well, say hello to him!"

I peer into the stable stall. "Ummm . . . Hello?"

Taran sighs. "Not like that! Look here." He reaches into a barrel and pulls out a carrot. "Remember Ulf, always keep your hand flat." He reaches out and Tallow gobbles up the offering, his big pink lips slobbering over my brother's hand.

"Urrrgh!"

Taran laughs. "Urgh? Really, Ulf? We both grew up surrounded by pig shit, and you wrinkle your nose at a bit of slobber?" He wipes his hand on my front.

"TARAN!" I try to push him away as he laughs.

"Speaking of shit . . ." He throws a wooden spade at me, which I miss and snatch up again from the floor.

"I'd like to pretend that this is a metaphor for learning respect for your mount, learning to care for it, and practising the knightly virtues of humility and patience. But it's not."

"Then why do I have to shovel all this shit?"

"Because my mentor made me do it, and his mentor made him do it, so now I'm making you do it."

"And why did they make them do it?"

"Because it's funny! Now get shovelling!"

"Ulf? ULF!" There was a knocking at my door. Dawn had broken, and the sunlight streaked across the sky outside my window, the colour of melted butter.

"Ulf!" Roderick's voice cut into me like broken glass.

"Fuck off." I snarled.

"For reasons known only to his Grace, Duke Colsarne desires your company. I would politely suggest that you make yourself presentable to his Grace imminently."

I rolled over and put the pillow over my head. "Can I politely ask you to fuck off again?" But Roderick was gone. I dressed quickly, and bumped into Decroix and Quentin as we headed to the study.

A plate with some crumbs sat on the corner of the duke's desk, standing against the tide of maps and notes flooding the table. Alexia and Siffisante were seated beside Colsarne, who was poring over the information arrayed before him and Roderick lurked by the door. The duke smiled at us as we entered. "Ah! Good morning, Decroix. I hope you and your companions slept well? Please, do take a seat." The smile and words were both as cold as midwinter.

Roderick proffered up a tray. "Pastry?" The two brothers politely decline, so I decide to take theirs as well. "I am glad to see that a brush with death hasn't affected your appetite." he murmured.

Alexia spoke up, "My father and I are most concerned about the developments in Carstock. Until recently, we considered it to be the most stable and prosperous town in Rusia."

"However, that is obviously no longer the case." Duke Colsarne said. He drummed his fingers on the desk. "We must make an example of Carstock and of this Elivar woman. Daughter?"

"Yes, father?"

"What would you do in such a situation?"

Alexia paused, considering her move under the hard eyes of her father. "Crush them. Utterly, completely, and without mercy. There can be no negotiation with fanatics. The loss of production and status of Carstock will be regrettable, but the alternative will fan the flames of rebellion throughout the entirety of Ashenfell."

Colsarne nodded, satisfied with her answer "Then, how are we to proceed? Would it not be prudent to rally our forces? Muster militias from villages and the countryside, to weight the odds utterly in our favour?"

She shook her head. "With respect, father, the longer a splinter is left, the more it will fester. Almost a week has already passed. We strike as soon as we can, to stop the enemy from consolidating their position."

For the first time I could recall, a genuine smile crossed his lips. He beamed at his daughter. "My finest creation." He stood up. "Lady Alexia will be more than able to advise you on the proper course of action. Roderick, have the stable saddle my horse. I wish to take a short ride."

"As you wish, my lord."

The two men exited and Lady Alexia paused for a moment, taking a small sip of watered wine.

"Siffisante?"

"My lady."

"I understand that you are . . . familiar with the brigand Azrael Bordane?"

I spluttered on my pastry, sending crumbs everywhere. Siffisante fixed me with a glare that could kill a goat. "Yes, my lady."

"Excellent." Alexia took up a quill and wrote out a note with a flourish on a parchment, finishing it with a large red seal bearing her family crest. Rolling it carefully, she placed it into a leather scroll case. "Siffisante, you are to deliver this to Azrael Bordane with your usual . . . charms."

I couldn't help but snigger.

"His band are to assist with our own forces in striking out against the traitors in Carstock. In exchange, they will be pardoned. You will leave immediately, and have Azrael's men join with our force on the march."

It was a cunning move. Why risk the lives of your own people when you can kill your enemies and get rid of some troublesome bandits in one clean blow?

"Decroix, you and your brother will take command of our main forces. Ulf?"

I looked up suddenly.

"You will accompany Siffisante to Azrael's encampment, to protect her virtue and make sure she is safe."

It took me a moment to realise my mouth was hanging open. I chose my next words with caution. "My lady, Azrael Bordane and I did not exactly part on the best of terms."

She smiled sweetly. "Then this will be the perfect time for you to make friends again."

She sat back and regarded us all with her father's eyes. Siffisante and I were to travel swiftly, to pick up new recruits while not slowing the others. It was a good plan, even if I didn't t like it.

"Make ready as soon as you can. Take what you must, the resources of House Colsarne are at your disposal."

I paused for a moment, looking at a large, ornate silver candlestick on the table. I picked it up and it felt reassuringly heavy in my hand. "My lady, do you have any more like this?"

"A few. Why?"

"I will need as many of these as I can get. Is there a mason or a joiner in the household? Someone who can carve with a chisel?"

"I believe we have a joiner employed at present, working alongside our carpenter on some new cabinets. But why the candles—"

"That will do nicely, thank you." With that, I swiftly bowed and left.

I sharpened my sword, and paid a servant a couple of Ecar to fix the hole in my shirt. By midday, we were ready to depart.

Colsarne had about two hundred men at arms. Fifty stayed behind and the rest marched with us. Over my shoulder, the flag of House Colsarne snapped neatly in the wind. The cruel looking eagle standing proudly on a silver field, wings displayed and ready for flight. They were grim looking men, dour and stern-faced. There were about thirty crossbowmen, fifty billmen with a range of polearms and forty swordsmen, shields clattering on their back as they marched along. The rest were mounted men at arms; some of them were armoured better than others, but all of them looked like they knew what they were doing.

We travelled due east for five days until we reached the outskirts of the Wallenpel. I had sincerely hoped to never see those bastard woods again, but fate is like a beautiful woman. It will always find a new way to fuck you.

I rode next to Siffisante in silence. When we had last been there, weeks before, she was over the saddle of my horse trying to get free. Now, I would live or die depending on what she said to that albino lunatic. I caught her looking at the dagger on my hip, which I had used to kill some of her friends and fellow cultists and I shifted uncomfortably.

"I think it's towards this way." She nodded at me and we altered our course slightly, continuing on foot when the forest got too thick to ride. I briefly wondered to myself why I was letting her lead the way. After all, I had been to Azrael's camp as often as she had. But then I'd much prefer to have her in front of me, rather than behind me in a position to put a knife in my back.

The branches twisted and spilled over each other like broken bodies, and after a while the canopy blocked out all but the faintest sunlight. Siffisante didn't press for conversation, and neither did I.

Navigation in woods is always a dice-roll. You're never sure how long anything will take; the dense trees make it hard to figure out your way. We were two days into the Wallenpel when I spied a ragged woman picking berries from a bush. Her fingers were stained purple and she popped one into her mouth, smacking her lips together. I put on my best smile.

"Hail! We're looking for Az-" I corrected myself. "*Lord* Azrael Bordane" She looked up in fright and the berries scattered to the forest floor. She bustled away as quick as she could, hands in the air with worry.

"Oh, for fucks' sake . . ." I muttered. "Here!" I thrust Reed's reins to Siffisante and chased after her. I'm a big man, but I can move swiftly when I have to. Certainly faster than an old woman with her skirts hitched up. "Hey, listen! We only want-"

Brigandine

She lashed out with a small knife, which skimmed across my armour. I grabbed her by her frail wrist and threw the blade clear away. She screamed at me and a drop of spittle hit my lip as she hit at me with her free hand. I grabbed it and winced as she started screeching and thrashing.

"SHUT THE FUCK UP!" I yelled at her.

"ULF!" Siffisante shot me a dirty look and I let go, dropping the woman to the floor.

"Please explain to me how it's my fault this old bitch is moon-touched?"

"Just fuck off for a moment, would you?" She picked the crone up, shushing her moans and sitting her down on a tree stump. I gave them some space and, once the silly wretch had calmed down, Siffisante took her arm and she led us deeper into the forest.

A few of the trees started to look vaguely familiar, that and my ear caught rustles in the canopy that I had no doubt were sentries readying bowstrings." "Wait here." she said. I nodded, and the two of them went into the camp clearing.

I loosened my sword and looked about me. Reed seemed fine, but I couldn't help but fidget. Don't get me wrong, I couldn't give less of a shit about Siffisante. I just worried I'd get an arrow in the throat if she decided to make a deal with Azrael behind my back.

After a quarter of an hour or so, Siffisante returned with two hunters flanking her. Both of them looked at me nervously with arrows nocked. I tied Reed to a tree and met them halfway.

"He'll talk to us." she said.

"Great." I replied. "Fucking marvellous."

The encampment didn't look quite as busy as when we were last there, and I could tell some of Azrael's hangers-on had fucked off. I wasn't surprised. I took his sword and embarrassed him in front of all his cronies. That's the thing about running a band of cutthroats: they don't tend to have a lot of patience for off-days.

Azrael stood at the firepit under his golden tree banner. He had a new sword on his hip, a simple blade of plain steel. Charon stood next to him, and his one good eye glowered with bitter hatred when he saw me. His face was a horrible mess of ugly red scars and twisted flesh. The eye socket was covered with a ragged scrap of cloth and one side of his lips were melted away, leaving him with a permeant evil sneer. I met his gaze and nodded in greeting, only to be met by a low, angry snarl.

Most men would find a giant like him intimidating. I was just happy that I wasn't the biggest and ugliest bastard there for once.

Azrael bowed low to Siffisante. "Once again we are humbled by your presence, my lady."

She extended her hand and he kissed it lightly. "My lord, the honour is mine." She curtsied and blinked her eyes slowly, her cheek turned demurely towards him.

I couldn't stand the bitch, but dammit if she didn't know exactly what she was doing.

"It is just a shame that you are not alone my lady. But we suppose that is the best. You are a rare jewel, my sweet darling, and need protection."

He glared at me coldly and, to my credit, I didn't smack him in his smug mouth.

Siffisante caught his eye and slowly reached into the scroll case. "I bear a message for you, my lord. The Lady Alexia App Colsarne, of the Proud and Fearsome House of Colsarne, sends her fond regards." She passed over the scroll and Azrael broke the seal with his dagger. His eyes darted over the page, maintaining a neutral expression.

He tapped at the parchment, running a long nail across Alexia's curled writing. "My good lady Siffisante, you are as wise as you are lovely." She simpered and I tried not to be sick. "We would value your council on this matter."

He tapped the word again and lowered the scroll. I caught a brief glimpse. "AND". That was the word he deliberated over. "AND". It was all I could do to keep the smirk off my face when I realized he couldn't read.

Siffisante picked up on this as well, and we exchanged the briefest of glances. "My lord, I am flattered to be asked. As you can see, the town of Carstock is in disarray. The Guilds' Council who run the town have become . . . unruly."

Azrael nodded his head, doing a decent imitation of understanding.

"That is why the Lady Alexia requests your aid. To supplement the household troops of Duke Colsarne in bringing this rebellion to heel, and restoring the natural order of things. As a fellow noble, I'm sure you understand the obligation shared by those who rule to bring peace and order to the land."

"Of course! You may let Lady Alexia know that her cousin Azrael Bordane, Lord of the Wallenpel, accepts her invitation." He paused for a moment. "However, as you are aware there are some members of my company who have had . . . disagreements with those in authority. Through no fault of their own, of course!" He quickly added.

Siffisante smiled demurely. She turned and addresses the clearing at large, holding her arms out wide, delivering her great speech like a strolling player.

"Then it is with the greatest of pleasure that I may extend the Lady Alexia's full pardon to any man or woman who participates in the liberation of the fair town of Carstock." The camp erupted in murmurs of greedy curiosity.

She continued "And of course, to say nothing of the riches and wealth seized by the cruel and corrupt, which would be far better off in the hands of the righteous and loyal." She turned back to Azrael. "And I am sure Duke Colsarne would want to reward those loyal to him. After all, his daughter needs protecting in this cold, wicked world . . ."

Azrael drew his sword and held it high. "BROTHERS! SISTERS! FREE PEOPLE OF THE WALLENPEL! TODAY WE MARCH TO WAR!" Azrael's proclamation was met with ragged cheers from those who remained. The camp soon bustled with activity as people packed up their weapons and belongings, ready to head off to wherever their mad lord wished. Azrael returned to his tent, but Charon lingered in front of me, his fists clenching.

I leaned in close and whispered. "Go on, fucking try it, big man. You and I both want you to." He twisted up his face with anger, spat on the ground and left. I muttered, "Didn't think so."

Within half an hour, Bordane's merry band of fuckwits had broken camp and departed. Azrael led a small mare at the head of the scruffy column. Next to him another thug held his faded banner as high as the forest would allow, occasionally dipping it under the branches.

The bandits knew the Wallenpel and the land around better than any man, so even with our extra company, we made good time. As we emerged, blinking into the sunlight, I looked back and could finally see what we had to work with, and my heart wasn't exactly filled with confidence.

They were a ragged looking bunch of fighters in mouldering gambesons with a hodgepodge of weapons. Everything from pruning hooks and war scythes to pitted swords which looked like they needed a few hours on the grindstone. They had some vicious looking archers among them, though, and every last one would be a thief, a killer, or both.

Exactly the type of people you want on your side in a fight.

I leaned towards Siffisante and hissed into her ear. "You've just promised away the looting rights to the town, and as good as swore the Lady Alexia's hand in marriage to some crazed C'targian with delusions of grandeur. So, what do we do when the battle is over and the survivors are tearing the town apart?"

She smiled, as if humouring a senile grandparent. "Oh, sweetie! 'Survivors' has a lot of implications."

"Like what?"

"Well, for one, it implies they survive."

Chapter 14:
The Boring Parts

It took us only three days to rendezvous with the rest of the army. They weren't exactly hard to track. Decroix and Quentin seemed both surprised and happy to see us, and, to my surprise, I was genuinely pleased to see them both.

Decroix rushed up to greet us. "Ulf! I'm glad you're back."

"So, how's it been?" I asked.

Decroix looked away. "To tell you the truth, it's not been easy."

I glanced around the camp. All around me, I could see bored men playing dice and passing jugs around - the things soldiers do when they're not marching, sleeping, or killing. I could hear shouting as someone decided to pick a fight, and it got louder until the corporal cracked their skulls together.

"Right," I said, "let's break camp and get going."

Decroix looked at me puzzled. "But it's the afternoon. We'll only get a couple of hours march at most before we have to stop and set up camp again."

"This isn't a fucking religious holiday, Decroix. Get these bastards on their feet and get them moving! Come on!" I walked up to the nearest group, a few crossbowmen sitting around a bubbling pot. "Get your shit together. We're moving."

"But we've just started to cook." He lifted the lid. "Fresh rabbit."

"Eat it on the march. Get going."

"How are we supposed to eat stew on the move?"

"That sounds a lot like a problem for you, not me. Now pack up your gear and get a fucking move on, we've got a war to win." I turned and walked off, but my ears pricked up when I heard one of them mutter. He stood up and folded his arms in a strop.

"What's your name?" I asked.

He paused. "Aiden."

"Aiden, unless the next words out of your mouth are 'Let's get all our gear packed up and get going, lads!' I am going to punch you square in the cock. Do you understand me, Aiden?"

"What?"

I punched him square in the cock. He went down like a cheap prostitute, and his friends rushed to help him.

I turned and yell out to the rest of the camp. "If you want to spend your time sitting around outdoors, doing bugger all then fuck off and be a charcoal burner. If you're soldiers who want to earn some good coin and kill some bastards who deserve it, then come with me."

I walked through the camp and helped get things sorted. Tents were dropped and thrown rapidly into wagons and belongings were bundled into sacks. I kicked awake anyone who was asleep and within half an hour we were on the road. I shouted to the captains of each unit to march them hard. Time wasn't on our side and we couldn't afford to fuck about.

I turned to Decroix. "Have you set watches and duty shifts?"

He furrowed his brow. "I thought the captains would sort that all out between them?"

I sighed. "Fuck me. You haven't spent much time with soldiers, have you? Unless you sort something out yourself, it's not going to get done. Unless you know it's been done, assume it hasn't. No-one volunteers for anything in an army, because being a volunteer can get you killed. No-one wants to be the first one over the wall because he's the first one to get stabbed. Same principle for everything from digging the shit pits to collecting firewood."

We pressed on until the sun started to bleed. I could hear some grumbling from the men and Azrael's band looked shattered as they joined up after a while. They had less to carry, but inexperienced troops can't be pressed as hard as proper soldiers.

I gathered the captains together and set a watch rotation. "Three shifts of three hours. Half to take a watch tonight, half for tomorrow and then swap back. That gives us twenty men on watch at a time. Pick five men each who have been slacking off and stick them on firewood and shit-pit duty."

Rouberte, the lanky, sour-faced captain of the crossbowmen, looked at me incredulously. "Why not make the rabble do it? Why should we be tired?" There was a murmur of agreement from the other two captains and I pinched my nose in frustration.

"Do you know who those buggers are?" I pointed to Azrael's band, now starting their own fires and unpacking sleeping rolls.

"No."

"Exactly. Neither do I. But I do know they are a bunch of murderous bastards with the discipline of a stray dog in a slaughterhouse. I don't trust them to watch over me while I sleep, and if you do then you're a fucking idiot." He nodded in reluctant acquiescence.

A tension settled over the camp as the two forces rested near each other for the first time. The neat canvas of Duke Colsarne's men a stark contrast with the rickety shelters cobbled together by Azrael's band. With a hard march, I reckoned we could get to Carstock within four days.

I found the brothers, and we met with the Captains in the command tent. Siffisante was nowhere to be seen, and I could only assume she was getting reacquainted with Azrael behind a bush somewhere.

Marl, the captain of the swordsmen, smiled and leaned over the map. "Thank Wilfred the Prudent that you remembered to grab a map before we left, eh?" He was a solid looking man, slightly soft about the middle, but with clear muscle underneath.

Johan, the captain of the bills tapped his finger on the main gate. "That's where we should strike. One strong blow, break the back of them. Send the swordsmen in first, then my bill block can follow up and take care of controlling the townsfolk."

Marl snorted. "Take care of the looting, you mean? And just what the fuck do you mean by sending my men in first like some decoy?"

Johan sighed and rolled his eyes like he was speaking to a child. "You have shields. If they throw anything down, you can just protect yourself."

Rouberte looked down gloomily at the layout. "I don't see why any of us should be risking our necks. Send the rabble in! Let them take a rock to the face or some burning oil down the gullet."

"Shouldn't we have Azrael in here as well?" Decroix spoke up. "After all, he will be commanding his own men."

Rouberte snorted and Johan stifled a smile. "Really?" Johan smirked. "What exactly does a C'targian bandit have to contribute to the discussion? If it were up to me, I'd just hang the bastard. Him and his thieving bunch of cunts."

I put both my hands flat to the table and met him eye to eye. "Well, it's not up to you, is it, Johan? Lady Alexia put Decroix in charge, so why don't you just shut the fuck up for a moment and listen, eh?"

Johan scowled and pinched his thumb but said nothing further. After a moment, I broke my gaze away and looked over to the brothers. Decroix and Quentin shifted uncomfortably. They were superb schemers, but military planning and strategy clearly wasn't their strong suit. I had no idea why Lady Alexia had chosen them to lead. Neither one was shagging her, or at least I thought not.

Time to help them save face. "May I make a suggestion?" I asked.

Decroix looked at me, relieved. "By all means, Ulf. I would value your council."

I studied the map in front of me, trying to recall the layout of the streets and buildings. "There are two gates - one to the south-east, one to the west - and the docks to the north-east. These are the ways we can get in, and where the enemy will try to get out when they realise that they're fucked."

Rouberte wrinkled up his nose. "So, you want us to split our forces?"

"Shut up and listen." I snarled. "We're not splitting the troops, not exactly. But for this plan to work, everyone needs to have their shit together and work as a team. Think your men can do that?"

He nodded. "Good. Right, we're up against a foe who is going to be well-armed, fanatically loyal and probably piss-drunk. We need to break them quickly and cut off the head of the serpent."

Marl frowned in concentration. "How?"

"Marl, you and the swordsmen will approach the south-east gate and break through. Rouberte, your crossbows will pick off defenders on the wall. Independent skirmishing fire. Target anyone with burning oil or who has the brains to try and kick the ladders away."

Quentin piped up. "Are we not better off going through the western gate? The walls are lower and it's less easily defended."

"I can see what you're saying Quentin, but look at the streets. It's a warren of alleyways and side streets. Great if you're trying to evade capture, but if you're a big unit of men trying to get through, all you'll get are daggers to the kidney. Azrael's men don't have the discipline to fight as a unit, but that's fine for this sort of scrap.

"Marl, once you break through, hold the gatehouse, spread your men so we control the gate but don't move too far out unless you want them picked off." He nodded in acknowledgement.

"Good. Once the way is clear, Johan will lead his block through the gate, pushing out to the left and right, then we quick march down this street into the main square. The power base is here; once we break it, the town is ours. After that, take half your men and head to the western gate. Azrael will be creating a distraction over there, and between the two of you, you should be able to capture it. Advance cautiously and don't get drawn into an ambush. I'll take the rest of the bills and leg it down to the docks.

"Meanwhile, you two work on controlling the mob. Crack some skulls together. Don't kill more than you have to, though. No looting and no buggering old ladies. Just tell your men to keep the peace as best they can."

Decroix looked at the docks on the map. "What time are we attacking?"

"Dawn. Nice and early, get it over with. Attacking from the east to have the sun in the enemy's eyes."

"We should wait for a couple of hours, for the tides. High tide should be in the very early hours. If we can delay a bit, we can wait till low tide and inconvenience any of the bastards who want to leave by ship."

"That's a good point. Agreed. Thank you, Decroix."

I gazed over at the others. "Is everyone clear on the plan?" I looked over each one until I got murmurs of agreement and nods of assent. "Good. Now I'm going to sleep and I suggest you do the same, because we're marching at first light and there are still days to go till Carstock."

We climb the tower and I cling to the side rope, following my brother's footsteps up the narrow stairway. At the top, he swings open a thick door, dark with age. The room is huge. A vast square table dominates the centre of the chamber, the surface covered in rich green cloth. On the top are hundreds of painted soldiers in red and blue, carved from wooden blocks and bearing swords, spears, and bows. Cavalry sit bolt upright on motionless horses, their manes made from wisps of wool stuck on with glue.

I burst out laughing. "Right. So, you've brought me up here to play toys? Are you trying to make up for lost time?" He smacks me on the back of the head. "OW!"

"These aren't toys, Ulf!"

"Really?" I say, trotting a horse along the table ledge. "They look like toys to me."

He snatches the horse away and sets it down in its place. "Use your brain for a moment. This is about strategy."

He opens a chest and takes out some small models of houses, sections of wall, and towers, arranging them carefully along the edge of the table. He takes some of the models and sets them carefully aside. "Ulf. Tell me, how would you go about taking these walls? These are the men at your disposal. Each piece is worth ten warriors."

I turn a man at arms over in my hand. The little wooden warhammer sits in his fist and the face is painted into a warlike grimace.

"Ulf?" Taran stands, waiting for my reply.

Brigandine

"Well. I would send them to the walls. Strike them from lots of points at once." I move the models up to the walls, spreading them along. "And I'm here." I pick up one of the models that looks a bit like me and stick it right in front of the gate. "Leading from the front to inspire and set an example."

Taran looks at my plan for a moment. "You and all your men are dead in about twenty minutes."

I roll my eyes at him. "How?"

"Well, your first mistake is spreading your men out too thinly. How are you going to get orders to them? What happens when one group break through without anyone else to support them?"

I don't have an answer to this.

"Secondly, how are you going to see what's going on from the very front rank? It's noble and heroic to fight from the front, but as the general, you need to be able to take a step back. Victory, and keeping your men alive: those are the marks of a good general. Not personal glory. There will always be a chance for that. It's better to win a slightly boring victory than to die a dramatic death and take your men down with you, no matter what the songs might say on the matter. As it stands, you're disorganised, blind, and you'll end up a greasy smear on the battlements."

We stand in silence for a moment. I stare at the models. Wondering about the little wooden families they could leave behind and the tiny graves to be dug. All due to my foolishness.

"Anything else?"

"As a matter of fact, yes." He picks up a piece. "How exactly is this horse going to get up the wall? Can it fly?" He waggles it in front of my face, and we both start laughing.

"Now come on." He moves the board around again and sets up two opposing armies. Blue for him, red for me. "Let's see if you've actually learned something, eh?"

I woke up to the smoke of cooking fires and the chatter of voices, the sunlight pushing through the canvas. I had taken the middle shift on watch and my head was still groggy. The men I was sharing the tent with were already up and about, and I was both annoyed and grateful they hadn't woken me. I pulled on my boots, and realized that, after having been worn a few weeks, the soles were finally in that sweet spot between stiff and worn out. You'd be surprised how many pairs of boots a solider can get through.

I remember one time, the rain had been beating down on us all afternoon. I couldn't remember exactly why we were fighting or who for, but it had been brutal. Close up, bloody work to wear the enemy down, hoping to break them before we did. The mud squelched underfoot and seeped into the soles, filling my boot with filth. The stitching had come undone and my left boot flapped as I walked, little stones stabbing into me with every pace.

We had withdrawn for the day as the sun was dying. As we trudged back to the camp, weapons heavy as lead in our hands, we went past heaps of mangled bodies. Limbs snapped at odd angles, jawbones hanging off of ruined skulls.

They were fresh, good boots, the soles thick and double stitched. I remember that. Streaks of mud splattered against the light tan. Twice I braced myself, foot against his groin and pulled back, jiggling it off while my cold, numb fingers undid the lacing. His naked feet flopped back into the mud and I jogged to catch up with the rest of the regiment, my new boots in hand.

There was a gentle knock on the tent post, and I looked up to see Siffisante standing just outside the open flaps. "I've briefed Azrael on his role." Siffisante said with a sly smile.

I pulled myself to my feet. "Was he happy with it?" The last thing I needed was Azrael having a strop and deciding to turn back.

"Oh, yes. Lord Bordane was most happy with his role in leading the decisive vanguard strike, to break the enemy line and liberate the fair city." Siffisante looked around the soldier's tent, at the discarded clothes and belongings, all stinking of smoke and sweat. She wrinkled her nose a little and made to leave.

"Thank you." I muttered.

She turned back. "My pleasure, Ulf. Any time . . ."

Once I was fully awake and all the men had eaten, we pressed onwards, marching hard. I kept an eye out for slackers. It was mainly Azrael's band who struggled to keep pace, so I did what I could to hurry them along.

That evening, I met with the captains to go over the plan again and make sure everyone was clear with it. We committed the map to memory, then briefed the sergeants, so they were all clear on what was expected of them.

As we marched onwards, we came across some of the ash coppices which make Carstock famous. There were vast barns filled with drying planks, boards and poles. We took them happily, turning the timber into ladders to scale the walls. I told the men to fell the thickest tree they could find. We fire-hardened the end and lashed it to a cart to make a battering ram for the main gates.

Three days later, the scouts from the crossbowman unit rode back to report that Carstock lay about three hours march away. I could just see the town in the distance.

Decroix turned in the saddle and looked at me thoughtfully. "Do we attack now? We don't want to give them the chance to run away." I shook my head.

"No. If they wanted to run, they would have already done so. We make camp and we attack in the morning. The men are tired from marching, and they know we are coming anyway."

You can't exactly hide an approaching army. I've heard some people say that you should deceive the enemy, hide your numbers and attack from the shadows like a thief. But I wanted them to know we were coming. I wanted them to know we were marching towards them, so they could shit themselves.

Night descended like a thick black mantle, cloaking the world in shadows.

I was shaken awake around midnight. I nodded in acknowledgement and dragged myself out of bed, moving as quietly as I could so as not to wake the others. It's not my turn, but I've taken the middle shift again. I needed the others as well-rested as they could be, and I don't sleep much anyway.

I walked to my post and waited to be hailed. "Who goes there?" He knew damn well who it was, but rules are rules.

"Ulf of Banrillar. Evening."

He raised his hand in greeting and slouched off to bed, glad to finish his shift. His name was Simon. Ugly bastard with a big nose, but a good man. His warty face spread into a grin and I smiled back. "I'll try to get a good night's sleep. Could be my last!"

"Go on, fuck off and get some sleep."

It was a quiet night and the breeze felt warm for the time of year. I could see the two other sentries, one each to my left and right, spread out in the perimeter. It took a few minutes for my eyes to adjust to the deep darkness. I stamped my feet, trying to wake up and stay focused.

Guard duty is one of the worst things about being a soldier. It's up there with marching and people trying to kill you as the biggest arse aches in the job. Marching is boring, but if you fuck it up no-one is going to die. People can die if you fuck up while fighting, but at least it's not boring. Guard duty is boring, and if you fuck it up, people will die. So, it's the worst of both.

The trick is to check, and to keep both your eyes and ears open; it's no use having one and not the other. Make sure you're looking at the other sentries. Are they still there? What's ahead? What's behind?

An hour later, the sentry to my right spoke the hour, just loud enough for me to hear and repeat it to the man to my left. Another one passed, then another. Finally, with a tone of relief in his voice, the fourth hour passed and I waited for my replacement. The man to my right shared a joke with his relief and headed off to bed. I sighed and bit my tongue hard to keep myself awake.

Half an hour passed. "For fuck's sake . . ." I snarled. "Stupid bastard . . ."

You don't leave your post until you're relieved. If the next bugger is drunk, still sleeping, or has just forgotten, that's your problem. I tried to focus on the fact that at least my replacement was getting a solid night's sleep, and I made a note to kick the shit out of him in the morning.

A scream of panic and a frantic yell broke the silence of the camp behind me. I sprinted towards the sound, and barked "STAY

THERE!" over my shoulder as I ran. Men were stumbling out of their tents, weapons drawn. My blood ran cold when I saw where all the commotion lay.

Simon stood at the front of the tent, his hands dripping with blood. Two swords were pointed at him and everyone started shouting. I shoved my way forward and grabbed hold of him. "What the fuck has happened?"

He stammered, so I slapped him hard across the face. "WHAT HAPPENED?" I roared. He pointed to the tent and I barged past him.

Inside was a mess of blood and meat. The six men we were sharing a tent with all had their throats opened, ragged gashes across their necks leaving their heads to loll horribly. I backed out and forced my stomach to stay down. Simon started screaming, tears pouring down his face. "I WAS PISSING! I WAS PISSING!" he howled.

"Everyone, up and armed! I want the bastard who did this found!" The cry went up around the camp. It wouldn't help–anyone who can sneak into a camp, slit six throats, and slip out again isn't going to be caught–but we had to try.

I grabbed three men. "You, clean Simon up, get him a drink of something strong, and see he's alright. You two, you're with me." I looked back into the tent, committing their faces to memory. I promised myself that the fuckers who did this were going to pay.

"Get some shovels."

Chapter 15:
The Battle of Carstock

Digging a grave is never fun. I should know, I've dug enough in my time. You always do a decent job, because one day someone will be digging yours.

It took a couple of hours, and we were dripping with sweat by the end of it. Wordlessly, we took the weapons and money from the bodies. The dead don't need it, and no proper soldier would want his companions to go without.

Marl stood silently by. All six men were his, so it was custom for him to help fill in the grave. His belly wobbled as he shovelled three clumps of dirt over each man. His heavy-set face creased in a frown. I could tell that he blamed me. I set the watch pattern, but he knew damn well there was nothing more I could have done. That wouldn't stop him being angry, of course.

Simon turned up near the end and started to cry. I took him away, shielding him as Marl rolled his eyes in contempt.

"First time seeing something like this lad?"

He nodded at me, his eyes bloodshot. "I got up to piss. I was only gone for a moment."

"And I was on watch. If you had a bigger bladder, then you'd be in that hole, too. As would I, if I was a lazy bastard and had decided to have a proper sleep."

"It's not fair. It's so stupid!"

I shrugged. He was right of course. "It is stupid. That's war. Sometimes people die because that's just where the arrow falls. Or because the person next to them fucks up, leaves an opening and the enemy gets a lucky blow in. Or they eat something dodgy and shit themselves to death. Have you ever seen someone shit themselves to death, Simon?"

"... no?"

"Well, you've got that to look forward to. Point is, people die. That's soldiering. Being a mercenary without death would just be a series of picnics and hiking." He nodded and I thought he just might understand.

I looked around, to make sure no-one was watching. "If you can't do this, leave. You swore an oath of loyalty to Duke Colsarne. But I'll lie for you. I'll say you had sword-sickness. Your mind broke when you saw your friends were killed and you ran."

He looked at me dumbstruck. I shrugged. "It's your choice. Or you can find the fuckers who did this and cut them out a new arsehole. Your call. Are you going to run away, lad?"

He shook his head and swallowed. "No."

I put my hand on his shoulder. "Good man. Now, get your shit together and get going."

The assassin wasn't found. I was annoyed, but not surprised. We left the camp where it lay. No point in taking tents with us. If the plan worked, we'd be sleeping in Carstock tonight; if it didn't, we'd be dead. Either way, no need for a tent.

We pressed onwards towards Carstock. The men were in a grim mood; angry about the attack in the night and eager to spill some blood in revenge. The perfect mood for a fight. I made a point of speaking to the captains about keeping the men under them in control, reminding them that we were here to liberate Carstock, not butcher it. Marl gave me a brusque grunt and turned back towards his unit. I met Decroix's eye and we both nodded in understanding.

We approached the walls of Carstock a couple of hours after sunrise. Azrael's force broke away from us, as per the plan. From the back of his mare, Azrael raised his hand in salute to the rest of the army. I returned the gesture, struggling not to laugh as his tatty banner snapped in the wind, wrapping itself around the pole. Charon walked beside him, glowering like a caged bull. We locked eyes for a moment before he strode off.

We waited for a short while to let the bandit forces get into position. I squinted, but couldn't make out any details.

"Quentin, your eyes are sharper than mine. Anything?"

He shrugged. "A bit of commotion on the walls, I think."

"You and Decroix, stay near the back. You're actors, not warriors. You can't fuck your way out of someone trying to stab you." Quentin opened his mouth for a second then closed it, nodding in agreement.

Around me, soldiers were hobbling horses at the tree line and readying their weapons. I threw the bag of engraved candlesticks over my shoulder and patted Reed on the flank. "Good girl. I'll be back, I promise." I scratched her neck, and she snorted in understanding.

I looked around at the men. Some of them grizzled, faces scarred like old chopping blocks, but a number of them are new. Probably their first proper fight against something harder than shitty bandits. No matter how this went, a lot of people were about to die.

Then we attacked.

"EXTENDED ORDER!"

The sergeants echoed the cry and the army spread out, a gap of three arm lengths between each man. As we approached, arrows and bolts started to fly from the palisade. I roared "DOUBLE TIME!", and we all quickened our step, moving in a wide formation to make life harder for the enemy archers.

Screams started to erupt as arrows found their mark. I winced as I stepped over a billman, balled up and clutching at the quarrel protruding from his guts. "KEEP THAT LINE STRAIGHT!" The sergeants prowled the line, shoving forward or dragging men back, keeping us moving together in good order. I could hear more howls around me as more men fell to the onslaught.

Rouberte sprinted forward, head bowed and shoulders hunched, followed by the rest of the crossbowmen. They spread out in a skirmish and returned fire, and several bodies toppled from the walls. The crossbows whined as they were frantically reloaded behind heavy pavises, and more quarrels lanced forward, some of them thudding into the wood and others finding their lethal mark.

"LOOSE ORDER!" We got closer to the gate and we moved into the centre, the gap between each man closing up so that there was only one arm span between them. Room enough to fight and support each other.

"COLUMN!" As soon as the men moved into position, the army shuddered into a long, brutal column and the battering ram thundered towards the gates like the tip of a spear. A group of swordsmen were clustered around it, protecting it with their shields as they advanced, drawing the bulk of the enemy arrows. The swordsmen at the front raised their shields and braced for impact as it slammed into the doors.

The ram rocked backwards and thudded hard into the gates One man fell, gurgling through a throat filling with blood, and I rushed up to take his place. My muscles strained as we drew it back.

"HEAVE!" The gate shook, but held. A rock crashed into the side of my helmet, driving my skull into the wood. I gritted my teeth and shook the stars away.

"HEAVE!" Once more the gate shook and splintered. Once more, the gate shook and groaned. My heart jumped as a splintered plank broke free and clattered on the cobbles behind.

"Harder, you sons of whores! Now, HEAVE!" With one more strike, the gate crashed inwards, twisting away on its iron hinges with a foul shriek. A huge cheer rose behind us and we forced the ram cart through, driving the doors asunder.

There was a clash of steel above me, and a handful of defenders were cast down onto the street as more of our men climbed over the walls. Swarms of bodies pressed against us as we staggered forward. There were dozens of townsfolk frantically trying to force us back. A man with a mace rushed in with a clumsy swing, so I took up a half-sword stance and stepped forward, thrusting through his temple. The swordsmen advanced over his still-twitching corpse while the bill block spread out to the left and the right, securing the gate, as per the plan. I stepped into the second rank as the shields locked together in a tight wall, bringing my sword up high so I could still fight over the top. Marl pointed his sword. "To the square!"

Villagers spilled out of the side streets and alleys as we marched forward. They hurled piss pots, rocks, and knives at us, and they darted forward to make frenzied hacks and slashes with messers and axes. They ran towards the shields to die broken and bleeding in the street, or threw themselves at the bill points, desperate to slow us down for a moment. A woman leapt into the shield wall, cracking her skull against a metal boss and laughing hysterically as she was cut apart.

As we pressed onwards, horrible sounds started to filter through around the chaos of battle. Hideous whines and chirping spliced into snatches of tickling music floated through the air. I ground my teeth as my skin started to itch uncontrollably, armour rubbing with every movement.

Each step became a labour as the marketplace came into view. The air tasted rank and stale. I could see those around me struggling as well and I gripped my amulet tight. My vision swam in and out of focus like I was drunk out my skull, a man to my left dropped his sword and clutched at his face, blood streaming from his eyes.

The Carstock guards were formed in ranks when we finally reached the square. Most of them were holding huge, heavy bladed halberds. The townsfolk were being kept at bay, but big professional bastards are different from half-mad craftsmen with second-hand weapons. This was going to be a hard fight, and we all knew it.

Now or never. Every soldier knew the words and right at this moment, I thought we needed it. I took in a lungful of filthy air and belted it out as loud as I could, the other voices echoing in reply.

"Swords and Daggers!"
"BIG PRICKED SHAGGERS!"
"Slay the foe-men!"
"ONE BY ONE!"

"Quick-pace, no lagging!"
"MORE TIME SHAGGING!"
"Why do we do this?"
"BECAUSE IT'S FUN!"

"Mean Skull-breakers!"
"MAIDEN-HEAD TAKERS!"
"Whores all love us!"
"GIVE THEM SONS!"

"Spear-shafts snapping!"
"BREECHES CRAPPING"
"Loot the corpses?"
"WHEN WE'RE DONE!"

"Bloody slaughter!"
"FLOWS LIKE WATER!"
"Sheathe our swords?"
"WHEN DAY'S WON!"

"Leave the field?"
"ON OUR SHIELDS!"
"Only go home?"
"WHEN WE'RE DONE!"

The words gave me focus, and as their voices joined with my own, I could feel their resolve growing. We forced our minds to cling to the words, belting them out with defiance. Our pace quickened and as one we slammed into the enemy block. The guards rained down heavy, brutal strikes and thrusts in between our shields. I scowled at a horrible scream somewhere to my left. One guard stepped forward so I jabbed my sword at his face, cutting him across the cheek. His hand flew up instinctively and the man in front of me stabbed him in the guts. We pressed as hard as we could, gaining inch by precious inch.

As the square widened, the rear ranks spilled out to the side, keeping us from being flanked. I glanced behind and I could see our bill block at the rear, stopping any nasty surprises.

More screams and flashes of red. We were losing men. I raised my sword above my head and parried a downwards swipe. My arms stung with effort as the blades crashed into each other. He had a sick grin on his face, and I could see the muscles bulging under his armour. I thrust towards him and he dashed away quickly out of my reach.

I dropped back a couple ranks for a breather, and grimaced as I inspected my sword. The notch left by the guard was nearly half an inch deep. All along the line, shields were being splintered. Some were hanging by tattered straps, worth nothing more than firewood.

I turned to Marl and hissed. "These bastards are hitting hard, Marl." He grunted in agreement and hacked down another blow. "We can't keep this fight up! They'll wear us down."

"Where are the fucking reinforcements!" He bellowed, face crimson with exertion.

Glancing behind me, the bills were fighting some stragglers. A desperate mob darting in and out with swords and knives. Not a huge threat, but stopping them from helping us. I could see the men on the left flank were struggling. A score of them had died under the halberds, and the rest were wavering.

"Marl, do you trust me?"

He snarled. "No. You're a filthy sell-sword and an enormous cunt."

"Good. Then just support me or we're both dead."

I burst through the shield line, swinging my sword in great arcs with both hands, stamping down on the shaft of one halberd and knocking aside another. I brought the hilt up just in time to parry a blow. I slammed my shoulder forwards and barged a man to the ground. My sword clanged on a breastplate and I kept pushing forward.

"FOLLOW ME!" Marl roared, and the men surged through the gap. Blades snapped to the left and right of me and I burst through to the rear. I hacked sideways, severing a head and stabbed another man through the back. My hilt became slick with blood and I gripped tight, delighting in the panic and confusion. The swords pressed through and looped around, crushing them like a bear trap.

Two guards broke away from the group to fight me, so I set my feet in a plough stance and laughed like a madman. The first rushed in, sword held high and leading with his wrists. I opened up his belly and he fell screaming. I parried the thrust from his mate and brought my pommel up, cracking his teeth. He slashed at me as he reeled away, and a lucky blow tore open the armour on my bicep. My next strike cut off his hand, and the backswing ended him.

I looked up, panting. Against all hopes, I could see that we were fucking winning. The cobbles ran red with blood and the air stunk like an abattoir.

In the centre of the enemy line, a middle-aged man struck out with his longsword, driving his blade through a billman's eye. He moved like a snake, ripping out throats with practised ease.

"OI, FUCK-FACE" I yelled. "SURRENDER. Throw down your arms and no more of your men have to die today."

He screwed his face up and levelled his sword at me. "Come and face me, dog! In mortal combat, if you dare!" He smiled horribly and hacked down another of our men.

"WITHDRAW!" I yelled out. Marl looked at me aghast. "DO IT!" I barked.

Our men backed off two paces, out of reach of the enemy blades.

I pointed my sword at the officer. "Name?"

He straightened and sneered at me. "Captain Caliban Rigal, of the Carstock guard."

"Captain Rigal. I, Ulf of Barillar, challenge you to single combat on the accusation of blasphemy and treachery to the Crown."

He spat. "Challenge accepted."

Marl ordered the swordsmen to part and Rigal stepped forward, eyes locked to mine. He took up a duelling stance and laughed wildly to the sky. "COME FACE ME, ULF OF BANRILLAR! KNOW THAT PAIN AND DEATH AWAIT YOU!" He brought a hand to his mouth, giggling, bright yellow eyes rolling in their socket.

I forced a laugh. "Death? I have walked with death since before I was a man. And pain? Pain is an old friend."

It's a cunt thing to say, but you have to play the game.

He howled with rage, and we charged each other. Our swords clashed and locked to a bind. He side-stepped, then swung round and behind me. I ducked the cut and then thrust, forcing him back. He danced a few steps on the slick cobbles, then bent down to run his hand through the gore. I watched him pull his bloody fingers through his hair, then suck on his nails with horrible glee.

My shoulders ached, and I felt pretty sure I was bleeding from my thigh. I had to finish this.

We exchanged blows, rapid strikes from the wrist and elbows. He was incredibly quick, moving far faster than his age should have allowed. Each time our swords rang together, my arms and back screamed in protest, but I forced them to keep going. Once again, he danced out of my reach.

A strange mewing sound came from his throat and he reached down to stroke the face of a soldier sprawled bleeding out in the street. I took the chance and charged him, sword held forward like a lance. I crashed into him like a bull, burying the tip of my sword up and under his breastplate, splitting the mail undershirt and into his guts. He staggered back, shrieking, and ripped the sword from my hands. He fell to a knee before rising up again, black blood pooling at the corner of his mouth. His face twisted up in a smile, and his pallid skin seemed far too big for him. He grasped the sword and ripped it out of his belly, showering the street with a cascade of foulness. He moaned deeply, eyes closed in private ecstasy before he brought my sword up and shattered it against his knee.

"Poor little Ulf . . ." He stepped towards me, the tip of his longsword dragging on the ground. "Was that a special sword?" His eyes fixed on him as he slowly paced, tilting his head. His mouth twisted up further showing a hideous maw of misshapen teeth. "A present? From your brother?" He opened his mouth wide and charged towards me.

I snatched up a blood-smeared halberd and swung it wildly. Rigal leapt into the air and landed perfectly before swinging down at my head. The blade bit deep into the wood, a splinter from caving in my skull. The next cut slashed through the shaft near the head and I threw the useless weapon to the ground. I circled backwards, all the while Rigal's hideous laughter tore through the air.

My head crashed to the cobbles and I realised I'd stepped in a man's guts. My boot felt wet and slick as I tried to yank it free. Rigal rushed over and stabbed through my left wrist, piercing my steel vambrace and pinning me to the ground. My howl of pain was cut short as he backhanded me, loosening my teeth and splitting open my lip.

He squatted over me, drool pooling from his unnaturally distended mouth. "He was screaming when he died, wasn't he?" The voice sounded like Rigal, echoing around in my head. "Crying like a whore . . ."

I slammed the bag of candlesticks into his face and he staggered back, howling.

Blood poured from my wrist. I was going to fall unconscious soon, but I wasn't ready to die. Not yet, and not at the hands of this cunt. I forced my arm up the blade till I could grasp the hilt and pull it free.

More blood. Everything felt numb, but I kept going.

He rushed me and I swung the bag, the heavy metal clanging against his skull. With my one good hand, I fumbled, grabbing out a candlestick. I tackled him to the cobbles and we thrashed around on the ground. He jammed a thumb into my eye socket, and I pulled back, hammering the heavy silver lump downwards with all my might.

"Flame of the mind!" He screamed out in agony.

"Flame of the body!" His jaw crumpled inwards, twisted at a horrible angle. My chest felt ready to burst, and the colour faded from my sight.

"Flame of the spirit. Oswald, grant me thy aid!" With the last blow, I caved in his skull. Fat grey worms poured out from a rent torn in his face and writhe obscenely on the cobbles. The silver candlestick crumpled into itself and twisted away to nothing.

I staggered to my feet and vomited spectacularly. It mixed with the disgusting pile at my feet, but I wiped my mouth and felt better. I blinked rapidly and my eyes came back into focus.

The guards had thrown down their weapons, and now everyone was looking at me expectantly, like they wanted me to say something. I gobbed onto the street again and coughed hard. "People who make speeches in the middle of battles are cunts. You lot, take away anything sharp they have, stick them in that house there and barricade the door."

Five men did as I commanded. "The rest of you, get a wiggle on! You've got a fucking job to do."

Marl gave me the slightest of nods. "YOU HEARD HIM." He barked out. "DOUBLE TIME YOU SACKS OF SHIT!"

I grabbed the bag and snatched up the broken hilt of my sword. "Fuck . . ." I retrieved Rigal's blade from the cobbles and hefted it. It was solid and well balanced, and the cunt had no further need of it.

I turned around and saw Decroix and Quentin arrived along with the other troops. "Ulf! What happened?"

"Who cares." I spat again, trying to get the taste from my mouth. "Got any water?" Decroix passed me a skin and I swirled it around, feeling it sloshing out of the hole in my cheek. It probably looked fouled, but I couldn't give less of a shit at that moment.

The units departed to their various roles. They knew what they needed to be doing, and one extra sword wouldn't make a difference now. We'd broken their back; the rest was just the bloody work of mopping up. Besides, I had something more important to do.

"Both of you. With me." They nodded, and we walked towards the centre of the town square.

"Where are we going?"

"We're going to The Pit, Quentin. That's where."

His face creased. ". . . why? There's no-one there to save, they've all been killed."

Brigandine

"Remember Cassioc and the Ouroboros?"
"Oh. It's like that again."
"Yep."
"Bugger."

Chapter 16:
Waking Up

The jagged rocks of the pit stabbed upwards, stained dark brown with gore. At the bottom lay some mangled piles of offal which, I fancied, used to be people. The stench of ruptured guts and stale meat wafted up towards us. I glanced back and saw that the brothers' eyes were watering, and honestly, I couldn't blame them.

Standing at the edge of the pit, I grabbed the rope and walked backwards, pulling it out. Eventually, a pulpy corpse flopped over the side. The face had been smashed against the rock, but it might have been a young woman. I fumbled with the knot, but my left arm was still useless. "Quentin?" He nodded and deftly untied it.

"Right, tie this around my waist and lower me down gently. When I'm at the bottom, tie the rope to something sturdy and fuck off somewhere safer."

Decroix frowned. "What are you going to do?"

"The stones power the magic. Each drop of blood, each scream, each death. They weaken What Should Be and make it easier to turn it into What Should Not."

"What are you-"

"It's been a long fucking day and it's not even noon. So why don't you and donkey-drawers just lower me down into this pit full of mangled human sacrifices and stop asking stupid bloody questions, eh?"

Brigandine

They braced the rope and I lowered myself off the edge. I plummeted about half a yard before the rope snapped taut, biting into my middle.

"Are you alright, Ulf?"

"Perfect. Now lower me down SLOWLY, you pair of fuckwits!"

I could hear Quentin grumbling, so I tried to focus on that rather than the tableau beneath me. After a few moments, my boots touched the spongy dirt. Flies buzzed manically, and pulsing white maggots burrowed through the whole mess. I reached down with my good hand and wiped away at the rocks at the bottom till I could see the edge of the carvings - strange, twisted symbols that writhed if you looked at them too closely.

If I had been more of a cunt, I'd have smiled knowing that I was right, but at that moment I was more concerned with not fucking up and dying. I scraped away at the rest of the stones. By the end, my nails were encrusted with filth and my knuckles scraped raw, but I had found three Waystones that bore the mark.

"Fuck . . ." I hissed to myself. Three. Whoever set this up wasn't playing games.

I looked up and listened. There were still sounds of fighting across the town. Ringing weapons, screams, and war cries.

I counted the remaining candlesticks in my bag. Four. A bit of good luck at least. Now I could banish an unimaginable force of evil from this world and still have a romantic dinner afterwards.

The sky above turned an angry black, with clouds forming like a massive bruise.

"Bugger it." I thought. If I died, I died.

I drew out a candlestick and hefted it, taking comfort in its weight. Good to know Duke Colsarne didn't buy the cheap stuff. I traced my finger over the symbol engraved on the bottom. It was crudely worked, but good enough to get the job done.

The words flowed from my mouth. "Flame of the mind, flame of the body, flame of the spirit. Oswald, grant me thy aid!" I smashed the candlestick down like a thunderbolt and the tip of the stone split in two.

The air shimmered and warped, and an ear-splitting whine echoed through the pit. My skin goose pimpled and burned at the same time and I pulled out another one. The whine reverberated around my skull and I squeezed the base of the stick as hard as I could, forcing myself to stay in the present.

I choked out the words, every breath an effort. "Flame of the mind . . . flame of the body . . . flame of the spirit. Oswald! Grant me thy aid!"

I drove the candlestick down onto the second stone. A blinding flash of light and a low roar like a dying bull. My head slumped with exhaustion, and I could see that the leather in my boots was now nothing more than flowing, writhing flesh. I ripped them off and threw them to the side of the pit, trying to ignore how they flopped and flailed about like drowning fish held in the air. I slumped down next to the final stone and felt a wet splash on my neck. I looked up and a drop of something foul fell into my mouth.

Blood. It was raining blood.

Huge, thick droplets hurled down from the sky, pounding the earth. The red streaked against the silver in my hand and despite the exhaustion and the agony I found myself laughing.

"Raining blood. That's a new one."

The words barely came from my lips, but I whispered them with as much strength as I could. The final Waystone squatted there like an angry toad, glowering at me. I brought up the candlestick, and I struck.

"But why? You haven't explained."

Taran shrugs and throws another log on the fire. "Why what?"

"Why does the silver work that way?"

He throws his hands up and sighs. "Why does the tide go out and in? How do birds fly? Why do you get a mule when a horse and a donkey shag each other? Who knows!"

"Come on! You know what I mean."

It's a cold night. The horses whinny and stamp to keep out the chill, and I can see their breath steaming. My brother holds his hands to the flame and closes his eyes.

"Taran?"

"I don't know. Sellor probably doesn't either, if it makes you feel any better."

I frown. "Is it because it's purer than other things?"

Taran scoffs. "Why not iron? Iron is pure. Or water? Or dirt?" He kicks a bit of dirt at me with his boot and I grunt in annoyance. "Look, I know you want a nice, easy explanation for why it works, but that doesn't make it so."

I tut in frustration and poke at the fire with a stick, more out of something to do than out of necessity.

"Just be grateful, Ulf. At least there is something out there that can even up the odds a little."

"What do you mean?"

He looks at me from across the fire with a sad face. I shuffle a little, uncomfortable. "I mean . . . look, there are some things out there which you'd much rather weren't out there."

"What, you're scared?" I give a little chuckle and then stop dead when I see his face.

"You're fucking right, I'm scared! And if you had a lick of sense in your thick skull you would be, as well. Men you can kill with steel and courage. A sharp sword will finish them off. It's when things get more complicated, when the world as we see and know it starts to . . . bend."

"What do you mean, bend?" I lean forward, curious despite myself.

"It's the only way I can describe it. Nature as you know it starts to run and fray at the edges, but with the right strength of will, some silver and a bit of luck you can send those things screaming back to wherever the fuck they come from."

My mind swarms with questions. "But what are they? And where DO they come from?"

He throws on a big log to burn till dawn and climbs into his sleeping roll. "That's enough questions for one night. There's a long ride tomorrow." He yawns. "So, shut up and get some sleep."

The fire spits and crackles as I lay there looking up at the stars. Thinking.

Pain. That meant I was alive.

My eyes swam into focus and the throbbing pain in my muscles abruptly rose. The stabbing agony in my left wrist shouted the loudest, and I glanced down to see it wrapped in linen, the limb bound to two wooden boards. The room was small, and the sunlight spilling through the open window was obnoxiously bright. Instinctively, I brought up my hand only to be painfully reminded about why that was a stupid idea.

"Good morning, Ulf! It's a bright new day!" Quentin looked frustratingly chirpy as he stood up from a chair and stretched. "Well, good afternoon, to be exact."

"Oh, for fuck's sake . . ." My voice sounded creaky and each syllable strained my throat. I could still taste the foulness from the pit in the back of my mouth. "What happened? Where's everyone else?" I tried to sit up, then immediately regretted it.

"ULF! Calm down! I didn't fix you up so that you could bugger it all up. Here, start by having something to eat." He passed me some bread which had seen better days. Chewing hurt my jaw, but frankly, I'd rather not been hungry.

"Better?"

I nodded. "Wait, you fixed me up?"

"Well, Decroix helped me drag you out of the hole and gave me a hand washing the blood off you, but I did the tricky bits. I even got us the room we like at the Old Rope!"

"Let's see . . . acting, wrestling, fucking, jumping, crossbow marksmanship, and leechcraft. Have I missed anything?"

"Remember that I've also got a great big wi-"

"Yes, I know. You don't need to go on about it."

"Why? Everyone else does."

"Fuck me . . ." I muttered.

He wagged his finger and frowns. "Not until your stitches get better."

"Shut up and tell me what happened."

Quentin threw up his hands. "Which one? I can't do both!"

"If I could get out of bed, I would punch you square in the cockshaft."

"Well, you can't. So there."

I closed my eyes in frustration. "Where's Decroix?"

"Alive and fine. Currently taking stock of what's going on in the town."

"The army?"

"Mostly fine, partly dead. We lost about a quarter. Marl's bunch had the worst of it. Most of them are liberating booze from the taverns."

"Captives?"

"Taken where we could. The guard are under lock and key. Most of them are pretty fucked up in the head at the moment, what with the rain of blood and all. The rest of the town, we just took away anything that looked like a weapon and told them to sod off back home."

"Elivar?"

He shook his head sadly. "Got away somehow. Decroix is speaking to the harbour master, trying to figure out if she left on a ship. Or she could have left at any point before we arrived. I've got men searching the town."

I nodded. "Good plan." The bread was coarse, and I picked out a chunk of grit from my teeth. "Speaking of evil-minded bitches, what's Siffisante doing?"

"She's taking an inventory: piles of weapons, any money lying around." he said dryly. "For Lady Alexia's benefit, obviously."

"On her own?"

He rolled his eyes. "Obviously not. Decroix gave her three 'helpers' to take care of any heavy lifting."

I couldn't help but chuckle. "How did Snow-face's lot fair?"

Quentin shrugged. "As well as to be expected. They did their job. A lot of them died, of course, but there are about half of them left."

"Are they behaving themselves?"

"Surprisingly, yes." Quentin stood up and looked out of the window. Peering over his shoulder, I could see some of the buildings smoking, but it was nothing the town couldn't recover from.

"Quentin?"

He turned around. "What?"

"Thank you."
"Any time, Ulf. Any time."

After a couple of hours, I propped myself up and got dressed. Quentin had left some fresh new clothes on the table in the corner, along with my gear. He was an irritating little bastard, but it was hard to be cross with him when he did things like that. I dragged the flappy linen shirt over my head awkwardly, wincing with pain as my arm caught. Trust Quentin to find something fashionable.

He'd also managed to lay his hands on a jerkin and a short cloak, which would have been perfect if any of the soldiers had decided to put on a small formal ball later in the evening. Growling at the difficulty, I buttoned up the jerkin and fixed the cloak. It was meant to be worn at a 'rakish' angle, but I tried to make myself look like less of a prick by wearing it over both shoulders to stay warm. He'd even found me a new pair of boots. They were a bit stiff underfoot, but they'd loosen up in time.

Finally, I strapped on my sword belt. It felt strange without the weight of my old blade, but I set off to get that sorted presently.

The streets reeked with the iron smell of fresh blood, even if most of it was washed away by last night's rain. Soldiers nodded to me as they walked past and I returned the greeting. I had to stop after a short while to catch my breath, wheezing like an old man and hoping no-one was watching.

I headed back to the sign of a helmet and crossed swords and knocked twice on the door.

"Bugger off!" The old voice from behind the door was edged with malice. "I've got a mace with spikes on it and I'll stick it right up your arse, son!"

"I'm not a looter! I need you to fix something for me." A hatch slid back and a pair of beady eyes peered at my neck. I bent down so he could see my face.

"Oh. It's you. I remember the hole in the cheek. Come in then, don't let the warm air out!"

Several bolts slid back and I heard a table scraping across the floor. He opened the door a crack then slammed it behind me as I stepped in.

"Sorry about that." He muttered.

"Not a problem, I'd be doing the same. "

"Not the door." He sighed. "The bloody guards and the fighting with the guilds." He shuffled over to a bowl on his workbench. "Oatcake?" I thanked him and took one. He chewed loudly with his mouth open. I know I'm not one to talk, but it looked pretty disgusting.

He looked down sadly. "Never would have sold them the weapons if I'd known. None of us would have."

For one horrible moment, I thought he was going to cry. I stood up and plonked down Rigal's sword and the remains of my own. "I need your help with something. Take the blade from this sword and put it on the handle of this one."

He picked up the sword and frowned. "Nothing wrong with this one." He thumbed the edge. "Nothing a bit of time with a grindstone couldn't fix. People don't have the patience to properly sharpen anything these days. Went to the tailor on Wednesday. Scissors were blunt! Imagine that! A tailor with blunt scissors." He shook his head in disbelief. "No patience!"

"Swap the hilt over and sharpen the blade." While my mind was on the topic, I pulled out my dirk and laid it on the table as well. "This too."

"Sword hilt would look bloody funny on a dagger . . ." he muttered.

"Not the re-hilting! Just sharpen this one." I counted out five Wyear into his hand, then gave him another five. He looked pleasantly surprised but didn't comment. "For a craftsman's patience." I explained. He nodded and got to work.

My legs were suddenly tired and I had to close my eyes. I tossed another Wyear onto the workbench.

"And one Wyear for a nice sit-down." And I slumped into a chair and dozed.

After a while, I woke up to the smell of polishes and balms. I grunted a little and sat up in the chair.

"Oh. You're awake now, I see. Looked like you needed the rest." He ambled over. "Look at this!" He thrust a bundle of leather cord under my nose. "See?" He asked accusingly.

". . . umm, yes?"

"Cracked! Cracked and dried out! Left in the rain, probably." He went back to his bench, his knobbly back turned to me. "Anyone can keep a sword sharp, but they always forget the grip. Let it get all dried and crackled. You'd be better off with some new thronging round the grip."

I shook my head. "Use the old stuff."

He shrugged. "Suit yourself. The customer is always right . . ." He fixed the sword in a vice, keeping it steady. I could see the freshly cleaned blade shimmering in the dirty sunlight.

"Mind you, most of the time they're not." he muttered. The old man bound the cord round and round the wood covered tang, tying it tight at the bottom. Satisfied, he sheathed the sword and brought it over for my inspection.

He scratched his nose with practised ease. "Stitching on the scabbard was coming loose. Leather was cracking, as well. Had to sort it out." He held his hands up, warding off an argument. "Don't worry, it's not extra."

I stood up and ran my fingers over the fresh linen stitches, then pulled out the blade. It was beautiful.

"Spot of grinding to get it to fit the guard, but no huge bother."

"Thanks." I said, moving to leave.

"What do you want doing with the other sword bits and the broken blade?"

"Smelt them down."

"Seems like a bloody waste. Y'mind if I keep them for my spares box?"

"Yes. I do. Smelt them down." I handed him another three Wyear and he shut up quickly.

I stepped out into the slight chill of the early evening. "Good evening to you."

He gave me a bow, low as he could with his dodgy back. "And to you to, sir." He closed the door and I heard the bolts sliding across, followed by a muffled "You mad bugger..."

I headed back. I had done nothing but sit in a chair and doze, but I was still exhausted. The others had everything under control, and if they didn't, it could wait until tomorrow.

Slowly. Firmly.

I run the whetstone over the blade, watching my face shimmer on the steel. It's late, and I should be in bed, but I can't help myself. I run my thumb over the edge of the blade, side to side, never up and down. It's wickedly sharp.

Looking up, there's a stub of candle left. I stand up as quietly as I can, wincing as my stool scrapes the flagstone. Holding the sword up to the flickering light, it looks even more beautiful. I take up a stance, bringing my wrists to the side of my head in a high guard before sweeping it down again and stabbing it towards an imaginary foe. I pull it back, twisting the blade and the pommel slams into the bed frame with a resounding thunk.

"Bugger!" I stagger back and trip over the thankfully empty piss-pot, sending it skittering across the floor. There is a knock at the door, and a moment later my brother opens it.

"Ulf, which is more embarrassing? People thinking you're up all hours at night polishing your longsword, or people thinking you're up all hours at night polishing your 'longsword'?"

I fumble with the sheath and put it back on the desk. "I was making sure it was still sharp."

Taran laughs. "Sharp? Really? In case the blade has dulled its edge after a long, trying day of being in a scabbard. If you sharpen that sword any more Ulf, you'll be left with a needle."

My cheeks flush. "Sorry."

"Don't be stupid. You were like this when you got your Federschwer. It's late." *He puffs out the candle and the tallow smokes and splutters. "Now, fuck off to bed. Big day tomorrow. You need to look like you know what you're doing."*

I frown in the darkness. "What? Why?"

"So you don't look like a ball-bag and show us both up? Is that enough of a reason?"

"*No, I meant- why is tomorrow important?*"

"*Oh, forgot to mention. It's a matter for the High Council. Routine, but we need to meet to discuss it. But look, get some sleep. I mean it. Anyway, night-night!*"

"*. . . Night!*" I manage. He shuts the door and I sit down on my bed, head buzzing. The door swings open.

"*Oh, and Ulf?*"

"*Yes?*"

"*Stop playing with your longsword! It will drop off!*"

I hurl my pillow as he slams the door, and then lie down try to get some sleep.

Chapter 17:
The First Time

We stayed in Carstock for a week, organising and re-building what we could. The army was fairly well behaved, but I had to hang three of Azrael's men: two for violence and one for buggery, which sounds like the start of a grim children's rhyme. Azreal didn't seem to care. Siffisante had shacked up with him in one of the nicer townhouses and they spent their time getting drunk and shagging. Couldn't blame them, but I still thought they were a pair of cunts.

Two messengers rode out to Duke Colsarne with news of the victory.

The mistresses and masters of the guilds were assembled and hanged for siding with the Elivar. The punishment for treason should have been torture and burning, but there had been enough bloody spectacles for a while in Carstock, so Decroix agreed that they should die in private. The new heads of the guilds all eagerly bent their knees to Decroix as Colsarne's representative. He took their oaths and Quentin jotted down their names in a ledger.

There was no point trying to punish everyone who sided with the Black Ram. If we had, then we'd have put the whole damn town to the sword. They were petty, selfish people who howled praises out of fear, greed, or bloodlust, but Decroix let it be known plainly to the new aldermen that this was the mercy of Duke Colsarne, and it would not be extended a second time.

Some of the other cultists were dragged from hiding, screaming as they were ripped from cellars and attics and tossed into the street. We only got hold of a few of them. The citizens of Carstock tore some of them apart, beating them to death with staves and rocks. We kept order as best we could, but the town needed time to settle down and let its blood cool.

All the guards were disarmed and their thumbs were broken. I did it myself, cracking them one by one on an anvil until my arm ached. I didn't enjoy it, not one bit, but I didn't want to fight these bastards again, and neither did the rest of Colsarne's men. Credit it to them, not one of them begged, pleaded, or cried. They knew that the bastards leading them would have done far worse to us if they'd won.

Johan stayed behind with enough men to keep order in the town as the rest of the army proceeded to march back. Impressively, Siffisante had managed to persuade Azrael to accompany her back to Colsarne's manse, to personally bring word of his glorious victory. It also stopped Bordane from getting any ambitions about stabbing Johan in the back and taking over the town.

My bruises were starting to fade, but my left arm was still heavy as lead. I could move my hand, but rolling my wrist was agony, so I kept the reins in one hand as we rode out the gates.

I looked back over my shoulder and saw the mess we were leaving behind: houses turned to charred skeletons, dried brown stains marking the timber. People were starting to rebuild now that the Black Ram had left, like waking up from some hideous, maddening dream.

They were better off now. They had to be.

We pushed ourselves hard and got back to Colsarne's manse in seven days. The rain was punishing, and the hooves and feet of the army churned the roads to mud. Marl and Rouberte's men grumbled about Johan's lot getting the soft option as we trudged along.

Around two-thirds of the survivors from Azrael's band settled into staying in Carstock. Some of them were loyal enough to their white-skinned lord to come along with him on whatever moon-touched quest he chose next, but for the rest of them, the chance to live in a house rather than a shitty forest was clearly too much to pass up.

I sent outriders ahead to let Colsarne know we were coming, and I'd be lying if I said I didn't feel glad when the scout reported back and told me there was a feast being prepared.

Darkness had fallen when we arrived at the manse, and a fine, cold drizzle lay in the air. The horses were stabled, and we trooped into the hall. We were all tired, but certainly not too tired for a hot meal. Roderick guided us towards the head table. Duke Colane and his daughter stood to greet us and Decroix bowed low, with the rest of us following suit.

"Rise." he said. "The Proud and Fearsome House of Colsarne thanks you. My daughter was wise to put her faith in you."

Something told me I would be wise to agree.

Duke Colsarne offered the first bowl of pottage to Decroix, which he graciously declined and proffered back to the duke. Like his daughter who sat to his left, Colsarne ate slowly and gracefully. When his small bowl was cleared, the rest of us were served. I could feel the angry beast that was my stomach roaring in anticipation.

The pottage dish was mixed with roasted duck, drizzled with dates and honey. I stopped myself from wolfing it down, but barely. The heat of the great hall fire licked at my bones, and it felt good to sit in a proper chair instead of on the ground, and to eat actual food instead of crappy rations.

I took a great draught of wine and my head warmed wonderfully.

A subtle cough brought me back to reality. The duke was looking at me. "Ulf. Decroix was just telling me about the role you played in Carstock's liberation. We are most grateful, despite the damage to the architecture."

Lady Alexia smiled and raised her glass to her lips. "Such are the hazards of siege warfare, father. Decroix and his men did well to break them when they did. After all, we would not want to delay our trip to Scandar more than is necessary."

"SCANDAR?" I spluttered, then quickly added, "My lady?"

She blinked softy. "Yes, Ulf. Scandar."

Duke Colsarne eyed me coldly. "We will bring this matter to the Autumn Court, before the Queen retires to Cassioc for the winter. If we delay till then, we would be in a worse position to counter this corruption, if it is as widespread as some of the wiser members of the council fear."

"Which wiser members, father?"

"Me."

Colsarne took a sip of wine. Decroix flashed me an uncertain glance, while Quentin pointedly avoided anyone's gaze. My eyes flicked over to Roderick, who wore an expression of grave concern.

I cleared my throat. "So, I venture we're leaving tomorrow, your Grace?"

He nodded and turned to the brothers and me. "The four of us will journey with fifteen men and five servants. Roderick will assist you, but I want you to see to the preparations."

"Five." Lady Alexia corrected her father.

"No, four. Myself, Decroix, Quentin and Ulf. Roderick will remain here."

"And me. So, five." She smiled sweetly at her father and he smiled back, thinly.

"Five it is. See to it, would you Decroix? Oh, and make sure to bring one of my daughter's handmaids to attend her." He glared at Quentin. "The ugly one. With the cleft lip."

After a few more courses, we finished supper and retired to our chambers. It was only after I finally laid down on a proper bed that I realised how much my bones ached. I forced myself to sleep, keenly aware of the long road that awaited us in the morning.

I look over my shoulder as The Hearth fades behind us, the rhythm of the horse's hooves sounding out across the road.

"What are we going to do?" Taran doesn't bother to look round, which is just as well as that means he can't see me roll my eyes.

"Observe and report."

"Observe and report." He echoes, satisfied.

Brigandine

I pull my horse up next to him. He wears his travelling armour, a lighter suit of plate with a coif instead of a full helm. I've oiled the steel, but it just takes one really wet night and I know I'll be scrubbing at it the next day.

He looks at me in false confusion. "Where are we going to again?"

I sigh. "You know where we're going." *He looks at me sideways with his mouth agape.* "CRAFTVALE!" *I snap.* "We're going to Craftvale."

"Oh yes!" *He beams.* "I remember now. What are we going to do when we get there?"

"Observe and report." *I drone.*

"Exactly." *he says.* "When we get to Craftvale, our job is to see what's going on. It's a small town, so it shouldn't take long."

"Why the fuck are we bothering with this?" *I'm grumpy, it's early in the morning and we've been sent on a fool's errand by one of the cooks, whose daughter thought she saw something.*

Taran turns to me, red in the face. "Firstly," *he snaps,* "we are 'bothering' with this because it's our fucking job. Secondly, it's right on our doorstep. Thirdly, because that was what the High Council agreed, if you recall. Finally, because if we don't look into it and it DOES turn out to be something we SHOULD have looked into, then you, me, and a lot of innocent people who we have sworn sacred oaths to protect are going to be FUCKED. Is that good enough reason for you, Ulf?"

"I didn't mea-"

"Answer the question! Yes or no?"

"Yes."

"Good." *He digs his heels into his horse's flank and it gallops quickly onwards, leaving me to catch up.*

I fucking hate rain.

We'd been on the road for a week and a half, and the rain had been incessant. My wool cloak kept the worst off for a few days, but once it soaked through it sat on my shoulders like a lead weight.

Every day was the same: wake up in the rain, eat, ride in the rain, eat again, ride in the rain some more, and finally make camp at the dying of the sun. The skies were drawing in earlier and earlier as the world prepared for winter. Reed's flanks were brown with puddles from the road, churned up into a mess. The tents were splattered with mud, the fine canvas now blooming with spots of black mold. The wind blasted through the camp, sending the bedraggled eagle banner of House Colsarne snapping and twisting in the wind.

I stood first watch. My back ached from the days riding, and I wanted nothing more than to go to sleep. At least the rain had stopped.

Another man stood with me. Buggered if I could remember his name. "Funny about old Marl, eh?"

I turned and glared at him. I knew he was just trying to make conversation and be friendly and all that bollocks, but right then he was just pissing me off.

Marl ended up joining us. He rode out from the gates, his fat face red, his armour clattering and practically begged the duke to let him accompany us. He gave me an evil eye as he did so. I knew he didn't like me, and to be honest I didn't care. If he thought he needed to be here to protect the duke, then fine. I wasn't too fussed.

"Cold evening, eh?"

I sighed. "Yep." Everyone else had gathered in their tents. Duke Colsarne and Lady Alexia had a large bell tent, flanked with iron standards bearing their house banner. The rest of us were crowed together in a large campaign tent, musty from storage.

Dark. Cold. Bored.

My feet squelched and I stepped over to a slightly drier patch of ground. I felt the mud seep into my boots. "For fuck's sake . . ." I muttered.

"What did you say, Ulf?"

"Nothing."

"Oh."

He was quiet for a moment, and I treasured the silence. Then, like a desperate man striking flint against steel in a rainstorm, he tried to get a conversation going. "Bit of a grim night, isn't it?"

"Yep."

"Carstock, eh?"

"Yep."

"That was a bit of a bugger, wasn't it?"

I scanned the tree line near to us. The stars were all out, bright and shining, and I blinked, peering into the gloom and shadows. ". . . yep."

"I mean, who would have thought it would be something like that!"

I turned to look at him. He smiled back at me nervously, then turned to stare into the distance. "First time, lad?"

Silence.

"Lad?"

He turned back and I could see tears running from his face.

"Yep." He croaked. He choked back something in his throat and-

Simon! That was his name. "Marl said you did a good job. Got three of the buggers."

He swallowed again and took some deep breaths. "They were looking the other way. Fighting other people, I mean." He wiped his big nose with the back of his hand. "I didn't stab them in the back - I'm not a coward - but they were fighting someone else so I . . . got them."

"Nothing wrong with that," I said softly. "You got the job done. Doesn't matter how. They all ended up dead."

"I suppose."

There came a long pause. I could hear a fox or something rooting about nearby. A few rabbits had been playing around there earlier, and it was probably time for nature to redden her claws.

He piped up. "What was your first proper fight like?"

"It was fine."

"Fine?"

"Fine."

I heard a muffled squeak of something small and furry dying at the teeth of something large and furry. Such is the way of the world.

We chatted a little more. He told me about his family. He was from some shitty village somewhere. His cousin worked in the Colsarne stables, and that was how he'd gotten into the duke's service. Didn't have a girl, always hated onions, the usual crap. After a couple of hours, we woke up the next ones on watch who staggered out of the tent, drowsy and blinking.

We took our armour off outside the tent so we wouldn't wake the others, then gently tucked the pieces into the jumbled heap of belongings. I lay down in the press of bodies and kicked the man next to me to stop him snoring. He spurted and snuffled, and the snores went down a bit. I rubbed my limbs under the blanket to coax some warmth into them, and eventually slipped into a fitful sleep.

"Excuse me?" Taran puts his hand to his sword hilt and tilted his head.

"I said fuck off. Are you deaf, you stupid cunt?"

My brother keeps his voice level and calm. "I asked if we could buy some food. Buy. Not take, not steal. Buy. You know, for money."

The farmer spits on the floor. "I heard what you said, you dozy bastard."

One of his sons pipes up. "We don't want your money. No-one round here does." The three of them are like their father-tall, broad, and holding big, heavy pruning hooks.

"Now hold on there, Jud." The farmer gives my brother a slow, lazy smile. "We're not going to sell them nothing. But we could still take their money the same."

We both draw our swords. "Don't be stupid!" The farmer laughs. "Four of us an' two of you?"

Taran shrugs. "Hardly seems fair, does it?"

I struggle to keep my horse steady as they all lunge forward. Taran jabs his spurs hard and leans in as Jud swings for him, cutting him across the chest. His billhook drops with a thud on the dirt and my brother brings his horse around. Jud's brothers rush him and he moves his horse expertly, putting one of them in front of the other and parrying their clumsy blows.

The farmer runs at me, bellowing with rage. I panic, fumbling to get out of my stirrups and fight him on the ground. He swings double-handed into my horse's neck, nearly severing it and drenching us both in blood. I slam to the ground hard, my foot pinned under the twitching corpse. He swings to split my head and I bring up my blade, arms jarring at the impact. I wrench my leg free and scrabble back.

I risk a glance at Taran, and see him thrust down into one of the brothers' necks. A spray of gore erupts as he draws his arm back, parrying the other's avenging strike.

I thrust forward and stab the farmer in the thigh. I'm younger and quicker, so he doesn't even have time to move. He howls out and one of his hands flies to the wound to staunch the bleeding.

"You little bastard!" *he cries. Rising to my feet, I slash upwards with both hands, biting into his arm and bringing it backwards to tear through the muscle. His weapon drops to the floor and he stumbles to the ground in shock. I hack down at his neck and the head rolls free. My feet are wet and the taste in my mouth is foul.*

Taran is blocking blows, moving his horse like a dancer. I rush up and tackle the last brother to the ground, a pile of gouging, kicking, and teeth. I land on top as we roll, slamming my gauntleted fist into his jaw.

"ULF!" *I roll off just in time, coming up into a crouch. Taran's big warhorse rears up, nostrils flaring. The man pushes himself to his knees only to be cracked the jaw by a flying hoof. He lands in a heap, neck lolling at a jagged angle.*

"Are you alright? Are you hurt?"

I'm panting, and my hands are shaking. I look over at the farmer. The stump of his neck oozes into the soil, the rest of his family around him like a grim woodcut.

I vomit.

It comes up fast and full, retching and hurling up everything in my guts. I'm on my hands and knees, nostrils stinging from the acid. I can't hear what he's saying but he forces a water skin into my mouth and I'm being led away.

We're in a barn, sitting on benches. A donkey looks at me, stupidly.

"I killed someone!" *I gasp out.*

"Yes. You did." *Taran says matter-of-factly.* "And he didn't kill you. That's the important bit." *He gets up and drags over a cask of water, cleaning his own face and hands and then helping me with mine.* "You've seen men die before. Remember on the road to The Hearth?"

"But I wasn't the one who killed them!"

Taran shrugs. "True."

"We should have done something else! We didn't have to kill them!"

"Like what?"

"Talk to them! Get them to be reasonable!"

Taran gently rests his hand on my shoulder. "They weren't in the mood to be reasonable, Ulf."

"What if we just rode off? They wouldn't have caught us."

"And then what? They brag to their neighbours. 'Oooh! The other day me an' pa drove off two buggers from the Order of the Cleansing Flame! Buncha softies!' Word gets around. The Order loses honour and respect. People start thinking 'Hmm, maybe the Order can't protect us!'. Or worse, what if some people start thinking, 'Hmm, maybe the Order is weak. Maybe now is the time to make a move. Maybe now is the time to come back.'"

Taran kneels down in front of me, making me look him in the eyes. "Do you see what I'm saying? The farmer and his boys weren't especially wicked people. I've known far worse. They were just greedy and stupid. But we did what had to be done."

I nod my head and Taran sighs. "This is what we are training you for, Ulf. Being a knight isn't just fancy poems and riding horses. What do you think the armour and the weapons and the hours and hours of training are for? Sooner or later, it's all for killing. And that's the horrible truth of it all."

I stand up, my legs wobbling. I take a deep breath and pick up a shovel from a jumble of rusty tools by the wall. "We're burying them."

Taran nods and takes off his armour. In the farmyard, we dig four graves and drag in the bodies. Taran mutters some prayers. Before we go, we take the food we were going to buy and let the penned animals free so they don't starve. Some lucky person on the road is going to get a free pig.

We stick my gear on the donkey and I walk beside Taran, leading the beast on a length of rope. I look behind me at the slicks of gore soaking the earth, and we press onwards to Craftvale.

Chapter 18:
A Long Night

The road to Auldcall wasn't too bad. Once we left behind the hills of Colsarne and Carstock, we moved out towards the plains and flats of western Rusia. We arrived in town at midday, Duke Colsarne slouched in the saddle, his daughter riding beside him. He turned to Decroix as we approached the gates. "We shall remain here for no more than two nights. We need to re-supply, and Marl tells me several of the horses need shoeing."

Decroix nodded and rode ahead to prepare for his lord's arrival. The guards immediately parted and let us through. Even though his retinue might not be much, they knew far better than to try and fuck with a High Duke of Ashenfell.

Auldcall is a wealthy town. The walls are thick-hewn grey stone, and even the cobbles look polished. We passed a merchant and his family wearing the gaudy clothes of the newly rich. I turned to Quentin with a sigh. "Look at the tossers. Fat, rich, and happy. Good farmland on the Grapean, and life is rosy. Wankers."

He turns to me. "Hmm? Did you say something?"

"Never mind . . ."

Decroix stood waiting for us on the other side of the gates. We dismounted and led our horses through the streets to The Falcon, a large inn with three levels and a cellar, and stables to the side.

Our horses were stabled, and arrangements made with a farrier to see to those that needed attention. Aside from needing new shoes, Reed was fine. I passed the stable lad a couple Ecar to make sure she got rubbed down properly . Two of the men stood on guard at the door, armoured and with swords readied, looking like the most overly prepared bouncers in the world.

The innkeeper sent us a fine dinner of meats, cheeses, fresh bread, and jugs of honeyed wine. After spending weeks on the road, I was happy to have a meal I didn't have to cook myself.

Quentin cut himself a generous wedge of cheese before passing the platter on. "By the way, Decroix, good choice on the inn. What's in the wine? It's nice."

"It's the honey." I said. "The lands around here are rich. Good fields mean lots of plants and flowers. Good flowers mean happy bees. Happy bees make better honey."

Decroix frowned. "How do you know so much about agriculture?"

I shrugged. "You pick bits up here and there."

There were shifts to stand guard: two outside the door and one each in front of Lady Alexia's and the duke's chambers. I was taking a shit when the shifts were drawn up, so I ended up getting the middle of the night shift with Marl. It was buggeringly cold out, so I stepped from foot to foot and rubbed my hands to stay warm. Marl stared out into the darkness impassively.

"Bastard of a night, eh?"

Marl snorted. "Been far worse." he says curtly.

"Shit luck getting stuck on the middle shift, isn't it?" I'm not good at smiling at the best of times, but I gave it a go.

"I volunteered. Commanders should take their fair turn, look after their men."

The silence was fucking deafening and after a few moments, I felt ecstatically grateful when a drunk staggered past, muttering to himself. I shook my head. "What a piss-head, eh?"

He grunted. I gave up and watched the drunk stagger into an alleyway next to us.

A few moments passed. Suddenly Marl looked confused and held up his hand to silence me.

"Marl?"

He wordlessly went inside the inn and I walked after him. He trod softly and gently despite his bulk, and silently drew his sword. He blew out the candle guttering on the bar and slowly moved down into the cellar. I unsheathed my own blade and followed him, my eyes adjusting to the pitch darkness.

I could just about make out when he led me to the edge of the cellar and pointed upwards at the trapdoor leading into the street. I saw the metallic glint of a thin blade, slowly lifting the bar of the trapdoor. Marl raised his eyebrows at me and frantically gestured to give him a boost. I put down my sword and winced as he put his foot onto my hands.

The trapdoor flew open and the grubby face behind it tumbled back in surprise.

"GOTCHA, YOU LITTLE BASTARD!" Marl roared. My arms strained as I flung his bulk upwards after the fleeing robber. I threw up my sword and then scrabbled into the street just in time to see them both turn a corner. I got up and ran after them, armour clattering. With our armour and Marl's belly, we were none too fast, but we kept up the chase as he darted from corner to corner, and we stuck to him like dogs on a bleeding hind.

We eventually cornered him, his path blocked by a vast pile of wool packs. He tried to climb up, but tumbled down to the cobbles with a thump. Marl stood panting and redder in the face than normal. I grabbed the shady looking man by the scruff and jumped back when he swung at me with a wicked-looking knife.

"For fuck's sake, not again." I groaned.

I slammed my fist into his gut, and as stood doubled over, punched him in the wrist with the crossguard of my sword. There was nice, clean snap and a tinkle as his wrist broke and the knife fell to the floor.

"You're not as good at this as your friends were." I slogged him again for good measure. "Either that or I'm getting better at knowing you're coming."

He curled on the floor then, so I kicked him a few times. It felt nice to be the one giving out the brutal beatings for a change.

Marl came over, still panting and shoved me out the way. "Stop that." He barked at me.

He looked the man over with contempt and put the heel of his foot down on the man's broken wrist.

"What the fuck were you doing sneaking around?" The man screamed then scratched and thumped at Marl's leg, but he wasn't an idiot. He stood to the side so the poor bugger on the floor couldn't punch him in the cock and I looked on in silent approval at how much of an arsehole Marl could be.

"I just wanted to see if there was anything worth looking at!" he whined.

"Liar." Marl said simply. Marl shifted his weight, and I was convinced I could hear bones scraping together behind the man's choking sobs. "Who told you to try and go spying on Duke Colsarne?"

"Please stop!" He started crying. "I'm just a petty thief! I swear! Mercy!"

Just as a piece of advice if you're ever being tortured by a big, angry, red-faced bastard like Marl: screaming "Mercy!", "Stop!" or "No, not in the balls! Please! Anything but the balls!" has literally never, ever worked. Feel free to give it a go if it makes you feel better, but just believe me when I say it's not going to help you.

Marl raised his foot and stamped down on his fingers. Despite myself, I couldn't help wincing. It's hard to do anything with broken fingers, but if your job is picking locks and purses then you'll need to find a new profession sharpish. Maybe something gentle, like goat herding.

"STOP LYING TO ME YOU LITTLE SHIT!" Marl screamed into his face, spittle landing like morning dew.

We both turned round at the sound of rapid footsteps and two of the night-watchmen were at the end of the ally. They look at us, dumbfounded.

"Duke Colsarne's business. Nothing to worry yourself over." I threw a handful of Wyear towards them. "Go and have a nice drink somewhere and remember to forget this, eh?" They nodded, slowly picked up the coins, and left. Marl turned back to our new friend.

Brigandine

"Why did you have a dagger?"

"Would you go out at night without a dagger?" he pleaded.

I shrugged. "He's got a point, Marl."

He turned on me, still crimson with fury. "He's one of those Black Ram bastards. I know it!"

"Marl, this is a little awkward, but I don't think he is."

He looked at me, face lined with confusion. "Huh?"

"Well, he could just be a petty thief. I mean, you do get petty thieves." I looked into the man's eyes. He stared back at me in silent desperation, knowing that I was the only thing keeping him from being brutally beaten to death.

"Marl, most of the time they're much better fighters than he is. Also, the Black Ram assassins tend to be cold, professional killers. This bloke looks like he'd struggle to cut cheese, let alone throats." He nodded at us in enthusiastic agreement. "And besides, proper assassins dress in black with a touch of class. This poor bastard is more tatty shades of brown with a few bits of grey. Also, no leather medallion with the symbol of the Black Ram. That's a dead giveaway."

Marl paused for a moment, mulling it over. I could tell he was thinking because his lips were moving. "Go on, then. Fuck off." He dragged the man to his feet before giving him a half-hearted kick up the arse.

"Thank you!" He sounded pathetically grateful, and, to be honest, Marl and I just felt awkward.

"If I catch you bothering His Grace again, I'll split your cockshaft with a tent peg."

The thief nodded in acknowledgement and scuttled off. I picked up the dagger and offered it to Marl. He shook his head, so I shrugged and tucked it into my belt. No point saying no to a free dagger.

We walked back to The Falcon. This time Marl broke the silence. "So. You've had dealings with those Black Ram buggers before, then?"

"Once or twice."

He grunted.

"So, how did you find out about them?" I asked.

"Decroix told me. That's why I came with. I didn't want his Grace to be out on the road with bastards like that abroad. He's not a bad one. Decroix, I mean. Moody, though."

I laughed at the irony of Marl calling anyone moody. "If I had a randy sod like Quentin to keep out of trouble, I'd be grumpy too."

"Heh." For the first time, Marl cracked a grin at me.

By mid-morning the next day, Decroix had sourced everything that we needed. The farrier wasn't going to be finished till sunset, so we would need the extra night in The Falcon.

Duke Colsarne reacted with apathy at the news of our midnight caller. "Ulf has a great deal of experience in these matters. If he considered him to be just a simple footpad-"

"Latch-pry, my lord." I couldn't help myself.

He turned his head. "Latch-pry?"

"Footpads are muggers. Robbery with the threat or employment of violence on a road or street. That's a hanging. Latch-prys are just breaking into buildings to nick stuff. My lord."

"A most useful distinction, Ulf." he said firmly. "But I'm afraid I don't care."

"As you wish."

For want of anything better to do, Quentin and I decided to take a stroll. There were no markets on, so we took in a tour of every alehouse we could find. We were at a hole in the wall, sipping on some sweet beer made by the plump widow who served us through the hatch on the side of her house.

I leaned my back against the wattle and daub and smacked my lips together. "It's good stuff." I wasn't slurring my words quite yet, but the world had started to glow quite pleasantly.

Quentin nodded "Yep. Sh'good." He slipped a little and staggered, spilling half of it on the street.

"You dozy bastard!" I laughed as he fixed me with a stupid smile.

"Quentin, Ulf. What the fuck are you two up to now?" Decroix rolled his eyes at us from the end of the street and walked up to us briskly. "You're a bad influence on him. You know that?"

Quentin furrowed brow. "D'you mean me or him?"

"Both!" he snapped. "We're riding out at first light tomorrow. You should be getting some rest, not pissing your money up the wall."

"Don't be silly. It's in the street, not up the wall."

I held up my hands. "Look, let's be fair. We'll have one more mug, then we'll call it a night."

Decroix sighed. "Fine, all right. But just one!"

Late at night, we staggered into the brothel. Cheap perfume hung in the air and a generously sized fire crackled in the hearth.

"Good evening, kind ladies." Quentin boomed, swinging off his cloak in an almost graceful movement. "Now, who wants to help me take off the rest?" The whores giggled and swarmed up to him.

"You know that you don't need to try and seduce them, Quentin. They are in fact, paid to sleep with you."

Quentin pouted. "Ah, come on, Decroix! Relax a little bit. You might like it."

"I am relaxed!" he snapped. Decroix had managed to catch us up fairly quickly, but was still a few drinks behind Quentin and me.

I spied a good-looking lass, just how I like them. She's plump and pretty and has a pair just like Mary. Well, maybe a bit smaller, but I didn't hold that against her. I slowly counted out three Wyear and pushed them onto the table.

"Hey. Hey! Come over here and say . . . something nice to me!" I really started laying the charm on thick and I fixed my best smile in place. She turned around and her face wrinkled up when she saw the gaping hole in my cheek. She then turned it into a horrible, painted on smile. I slumped down in my chair a little.

"Good evening, sir . . ." she purred close to me and nibbled at my ear. Her breath was sweet, like too much honey. "And what do you need? My big, brave man."

I suddenly felt sad. I couldn't explain why, but I missed Mary right then and I felt myself wilting away like an old pear.

"Jug of wine." I pushed the coins towards her.

She faked a little pout. "Don't you want something a little more . . . interesting? There are plenty of fun things we can do." She rubbed a hand up and down my knee and I pulled my leg away.

"Just wine."

She took her hand away and turned, muttering to herself.

I slumped down in the chair and scratched at my jaw. Decroix said something, but I couldn't hear him, and couldn't be bothered to check. Out of the corner of my eye, I could see Quentin wondering off with a couple of them, two girls and a man with one of those stupid beards everyone had those days.

There was a thunk on the table and the clink of a few cups. She came back and blew me a kiss. "Are you sharing?"

"No."

She snatched up the coins and stomped away, bottom waggling. I slopped some onto the table, but most of it went into the cup, so I counted that as a win.

"Ulf! Did you hear what I said?" Decroix was talking again. He waved a hand in front of my face. "Ulf?"

I poured out another cup for him and slid it over. It rolled on its side and spilled, deep red wine filling up the cracks and scars in the woodwork.

"ULF! For fuck's sake . . ." Decroix stood up to dodge the wine dripping over the side.

"Don't worry . . ." I could hear myself slurring, but I didn't care anymore. "There's plenty left!" I grabbed another cup and poured some out carefully before sticking it in front of him.

"I don't want any sodding wine!" he snapped.

I squinted at the bar, forcing it to focus. "I think they do beer. Or is the mead behind there? Hey, you!" I waved my arms. "Is that mead? Why didn't you tell me you had mead! I want some mead for my friend!"

Brigandine

I could see the woman with the nice bottom talking to the abbess of the brothel. She didn't look happy, but she was smiling as she came over, so I assumed must be good.

"Good evening, sirs. I'm glad you're having a fine time in our little hostelry, but could I entreat you to keep your voices to a sensible level? For the comfort of the other patrons."

I grinned like an idiot and held my finger to my lips, leaning over to Decroix. "SHUSH! Keep it down Decroix! People are trying to fuck!" I threw back some more wine, forgetting to tilt my face so a thick trickle spilled out from the hole in my cheek, down my neck and under my shirt. "Anyway, Decroix wants some mead!" I grabbed Decroix's hand and held it tight. I thought I was about to cry.

"Certainly."

She smiled, hiding her disgust a lot better than the other one did. I fumbled around in my pouch and pulled out a coin. I half passed, half threw it at her, and only realised it was a Guilder after she'd fucked off, but I didn't care too much.

I pulled Decroix up close, and he let out an exasperated sigh. "What's wrong! Come on, what's the matter? We're having fun, aren't we?"

Decroix pushed me away. "Yes, yes. We're having fun." he said soothingly. "I'm just trying to keep a lookout for my brother."

I burst into tears. I felt like a fucking idiot, but I couldn't help it. Decroix looked confused and started patting me gently on the back. The abbess was back, looking angry now.

"Right! This is a knocking shop. People come here to relax, to have a few drinks and a good shag. They don't come here to listen to some moon-touched idiot with half a face cry like a buggered goat. Now, fuck off!" I stood up shakily.

"No! You fuck off!" I shouted.

"This is my brothel, get out!" She yelled. There were lots of people looking at us. Decroix was saying something and I'm pretty sure there were some rough-looking heavies with clubs stepping out of the shadows.

Decroix started dragging me somewhere and I began fumbling with my pouch, furious. "It's MY brothel now! I'm buying it! You work for me now! You, hired thugs! Arrest this woman!" All my coins spilled across the floor, and I suddenly sobered up as the door slammed in my face. We were both in the street, and a light drizzle began to spit down from the night sky.

Decroix shot me a murderous look and he slumped down, his back against the wall of what I thought was a candlemaker's shop. I sat down next to him.

"We're waiting for Quentin, then we're going back to The Falcon."

"I'm sorry." I muttered.

"Don't talk to me!" he snarled. "It's bad enough having to take care of Quentin all the damn time. It's like trying to piss in your own mouth. Nearly impossible, and not exactly fun when you manage to do it." He jabbed a finger at me. "You're normally the sensible one. What the fuck happened?"

I shrugged my shoulders. He rolled his eyes at me and we sat in silence for about half an hour, till Quentin staggered out with a big smile on his face.

Decroix stood up and sighed. "You took your bloody time!"

Quentin gave a low bow. "Thank you, I tried my best." He turned and blew a kiss to the two women and the man with the stupid beard waving out the window. He threw down a belt with a dagger in it.

Quentin picked it up and waved cheerily. "Thank you, Ballson!" They then closed the shutters and presumably went away for a long bath.

Decroix frowned. "Ballson? That's an odd name."

"It's a stage name." Quentin smiled. "Because he puts his 'balls-on' your-"

"That's as much as I need to know, thank you." Decroix gritted his teeth, and the three of us staggered back to The Falcon.

"Quentin, why are you so happy?" I asked.

"Well, you know my todger?"

"Only by reputation."

"It's like a massive salami."
"Butchers cut slices off?"
"No! Although to be fair, one did try."
"Were you shagging his wife?"
"No, I was shagging her husband..."
The two men by the door looked straight ahead. Deliberately not looking at us as we walked up the stairs to bed.
I felt tired. So damn tired.

Chapter 19:
Pretty Fucked

"*Craftvale looks like a bit of a shithole.*"

Taran gives me a dirty look. We've been getting on each other's nerves recently, so I'm acting like a spoiled little bastard. My feet hurt from walking beside the donkey, and I can't help but resent Taran for having a horse to ride.

"*Go on, tell me about Craftvale.*"

I grit my teeth, regretting opening my mouth. "*It's a town. Lots of town stuff. People selling and buying things. The normal crap.*"

"*What's it near? What does it do, who are its allies? Where-*"

"*It lies on the north bank of the river Grapean. Goods come from the south and onto Auldcall. Or they come from the port of Melpapier on the North Coast and head further inland.*"

"*What else is nearby? What makes it especially important?*"

"*It's near The Hearth?*"

Taran sighs. "*Come on, Ulf. Don't be thick. Who lives there?*"

"*At The Hearth? Well, we do.*"

"*And?*"

"*The horses?*"

"*If I wasn't riding, I'd lean over and smack you in the mouth.*"

"*Yeah, but you are. So there.*"

"*Who else lives at The Hearth? Please use your fucking brain, Ulf.*"

"*The servants, obviously.*"

Taran throws his hands up. "*Finally!*"

"*That's why this is important, isn't it? Their families and kinfolk must live here.*"

Brigandine

"*The Ecar stops spinning! At last, he gets it!*" Taran shouts. "*Yes, Ulf, that's the reason why it's important we look into this. Craftvale is where most of the craftsmen, labourers, farriers, smiths, seamstresses and all the other hundreds of people who make all the things we use and ensure we don't starve to death in a ditch come from.*"

"*Well, they need us more!*" I'm still itching for a fight, so I press him. "*Without the Order protecting them, they'd be fucked! That's what Sellor always says. 'The light that burns away the wicked darkness' and 'Those who do what must be done'. They work for us! We basically own them.*"

He turns and looks at me, full of disappointment, and it cuts me like a fucking dagger.

"*Ulf.*" He says quietly. "*Remember, we are their protectors. Never, ever their owners. Horses are owned. Dogs and pigs are owned. But never men. That's the difference between us and them.*"

"*Between us and the beasts, you mean?*"

"*Yes, but not the kind of beasts you mean.*" He says quietly.

We head on for another half an hour in silence. We ride up to the gates of Craftvale just as the sun is dying. Like all good towns, there is a statue of Queen Karidine standing over the gates, reminding those who pass under that they are under the Queen's protection and mercy - but also her authority and law.

"*HALT!*" A gruff voice shouts out at us and two guards bar the entrance with crossed spears. "*Name and business.*"

My brother flashes them his winning smile. "*Sir Taran of Banrillar, of the Order of the Cleansing Flame, and my squire, Ulf of Banrillar.*"

The guard glares at us. There is a long pause and he sneers at us from under his helmet. I catch sight of his face, thick-lipped and drooping. "*And what, pray tell, is your business in Craftvale?*"

Taran smiles again, pointedly. "*My business is that of the Order. And my business is my own. Now, good sir, be kind enough to let us past. Please.*"

There is a moment's hesitation. Taran's hand drops casually to his hip and his shoulders flex, like the creak and shift of thin ice.

"*Enter.*"

He nods and we go through. "*Thank you, friend. Say, you couldn't recommend a nice inn, could you? Somewhere with room for our mounts.*"

"*The Wrestler.*" he says gruffly. "*It's got a stable and it's a goodly, quiet place.*" He stresses the last few words and we get the hint. "*Weapons bound!*" He calls after us as we head down the street.

Taran tosses me a strip of leather from his pouch and we strap up our swords. Looking around, most of the shops are shut up. There's a butcher nearby with the windows boarded, a rotting pile of offal in the alley to the side. I slap away a fly as we walk past.

I'm used to people staring when we travel. It's rare to see someone wearing the shining plate harness of a knight, clad in blue and gold. When you live your life in shades of brown and grey, to see someone clad in the spender of war . . . well, that's something to gawp at, isn't it?

But this time, folk shuffle out of our way. There aren't many people around and the streets are quiet. Those we do see keep their heads bowed down and their eyes fixed firmly on the cobbles.

As we venture inwards, the rot and decay of the town becomes obvious. Doors are boarded up, and broken windows stand unmended. What should have been a prosperous and thriving town seems to be slowly oozing into a sump.

Taran tries to get the attention of a woman, a child clutched to her breast. "Hail friend! Do you know where The Wrestler is? We need rooms."

She turns to us, and I am taken aback by her face. Her mouth hangs over her bottom jaw, which is almost non-existent, and she blinks slowly with bulging, pale eyes. The light is bad, but I can see she is nearly bald, with only a few dank wisps of hair beneath a ragged shawl.

"Um . . . hello?" I venture.

There is a thick, gulping noise and a high-pitched whine. She looks down at the bundle clasped to her chest and makes a slow, guttural soothing noise. She glares at us, jabbing her finger down the street, and then scuttles into a nearby house, slamming the door behind her.

"Friendly folk, aren't they?" Taran whispers.

The night is settling in now. There are precious few lights in the windows of the town, and the bleeding sun is all but gone, giving way to twilight gloom. People all around are moving quickly, bustling into their homes. We tread onwards, the grime on the cobbles soaking through the leather of our boots.

"There!" I point to the tavern. It's a simple inn, with stables to one side. Above the door is a cracked and peeling mural of two men stripped to the waist, twisting and snarling at each other. One has a snake wrapped about his leg, and I wrack my brain to try and remember the old story.

Dismounting, Taran raps his fist on the dried-out door and I peer through the greasy, scratched glass at the hunched figures inside.

"SHOVE IT!"

"Pardon?"

"THE DOOR. SHOVE IT." A meaty voice bellows from within.

Taran turns to me and shrugs before driving his shoulder into the wood.

Brigandine

The door swings open with a crash. Spluttering candles cast long shadows across the room.

It's a shitty little place. The air is filled with stale beer and the earthy smell of unwashed bodies. Dozens of eyes are rolling over us, and the silence squats like a toad.

Taran strides into the tavern, leaving me with the horses. "Stabling for two and a bed for my squire and me, please."

The landlady snorts and swallows, making a foul noise. "It's getting on late."

"I know." says Taran. "That's why I'm paying you good money." He takes out a shiny Guilder and flips it onto the bar. It's gone in a flash. "We'll be here for a few days. I'll take a bath and food in our room please."

She nods and yells at a youth cleaning out tankards behind the bar. "Samiel! Get the horses." He shuffles to the door, walking painfully on bandy legs, with one foot twisted onto itself. Taran smiles at him and presses a W year into his hand.

"The animals are outside. But the one on two legs is my squire."

I bristle a little but keep my mouth shut. Samiel leads the animals towards the stable, and I close the door behind me, forcing it back into the swollen frame.

"Come along!" The woman leads us upstairs with a candle, and I can sense the gawps and sneers of the patrons below reaching up after us as we turn a corner on the landing.

"Need to heat the water . . ." she mumbles. She takes out a thick iron key and unlocks the door, then moves over and lights the two candles in the room. The smell of rancid tallow swells up as the tiny glow fills the gloom. The room is small, with most of it taken up by a stout bed, its mattress stuffed with straw. Taran dumps his gear in the corner of the room and I do the same.

"Spaulders." He holds out his arms and I fiddle with the buckles, squinting in the light.

"Vambraces." I put the rest of his arm protection carefully onto the floor to one side.

"Breastpla-"

"I know how it goes . . ." I mutter.

"Well, at least you've learned something." He teases. "Now hurry up! Supper should be here soon."

I strip him of his travelling harness, and when I'm done, he flops onto the bed with a satisfied grunt.

Just as I unbuckle my own armour, there is a knock at the door. The landlady has returned with a jug of wine and a platter of meats, some hard, dark bread and a wet-looking pale cheese. I take the platter and pour two glasses of wine. Taran takes a deep drink and winces.

"*I wonder how they managed to get the goat to squat over the barrel . . .*" he murmurs.

After my first cautious sip, I'm inclined to agree. The food is just as bad: dry, nasty bread, and the cheese leaves a greasy film on the roof of my mouth.

"*Sausage isn't great either.*" Taran munches.

"*What is it made from?*" I wrinkle my nose at the dull, sour taste.

"*I don't know, but I fear the wurst . . .*"

I roll my eyes and push the platter away.

The landlady returns after a few minutes and wordlessly moves to take away the dish. Taran stays her hand, pointing to a morsel of bread still clinging to the plate. She shrugs and returns with an old wooden tub, filling it right to the brim with steaming water.

Taran throws his shirt at my head and hops in, splashing the water over his face. "*At least the bath is good.*" He flicks the water at me before pouring it over his head.

When he's finished, I wash myself in the now slightly grey water. It feels good to get rid of the sweat and dust of the road. Taran flicks the remnants of the dry bread into the corner of the room picks up the round wooden platter. I frown at him, but I'm too tired to care what he's up to.

He takes the tiny hatchet that we use for kindling and splits the platter down the middle, coughing loudly to mask the noise. He slices again, making a wedge. "*Taran, what the fuck are you doing?*"

My brother smiles and shoves the wedge firmly under the door. "*Just in case . . .*" he says.

After washing, I pull my shift over my head and climb into the bed. Taran does an exaggerated yawn and stretches out, knocking me in the face.

"*Ow! Sod off.*" I pull the blankets over me and roll up as tight as I can. The cold air whips through gaps in the floorboards and the evening chill wrap around me, cutting through the bedding and into my bones. I hug my arms around me and grit my teeth to stop myself from chattering.

My brother sighs. "*Oh, come on, Ulf. Don't be a baby.*" Taran gets out of the bed, careful to not let the cold air in. I can hear his footsteps in the dark, rummaging around in his pack. I feel a weight on me as he spreads his travelling cloak on top of the blankets, the thick wool trapping in the warmth.

"*Better?*"

"*Thanks.*"

Whispered conversations and the smell of reek of ale drifts upwards from below. I strain my ears, but I can't make out the words. Harsh whispers and guttural, raspy grunts mix with thumped tankards and unpleasant laughter.

Brigandine

Eventually, my eyes get heavy. The middle of the bed is warm, and I pull myself down deep under the covers. I can still hear things-voices-but they drift away, and I find myself dragged down under into a swirling mess of black and purple.

The landscape around me is jagged, like broken glass. I find myself running. The looming flanks of my surroundings leap and snap at me making me jump and dodge to the side.

My feet are bleeding. Tiny pricks of insect bites are suckling away at my heels and thorns tear at my skin. I desperately shield my eyes, turning and sprinting from whatever is lunging at me from the shadows.

There's hot breath in my hair. Wet speckles hit the back of my neck and I roll to the side, sinew and lungs screaming with the effort. Every step is hard now. Jagged pain arches up, running along my ankles, knees and legs until I thrash around in vain.

Something is holding me. I can feel nails digging into my skin, pinching at my legs until they creep up over my loins and buttocks, groping at me obscenely. I scream out in rage and terror, scrabbling with my fingernails against whatever is holding me. My hands are bloodied, feeling like they have been scraped across burning, jagged metal.

My arms are bound. Chained down and pulling at my shoulders so hard I fear they will rip from their sockets. I open my mouth to scream, only to have it filled with something foul and viscous. Pushing through my lips and rasping along my teeth with hideous curiosity. I wrench my head from side to side as it floods over my head, blinding me.

"Ulf!"

Head pounding, my vision swims into focus. Taran is shaking me gently. He raises a finger to his lips. I can see a faint and flickering light from the gap under the door. There are whispers. I can't make them out, but from Taran's expression, it's not good. I start to speak and Taran shoves his hand over my mouth. He raises his finger to his lips again and I nod as he takes his hand away.

We slip out of bed as silently as we can, feet cold on the wooden floor. Taran takes up my sword and hands it to me before grabbing his own, tossing the baldric over his shoulder. He gingerly opens the shutter, the silver hilt glinting in the moonlight.

"I don't have it, I thought you did!"

"I'm trying the key! It won't open!"

The voices get louder. I recognise the landlady.

"You stupid cunt! What are we to do now?"

"Break the door down, you damn fool!"

The door rattles with heavy thunks against the wood, joints groaning and creaking with each blow.

Quickly, he waves me over to the window and points downwards. Across the alley, there's a pile of animal shit piled against the wall mixed in with filthy straw. The nightsoil man clearly hasn't been yet, and the stench wafts up into my nostrils.

We exchange glances and nod. Taran leaps first, landing in the middle of the filth. He springs to his feet and holds up his arms. "Lower yourself down!"

I scrabble to the windowsill, suddenly aware of how high up I am and swing my legs over the edge.

There is a screech of metal as the door is burst from its hinges and sent flying to the floor. A boulder of a man stumbles into the room, holding a wicked-looking messer. The landlady and three others are behind him as he lunges at me. I shove myself off the ledge just as he swings for me, the blade biting into the windowsill. Taran grabs me and we fall into a heap in the alley.

"Get up!" *He barks, dragging me to my feet and drawing his sword.* "Horses! Go!"

I pull my sword free as we sprint around to the stables, and a moment later a hatchet swings at me from the shadows. I bring up my blade and the steel rings out in the darkness. He hacks at me again and I dart away, nearly slipping on the filthy cobbles. Taran spins round, cutting downwards. There is a brief, horrible scream and then Taran cuts his head from his shoulders, sending it rolling into the darkness.

He bends down and grabs at an iron ring of keys, cursing as they won't come free. I grab the belt and cut it in half. He grins, "Good thinking! Now, hurry the fuck up!"

The voices are shouting now, rousing others. Taran fumbles with the keys at the stable door before shoving the right one into the lock and bursting into the gloom.

All around is the smell of blood and shit. I feel something wet beneath my feet. Though the open door, I can see twisted, snapped limbs and piles of ropey guts. The glassy eyes of Taran's horse gaze up at me, skull split down the middle.

"Bastards!" *Taran snarls and grabs me by the arm.*

"Where are we going?"

"Away!"

"Away where?"

"From here! I would have thought that would be fucking obvious!"

We fly through the streets, stones stinging my feet. We dart into a side alley, hearts hammering from the sprint. We duck behind some woolpacks and Taran peeks up.

"Bugger!"

"What?"

"Those bastards are everywhere . . ." *he murmurs.* "Look."

I raise my head above the woolpacks and I can see figures pouring out into the streets. A hue-and-cry is echoing across the town, bidding all able-bodied men and women to find weapons and bring us to justice.

"Fuck me . . ." I mutter.

Taran smiles grimly. "My sentiments exactly. Right, what's the plan?"

"Pardon?"

He looks at me expectantly. "What's the plan, Ulf? It's a fairly easy question."

"What? I don't have one! You're the knight!"

"Well, you have about, ooh, I'd say, twenty seconds to think of one before that guard over there finds where we are, lets all his pals know, and they kill us."

"Taran," I hiss, "now is not the right time to try and-"

"Probably nearer ten seconds now." he says casually. "Do you want to be a knight or not?"

I kick out at the woolpack in frustration, stubbing my toe and bending back the nail. "Fucking- wait, that's it! This way!" I grab Taran by the arm and lead him round the back of the building.

He smiles. "Go on . . ."

"The woolpack. Where do you find woolpacks?"

"Near wool combers."

"And before they can comb it, you need to?"

"Wash it. And to wash it you need-"

"Water. And lots of it."

Taran grins. "And where does the river lead?"

"Out of this shithole." I finish.

After finding a door, I use my sword to carefully lift the latch into the warehouse, thanking Oswald the Fierce that the owner was too cheap to pay for a decent, locking door. But, to be fair, who the fuck would break into a wool comber?

"If we can make it to the end of the warehouse, there'll be a part that goes underground, meeting up with the river. If we can get to that, we'll be fine."

"Lead on!" Taran bows. "After you."

I check round to the right, then the front. Looking behind the door last. I wave my hand and Taran enters behind me.

The warehouse is a cavernous wooden building. The sound of rushing water and the smell of damp fleece fill the air. My eyes adjust to the deep gloom, grateful for the shard of moonlight through the high windows. I walk around slowly to the left, my sword arm held out into the darkness as we hug the wall. Taran clicks his tongue softly and I turn around. He points and I catch a glimpse of a shambled, hunched figure in the shadows. I grit my teeth and curse. I double my pace, keeping as quiet as I can as

we dart through the shadows. There is the heavy, metallic sound of bolts being drawn back and my head swims for a moment with a rancid smell.
"Ulf," Taran whispers. "Run!"
Taran sprints past me, his face painted with terror. He screams, all efforts of stealth are forgotten. "HURRY UP! COME ON!"
"Taran, what are you-"
"No time! Run!"
We hurl ourselves forward, the crates streaming past us as we dart from shadow to shadow.
The smell is getting stronger now. The sickly-sweet smell of rotten flesh combined with the reek of wet fur. Snapping back into the gloom, I catch a glance of a twisting, writhing member, as thick as a man's arm and ending in a lumpy, engorged phallus. It cracks like a whip, leaving a whine in the air before slithering backwards. We hide behind a crate; the snuffling, rooting sounds seem to echo from all around us.
"Taran, can you tell me what the fuck that is?"
"Yes. But I'm not going to." Taran shifts the grip on his sword, holding the blade in a murder-stoke stance. "Here's what's going to happen. You're going to run and dive into the opening into the river. Stay still, float along with the current and get out when you leave the town."
"What? No! You said I was in charge!"
He grabs me by the front of my shift, bringing our faces close. "That was then, this is now. You're my squire Ulf, and I'm also your big brother, so do as I bloody well say!" He hisses, throwing me down.
I scrabble to my feet, dumbfounded. He shoves me. "GO!" he yells, breaking from cover with a war-cry.
I dart outwards, following the sound of the rushing water. There is a deafening mew which ends in a hacking, phlegmy gargle. A massive tentacle smashes into a crate, breaking it to splinters. Turning around, I see my brother dart from side to side, his footwork perfect. A mass looms out into the shaft of moonlight, a bulbous lump of rolling eyes which pop and vanish under the oily bulk.
Taran smashes his sword hilt down. Acrid smoke curls up from a dried and withered stump. Suddenly the entire mass rumbles forward, sending boxes flying as the hideous creature squats before us. More eyes. A mass of thrashing limbs of all description and a huge central orb the colour of a festering wound. It rolls unblinking in the socket, fixed on Taran.
Taran bellows, striking out at it as a tendril licks across his forearm. He shouts out in pain and even over the foulness of the creature I can smell his burning flesh.
"Hey! HEY! Over here you ugly cunt!" I wave my arms wildly and run around to the side.

Brigandine

"ULF! FUCK OFF! DO AS YOU'RE TOLD FOR ONCE IN YOUR LIFE!" I see the fear in Taran's eyes. For me, not for him.

"I can't hear you!" I yell, grabbing up a lump of wood to hurl at the beast. The splintered wood catches it in an eyeball and it bursts like a boil. It makes rumbling gurgle and lurches towards me.

I swing my sword in desperate arcs, trying to keep the tendrils away from me. One wraps around my sword and I wrench it free, the metal subtly glowing and pitted with the heat. As it's distracted, Taran leaps forward, bellowing the name of Oswald. The murder-stroke hits and the sword hilt buries itself into the central eye with a terrible sound, akin to dozens of animalistic voices screaming at once. The mass shrivels into itself, curling up like a dead spider before slinking back into the shadows.

I run to Taran, seeing him doubled over and gasping with the effort. His face is pale and drained, eyes bloodshot and streaming. "Come on!" he manages. "The river!"

The wool washing pit is a few yards away and we stop before the hatch over the river, looking down at the black, swirling water. Taran sheathes his sword and plunges into the depths, and I follow after. We drift frantically, keeping our movements to the bare minimum to avoid drowning as we are bashed against the river bank and the floating filth of the town.

All around us we can hear the hue-and-cry. Misshapen forms prowl the town, grasping hefty cudgels and crossbows. I make out slurred curses and weird, misbegotten oaths as the entire town searches for us.

When it is safe, Taran forces himself onto the bank, grabbing my outreached forearm as I hurtle past. He drags me ashore and we both lie gasping for air, shattered and exhausted.

Taran leans over and punches me as hard as he can in the shoulder. "You stupid cunt!" he yells. "You could have died!"

I force myself up, still spluttering. I hack up some water and take some deep breaths before turning to his furious face. "Yes, but I didn't. So there." I fall back down and I hear Taran break out into hysterical laughter. I join in as we lie under the bulging moon, soaked to the skin and shivering with cold.

I swear loudly as I remember Taran's armour was left behind, and is probably being pawed over by some degenerate.

"Taran?"

"Yes, Ulf?"

"How fucked are we, exactly?"

Taran gets his breath and staggers to his feet, dragging me upright.

"Pretty fucked Ulf. Pretty fucked."

Chapter 20:
Fire and Ashes

"I'm just glad to have found you, my lord."

The muffled words stabbed into my aching head and the room was tilting dangerously from side to side. My mouth felt like a badger's arsehole and my guts squirmed and rumbled.

"Yes. And now you will un-find me."

"Lord?"

The voices were coming from outside my room. Duke Colsarne and someone else. I sat on the edge of the bed and eavesdropped.

"You couldn't find me. You don't know where I am. I should have thought that would be obvious."

"But, my lord! This message comes from Queen Karidine's own hand. I was to deliver it to you and take back a reply bearing your seal."

"Yes. It is such a shame that you couldn't find me."

"But, my lord, please! You don't know what you ask of me. To lie to the Queen's seneschal, to break my bond as a messenger . . ."

"You only get paid if you bring back my seal, correct?"

"Yes, lord."

"Tragically, you couldn't find me. However, you did stumble across five Guilder in the road on your journey back. Also, no-one had to break your legs."

There was the soft clink of gold followed by the rapid footsteps of a man who knows a good deal when he hears one.

I waited a few minutes, then dressed and headed downstairs. The brothers were sitting at a table in the corner, both looking sorry for themselves. Decroix looked up and gave me a thin smile. "Good morning, Ulf. Did you sleep well?"

"No. Not really." There was a jug of water on the table, so I downed a big slug and swished it around my mouth, spitting it out onto the floor.

Quentin winced as a bit of water dribbled out the side of my face. "Do you have to do that here?"

"Yes." I sat down next to them, closed my eyes, and rubbed the sides of my head. Quentin said something to me, but I didn't hear, and didn't care enough to ask him to repeat it. Marl started talking about something. Loudly. I thought seriously about throwing a chair at him.

A wonderful smell filled the room, and was accompanied by a soft clunk on the table before me. I opened my eyes and saw a wooden bowl, filled with fried ham and three big, fresh rolls.

I grabbed the serving maid's arm before she left. "I want you to know: right now, you are without a doubt the most beautiful woman in the world."

She smiled at me awkwardly. "Ummm, thank you, sir." she said, gently pulling her hand free.

"Hold on, let me give you something." I reached into my purse, then remembered that I had spent all of my money trying to loudly purchase the brothel we were in last night.

Decroix sighed and handed me five Wyear. I pressed one into the girl's hand, and it disappeared instantly. She scuttled off and left us to breakfast.

Quentin smacked his lips. "This is good! I haven't seen baps this lovely since-"

"Yes, yes. You're very clever, Quentin." Decroix sighed and took another bite. "We're headed off in about an hour. Just the final preparations to make ready.

"I'm not complaining, but why did we need the two nights?" I asked. "We could have had the horses shod in only a few hours, and it doesn't take that long to pack some sacks with food."

Decroix shrugged and gave me a wry grin. "You'll see."

"So, it's due west to Missden, and then the north-west road to Scandar?"

Decroix nodded. "Yep."

I patted the side of Reed's neck. A couple of days rest had done her good, and her coat was gleaming. The new shoes clattered along the road. The western route was an easy road to travel, and despite the autumn weather the going wasn't too bad. The money that passed between Auldcall and Missden meant that the sensitive arses of merchants had paid for a half-decent road to be laid.

Three weeks went by quickly as we travelled onwards. The land was rich and fat, and the weather stayed fair. Amongst the farmsteads were coppiced woods, saplings planted neatly in a row, destined to end up on someone's cooking fire.

The inns we stayed at were not quite as grand as The Falcon, but they did for the night. When we were between beds, the nights started to get bitterly cold. We stopped at farms to refill our water skins, taking it in shifts.

Smoke.

We were five days' ride from the town when Quentin spotted it. He yelled out, pointing. Decroix's gelding reared at the sudden noise and he pulled on the reins, cursing. I could barely make out the rising plume, but it was there, alright.

I sighed. It had been far too long without someone around me dying horribly, so I suppose it was just a matter of time.

Duke Colsarne and his daughter stopped at the side of the road. Lady Alexia smiled at me grimly. "Ulf, if you would be so kind, please take two men and ride ahead to ensure our safety."

I nodded in acknowledgement. Decroix was shushing his horse and patting its neck, glaring at Quentin. "Come on, let's go."

"Where?"

"To find out what the plume of smoke is."

He sighed. "I thought so. Bugger." We spurred our horses and rode hard ahead of the group, Reed's hooves clattering on the cobbles.

The inn was a blackened wreck when we arrived, a heatwave shimmering over the gutted remains, dying warmth from the shattered timbers.

Quentin whistled and sucked his teeth. "Fuck me . . ." he muttered.

We dismounted and tied up the horses. The embers were still glowing with a blanket of snowy-ash over the skeleton of the inn. I poked around the debris with the tip of my sword, turning over a fallen beam.

"Quentin, Ulf, over here!" Decroix waved us over. "No bodies, but look at this." Decroix kneeled to the ground and rubbed at some of the dried mud, baked by the nearby inferno.

My knees briefly grumbled as I bent down. "What exactly am I looking at, Decroix?"

"See the little brown flakes? Dried blood. Lots of it. Here outside where the door would have been."

Quentin looked worried. "So, it wasn't an accident then?"

Decroix pinched the bridge of his nose and sighed. "Well, Quentin, it is possible that someone dropped a candle, couldn't figure out how to pick it up again, set fire to the inn, ran out the door, tripped up and fell on something incredibly sharp, bled everywhere, and then everyone else ran out, fell over them and proceeded to bleed everywhere, then they all went back inside and burned to death out of embarrassment. However, a more likely hypothesis is that some bastards set fire to the inn, killed everyone who ran out, and chucked the bodies back into the inn."

Quentin paused for a beat. "But it's not impossible, right?"

"Please, just for a moment, shut up and let me think."

Quentin gave me a shrug and started looking around in the bushes. I strolled round to the side of the building, where the storage entrance normally is. There was a blackened, heavy branch with two iron loops around it. "They must have blocked the cellar, too. Stop anyone getting out that way."

Decroix nodded in agreement and clicked his tongue. "Two questions. Who-"

"-and why." Quentin finished for him. "If they were just going to rob the place, why burn it down? It attracts attention. Why not just kill whoever's inside? There must have been a few of them to be able to slay an entire inn's worth of patrons and staff."

I piped up. "A band of brigands would have just killed them and taken their stuff." I moved forward gingerly across the hot rubble. "Here we are . . ." I wiped away some hot ash with my boot and bent down, pulling at a loose flagstone. "Under the hearth. That's where the good stuff is. Petty cash and day to day money you can keep in a strongbox, but you want to hide valuables. It's an old trick."

Sure enough, there lay a small box, the hinges bound in iron. It was locked, so I smashed it against the ground until it sprang open. I found few Guilder and about fifty Wyear, which I scooped up into my pouch. I'm no grave robber, but dead folk don't need money.

"That has to help us with the 'who'. Robbers and thieves would have known that trick. Or, at the very least, they would have held a knife to someone's cock till they talked."

Quentin cleared his throat. "So, with that in mind, let us consider the 'why'. There aren't many villages about. That's the point of a roadside inn. They're isolated."

"Trap." I said flatly. "It's a fucking trap."

Decroix looked at me puzzled. "Go on."

"Think about it. What's the time?"

"Late afternoon."

"Exactly. This is about the time we would be looking to stop at this inn to rest up."

"So?"

"My point is, I will bet my left bollock that a little further along the road, we will find a clear patch of ground, a convenient if slightly messy pile of firewood and a campsite ready for us to stay at. Then, during the night, one or all of us end up with our throats slit wide open."

There came an awkward pause while Decroix weighed up what I said. We mounted up and rode off back to the main party. Duke Colsarne looked less than pleased with our report.

Brigandine

"Father, I have a plan." He turned in the saddle towards his daughter. She explained her idea and he nodded in agreement.

"Marl, Decroix. Make it happen."

I was right. We came across the trap just before dusk. I felt slightly touched by the fact that there is even a gralloched deer. Personally, I thought they were overdoing it. After warning everyone not to eat it, I found some sticks, set up a spit and soon the venison fat started dripping into the flames with a maddening smell. Marl kicked up a fuss, but I told him that firstly, it was probably poisoned, and secondly, he was quite fat enough as he was. He grumbled but took my point.

So, there I was, in a comfy bed. Duke Colsarne had that magical combination of being very old and very rich that meant his bed was warmer and softer than any other I've ever slept in.

But I wasn't sleeping. No-one was.

Quentin lay near to me, acting as a double for Lady Alexia. Marl wanted to take the place of bait, but I tactfully pointed out that we would be better off with him on his feet to fight off the attackers. After my joke about the deer, I didn't think it was fair to point out that unless Lady Alexia had recently eaten half a dozen salmon and started farting like an angry bull, Marl would make a poor substitute. Quentin was lithe with fine, long hair. He was also a fair fighter, so I felt happy to have him with me.

I blinked hard to keep my eyes open. The only sound was the wind, whipping through the camp and snapping at the canvas. I heard a soft rustle. Not the sound of trying to slip out in the night to piss without waking the rest of the tent. No, this was the sound of someone being very, very careful. Quentin nodded to me in the darkness and we lay still.

Moonlight spilled through the rip in the canvas. He was good, certainly better than most, but we were expecting him. I heard a small clink as he knocked over the piles of coins I left on the floor and Quentin jumped up like a cat, dagger in hand.

Quentin stabbed quickly, cutting him across the forearm only to get a punch in the jaw for his troubles. He sprawled on the floor and I darted forward, sword point first. The assassin jumped back out of the tent and I barged after him, slashing aside the canvas.

He stumbled on the ground and I hacked down between his shoulder blades.

"TO ARMS!" I bellowed, and men came spilling from their tents, weapons readied.

There were about a score that I could see. Some in the trees, others lurking in the shadows.

We had fifteen warriors, but they hadn't expected us to be awake and armoured. I ran forward, followed by Quentin. Two of them charged us, pulling swords from beneath their cloaks.

I swept my sword in a low arc, biting into one man's calf, then wrenched it free and severed his arm at the elbow. Quentin swung his short sword overhead, cutting the other across the brow. He staggered back, blood in his eyes, and Quentin tossed him over his hip before stabbing him through the ribs.

I glanced around. One of our own lay spread out in the mud, fingers twitching. Next to him, Marl stood fighting a big man with a felling axe, and I could see he was struggling. An axe can be every bit as dangerous as a sword in the hands of someone who knows what they're doing, and this bugger did. Marl blocked and ran his blade down the shaft, trying to sever the axeman's fingers, but he pulled back for another swift attack. Marl made a high guard and struck out the meet the blow, the axe head biting deep into the blade.

I sprinted over to Marl's side and we cut him down together. I tore his throat out and blood spilled down into his jerkin. He tried to say something to me as he died, but I didn't care enough to listen.

Another of our men fell with a scream, and I could see him bleeding out from the corner of my eye. Two of the attackers jumped over the body, running towards the last sealed tent. The food store where Duke Colsarne and his daughter were hidden.

"TO ME!" Marl whirled his sword above his head and barrelled through camp to his lord's side. Others were running to join him.

Brigandine

I saw Simon fighting two of them, trying to run around their sides to keep them in a line, but they weren't having it and were driving him back with savage blows.

Fuck it, Marl's had this one sorted.

I pushed through the swirling chaos towards Simon. My blade clashed against another and I pushed the hilt forward with all my strength, making my enemy stumble. Simon lunged and took him in the side, darting back to a guard. With the two of us, we cut the other bastard to pieces and left him to die.

We turned back to the supply tent. Steel flashed in the moonlight and the first attacker fell, doubled over on the end of a longsword. Duke Colsarne stepped out of the supply tent and took up a fencing stance, point raised. Swords clashed and I could see his arm knocked aside from the blow, only to swiftly parry the second strike. Colsarne brought his sword round in a great arc, feinting at the last moment to score a hit across the chest.

That was when Marl reached the tent, charging and snarling like a boar, and ran the bugger through. I arrived a moment later. The duke was panting with the effort, but still alive. The rest of the bastards were fleeing now.

Marl rallied our men to his side and counted heads. "Bastards!" He spat, shaking with rage. We brought back three bodies, and six of their friends wordlessly carried them away for burial.

Colsarne stood breathless, hands on his knees. He waved away Lady Alexia and stood up tall, glancing over his household. "Thank you." He took a deep breath, chest still rising. "Thank you all for your courage." He glanced at Marl and the big man bowed his head.

Decroix ran into camp panting, his sword glistening wet. "They've legged it!" He shouted. "Fuck knows where they are now." Decroix snarled and wiped his blade on the grass. "Light a fire. Dawn is only a few hours away, so there's no point going to sleep but get some rest if you can. We break camp at first light."

I scraped my flint and steel together, and managed to spark up a decent fire to chase away the chill. We had plenty of wood about, so it blazed away merrily. I felt the warmth lick at my face and spread over me, and tried not to think about the three men who had died. Simon dragged over a few decent sized logs and joined me.

Duke Colsarne held out his hands to the flames and rubbed them together. It was only then, in the firelight, that I noticed just how thin they were, his fingers like pale twigs. He wrapped his great fur cloak around himself, shivering in the cold air.

"Ulf?"

"Yes, lord?"

"Common bandits don't try to kill a heavily protected man with an armoured retinue."

"No, lord."

"So, to the question at hand."

"Lord?"

"Ulf. You're not stupid. And neither am I, so please don't pretend you are."

"Well, my lord, the main question that leaps to my mind is, who hired them?"

He smiled thinly and turned back to the fire. He lowered himself down slowly onto a log, wincing as he did so. "Thank you for playing your part, Ulf. You delivered an admirable performance as a sleeping duke."

"Thank you for trusting me to do it."

"I'm sorry? Do you think I trust you? Then I am afraid you have misunderstood our relationship entirely."

"With respect, lord, is there a person you do trust?"

He looked into the fire, throwing on a small log. The sparks leapt up and swiftly died on the ground. "Do horses count as people?"

"I prefer Reed to most people, but she doesn't have anything particularly useful to say."

"Neither do most people." He flicked a small twig into the fire with his foot and it twisted and crackled. "Most people are idiots, Ulf. Happy to go along with whatever keeps them fed, warm, and distracted. But most importantly, they want whatever keeps them safe from the vicious men of this world. Even if that means they have to be vicious to other people first."

There was an awkward pause, and I worried for a moment I had heard more than I should. Then I remembered that Duke Colsarne had never once told me anything more than exactly what he needed me to know.

"We ride onwards to Scandar, as quickly as we can. Queen Karidine must be informed. I have no doubt that her Majesty is aware of the situation, but she has yet to act. The extent of the threat must be made apparent to the court, and I will force her hand, if I must."

I nodded in acknowledgement.

"The world is full of bastards, Ulf. Some of them are cruel, murderous bastards. Wicked, honourless men who would burn us all to cinders if they could get a good price for the ash."

I threw on another log. Fuck it. Might as well use it up.

"There are spineless bastards. Cowards, sheep, and weaklings who will flock to the banner of any who promise them a bigger food bowl or a shinier chain."

I nodded again. He wasn't talking to me, so it didn't matter, but I felt like I should.

"And then there are bastards like us. Human enough to need to protect the world, but enough of a bastard to do what must be done, for all our sakes."

It was in that moment that I saw him for what he really was: an old man playing a dangerous game, where the stakes were the lives of his family and everything they had ever built, ready to be dashed to pieces in an instant. Someone who must watch men die to protect him and spend their lives like tokens on a playing mat. Someone who has to live with that weight, every day.

Then I remembered him gutting the first unlucky bastard who tried to murder him and his daughter, and I recalled that he was, first and foremost, a ruthless, cunning old sod.

Chapter 21: Meef

"So, what's the plan?"

We've survived the night. Which is good or bad, depending on how you look at it. Now, Taran is looking at me expectantly.

"Seriously?"

"Yep."

I sigh and roll my head. My body is aching all over, but for some reason, my neck is worst of all from sleeping on the cold, hard earth.

"Well, we need to get back to The Hearth."

"Agreed. How?"

I look around the landscape. It's ragged, bare looking land. I see a few mangy sheep clinging to the scrub, teeth tugging at a few good patches of grass. "Well, we don't have any horses, so I suppose we're walking."

"An excellent plan. Except neither of us has any shoes."

I look down at my mud-splattered feet. "Bugger..."

"Bugger indeed! Plus, we don't have any clothes, so we'll probably freeze to death. Plus, the entire town is probably hunting for us."

"So, go on then."

"What?"

"What are we going to do?"

"I don't know what you mean. This is your call."

I roll my eyes. "Come on, Taran. We both know you've got an idea."

He tries on a mock innocent look which doesn't fool me for a moment. I fold my arms and treat him to a withering glare.

"Do you want a clue?"

"Go on. Give me a clue."

"Sheep."

I look again at the slightly pathetic looking animals. One of them is hobbling with a foot swollen up like a handful of strawberries. I'm not an expert on animal husbandry, but I'm sure they have seen better days.

"Even if we could catch one, how are we going to get a fire going? We could wear the skin, but it would still be bloody and-"

He holds up a hand to cut me off. "Ulf, this is painful to listen to. Please, come on. I know we're both tired, but think."

I curse under my breath, which Taran pretends not to hear. "Sheep. Sheep. Sheep . . . they're stupid, woolly. You can eat them . . . too small to ride . . . live on a farm-"

"Yippie!" Taran shouts out with joy. "Where there are sheep there is a farm. And where there is a farm you will find . . ?"

"Farmers?"

"Exactly. People we can ask for help. People who might have some old clothes and a hot meal for travellers down on their luck."

I furrow my brow. "Why exactly would they give a shit about us?"

He shrugs. "Why wouldn't they? Besides, do you have any better ideas?"

"What if there are guards from the town waiting there? They'll have sent out patrols."

"Easy! Then we kill them and take their boots. Or they kill us. Either way, we don't have to worry about having cold feet. Now hurry up and get walking, time is wasting!"

The farm is a shit heap. It takes us about an hour's walk to get there. A half-blind dog looks up as we step over a stone wall and into the yard. He makes a sort of a cross between a whine and a fart and settles back down as we walk past. Taran bends down to scratch him behind the ears.

I wrinkle my nose. "Careful, he'll have fleas."

Taran shrugs and walks up to the farmhouse door. It's a small home with the wattle crumbling away in places, and the thatch sags like a paunch. He raps once on the door and it swings open.

"You're back early my love-" An old women looks up at us with a start and takes a step back. "Ikka blind me!" she swears.

Taran takes a step back and smiles at her. "I'm sorry to have startled you, young lady. Is your mother at home?"

Rather than slamming the door in our face, she laughs and opens the door wider. "Well, come in, come in!" She looks me up and down disapprovingly. "You'll freeze to death! Sit down, I'll build the fire up."

I have to duck as we step through the portal and blink hard as my eyes accustom themselves to the gloom. Taran follows a moment later.

"Thank you so much. It's deeply appreciated, my lady." He smiles as she throws a fat log onto the hearth.

"Oh stop! I'm a married woman, I'll have you know."

"And you're a married woman I know I'll have!" he quips back.

She gives Taran a mock frown and wags her finger. "Less of that, young man! Anyway, what are good people like you doing out in weather like this, dressed like that?"

Taran slaps the side of his head. "Where are my manners! Lady, I beg your pardon." He stands and bows low. "Sir Taran of Banrillar, of the Order of the Cleansing Flame, and my squire, Ulf of Banrillar." He rises, a brilliant smile on his lips.

She scrabbles up to courtesy and he raises her hand to stop her.

"Please, good lady, we are in your debt."

"Well! Fancy me! A couple of young, handsome knights wearing nothing but bedclothes calling at my door." She sighs. "You're a few years too late, mind you."

"Don't be silly! Only one of us is a knight. Ulf is just a grubby squire." I roll my eyes at the mock flirting, but I can feel the cold leave my bones, so it's not all bad.

She moves over to the hearth and my eyes are drawn to an iron pot hanging from a chain in the chimney. She pours in some more milk from a jug and two big handfuls of oats.

"You look half dead, Aeder bless you. We'll be having luncheon in an hour when my husband returns from fields. You'll join us? It's rare we have company."

"It would be an honour." he says gallantly.

The old woman fetches some shirts, both in desperate need of patching, and a pair of breeches worn thin as a miser's ham slice. Taran passes the trousers to me, on the basis that his legs are better looking than mine. *After a while, a bent old man opens the door and beams at us in surprise and delight.*

"Magara! You didn't tell me we had guests." *He hangs up a woollen hood on a hook by the door and shakes my hand warmly. I smile weakly and stand to receive him.*

"I'm Illias. Has she been looking after you?"

"Thank you for your hospitality." *I mutter.*

"Our pleasure, boy. Our pleasure." *I can see Taran struggling to stifle a chuckle as I bite my tongue.*

The pottage is plain, but it's hot and it fills my stomach. I scrape the spoon across the bowl for every last morsel.

"Growing lad, eh?" *The old man jabs me in the ribs.* "All boys are the same. Walking stomachs!"

He chuckles at his own joke and I force a grin. "Yes, sir. I suppose so."

"Don't you worry, my boy." *He stands up and for one awful moment I think he's going to ruffle my hair, but instead, he puts another scoop of pottage into my bowl with a warm smile.*

"Meef?"

"Pardon?"

He beams with pride. "It's my own special little secret. I'd love to show it to you!"

My hand moves to my sword hilt in cynical wariness but he gets up with a grunt and potters over to a large sack by the chimney breast. He slowly pulls out a joint of meat and places it reverently onto a nearby table. "It's my own masterpiece! There's nothing like it in all of Rusia. Probably Ashenfell!"

Magara gives us an apologetic look and Taran nods kindly at her.

"Now, young man!" *He turns back towards me.* "What's the best thing about lamb?"

"You can eat it?"

"AHAH!" *He waggles a finger at me.* "Yes! Lamb is tender and lovely, but there's not much of it. And you don't get the wool for years as you do with sheep." *He leans forward.* "But mutton is tougher and harder to chew, isn't it?" *He takes a long knife, the blade worn thin by decades of sharpening and carefully shaves away a slice and stabs it onto the point.*

"Careful, my boy! The knife is very sharp."

I hesitate for a moment at the grey, slightly furry looking meat in front of me. Taran raises his eyebrows at me and I gingerly pick it off the knife.

"Careful." he says again, worried I might slip and cut my own throat.

"Yes, sir." I mutter, wondering if we were better off with the cultists. "Thank you." I take it all in one bite and push it into my cheek, the tip of my tongue wilting at the taste.

"Now," he continues, turning to Taran who sits in rapt attention, "you're wondering about the name! 'Well,' I thought to myself, 'What's the finest meat of all?'"

"Venison?" I venture.

"Beef." He gently corrects me. "But it's a rich man who can kill a cow for the meat while it's still young and fresh. So, I came up with this little gem of an idea! Meef! The husbandry of mutton with the taste of best fresh beef!"

I've eaten fresh beef, red and bloody, with the juice running down my fingers. Baked into a pie with spices and wine. Roasted on a spit and slathered with sauce. As I force my teeth into action and feel the grit rub against my palate, there is one thought shouting louder than any other in my skull.

This does not taste like fresh beef.

"I can't tell you the full recipe. That's my little secret. But I will tell you this. One word, lad. One word." He leans in so close I can see the hair in his nostrils. "Rainwater!"

Taran stands up. "May I?"

"Of course, sir! So rude of me." He hands my brother the knife handle, and Taran cuts himself a dainty sliver before popping it into his mouth. He swallows it almost instantly. "My compliments, sir! It is quite simply, unique! Like nothing I have tried before."

"See, Magara! I told you! Didn't I tell you?"

"Yes, dear, you were right."

"I told you people would love it once they tried it."

"Yes, dear." As he puts the joint back into the sack and onto the chimney breast, she gives us both an apologetic look.

"You're welcome to stay as long as you need, good sirs." he says.

Megara chimes in, "Oh, yes! We'd be happy for the company."

Yet again, Taran smiles. There's a genuine warmth in his eyes. "Thank you both so much for your help, but we need to leave at nightfall. Our journey is an important one, and we cannot delay any longer than we must."

The old man nods sadly, and his wife tries to hide her disappointment. He sucks his teeth for a moment, probably probing for a stray thread of meef. He drums his fingers on the table before he sighs and stands up. "Well, you can't walk for however many miles without shoes. Where's that old hide we were saving for the winter? The one we got from the peddler with the lazy eye."

"You left it in the barn, Illias. But you can't be thinking to make shoes! Your own pair is falling apart. You've worn them for years."

"Then they'll probably last a few more. But if we don't do something this little boy's toes will freeze off, and how could we live with ourselves? An innocent child, in the freezing cold of winter."

There's not a trace of sarcasm in his voice. He fumbles for a bit of sting and measures my foot, shakily tying a knot in the right places. "There we are . . ." he mutters. "Sir Taran, I hate to ask, but could you help me with the cutting? The knives are sharp, but my hands aren't what they once were."

My brother puts a hand on his shoulder, then embraces him. "Sir, it would be an honour. We thank you."

They step outside the hovel, and I blink at the sudden sunlight. Magara tuts and closes the door behind them. She beams at me and puts her hand on mine. She pats my forearm and I look down at her wrinkled, spotted hand. "While the men are making you some nice new shoes, you can help me stitch up a pair of trousers. Mind you, I'll need a bit of help with threading the needle. I can do it, don't you worry. But you're in a hurry so it might be better if you do it."

She pokes around in the corner, which smells strongly of dog. "I know it's not grand, but your brother would rather be warm than not, I'll wager." She brings out a box of worn-out scraps. Tattered rags and strips of cloth in every colour. Every piece is small. "He doesn't have trousers and its way down in the fall . . ." she mutters.

So, with patches on our britches, stiff but hole-free shoes, and Taran with his trousers of many colours, we hurry off towards The Hearth. We manage to get about twenty yards away from the farm before I start laughing and making fun of him.

"Taran!"

"Yes?"

"You look so stupid. You know that, don't you?"

"Yes."

"As in, absurd. You realise that, don't you?"

"Yes."

I sigh. *"Taran, for fuck's sake. You look like a cut-rate jester who got dragged through a hedge and you smell like a dog's fart. Don't you understand?"*

"Yes."

I give up. We walk for a few minutes. The moon is shrouded by clouds and our breath streams in the night air.

"Ulf?"

I stop. *"Yes?"*

"You realise that those people gave us food when they didn't have to, gave up the goods that were going to keep them warm in winter, and spent the best part of a day in labour to make sure we wouldn't freeze to death. You know that, don't you, Ulf?"

There is a horrible pause, and I feel like an arsehole. *"Yes."* I say quietly.

"And that they treated us with kindness and hospitality when most people would have slammed a door on us and left us to die? Do you realise that?"

"Yes."

He turns and holds me by the shoulders, his eyes full of disappointment.

"Ulf, without them, we would both probably die of exposure tonight. Without that man's disgusting 'meef', our bellies would be empty. They are good people, Ulf. These are the people we have sworn to protect. To fight and die for if we have to. Do you understand?"

I grunt with frustration. *"Fine! FINE! I understand, Taran! I fucking understand!"* I throw my hands up. *"I'm sorry for acting like an ungrateful cunt. They are good people and we need to protect them. There, I understand! Happy?"*

Taran lets go and looks at me. *"I honestly don't know if you do, Ulf. I really don't."* He turns away. *"Now, get moving. There's a lot of miles to cover before dawn."*

Chapter 22:
Red

"Fuck me . . ." I sighed as I rubbed my neck. I had drifted off for a moment with my head at a weird angle, and it felt like I'd been strangled by a bear. We packed with haste and readied ourselves to go. Luckily Marl had a needle and some waxed linen thread for stitching up boots, so I sewed up the rent in the duke's tent as quickly as I could. Better to do it then than in the twilight when we were setting up camp.

The ride was hard going. We were cursed with a cold drizzle throughout the day, and the droplets hung heavy from the fur on Lady Alexia's mantle. I snuck a look at her and I could see faint worry lines, which matched the deep creases on her father's face.

After a week we arrived at Missden. It was a booming town has been thriving ever since the fall of Craftvale. The town had been successful since long before then. The kings and queens of Ashenfell have stocked their larders with the goods of Missden for ages, and bulging wagons churning the road between Missden and the royal seat at Scandar for centuries.

We reached the first of Missden's famous orchards several miles outside of the city, and rode between neat rows of fruit trees of every kind all the way to the gates. When we crested a hill just before the city, I could see a new road, cutting southwest to The Hearth, lined with vineyards where workers were busy picking the last of the grapes, their deep red contrasting with the vines.

I glowered at the distant sight of them and spat on the ground. Bright red fucking grapes. Shouting it out to the whole fucking world, so that when we are all nothing but dust and bones, people will still talk about Windor Decare.

"Fucking cunt . . ." I muttered.

Decroix looked at me bemused. "Ulf?"

"Doesn't matter."

He shrugged and turned back in the saddle.

It didn't matter. Not anymore.

The guards saluted as they waved us through. The painted statue of Queen Karidine was particularly grand. On a plinth directly below, looking up at her with devotion was a much smaller statue of the local guild alderman who commissioned it. Although, if I was feeling cynical, I'd say he was looking up her skirt.

Past the eastern gate lay a wide boulevard flanked with tailors and clothiers. Each shop had an intricate, gaudy banner hanging from its upstairs window to demonstrate their skills. A patchwork of colours and stitching, each bearing twisting vines, dancing beasts, and graceful kings and queens dancing, hunting, and fighting.

Quentin whistled. "Would you look at that, Ulf!" I could see him starring, so I followed his gaze to the fountain in the central square ahead.

There were dozens of people staggering around, and the water was bright, bright red.

I swore under my breath as we rode up into the square and the sweet smell hit me in the nose. Wine. The fountain was full of fucking wine! It says something about how much I hated the bastard that I was grumpy about the prospect of a free drink.

Decroix organised an inn for us just off the side of the square, a new building with a pair of crossed wooden swords as its sign. Typical. Just my fucking luck.

I forced myself to stop grinding my teeth and we stabled the horses. The stablemaster avoided my gaze as I handed over the reins. When I caught sight of my reflection in the smoked glass windows of the inn, I wasn't surprised.

Brigandine

Duke Colsarne went to his private room along with Marl and a couple of the more competent men at arms. I fished out a few coins and slapped them down on the bar.

"Ale. Now."

He looked up at me puzzled. "You realise that's wine in the fountain outside, don't you?"

I snarled. "What part of 'ale' are you too thick to understand?"

He shrugged and brought out a jug and filled it to the brim. "Thank you, sir. Bloody guilds always think filling fountains with wine an' giving away food is a plentiful an' kind thing to do." He snorted. "Well, it isn't for the bloody innkeepers, I'll tell you that!"

He handed me a flagon. "Why pay for something when we can just drink it from a fountain like a common horse with a trough!" He threw up his hands and leant forward, forearms on the bar. "Between you and me, the Decares are a right bunch of cunts, the lot of 'em!"

I nodded and a thin smile spread over my face. "So, what's with the wine? Can't be cheap for the guilds."

He shrugged. "They do it every time he visits, to show our allegiance to the head of the Decare family and the Knight Commander of the Order of the Cleansing Flame. If it weren't for them, the town wouldn't be as rich as it."

"Red for the Decare livery? How subtle." I said sarcastically.

"Same with this inn. Crossed swords." He pointed to the sign swinging in the window. "Statues. Inn names. Streets. Anything new has to have a tie in to the family for the guilds to give approval."

"I'm surprised he's not staying here. Thought he'd love it."

He shook his head. "No. He's down at the Bloody Pelt. Big place. Just off the corner of Armourer's Way. Good pies, but the beds are too soft, so I've been told."

I placed a Wyear down and walked back to my table.

"What's this for?"

"A good tip!" I called back.

I left Decroix to organise the supplies for the last leg of the journey, and grabbed Quentin for a stroll. Specifically, we went for a stroll around all the taverns I could find.

I concentrated on getting as drunk as I could and left the talking to Quentin. He told a few jokes and did a bit of tumbling to get the crowds going. He even picked up a few Ecars as he passed his hood around. The beer spilled out from my cheek as I downed another tankard and wiped my face. He started eyeing up the barmaids in the same way a practised merchant might judge a bolt of cloth.

Going from inn to inn there were a few older buildings with proper names, but most were like the Crossed Swords. Stupid names like The Noble Purpose or The Ardent Defender. Later into the evening, we came to a packed place called The Swift Hunter and the room was starting to feel warm and spinning a little, but I was still a grumpy sod.

"Why isn't there an inn called 'The Compete Bastard?'" I shouted above the noise at Quentin.

"Sorry, just remind me again why you hate this man so much?"

"Fuck you! That's why!" I snapped.

He rolled his eyes and took a swig. "Not bad. Nice malty notes with a good aftertaste." He mummers. "How's yours."

"STUPID AND POINTLESS!" I yelled in the tavern wench's direction. "It's shit! Like this whole town!" She ignored me, which was probably for the best, because I was a drunken arsehole at that point and I really just wanted to fight or fuck something. A couple of off duty guards gave me a dirty look, so I sneered back at them, showing off the mess on the side of my face. Quentin read the room quickly and dragged me out by my arm. "Come on, Ulf! Not again . . ."

We staggered out into the street and the door slammed behind us.

"Tossers!" I yelled and kicked at a loose cobble, watching it scatter into the night. I held up a finger. "One more tavern. Then I'll go back to the Crossed Swords. Deal?"

Quentin gave a small sigh and rolled his eyes. "Go on, deal."

It took us a while to find Armourer's Way, but we got there in the end. The Bloody Pelt was a three-storied inn with a stable on the side. All around were men at arms wearing the Decare colours. Two black swords on a red field. I 'accidentally' walked into one on the way over.

"Watch where you're going there, friend!" he yelled, stumbling into a wall.

"Why don't you stick a knife up your arse!" I called back.

He looked at me and walked away muttering under his breath.

"Cunt!" I spat after him.

"Ulf, I'm not sure this was a great idea. Maybe we should just get back? There's a long ride tomorrow and we've both had enough to drink for one night."

I held my finger and tried to stand steady. "You said one more drink! You said one more!"

Quentin smiled desperately. "Please, Ulf, come on! Nothing good is going to come out of this, we both know. What are you going to achieve? You'll end up with the shit beaten out of you and spending the night in a cell."

I held up my arms. "How do you know? It's might go perfectly!" I pushed open the door and scanned the room and sure enough, there he was. The smug bastard.

Ulric App Decare.

He sat in a corner chatting to two of his men. They had a platter in front of him: spiced sausage, runny cheese. I think there were herbs in the bread but I couldn't be sure. He poured out some wine for the three of them and laughed.

"Look at him there." I snarled to Quentin. "Laughing. With his friends. I told you he was a cunt."

He sighed. "Yes, Ulf. Why anyone would want to be in a tavern for any reason other than sitting alone and scowling is beyond me. Who would want to speak to people and have a nice time? The inconsiderate prick."

I turned around to tell him to piss off, but he'd already walked away. Sod it. I didn't need him.

Ulric was six years older than me, but he looked far younger. More hot meals and nights in warm beds and less stolen food and sleeping in ditches will do that to a man.

He looked up as I walked over and I saw the realisation slowly spread across his face.

"ULF?"

I nodded.

"Ulf! By my life! I haven't seen you in, well, years!" He gestured to the men to his left and right. "These are my friends and men at arms, Carter and Artimus." He stood up and smiled at me. His hair was still full and long, framing his face. "Ulf, please come and sit with us. I know things were very bad in past. Especially with your brother, and how you left the Order." He looked down. He couldn't meet my gaze. I ground my teeth and I knew he can see it through the tattered mess of my cheek. There was a pause. The two men with him shuffled awkwardly in their seats.

"Ulf, listen. Times are hard in the land. Things are changing. My father says the kingdom needs good men who will fight for her." He gestured to the table. "Please Ulf, sit down and drink with-"

I smashed the bottle into his face.

The glass shattered, spraying across the table with a wave of wine. His nose crumpled inwards, exploding with blood and shards of brilliant white teeth went flying. Artimus was up in a heartbeat and he punched me hard in the side of the head. I staggered back and lunged for Ulric, who was still reeling and wiping gore from his eyes.

"ULF! WHAT THE FUCK?" Quentin started doing something. Carter tackled me by the waist and I grabbed him by the throat as we rolled on the floor. I kneed him in the balls, then I was on top of him, pressing my thumbs into his gizzard.

My skull rang as someone punched me in the back of the head. Quentin had someone in a wristlock, pushing a dagger away from me. My head rattled again and sparks and stars danced in front of my eyes. I squeezed down on his throat once more and I could nearly hear the death rattle when there was a final sharp pain and then darkness.

The first thing I noticed was the throbbing pain at the top of my neck. I put my hand to it and I could feel the crust of dried blood. The second thing I noticed was the grimy light on the floor, streaming in from a grill in a thick, oak door.

"Fuck..."

"Fantastic! You're awake now! Well done." I heard the sound of sarcastic applause and I managed to place the voice.

"Quentin?"

"Yep. That's me."

"Are you alright?" I staggered to my feet. My sword and dagger were both gone and my clothes stuck to me unpleasantly.

"Oh, yes! Never better. You know, I was really worried for a moment. I had a nasty sneaking suspicion that I was going to end up in bed with the barmaid from The Noble Purpose. You know, Sally. The one with the perfect tits? Do you remember her?"

I winced. "Can you shut up a bit? Every word is like a kick in the balls."

"Oh no, Ulf! I need to let you know how grateful I am that instead of being up to my eyebrows in quim, I was able to get into a brawl with you and some other halfwits over fuck knows what and spend the night in a cell that smells like several types of piss."

More sarcastic clapping. "So, thank you, Ulf. Thank you ever so much."

"Are you done?"

He sighed. "Yes, I think I've got it out of my system now."

We waited for about an hour before the door swung open and we were dragged out into the glaring sunlight by a couple of the town guards. They flung our weapons at our feet and told us to bugger off. My coin purse felt a lot lighter than it should have, but by the expression on their faces, it wasn't the best time to press my luck.

Marl was waiting for us when we got back to the Crossed Swords. He had a face like February and wordlessly opened the door.

Decroix stood up from a table. "Quentin! What exactly were you playing at last night? I expect this kind of bollocks from Ulf, but come on!" He ran his hands through his hair and glared at the pair of us. "He wants to see both of you. Upstairs. Now."

"Decroix?"

"Quentin, you and Ulf committed mayhem when you knocked that man's teeth in! Mayhem! You know, the deliberate mutilation of a freeman or woman? It's a hanging crime. The fact he's Duke Decare's adopted son doesn't exactly make it easier." Decroix sat down, cheeks red with anger. "Just . . . get it over with."

Quentin and I exchanged glances and we headed upstairs. I could feel everyone's eyes upon on us as we reached the landing. I reached out and rapped on Duke Colsarne's door.

Simon opened the door immediately and we stepped inside. The duke stood at his desk, packing away a writing kit. "Thank you, Simon. You may leave us." Simon bowed and was gone in a flash, and I can't say I blamed him.

"Quentin. Ulf." There was a horrible pause. The duke closed a small vial of ink and carefully placed it into the specific drawer.

"Your Grace-"

"Quentin, I would like you to tell me something."

"Yes, lord."

"I would like to know this. Given the incredibly delicate matter at hand and considering what is at stake," His voice was steady, but I could hear the irritation creeping in at the edges, "taking into account the extreme importance of our sojourn to Scandar and what we need to achieve there, what I would very much like to know is this: what exactly were you thinking?"

"I'm sorry, lord! It was-"

Colsarne rapped his knuckles on the desk, flicking a fingernail. "Because I like to think that I have been a fair and magnanimous patron to you and your brother. Would you say so, Quentin?"

"Yes, lord! Of course you-"

The duke slammed down a paperweight. "That's why I am confused, Quentin! That is the exact source of my vexation and befuddlement. Because if I had been, as others in my position would have, cruel or neglectful to you and your brother, then I could certainly understand a particular resentment towards our house!"

"Please! We didn't mean-"

"HOWEVER," he boomed, "as I have not, and in fact have been both indulgent and kind to you both, the puzzle quite remains as to why exactly you would jeopardise what this house has built over centuries of blood and toil, sabotaging the lives of all the people you know."

Quentin stood silently, his body shaking. There was a dull click as the writing desk snapped closed.

"I love you. I love you and your brother like I love the fingers on my own hand, Quentin. But I want you to know this: if one of those fingers should become infected, I would tear it from the socket and cast it into the fire without a second thought."

He turned to me, eyes burning. "Ulf, if I could kill you then I would. You're ever so slightly more useful to me alive than dead. Now the pair of you, get out of my sight." We bowed and left the room, walking downstairs in silence.

Decroix pinched his nose and sighed. "Well, you're both alive, so that means it went well. Ulf, I'm docking your pay until the fine is paid back."

"How long will that be?"

"I'll let you know." He put two Wyear on the table and I pocketed them with a sinking feeling.

Quentin left and I followed him out the door. "Listen, I'm sorry-"

"Shut the fuck up."

"Quentin!"

He spun on his heel. "Ulf, I like you. You're a good laugh, and I'm reasonably sure you've saved our lives a few times, but for fuck's sake man! What is wrong with you?" He grabbed me by the arms. "I don't know what kind of shit is going on. That's what Decroix is for. He does the thinking, I do the talking. But whatever buggering mess is happening at the moment, it is sure as balls more important that your own little problems that mean you can't have an ale without getting roaring drunk and starting a fight!"

It felt like he stabbed me. I stepped back and he let go, turning away.

"Wait." I called after him.

He turned, red-faced and angry. "Leave me alone, Ulf! Just because your life is a fucking mess doesn't mean mine needs to be!"

Chapter 23:
Regrettable, But Necessary

"*Sausages. A fat, sizzling plate full of them.*"
    "*That's what you always say!*"
    "*It's still true, though.*"
    It's in sight. It's been the best part of two weeks, and we can finally see it. The dark grey stone stands out against the skyline like a beacon. The light is dying, but we will be there by nightfall.
    "*What about you?*"
    Taran thinks for a moment. "*Fish.*"
    "*Fish?*"
    "*With garlic. Slathered in it. On a bed of green kale.*"
    "*Really? After the things we saw in Craftvale, you want fish?*"
    "*Yes. Specifically, trout. Specifically roasted and specifically slathered to within an inch of its life in garlic and lovingly placed on a bed of green kale.*"
    We're getting closer. I can ignore the raw skin of my feet rubbing through my soaked shoes. I can ignore the growling of my stomach. Taran's clothes hang loosely about him and our bellies snarl at us like angry wolves. We had a few mushrooms and some bitter wild hops yesterday, but dammit I can't wait to eat something that isn't covered in shit.
    "*I'm going to miss this game, Ulf. I sincerely will.*"
    "*Really?*"
    "*No! Of course I fucking won't!*"
    "*I did wonder.*"

Taran turns and smiles at me. He's tired. We both are. I can see the battlement flags snapping on the wind and we wave our arms to the black outlines on the gatehouse.

We trudge onwards and I can see Windor App Decare and Ulric mounted at the main gate.

"Oh, fuck . . ."

"What is it?"

I point.

"Oh, for the love of . . ." Taran curses repeatedly as we for our way towards The Hearth. Windor and Ulric ride out to greet us. His great brown destrier snorts and paws as they stop in front of us.

"Sir Taran! What happened? Sellor told us to ride out to find out what was occurring at Craftvale. You look half-starved to death! And what happened to your horse and armour?" He smirks at my brother's clothes. "And what on earth are you wearing?"

Taran strides past them both.

"Sir Taran?" Windor calls, turning his horse.

"The Inner Chamber! Half an hour!" He snaps. "Oh, and Windor?"

"Yes, Sir Taran?"

"Shut your cunt mouth. I'm not in the mood."

I can't be bothered to listen to their reply as we walk through the gates.

Taran yells to a serf to summon the other Order masters and the patriarch to the Inner Chamber, and they run with their heels spinning. "Get washed and dressed. Quickly. I'll see you there."

"I'm sorry?"

"You're coming with me."

"To the Inner Chamber?"

"No, Ulf. To a cattle auction. Of course, to the Inner Chamber!" he snaps.

"But I can't! That is for-"

"Order masters. And what am I?"

"A master of the Order. But-"

"And I say it's fine. If anyone disagrees, I'll lop their bollocks off. Happy?" I nod. "Good. Now hurry the fuck up!"

I hobbled to a well and splash my face with water before heading to my chamber to dress.

Where is it? I know it's only for tournaments, but it's the smartest thing I have. I feel the soft dark blue cloth and I pull the tabard over my head. I hold the silver buckle in my hand and wind the belt around twice, tying it at the front. The golden cup shimmers in the candlelight. I think hard for a moment about which sword to take. The Federschwert has a finer scabbard by far and my sharp sword is rusted from days of wet travel, but that sword has saved my life a couple of times, so I owe it that much. I still snatch up a piece of dogfish skin to quickly rub out the worst of the rust.

The Inner Chamber is at the very heart of The Hearth, the place where Oswald the Fierce laid the foundation stone of the Order, and where he breathed his last. Taran is waiting for me, face grim. He looks me up and down and gives an approving nod. After a few moments, Windor arrives. "Any sign of the other Masters of Arms?"

"Not yet." *My brother answers curtly. Although, after a moment we are joined by Ichabod of Cassioc and Cain Bairflute. The pair of them offer Taran a friendly nod, which he repays in kind.*

"Sir Taran." *Bairflute smiles, his face criss-crossed with faded scars,*

"Good to see you, Ichabod. Cain, keeping well?"

He shrugs. "Well as to be expected.

Bairflute and Sir Ichabod suddenly wrinkle their noses, and a moment later I smell it too.

"Thomas." *They say in unison. The smell of animal shit and dander getting stronger as the Master of Horse approaches.*

I hear two bickering voices echoing down the hallway. Shuffling along the corridor comes Derrik Fairbourne, marked by the jangling iron bunch at his waist as Master of the Keys, arguing with another old man.

"As the Master Seneschal, surely this falls under your dominion, Auldmoon? 'All matters regarding servants and running of the household' isn't it?"

Auldmoon grunts, walking past him, with his staff of office rapping on the floor.

Taran nods respectfully. "Master Seneschal. Thank you for joining us."

The four Masters of Arms. The Master of Horse. Master Seneschal and Master of Keys. That just leaves Uther Skien, the Master of Lore, and-

"Brothers."

Like he could sense my thoughts, Sellor, the Supreme Patriarch of the Order, strides down the corridor, Uther following meekly in his wake. Sellor stares calmly at my brother, his cold grey eyes set in a grim frown. I look down at the floor, willing myself to keep still. "Brothers." he says again with a nod. The other eight bow deeply. I join in with them, unsure if it would be respectful or arrogant to move as they do.

"Taran of Banrillar, Master of Arms and knight of the Order of the Cleansing Flame. You have summoned this council. Speak now and name your cause so that the door may be opened."

Taran bows again. "Brother Patriarch, I name my cause. The town of Craftvale and the rise of our ancient enemy."

I hear a muttered curse from one of the company.

"And the boy? You know the law of the Order as well as any, Sir Taran. Why do you presume to bring him into the Inner Chamber?"

Taran turns to me. "Ulf, do you know what a shoggoth is?"

I feel every eye upon me and I swallow hard. "No, lord. I do not."

Taran turns back to Sellor with a troubled look. "Exactly, Brother Patriarch. But my squire has seen one. And fought it at Craftvale."

Uther splutters, his ink-stained knuckles white around his amulet. "A shoggoth! Brother, you are mistaken, surely. One has not been seen for centuries! For the wall between worlds to be that thin, it would take-"

"Hundreds of bloody, violent deaths to awaken the Waystones, and awful, dark rites to bring it into this world?" Taran finishes. Uther nods, his lips shaking. "Brothers, we waste time."

Sellor nods. "Agreed. The boy may enter."

The Master of Keys steps forward and takes a vast silver chain, bearing a simple iron key, from around his neck. He unlocks the door and Sellor steps through. Taran gently holds me back as the rest enter into a large round chamber.

A vast oak table fills the centre of the chamber. The surface, dark and smoothed with age, bears a carved map of Ashenfell, the names of each town and province inlaid with polished bone. Ten seats line the walls of the chamber, equally spaced around the table. The first nine are thrones made of the same dark oak as the table, a lineage of every man who had assumed that seat carved into the arms. The final seat, directly across from the door, was a simple wooden stool bearing only a single name: "OSWALD".

Taran guides me in and I stand by his side, willing myself to be still. Sellor raises then lowers his hands and the council are seated. His eyes meet mine and there is a moment that seems to last for an hour. "Sir Taran. Speak."

My brother stands up, his gaze moving across the room before resting on the Patriarch. "Brothers. As you are aware, I have travelled with my squire to the town of Craftvale."

Sir Windor speaks up. "Brother, for the clarity of this council, why did you travel there?"

Taran glares at him. "My brother, if you were able to attend the earlier meeting of this council, you would have heard Master Auldmoon express his concern."

"The mark!" Uther cries out. "The witch's mark!"

Sellor raises a hand. "Yes, brother. Allow Sir Taran to continue. Please, go on."

"Master Auldmoon, you discovered a mark upon the body of a servant, did you not?"

"A young girl." Auldmoon grunts. "Serving wench. A black ram upon her buttock."

"THE BADGE OF THE RAM!" Uther shrieks. "SHE BORE THE BADGE OF THE BLACK RAM!"

"UTHER!" Sellor shouts, leaning over and grabbing the Master by the wrist. He continues, "Master Auldmoon, kindly tell me, brother. How did you come to see the mark upon her buttock?"

"I was fucking her." he says.

I try not to laugh, and a pre-emptive elbow jab from Taran stops me. "May I continue?" Sellor nods. "Thank you, brother Patriarch. The girl was from Craftvale, and the Council agreed that I should investigate the town. The extent of the corruption and the Black Ram's influence was not yet known. We had hopes that this was merely an isolated occurrence, or a small band of cultists which could be easily dealt with. Sadly, this was not the case."

He lets the words hang in the air for a moment, and I could see the council exchange glances. Taran turned to me. "Ulf of Banrillar. Do you know the signs of the Black Ram?"

"What? No! You know I don't. Only knights are taught the signs to look for."

Taran nods. "Exactly. Ulf, tell the council what you saw in the town of Craftvale. In the people, their look and manners."

I swallow and I can see everyone looking at me.

"Ulf?" Taran prompts me.

"I . . . it was dark. We came to the town at night and-"

"Speak up, boy!" Sellor barks, making me jump in shock.

"It's fine, Ulf. Carry on." Taran nods and me and I clear my throat.

"It was dark when we went to Craftvale. The men on the gate were . . . different."

"Different? How?" Sellor peers at me, clearly mulling things over.

"Their faces." That's the first thing that came to mind. "They seemed off. Their eyes were too big. Either dark or milky white. And their teeth were all small and rotting."

The is a moment silence and Sir Windor scoffs. "Bad teeth and a few blind eyes hardly seems cause to condemn a town, brothers."

"Windor, when you have something useful to say, please speak. Until then be silent." Sellor pins him to the wall with a stare and he mutters an apology.

I continued. "There was one woman. Her jaw was too small. She was bald and she moved her mouth in an odd way. Like she wasn't good at speaking. Everyone was like that, some worse than others but they all had that feel about them." Uther is still shaking and I see Sir Ichabod and Sir Cain exchange a glance.

"The buildings were all rotten. They'd left piles of shit in the streets to fester. There were flies everywhere, buzzing away all angry-like. We went to an inn. After we went to bed, they tried to kill us. We leapt out the window to the street and ran for it. The whole town was after us. They didn't speak to each other, at least not like ordinary folk do. It was a wet sound, like a gargle. And we could see them from the shadows."

I think back to that night. Trying to piece it together. Desperately trying to figure out what was the actual event and what was my imagination.

"When they walked, it was sometimes on two legs like a man, and sometimes on all fours. Dragging themselves through the dirt."

"And how did you escape?" Cain asks, scratching his cheek with a long fingernail.

"Through the wool works, my lord. We broke in and were creeping through the warehouse when we saw it."

Brigandine

"What?" pipes Sellor. "What did you see, boy?"

I try to focus, but each time the memory slips away. I try to picture the writhing shape, the fetid smell. But nothing comes. I get snatches, but as I try to recall it slips from my mind a piece at a time.

"Arms. Legs. Lots of them. Long and slapping about. Pricks too. There were eyes, I remember that. Taran-" I halt, correct myself, "Sir Taran drove it back with a murder-stroke from his sword. It made a sort of whine like a dog and went back into the shadows with its flesh singed. We clung to the woolpacks and used them to float down the river. I remember that part."

Cain furrows his brow. "Brother Taran, if what your squire says is true, you are aware of the consequences, aren't you?"

"Yes, brother. I am aware."

"Sir Taran, Craftvale is vital to the strength of the Order!" Sir Windor grips the arm of his chair, nails biting into the dark wood. "The town provides men, food, supplies - all that the Order requires."

"All the more reason to purge this stain on our honour." My brother says flatly.

"My point is that this needs far more investigation than the testimony of a single squire!" He jabs a finger at me. "Brothers, Sir Taran is an intrepid and courageous knight. None of us doubts his prowess or bravery. But to sign the death warrant of so many people - the families and kinfolk of many of our serfs and retainers, no less! This is reckless!"

Taran walks across the room and rips the collar from Decare's tunic, then slaps him once across the face, the noise echoing across the chamber like a whip crack.

"Then duel me. Meet me tomorrow in the central square. Single sword, unarmoured."

"Sir Taran!" Sellor yells. "That is quite enough!"

Taran turns. "No, brother. If Sir Windor believes my proposed course of action is 'reckless', let him prove it. It's only fair. Unless, of course, I am mistaken." Taran turns his head in confusion. "It might be possible that I misheard. Did you say 'reckless', Sir Windor? Or did you say, 'regrettable'?"

I can see the hatred in Sir Windor's eyes as a low snarl builds in his throat. "Brother, I was about to say, 'regrettable, but necessary.'"

"Then I offer my sincere apologies, brother. Pray, forgive my rudeness." Taran bows and returns to his chair.

Sellor drums his fingers and glowers. "If you have quite finished, Sir Taran?"

Taran nods.

"Good." *Sellor stands, his old bones moving slowly.* "Brothers. We are all mindful of the significance of the task before us. We all know what will be required. We are all aware of the consequences."

They vote.

A plan is made.

Chapter 24:
The Price

We made the final preparations and readied ourselves for the last part of our journey, the long north-west road to Scandar. Reed's hooves beat steadily, glad to have some movement after our rest in Missden. Quentin kept his distance from me, and I can't say that I blamed him. The journey was fair; the Queen's Road was well looked after, as you'd expect, and the weather held. It was still getting colder each night, but at least the rain stayed away.

After six nights, we came to the crossroads. The fork in front went to the north-west and Scandar, weaving through the rugged hills of Orne. The road west led to Lerd, and to the north-east lay the final road, a passage which went round the hills and stopped at Usk before either continuing west to Scandar, or east to Melpapier on the coast. Usk is a shitty little trading post, nothing more than a few sheep farms and overpriced inns, but folks will often stop there on their way to Scandar. All the lords do, certainly.

So, when Decroix led us to the north-west road, I rode up beside him and frowned. "Decroix, why exactly are we heading this way? It's slower than the Usk way, and the hills are going to play havoc with everyone's piles."

Decroix gave me a thin-lipped smile. "Don't worry, Ulf. It's all in hand."

I shrugged and shuffled my arse round in the saddle. As I stepped down from the saddle that evening, I took a grim satisfaction in being proved right. I could see from the duke's face that he shared my discomfort. Bumpy terrain and an old man's arsehole are not the best of friends. Not for the first time, I wondered exactly what his plan was, though I probably wouldn't have understood it if he had told me.

We pressed onwards for another week, buying food from peddlers and roadside inns. At the pace we were setting, there was still enough time to reach the Autumn Court before the end of November.

On the last morning of travel, Simon rode up beside me, 'Have you been there before?' he asked, voice giddy.

I shrugged. "Once or twice."

"What is it like?" he asked. "Scandar, I mean. The courts held by the Queen."

I looked him over with a frown. He wasn't taking the piss, he was genuinely excited about this. "A lot of talking. Not much else."

He slumped in his saddle. "Oh."

We trotted along in silence for a few moments. "Look, it's not a huge amount of fun, Simon. The great houses gather four times a year to discuss the fate of Ashenfell. Most of the lords don't even bother to go because it's up in the far north. Most of them send a representative or a son they don't particularly like. All lords are required to attend at least twice in their life. First to swear allegiance to the Queen when their father either goes simple in the head or dies, and second to name their successor."

"There it is!"

We could see banners snapping in the cold air over the battlements. The royal standard of three golden fish representing House Fairbourne was visible even from our approach. It was much larger than the others, flying proudly above the main gates. I squinted, but I couldn't quite make out the others.

"Simon, your eyes are better than mine. What else can you see?"

"Umm . . . there are two crossed swords on a red field. That's Decare."

"Bunch of cunts. Who else?"

"A slaughtered bull, throat slit and head on the ground?"

"Witherhide. Poor bastards. Hardly a Wyear to the name."

"There's a rose. Green stem, the thorns dripping with blood."

I snorted. "House Skien. Used to be warrior poets. Now they just fuck each other. The son of the duke can't even chew his own food."

"The swan looks nice."

"That's Bairflute. No better than merchants. Their lands make the finest linen. Soft and white as a swan's feather, you see."

"Ah. What about the charging black boar?"

"House Spechal. Raiders and sailors. They're far east of Rusia, taking silver and murdering and raping as many foreigners as they please. Nasty bastards. They hate House Shayne, a lot of bad blood."

Simon tilted his head. "Why"?

I pointed at the other banner. We're closer now, and I can make out the shattered links of a broken purple chain on a yellow field. "Shayne are scholars. Famous for it. They break the chains of ignorance. They've spread the word of the Virtuous Ones to the lands across the sea. Old edicts say you can't raid and murder people of the true faith, even if they are foreign bastards. Hence the bad blood."

"Ah."

"The net one over there with the blue field is Mistport. Rich from trading along the rivers and the coast. Hard bastards, to be fair to them. I worked as a marine for a few months on a Mistport ship. They can drink and fight and fuck as well as anyone."

"Why did you leave them?"

I changed the subject fairly quickly. "Jundwood have the best archers around. Bunch of arrows on a green field is a bit unimaginative if you ask me, but it gets the point across."

"Why are two of them black?"

I gave Simon a thin smile. "Kaldar and Enk. About a hundred years back they fucked up quite spectacularly and rebelled. The heirs to both the houses slew their fathers and swore loyalty to the crown, but the colours were burned from the record. Ink splashed over books. Banners torn down and carvings defaced. All across Rusia. Apart from a few people, no one can even remember what they once were."

"Does that not get confusing when the two houses meet?"

"Not really. Look- Kaldar wears black-black. Dark as midnight. And Enk just wears very, very dark blue."

Simon peered at the distance. "That flag up there looks a little small."

I sighed. "No Simon, it's just far away."

"Oh?"

"The closer the flag is to the royal standard, the better. It's a sign of being within the monarchs' favour. Kaldar and Enk have never really gotten over the disgrace, so that's why they're near the back."

"Where will we be?"

"We'll find out in a moment."

We had nearly reached the main gate. Marl rode at the head of the column, his face set into a proud rictus, the Colsarne pennant flapping merrily from the end of his lance. I could see the guards, who recognized the colours, and watched one race off along the wall.

Simon made a little gawping sound as he saw the massive shape looming up close, the masonry of the inner keep shimmering despite the clouds. The stone of the Shining Keep of Scandar is a mystery. It's smooth as silk to touch, and its colour shifts in the light. No-one is sure where it comes from, but even I'll admit it's beautiful when you see it for the first time. Different sages have different theories, but most think It was brought to Ashenfell centuries ago when the people came across the sea to settle. It makes sense, because it can't be found anywhere else in the land.

All of the usual buildings could be found within the walls, all built with mundane wood and stone quarried from the nearby hills. But the Shining Keep at its heart is the true Scandar, and has been the seat of the Kings and Queens of Ashenfell through the centuries.

I heard some muffled shouting as we rode up to the gates, and looked up to see the standard of House Colsarne displayed on the battlements, just in front of the black cloth of Kaldar. Not an auspicious sign. I glanced at Lady Alexia, and watched a frown spread across her face.

Decroix approached a servant armed with a stylus and tablet who took a tally of the men and horses. The woman bowed and left, returning with grooms for the horses and attendants for the baggage.

We had arrived last to the court, so the guest house for Duke Colsarne and his retinue would be the one furthest away from the heart of the keep. It was still a fine building, but the one nearest the gatehouse and furthest from the centre of the castle. It seemed odd to give the best rooms to those who turned up first, rather than who's not a complete tosser, but I suppose it encouraged people to be on time.

"Shame we got here late." Marl grumbled, unhooking his foot from the stirrup. I nodded, although I had my suspicions as to why the duke chose to take the longer route to Scandar.

Grooms took the horses and I patted Reed on the side of the neck. I passed a Wyear to the lad to make sure she got a few extra apples. Nodding, he clicked his tongue and led her away with the others.

Quentin screwed up his nose. "This place reeks of shit." he mumbled. The hall was next to the stable complex. There must have been over a thousand horses from all the dukes and their retinues, not to mention the Queen's own beasts. Each one of those stallions and mares needed to piss and shit, and even with the most enthusiastic shovelling in the world, you're going to get a stink.

The duke and Lady Alexia were shown to the better rooms in the hall, with the rest of us sleeping together in the broad common room. Marl farted in his sleep, so I put my gear down in the corner opposite. Servants of the Queen brought bowls of warm water, scented with perfume. Some of us went for the platters of cheese and fruit on the long table, but I needed a wash, so I stripped off, throwing my clothes and armour into a pile.

"Ulf?"

I turned around, and saw Simon standing there. "What?"

"I was just wondering, what do we do here?"

"The duke will go to the main court, which is in a few days, if my maths is right."

"And if you're wrong?"

I shrugged. "Then it will be a few days more. He gets to take in thirteen other people into the privy chamber to stand at the side and be bored shitless. Ten men at arms, one cupbearer and the holders of the wax and seal."

"That sounds like a lot of people . . . fourteen including the duke. And there are twelve noble houses left in Ashenfell so that's fourteen lots of twelve which is . . . umm."

"It's a big room." I said, stopping him before he needed to take his shoes off to count. I ran the cloth over me and the sweat and the grime peeled off my skin.

Simon was still there when I turned back around. "What?"

"Why so many?"

I grit my teeth. "Back when the noble houses were basically just a bunch of thugs killing each other and stealing cattle, no-one would meet unless they had some armed men to watch their back. It's strictly limited to ten men at arms so that no-one comes along with an army to threaten the others. The cupbearer is to make sure the lord has enough wine so he doesn't die of boredom, and the holders of the wax and seal are there to stop him from fucking everything up."

"I don't follow?"

"He picks two people he knows well, one for the wax, one for the seal. It's usually a relative, or sometimes a seneschal. If they think he is about to give is approval or consent to something stupid, then they refuse to pass him the seal or the wax, or sometimes both. That way he has deniability. He wasn't able to put his seal to the charter because some tosser wouldn't pass him his stick of wax."

"Why wouldn't he just borrow someone else's wax? It's all the same."

Brigandine

"You're rather missing the point!" I snarled. "Now fuck off, and let me wash my cock and balls in peace."

He turned red and mumbled an apology before turning away.

Scandar is big. Over the years different rulers have smashed down walls, built up towers and added kinks and turns to the defences so that the whole thing is like a pile of snakes. Portcullises, murder holes, and thick, studded doors split up the rhythm of my stroll. Men with the royal colours, wearing the grim face and bored expression of every guard through history, waved me through at each gatehouse.

There were wagons everywhere, carrying bulging loads under waxed canvases, filled with everything the court would need when they departed to spend winter in the great city of Cassioc.

It wasn't just the lords of the realm here, obviously. Wherever people gather, there will be other people to sell them things. There were hundreds of stalls lined up again the stone walls, selling wine, women, and a dozen other things, all at grossly swollen prices.

I spotted a large and gaudy marquee, streamers of colourful cheap fabric adorning the entrance. A flushed man walked out with a wide, stupid smile and a slight stagger. He had the House Decare badge on his tabard, and he straightened it as he jauntily walked off. Straining my ears, I could hear a few plinking notes of a harp.

A prickling started under my fingernails, and a sharp smell, like soured milk, stung my nose. Focusing my eyes, the colours of the tent were too vivid, shifting slightly in the sunlight from shade to shade.

"WE?"

"Yes, Ulf. We. As in you and me."

"So, is this going to be my-"

"Your Rite of Mettle, yes. You know what that means, don't you?"

"Of course I do! It means I'm a knight!"

"It means if you pass the test set to you, you're a knight." There's a knock as the door. *"Speaking of which, would you get that?"*

I put down the gauntlet I am scrubbing, and open the door to see Ichabod of Cassioc and Cain Bairflute staring back at me. I freeze for a moment then bow quickly. "My lords!" I move out the way and they stride into my brother's chamber.

Taran smiles. "Brothers." They return his nod. "Thank you for taking the time. I appreciate we all have urgent business, but where would we be without tradition, eh?"

Ichabod chuckles. "Very well, Sir Taran." He turns to me. "Ulf, we two both bear witness to your oath. Do not make it lightly, for the Fire of Oswald burns away all mistruth." The ritualistic words flow off his tongue.

Taran put a hand on my forehead. "Ulf of Banrillar, as your lord, I charge you with this. Fight well in the battle to come. Return covered in glory and bring honour to yourself, our family and the Order of the Cleansing Flame. Do you accept this charge?"

I nod. "I do."

Ichabod and Cain each place a hand on my shoulders. "Your oath is witnessed, Ulf of Banrillar. We bid you hold to it." They intone, voices echoing into the stone.

Taran releases his hand and they do the same. "Thank you, brothers."

"Any time." grunts Cain. They both bow and take their leave.

Taran sits down and pours himself a small cup of wine before handing one over to me. "But I pour the wine? That's my job."

He shrugs and takes a sip. "I'll have to get used to it." He sighs, swirling it around. "Pouring my own wine. Polishing my own armour. Wiping my own arse. I'm not going to lie, Ulf; it will be hard."

I roll my eyes. "Very funny."

"Thank you. I rather thought so."

I get back to work on the gauntlet I was polishing. Taran's war plate. Not the fancy stuff for the tourney field, or lighter stuff for travelling. This is the heavy, brutal armour of battle, designed to keep a man alive, and built to help him with his killing.

I dip the rag in oil and work it into the knuckle joints. "This is always bastard of a spot." I mutter. I rub away with a handful of piss-sand and manage to get something approaching a shine. "Bugger. I can't get into these sodding pits! Look, there's still black bits!"

"It's fine. Don't' worry about it." He picks up the gauntlet and rolls the joints back and forth. "Thank you."

"Are you sure? It's still-"

"Ulf, it's fine." Taran drains the rest of his glass.

"Is your sword sharp? I should take another-"

"I could shave with it. It's fine. You did a great job on it, look." He takes a small piece of parchment from his writing desk, running it across the blade and it falls into two neat halves. He sheathes the sword and puts it carefully onto a stand.

"It's getting late. We ride out tomorrow at first light. You should get some rest. Even with us all on horses and moving quickly, it will still take at least a week to get to Craftvale. So, enjoy some time in a proper bed, because it's going to be a while till you get to do so again."

Taran rubs his temples and sits down at the writing desk. He takes out pen-knife and starts cutting a goose feather into a quill.

"I thought we had to get some rest?"

He looks up. "No, you have to rest. I have some work to do." He slices into the quill, making a sharp nib before splitting the end. "I'll see you in the morning."

I don't sleep. Not at all. The bed is warm and I'm more tired than I thought was possible, but I don't sleep. I get up out of bed and fumble with a tinderbox, relighting the candle. I go through my war gear again. The sword is sharp, polished to a gleam.

I take it out. I can still see the scratch on the blade. I've scrubbed away at it for over an hour, but it's still there. Not deep, but enough to mar the perfect surface of the steel.

The moon is high and heavy in the sky. The moonlight falls on my new armour, sitting on a stand in the corner, like a lumpy parody of a man. The flickering light from my candle makes the shadows dance across it.

I walk over and run my hand across it. Every rivet is tight and the leather on the front is soft and oiled. There is a small clink as I hold up the collar of the coif, the hard rings running between my fingers. I look up and stare into the eyes of my bassinet. Cold, expressionless.

I try to imagine myself on the field, clad in my brother's colours, the two of us in blue and gold hacking down the enemy, side by side like heroes. Or all of *us together, the whole Order, charging as one mass of men and horses, routing them and driving them away.*

Then I remember the farmer and his sons. I remember the blood and the reek of shit. I can see the scar on my sword blade where the pruning hook cut into it, and I remember that look in his eyes as he tried to kill us.

I think about our mother. Not for long, just for a moment or two. I know she'd be proud of me. Of both of us. There was a song she used to sing, but I can't quite remember how it goes, so I just start to hum the tune to myself.

Without waking anyone, I pull on my clothes and armour. It's awkward at first, but I fasten the buckles, then feel the stiffness as I bend and move around the room. The only sounds are the gentle rasp of leather on leather, and the soft tinkle of the mail coif as I drape it over my neck and shoulders.

The last thing is the belt and tabard. I bind the belt as tight as it will go, pulling in my brigandine and taking the weight from my shoulders.

The sun slowly rises and bleeds over the sky. I see movement in the courtyard below. Black silhouettes fitting saddles. The whinnies of horses cut through the quiet, and The Hearth comes to life. I shut the door behind me and make my way to the courtyard.

There are two rouncies per man, with destriers for those in full plate, and a few coursers for good measure, as well as mules for our gear. One of the stable servants leads me to a pair of rouncies which have been set aside. They are beautiful, clean-limbed and well-groomed, like all our horses. The names on the bridles are "Smoke" and "Ruby". I pat their necks and stroke them both gently, hoping we can bond before the battle. I put my gear onto Ruby and mount Smoke, feeling his power beneath me. Thomas, the Master of Horse, catches my eye, and I nod my gratitude.

In time, the full might of the Order assembles. The knights, their squires, and hundreds of men at arms, all gathered in the central courtyard. There are no wagons or camp followers; the Order is moving for one purpose, and one purpose alone. The sun is higher now, glinting off armour and making buckles sparkle in the dawn. Taran and the other Masters of Arms are at the front, facing us in silence. Chatter and muttering die away as Sellor rides to the front, clad in crimson robes and riding a white stallion.

"BROTHERS!" The word echoes, sounding out through the whole of The Hearth. The old man's face is torn with a frown, and his horse paws at the earth.

"*Today we ride forth. To battle. To glory! We ride to honour the oaths we have sworn to protect the land and its people. The sacred vows first made when Oswald himself walked this land at the forging of Ashenfell. As the founders of our Order did, as we do, and as those a thousand years hence shall do!*" He raises his arms, the sun rising from his shoulders like a halo. "*Brothers! We ride!*"

He shrieks to the sky, and a cheer rises from the Order. Mailed fists pound the air, and deafening whoops ring in my ears.

Chapter 25:
A Tall Order

"Ulf?"

"Huh?" I started, clearing my throat. "What?"

Decroix sighed. "I said, he's been in there for two hours now!" I looked up at the brothel tent. A pair of men were arguing if the price was worth it while a harlot looked on with a forced smile. "Two hours! What is he doing in there?"

"Do you want the obvious answer? I mean, this is Quentin we're talking about."

"Very funny."

"Who's joking?"

Decroix drummed his fingers on the table. We were under a beer tent, a pavilion that had been set up for the court. There was an alright view of the brothel, and we were waiting there until Quentin finished and returned. Not a bad little mission; I got to drink, Quentin got his cock wet, and Decroix got to worry. Everyone was happy.

Well, not quite. I felt some apprehension about asking Quentin to investigate, but as he had pointed out, he was much better with people than me, and knew a brothel better than anyone.

"Finally!" Decroix said through gritted teeth. I looked up from my drink and saw Quentin happily whistling a tune as he walked out the tent. Decroix tried to grab his attention, but from Quentin's smile, his mind was elsewhere.

After a bit of loud coughing, Quentin noticed and headed over.

"Well?" Decroix asked.

"Yes, thank you brother. And yourself?"

"You know what I meant! What happened?"

"What do you think? The same thing I normally do in a brothel."

"Or, indeed, literally anywhere else." murmured Decroix. "What I mean is, was there anything unusual."

"Oh very! But nothing I haven't done before."

Decroix turned to me. "Ulf, how much would I need to pay you to smash my brother's head into the table very hard?"

"Couple of Ecar should do it." I took a swig of ale and wiped the spillage from the hole in my face.

"Fine!" Quentin raised his eyebrows to the barman and he started pouring out another flagon. "I couldn't see anything odd. It was worth following up, obviously. We got to look at a lead, and I managed to get a decent shag out of it, so it wasn't a wasted afternoon."

Decroix tapped his fingers and chewed his lip. A clear sign he was thinking, or annoyed with Quentin. Or both, in this case. "But why?"

"Why what? Why was it a decent shag? Probably because she got her finger and-"

"Shut up for a minute!" he snapped. "Ulf, are we just being paranoid? I mean, there are plenty of people around here who could be in league with our enemies. We don't know what anyone else's motives are, and I don't know if we're just wasting time."

I shrugged. "Before the main court, do you have any better ideas?"

Quentin put up his hand before his brother gave him a cold, withering stare.

Decroix leaned in close, subtly looking around. "Right, until we know for certain, tell you what- let's just assume something dodgy is going on with the brothel. Ulf, what kind of things can be done in a place like that?" He pre-emptively kicked his brother to stop him from sniggering.

"Well, assuming you didn't see anyone brutally murdered and their blood smeared into a stone inscribed with twisting runes which make your eyes hurt, we can rule out the obvious."

"Nice to know . . ." Quentin mumbles.

"Anyway, I'm off."

"Where to?"

I drain the rest of my tankard and smacked my lips. "Where do you think?"

The first thing I noticed was the smell. Soft, like lavender. Most places like this smelled foul. The reek of sex and violence in varying fractions, or sometimes the waft of cheap perfume to cover it up. But this was deeper. Soporific. I blinked my eyes hard as they adjusted to the gloom.

The tent was split off into about a dozen or so chambers spilling off from the centre, great walls of scarlet fabric dividing them. I could hear the low moans and grunts of the other patrons and the false laughter of the whores cut through in sharp contrast to the bestial rutting.

In the middle was a vast heap of soft cushions and thick, plush furs.

"Hello there." A voice came from the darkness. Soft and quiet. My hand moved to my sword but I forced it away. "And what do you need, good sir?"

She stepped forward into the light spilling in through the flaps into the marquee, and I could her more clearly. She was C'targian, but her hair was raven black. Her hips moved in just the right way to make my hose strain at the seams, and her smile was subtle as a dagger. "What's your name?" she purred.

She pressed against me, running a finger up my front. She rubbed her hands against the side of my neck, and I flinched a little as she ran a nail along my cheek. She frowned and sighed in concern when she got to the hole in my face. I looked at her but there was no disgust in her eyes, no fear. She stood on her toes and kissed my jaw.

Smoke came from somewhere. Sweet and thick. I remembered the steam in Mary's bathhouse and tried to shake my head free of

Brigandine

the musk. She led me by the hand into a chamber, parting the curtain and slipping inside, taking me with her.

"You're the quiet type, aren't you?" she whispered. "That's all right, I don't mind." She pushed me gently and I stumbled back, falling onto a large, soft bed, sword clattering against the frame. She prowled towards me on all fours, eyes fixed to mine. Her hands moved to the straps and buckles of my armour, taking each piece and placing it gently onto the floor.

She was on me now. Her skin softer than anything I've felt. Her lips, her tongue, her body. All of her, over me. She ground her hips and cried out softly. A sharp pain. I looked down to see thin lines of blood on my chest as she dragged her nails across me. She pushed my shoulders down and I could feel myself inside her. She rose up, placing my hands on her breasts.

I heard a low moan, like a dying bull, and I realised that it was coming from me. Her eyes were closed, face a mask of ecstasy and she shuddered. I felt myself coming at the same time. I lunged up and grabbed at her, kissing her all over like an animal. She ran her hand through my hair, kissing my forehead and I fell back, panting and exhausted.

I held her close, drinking in her perfume with every breath. She purred, a soft growl of satisfaction and her beautiful eyes sparkled. Each breath felt ragged, my heart tearing with every beat, and her skin was cool against my burning flesh.

"I-"

"Shush now . . ." She murmured, legs across my body.

I tried to rise, but my arms were like lead. Then, darkness.

Nothing. I feel nothing. Cold, stretched out, and angry. I try to remember and I can't. Pressure builds around my head and there is something around me. Tight and smothering. It's all over me, creeping across my skin and forcing its way in. I try to scream, and it fills my mouth with a hideous bulk as something wraps itself onto my face.

I woke with a start, the sheets clammy and sticking to my body. The air was chilled as I threw back the covers. A bowl sat on the floor, holding a few Ecar and a Wyear, my empty purse sitting beside it. I yanked on my clothes and gathered up my things, rushing out with armfuls of metal. I heard tinkling laughter from all around the tent as I burst into the sunshine and hobbled to the tavern.

"Drink." Quentin said, staring at Decroix with the smile of a victor.

"I should never have agreed to this stupid game!"

"But you did. So, drink."

I threw my stuff on the floor and panted, my hands were shaking. I reached up for the amulet around my neck and found it gone. "FUCK!" I snarled.

"No, it's called 'drink'." said Quentin. "It's a game I made up, where if you can't think of a word that rhymes, you have to drink."

"Can I play?"

"Sure!" He beamed. "Cat."

"Not fucking idea. Time to drink." I drained the tankard and slammed it down.

"Your sort of missing the point here Ulf. You take a little sip-"

"Come here! You too, Decroix!" I dragged them both into the sunshine and grabbed Quentin by the collar.

"ULF! What the-"

"Bugger!" I spat. I jab a finger to Quentin's temple. "Decroix, look at this."

Decroix peered at it, puzzled. "It's . . . Quentin's head? His ear? Hair?"

"Exactly!" I probed at an ache in my mouth, I winced at the pain as I felt a tooth coming loose.

Decroix looked at me, baffled. "I don't understand. What do you mean?"

"GREY!" I shouted. "Look at it, Decroix! Fucking grey!"

"WHAT?" Quentin yelled. "I'm twenty-three! I'm too young to start-"

"How many times?" I growled.

"What?"

"How many times did you fuck them, Quentin?"

"That's a bit personal, isn't it?"

Decroix sighed. "Just answer him! And Ulf, please get to the point."

I took a deep breath and tried to calm down. "How many times, Quentin?"

"Three." he muttered.

"What? Three times? You're sure?"

He threw up his arms. "I'm still tired after the journey! It was a long ride, and pardon me if it wasn't up to my normal standards!"

"Nine . . ." I cursed under my breath.

Decroix looked worried now. "Ulf, what exactly are you saying?"

"I'm saying your brother has aged nine years."

I grabbed Quentin as he fainted and threw him over my shoulder, his limp form still heavy. "Decroix, get my crap from the tavern!" I barked. "We need to get him to bed."

We found a side room in the hall and made him as comfortable as we could. I told Simon to fuck off and leave us alone when he offered to help. He woke up after about an hour.

"What the . . ."

"Nine years." I said flatly. No point in trying to sweeten it. "You're nine years older."

He put his fingers to his face and screamed.

I rolled my eyes in a fair imitation of Decroix. "For fucks' sake! You're in your early thirties, you're not a skeleton."

Decroix shushed his brother and pulled the blanket back over him. "Why nine?"

"Three times three. Basic rule of magic."

"So, why don't you look older?"

I pulled out the loose tooth and spat out a little blood. "See. This little bugger was only a little rotten a couple of hours ago. It was probably meant to come out in a year or so. I only spent myself once, so one times one, I only lost a year." I flung the brown stump into a corner, running my tongue over the painful gap in my mouth.

"Bastards!" Decroix snarled. Quentin was having a bit of a cry, so I left his brother to the comforting.

"It's a pretty good idea. Evil and sickening, but clever, you've got to give them that. Most blokes will only go once, pull their tights up, and sod off again afterwards. It's only because he's such a randy sod that Quentin got buggered by this. Well, technically they got buggered by him-"

"Not funny!" Decroix snapped.

"All right, point taken."

"Right, so people can make magic from . . . emissions?"

I nodded. "Same as blood, bile, and marrow. The four waters that make up life. They steal the essence and use it for the desired effect. Blood keeps you alive, so it can be used to kill or bring about a false animation. Bile protects you from disease, so you can curse people, wither crops, and poison. Marrow can stiffen the sinews for a fight, giving fearsome strength-"

Decroix sighed. "Yes, we understand! Sorcerers use bits of people to do magic! But why do they want . . . that stuff! It's disgusting!"

"So, blood and human sacrifice you're fine with, but people fucking makes you feel all icky?"

"None of your business!"

I coughed, and spit out a little more blood. "As I was saying, man-juice can be used for magic. They use it for youth, vitality. But all magic has consequences, so it's stolen from others. In this case, Quentin and me."

My knee was a little stiff, and the gap in my mouth where a molar once was had started to scab over. Quentin was holding onto Decroix and shaking a little. He'd never had magic cast on him before, and I felt a bit guilty about being blunt with him.

Decroix ran a hand through his hair. "Right, so how do we fix this? How do we reverse it?"

I knew he wouldn't like the answer, but I gave it to him anyway. "You can't. Not unless you're willing to steal the life-force and energy from someone else."

"No!" Decroix looked appalled.

"Exactly. I didn't think wanking off blokes to steal their power was your style, anyway."

Decroix sprang up and got in my face, nose pressed to mine. "They stole a decade of my brother's life! How the fuck could you understand something like that?"

I met his gaze. "Better than you'd think. So how are we going to do this?"

"What?"

"Kill these cunts. That's what we're going to do, right?"

He nodded grimly and looked down at his brother. "Yes, I think so. I really do. Quentin, try and get some rest. We're going to get these bastards."

"I need to get myself a new amulet. Let's meet back in about an hour."

"Done."

We told Simon to look after Quentin. He asked what wrong, so Decroix lied that he'd gotten a fever from some bad chicken.

After a little asking around, I found a woodwright, an old, fat man turning some beads, his belly rising up and down from the effort on the treadle lathe. There wasn't much daylight left, so he was trying to get done what he could.

He stopped and wipes his forehead as I approached. "Good day." He panted. "What can I help you with, sir?"

"Got any sycamore?"

"Why yes, sir! Some lovely platters and I've got a few-"

"No, I need a little circle." I held my thumb and forefinger. "This big and about one cubit thick."

He frowned. "What for?"

"Then I need you to carve a symbol. Three flames dancing in a circle, with a hole in the top for thonging."

"Light's getting bad." He muttered. "Have to be tomorrow. Cost you five Ecar and I can-"

"You're doing it now and the price is three Wyear."

"What? For a bit of wood?"

"And the carving. And the hole. And you're going to do it right now. And you're going to keep your mouth shut." I counted out the coins and pressed them firmly into his hands. He put away a half-made bead and carefully cut out the disk from a shaft of sycamore. I watched him round it with a rasp before smoothing the surface with dogfish skin.

Once he was finished, I threaded a leather cord I'd bought from a peddler through the hole and hung the medallion around my neck. The light had nearly gone now, with the sun bleeding across the sky. The woodwright shook his head and sighed as he tidied away his tools for the day.

Decroix was waiting for me back at the hall. I'd never seen him look so serious, and apart from Duke Colsarne, I'd never known a man as serious as Decroix. Wordlessly, we walked to a quiet place, out of the way of prying eyes.

I sucked my teeth. "Well, let's talk through options."

"You're the expert on the esoteric, Ulf! You tell me!"

I scratched my chin. "Hmmm. Well, I've got an idea."

"Go on . . ." He said cautiously.

"What's the budget?"

"Duke Colsarne said we have the entire resources of the house at our disposal. Just tell me what you need."

"You told him!"

"Yes, Ulf. You and Quentin are not in his Grace's best graces at the moment, to put it mildly. He hasn't forgotten about Missden."

I threw up my hands in exasperation. "That was ages ago!"

Decroix pinched his nose. "You smashed a noble's face in! Now is not the time to be keeping secrets."

"We are planning to murder a load of people. Now is *exactly* the time to be keeping secrets!"

"Murder? I thought you had a plan?"

"That's the end goal, not the plan. The plan is how we are going to get away with it." I told him the plan, and Decroix smiled for the first time in a while.

"Oh, Ulf. That is very good . . ."

Chapter 26:
Words In The Shadows

The next evening, we were all dressed up and everything was in place. I wobbled a little bit, and it took me a few minutes to find my footing.

"Careful!" Simon fussed.

Decroix gave him a withering look. "Simon, when has saying 'careful' ever helped anyone? Do you sincerely believe that Ulf was planning to go arse over tit and fall off the stilts before you reminded him to be 'careful'?"

"Sorry . . ." he muttered.

"Just you be careful with your part and we won't have any problems." I grumbled. "I came up with the idea, why do I have to be up here?"

Decroix shrugged. "Because you don't have the looks to pull this off?" He adjusted his mask, hastily hacked out of some scraps of leather. "Anyway, how do my tits look?"

I rolled my eyes. "Lady Tall, they are bouncing majestically."

There were a few others about. Marl looked furious at his part. To be fair, Guffle the Farter was an old favourite. And Simon was the one who had to carry the bladders.

Runners had been sent to all around the castle, letting everyone know that Duke Colsarne was putting on an impromptu performance, with free beer for everyone. A dozen Guilders had been put behind the bars of each of the pubs on the planned route, with open barrels in front. Some dozy bugger had stuck his head in one for a laugh, which was always hilarious until his mates found out they were drinking nits.

It wasn't unusual; a lord displaying his prosperity as a gesture of friendship on the eve of a big diplomatic summit. Of course, that was absolutely not what was actually happening, but no-one else needed to know that.

"He's nearly finished." Simon peered from behind a wall which functioned as our backstage area.

"Ready, Ulf?" I nodded and Decroix gave a sly grin. "Let's show them the magic of theatre."

Decroix pulled the yellow scraps over his head, giving himself a crude, long blonde wig and bumbled out in front of the crowd. They gave a huge roar and a few flirty whistles before he scolded them to be quiet.

"OH WHERE, OH WHERE IS MY SILLY HUSBAND!" he shrieked. "GRUFFLE! GRUFFLE!" Marl stomped out sulkily, accompanied by Simon as I swayed dangerously on the stilts. I could hear the laughter. Marl was a moody bastard, so in a way, he was perfectly cast for this.

"GRUFFLE, HAVE YOU SEEN MY HUSBAND?" Simon squeezed the bladder making a fairly decent parping noise. He'd been practising all afternoon and he got a smattering of applause.

"OOOH! GRUFFLE!" Decroix slapped Marl round the face. "THAT'S ENOUGH OF THAT!" He turned to the audience. "HAVE ANY OF YOU SEEN MY HUSBAND, SIR TALL? HE'S VERY, VERY TALL!"

That was my cue. I moved out behind them, shaky as a newborn deer. I managed to put a finger to my lips to tell the crowd to keep quiet to my harridan wife that I've been out shagging the milk-maid. I snarled "FUCK!" as I nearly fell off.

The crowd loved it, though, and we got a big, drunken cheer, just like we wanted. We moved down the route we had planned, Decroix asking where Sir Tall had gone. I followed behind, taking crusts of bread, finishing drinks, and generally acting like a prick. All the while, Marl's face got redder and redder and Simon walked

Brigandine

beside him, farting away merrily on the bladders. I picked up small little items, playing the part of Sir Tall, the loveable thief - grabbing hats and caps, knocking over woodpiles, and other such larks.

It's amazing, in a way. Put on a pair of stilts and paint your nose red, and everyone greets you with a smile and a wave. If I'd been doing that dressed normally, they would have kicked the shit out of me.

After half an hour, we got to the right spot. I could see Quentin ahead, holding an oil lamp. He was chatting with another one of Colsarne's men. I couldn't hear the conversation, but I hoped it was nice and inane. He leaned up casually and I snatched his lamp, wiggling my fingers as I went by. I only needed to go a few more yards on those bloody stilts.

Lady Tall and Gruffle were standing near the brothel tent. Judging by the cheers, Simon had gotten a lot better with the bladder. Decroix looked over his shoulder, nodded at me and kicked Marl in the shin. "I DO SAY, MRS TALL." Marl droned. "I THINK THIS IS GOING TO BE A WET ONE."

Simon swapped bladders and squeezed with all his strength. The grease, tallow, and oils contained within sprayed outwards, hitting the canvas in a perfect splatter. Their part now done, I staggered on the stilts, reaching down to grab a proffered tankard. I threw it at my mouth and lurched sideways, crashing into the tent.

I grabbed hold of the ridge seam, balancing precariously on one of the stilts. I felt a hard bulge under the material, likely a pole or support beam. I flailed with my other hand, smashing the pottery lamp against it as hard as I could. The oil splashed out, and the flame spread across it hungrily as it rolled down the side towards the greasy mess left by the bladder.

There followed a fair bit of screaming and yelling. People started running off to fetch water as the fire started to flicker and smoke. I felt fire licking at my feet and I let go, crashing to the ground. My shoulder cracked hard on the impact and I forced myself up, head spinning.

Half the tent was ablaze now, sparks being carried on the breeze. I could see those nearby desperately throwing water over their own pavilions, eager to avoid the same fate. I could also see out of the corner of my eye that there were people in the way, stumbling around drunk and stopping anyone forming a proper chain.

I reeled round the back of the tent, drawing my dagger as I went. Decroix had beaten me there and I saw him pull back a bloody blade, shoving a flailing woman back into the inferno. The C'targian bitch leapt towards him from the shadows, holding a curved knife. Her beautiful face twisted up with hated as she lunged at Decroix and he barely parried the blow. She sidestepped his returning strike and plunged the knife into his chest, right to the hilt.

"DECROIX!" I shouted. I rushed up and stabbed her in guts, wrenching my dirk upwards.

With a strength she shouldn't be able to muster, she pulled the blade free and stepped into the burning tent, disappearing into the shadows, laughing horribly the whole while. There was a foul stench like rotted meat, standing out even above the smoke and flames, and her outline disappeared.

I grabbed Decroix by the shoulders and shook him. "Stay with me!"

"Ulf! Get the fuck off me."

"What? I thought she stabbed you through the chest!"

Decroix scrambled to his feet and picked up his knife. Then I noticed one sad, partially deflated tit. He tapped at it with the point of his dagger, and we turned and sprinted away in the chaos.

Everyone was on edge when we met up back at Colsarne's hall. Weapons were either worn or readied, and the air was more tense than a sheep at a pervert's party. I armoured myself up, cursing at the hard-to-reach bits like the pauldron buckle. I still felt stiff from the fall, and was all fingers and thumbs.

"Can I help?" I turned to see Simon, his face a mixture of earnestness and caution. Like a puppy who's not sure if he'll get a scrap or a kick up the arse.

"Sure, why not." I threw him one of the arms and pointed to the shoulder buckle. "Middle hole to that one, the well-worn one."

Brigandine

He nodded. He'd clearly been watching, as he didn't cock it up once. Which was annoying, as I had been looking forward to swearing at him.

After a while, someone came back to let us know that the fire was put out and all that was left is a soaked, smouldering canvas. Shortly after, Windor Decare burst into the hall, flanked by Ulric and a flock of knights and men at arms. He snarled at the sight of me, and the beast inside me started snapping at the leash, yearning for a fight.

"YOU!" he bellowed, red in the face. "You little bastard! You did this, didn't you? Your brother would be ashamed to see what you've become."

I glared at him. "Right on two out three accounts, my Lord. Ulric! Nice to see you. How're the teeth?" I slowly drew my sword, and they both took up a fighting stance.

"Ulf. That will be quite enough, thank you very much." Duke Colsarne swept out of his chamber, draped in a grey greatcloak lined with black fur, and the room fell silent. His daughter was on his arm, smiling her sweet, cunning smile. She offered both Ulric and Decare a perfect bow, meeting both their gazes as equals.

Colsarne nodded slightly and Lady Alexia resumed her place by his side. He gave them both a welcoming smile. "How good to see you. How might I assist you this evening?"

Decare pointed his sword towards me, knuckles white. "You mean, aside from your men staggering around drunk, creating mayhem? Apart from that, I'd have to say my main concern has to be that piece of shit setting fire to a fucking tent!"

Duke Colsarne blinked slowly and took a single step forward. "I apologise, but I do believe you are mistaken. I have heard from my men that, as part of a celebration praising our gracious Queen, there was an unfortunate accident."

"An accident!" He snorted.

"Yes. An accident. Very regrettably, one of my bondsmen tripped and fell while portraying a traditional comedic character. Sir Tall, wasn't it, Ulf?"

"Yes, my lord." I replied.

"Ah, yes. Ulf here was lucky not to have been seriously hurt after falling from what I assume were some very tall stilts."

"Yes, lord." I said, trying to keep a straight face. "They were very tall."

"Very tall. Very tall indeed . . ." he muttered, shaking his head. "Well, I am sure I speak for Decare, myself, and in fact all of Ashenfell when I say that we are most grateful for your valour and bravery." He started a small round of applause which all our men joined in, with a few whoops and cheers for good measure from Marl.

"Decare? You dare to presume and address me by my house, as if we were equal?"

Duke Colsarne shrugged. "I know it is not the case, but I always feel it is best to flatter one's house guests. Even the ones whose presence is a surprise." Looking at the imposing cloak with the vicious silver eagle on the back, there was no way this was a fucking surprise.

"Duke Colsarne, there has been a crime committed and there must be punishment and justice. You cannot stand in the way."

"Yes, but as a duke of the land, I'm sure you'll be forgiven."

Windor Decare narrowed his brow in fury. "What are you blathering on about, you old fool?"

The smile on Duke Colsarne's face fell away like a burning tree. "The Weal of The King's Way. The road to and from Scandar is under the protection of the Order of the Cleansing Flame, is it not? For trade and craftsmen building and serving our glorious castle of Scandar?"

"That's got nothing to do with anything and you fucking know it."

He cracked his knuckles, and if I didn't know better, I'd have sworn there was a smirk. "As the knightly master of that most noble order, you are aware of your obligations. Ulf was practising a trade! Acting, to be specific. A true and noble profession. He tripped on a poorly maintained cobble and is lucky to be alive, no thanks to your negligence."

"What? Yes, but that's an ancient law! No-one has cared about that rule for centuries!"

"I'm afraid I must beg to differ. I care about it. In fact, I care about it rather a lot right now. As Her Majesty will, when you failed to take control of the situation, I am sure. And then further, when you breached the Queen's peace by barging into my home and threatening my bondsmen. Or, you can say that I am quite mistaken, and you merely came in here to wish me goodnight before departing."

". . . good night, Colsarne."

"Good night, Decare."

I waited a couple of hours after he left. People were still on guard, but a few drinks had been passed around. I weighed up my options. If they caught me, I'd be dead. Definitely. But I considered that Decare couldn't possibly hate me any more than he already did, and also, that I hadn't risked my neck enough for one day.

I stuck to the shadowed edges of buildings, moving slowly and surely. I only had my dirk on me. The bulk of my longsword would have been a big clue to anyone watching, and armour would have been madness. I stepped cautiously, moving at an irregular rhythm. Step with your toe first, don't make a silhouette, and don't brush against anything.

It took me a few guesses before I was standing under the right window. I crouched down in the filth of the gutter and sharpened my ears.

"It just feels so wrong." Ulric. The slur of his voice put my teeth on edge.

"Compromise, Ulric. It is a vital skill that you must master." Windor Decare. I'd know that cunt anywhere.

I heard a slosh. Wine being poured? Or maybe they were pissing on each other. Who knows?

"You are App Decare. One day, you will rule over this House and shape its future. You have promise; that's why you were chosen. But you must learn when to stand firm and when to bend to the will of another. And the true mark of leadership is doing one while appearing to do the other."

A pause, followed by the clink of a wine glass on a table. "So, with regards to the Queen, what are you-"

"The situation with the Queen is under control." Decare said firmly, cutting him off. "You do trust Sellor, don't you?"

"Well, obviously. But my lord, you must see how this stings. Think about what we stand for. Yourself, the house, the Order!"

Decare's voice went cold. "Pragmatism. Sound judgement. Fortitude. That is what this house stands for, Ulric. A house or nation that cannot adapt, cannot compromise, is doomed to by broken and plundered by one that can."

"Yes, lord." Ulric muttered.

I heard some garbled voices, and two drunks started wondering past. I tried to slow my breathing and willed my limbs to total stillness. By some miracle, they walked right past me. I bit down on a sigh of relief and turned my attention back to the pair of cunts above me.

"I know what he'll do. I know how Colsarne will act. For all his wits and quick tongue, he's as predictable as sunrise, the stupid old bastard."

"He can't stop us. What exactly is our aim here?"

"Our aim? My aim is simple. I plan to break Colsarne's knees and make him grovel in his own shit and piss whilst I and a dozen men rape his daughter half to death and we get a cart-horse in to finish the job."

"You . . . you really hate him that much?"

Decare snarled. "No, Ulric. I hate her that much. No one says no to me. Not now. Not ever."

"My lord?"

"We were allies. once. Friends, even. But that was a very long time ago. It would have been perfect. His only daughter and my adopted son. It would have silenced any critics to your lack of noble blood, and it would have forged together the two most powerful houses in Ashenfell. When the Queen finally has the decency to fuck off and die, it would have been the two of you, ruling together. Your children the legitimate heirs to the kingdom."

"But, why did she say-"

Brigandine

"I'm tired, Ulric. Go, leave me. We will talk more on the morrow, but now I need to get some sleep."

The ground ahead is churned into a thick, sloppy mess. Hours of rain and the passing of over a thousand horses has seen to that. Last night it poured, and today isn't looking any better. The air reeks of sweat and shit as we march onwards.

I pull my hood up. The reek of damp wool is horrible, and I try to cover my sword hilt with my cloak to stop the rain getting to it. A drop of water finds its way down the back of my armour, and the cold chill runs down my spine before nestling into my arse crack.

Shouts. Screams. I jerk my head up and I can see a horse ahead, flailing in the mud. Its front leg is twisted and the white gleam of bone is showing. The rider is nearby, caked in mud himself and desperately trying to calm the beast. The front hooves are lashing out and one strikes him on the hip. He falls down crying out with shock before a footman takes a halberd to end the creature's suffering.

I keep Ruby steady and tighten my grip on Smoke's reins as they whinny at the sounds of confusion and annoyance. The rider is helped to his feet, and even from here I can see he is limping badly. There are angry shouts as the column grinds to a halt, men and horses bumping into each other.

Gradually, we untangle ourselves and start to move again. There are at least six more hours in the saddle to go, and my back already aches. Riding past, I can see the horse's blood pooling at the side of the road, steaming in the cold. Its mad eyes stare up at me, unblinking.

When the army makes camp, there are no songs or stories told at the fire. Men huddle together for warmth, preferring the choking smoke of the bonfires to the chill of the night.

I point to the treeline. "Something moved!" I'm sure of it.

Taran nods to me plainly. "I'm sure it did, Ulf."

"Not an owl or a fox or something! I mean a person."

"Yes, I know."

I look at my brother in confusion. "What?"

"The sentries know what they're doing. They'll make sure no-one gets into the camp and we can all sleep safely. Well done for spotting him, though; that was a tricky one."

"So, you knew they were spying on us?"

Taran laughs and throws another soggy branch onto the fire. "Ulf, you can't hide an army. And anyway, they know we're coming. The cat is very much out of the bag with that one, I'm afraid." He jabs at the fire with a stick, the embers briefly flashing. "We know why we're going. They know what we are going to do when we get there. They have had time to prepare, and so have we."

There's a bit more warmth from the fire now. I move my hands closer and rub my wrists.

"So, what's it going to be like? There is so many of us, they would be wiser to just yield, wouldn't they?"

"Hah!" Taran chuckles a little and takes out a bottle. He pulls the cork and takes a swig, passing it round. It's mead. Old, strong stuff that warms my insides.

"Ulf, the Black Ram don't care too much about their own survival. They're fanatics, and if they die, that's not too much of a problem for them. All in the greater glory of their mad god." He rolls his eyes. "Followers are just that. Pawns to be used and thrown away. A good commander cares about his men, Ulf. He will never risk the lives of his soldiers without a bloody good reason, and will never sacrifice them on a whim. When you're dealing with the Ram, you can't count on that."

"So, what does that mean? What is this fight going to be like?"

Taran stares into the flames, eyes heavy with worry. "Ulf, it's going to be a fucking bloodbath."

Chapter 27:
Faith

Knocking. That sort of light, hesitant rap that comes from someone who knows they need to get your attention, but they still feel guilty about it.

"Leave the fucking bench alone." I growled. I'd been awake for an hour or so. I never sleep well with everyone packed around me. I need space to scratch my balls and fart in peace, like a gentleman.

Simon smiled with relief when he saw he didn't have to rouse me. "Good morning, Ulf."

I nodded and stretched my neck. I had slept at a queer angle and I had a dull ache at the base of my skull. "What's that?" I asked, pointing to the bulky linen bag Simon was holding.

"Oh, yes." He handed it to me. "This is for you, from his Grace."

I muttered my thanks and took it from him, emptying it out upon the bench. Out tumbled a mass of soft, grey wool. I rolled the beautiful, fine cloth between my fingers, then held it out in front of me.

A long surcoat edged with black fur and bearing a resplendent eagle embroidered in silver thread. I hesitated, feeling the weight of the garment. The eagle stared at me, bale-eyed with claws sewn to savage points.

"Is everything all right, Ulf?"

"Hmm?" I turned to Simon, who was lurking. "Fine. Bugger off, I'll be out there in a bit."

"Shall I let his Grace know you'll be there soon? We need to get going-"

"Yes, yes." I snapped. "Now, fuck off so I can get dressed." I bustled him off. Turning, I could see the surcoat lying on the bench, fur shimmering in the sunlight filtering through the window. I put it off for as long as I could, strapping on my armour and putting on absolutely everything else.

"Fuck it." I sighed, picking it up. I slipped it over my shoulders and drew it in with my belt.

It felt warmer and finer than anything I'd worn in a long time, and it fit me almost perfectly. The cut made my waist look slim and my shoulders broad as an oak. So, this was why we spent all that extra time in Auldcall.

I stepped out of the hall, and saw Duke Colsarne and his retinue milling in the courtyard. All of us together in the same rich fabric, with the same fearsome eagle. I'm not one for theatrics, but even I thought we cut a pretty imposing sight.

Lady Alexia stood beside the duke, holding a great bronze seal, with Decroix on his other flank with a tinder box and a blood-red sealing candle. Marl stood stone-faced with a banner pole perched on his belly next to Quentin, who fidgeted with a goblet and glanced around nervously. I took up my position next to Simon and seven others and we marched for the Shining Keep.

We passed through warrens of corridors and passageways. Like House Colsarne, the walls were bedecked with looted banners and pennants. The stones hung with the mottled colours of House Fairbourne's defeated enemies. Rebels, traitors, and all those who have dared to bare steel against the ruling house over the centuries, right back to the founding of Ashenfell. Each of their names had been buried and forgotten, save for the silent ghost of their heraldry, draped here as an eternal warning.

Eventually, we arrived at the council chamber. Unlike the High Council of the Order, there is no pretence of equality at the Queen's council table. The Royal Seat squatted at the head of the table, back to the fireplace to warm the royal arse. The throne was a multi-limbed monstrosity of gilded oak, studded with precious stones worn smooth by the centuries. To each side stood twenty-five men in glistening armour. She had no bearer for wax or seal, for the judgement of a monarch is absolute and infallible. "Fuck, are we the last?" I muttered.

Each lord was seated on arrival, to discourage tardiness. As we entered and bowed before the empty throne, I could see that we were stuck with the worst seats by the door, draft to our backs. Even Enk and Kaldar had better seats than us, the dark blue on our left and black to our right. Both of them have dressed humbly, in simple, well-made robes, but the other nobles were clad like randy peacocks, shining with pageantry and dripping with finery.

Windor Decare glared at me, and I returned the sneer with interest. He touched a hand to his cheek where my scar is and winced sympathetically. I caught Ulric's eye and make a pointed show of running my tongue along my mostly-intact teeth. Although, rather than intimidate it probably just looked like I wanted to fuck him. To be fair, I would happily fuck him if I knew he would hate it a little more than I would.

Duke Colsarne took his seat. Only the high dukes of the land are permitted to sit in the presence of the crown. The dukes engaged one another in some awkward conversation. The first few blows were struck, subtle questions to find out exactly what the others knew and where they stood.

The chatter fell to sudden silence at the cry of the Queen's herald, and the dukes each rose to regard the woman striding slowly into the chamber. She wore a gown of cloth-of-gold embroidered leaping fish and dripping with seed pearls and topaz. Her ash blonde was bound in ribbons, with folded braids tucked into the emerald-studded crown of Ashenfell.

There was no doubt in my mind: as improbable as it seemed, this woman - who couldn't have been more than forty - was Queen Karidine. Or, if she wasn't, she had a fucking cheek sitting on her throne.

A figure shuffled after her, the vast golden cup of House Fairbourne in his hands. I knew that gait. I knew that wrinkled face and those flint-grey eyes.

Sellor.

The Decares inclined their heads in respect, and Sellor responded with a bow of his own. He stood by the throne, and apart from the slight shaking of his hands and a few more creases to his temple, he was the same old bastard from all those years ago. For just a moment our eyes met and he looked at me, puzzled. It only took a moment for the recollection to dawn and he furrowed his brow in contempt.

The queen lowered herself into her throne with the practised grace only a monarch can manage. "My council. It is good that we meet this day." There came a murmur of agreement. Duke Spechal tugged at his collar, and I could see the glint of mail links beneath his tunic.

She gazed across the room. Duke Colsarne's face remained expressionless. "There is much to discuss, my lords. We come to a time when decisions must be made. Hard choices for the good of the realm, and for all the people of Ashenfell." Her voice sounded light, but firm and powerful. Every word chosen like a carpenter selecting a tool. "But first, there is an account to be made. Colsarne, you know of the matter I refer to." She fixed the duke with a viper's stare, and he coolly blinked it aside.

"Does Her Majesty refer to the situation in Carstock?"

"Your perception serves you well, my lord." she said. "Now, explain."

Duke Colsarne arched his fingers and took light breath, the eyes of every man in the chamber upon him. "Your Majesty. After investigations by my agents Decroix and Quentin, we revealed evidence of an uprising against your person, and I took it upon myself to quell the rebellion without mercy. I deployed my own household troops-"

"And the bandit, Azrael Bordane? I am told that this common footpad played a role in the liberation of the fair town of Carstock.

Common thieves and murders fighting alongside your own men. Hardly the mark of chivalry."

Duke Colsarne tilted his head in consolation. "I may have utilised other resources to ensure a decisive victory. Given the nature of the rebellion, I hope your Majesty will consider my actions justified."

She put a hand to her chin and a thin smile started to spread. "Yes. Please do tell us more about the nature of the rebellion. What, pray tell, warranted the employment of such unorthodox tactics?"

"My gracious Queen and my lords of the realm. I will speak plainly. The Black Ram has returned."

Windor Decare snorted. "Outrageous." He turned to the throne, rolling his eyes. "My Queen, the mismanagement of his own lands and the rebellion in Rusia should be embarrassment enough for Duke Colsarne. But to try and claim that, after many years, The Black Ram rears its head in Ashenfell is nothing short of absurd."

"It seems strange that you would so readily dismiss such things, given your status as a master of the Order of the Cleansing Flame, Decare." said Colsarne.

"It is precisely because of my rank that I dismiss it!" He snapped. "You are attempting to whip up panic and discord amongst this council to cover for your own incompetence. Such naked ambition is unbecoming, even for you." Windor folded his arms, sitting back in satisfaction. I could hear a low growl in Marl's throat and a grunt as Decroix elbowed him.

Duke Colsarne blinked slowly and rapped his finger on the table in front of him. "Thank you Decare. Your comments are as valuable and intelligent as they always are."

The Queen sighed. "Colsarne, although I appreciate your overwhelming need to show how clever you are, may I suggest returning to the matter at hand? He does raise a rather good point. What proof do you have exactly that the Black Ram is part of the upheavals? There are always such rumours. Many have attempted to harness the power and might of The Black Ram, but seldom are they anything more than malcontents whose reach exceeds their grasp."

"Your Majesty makes two excellent points. However, I do feel that this matter is worthy of the consideration of- "

"What about the Waystones?" I looked around to see who had just spoken, then realised with horror that it had been me. Everyone's eyes were upon me and I swallow hard. I had better make this good.

"Your Majesty. There were Waystones in both Cassioc and Carstock. In Cassioc, it was part of a hidden cult, just beginning to develop their power. But in Carstock, they used public execution as a guise to offer up blood to the stones and draw forth the magic within."

Decare slammed down his fist. "Your Majesty, I must protest! Colsarne, for all his flaws, is at least a duke of the realm. It is his right by blood to speak on this council." He jabbed a thumb at me and snarled, "This vagabond is nothing more than an itinerant mercenary, and nothing less than a traitor to the Order of the Cleansing Flame. His word should carry no more weight than that of a donkey!"

I would have gone for 'complete and utter cunt' rather than 'vagabond', but that's just my personal preference.

Duke Enk glared at him coldly. "To be fair, Duke Decare, there are some members of this council I would deeply prefer to be replaced by a talking donkey." Decare sputtered as several of the other dukes chuckled at the quip.

The queen raised her hand and the laughter died away instantly. "Perhaps it would be prudent for certain members of this council to remember that they are lucky to be sitting here at all."

Enk's eyes fell to the floor, and I could see Duke Kaldar adopt a similarly contrite position. Eventually, Bairflute broke the silence. "Well, regardless of the cause, this is troubling." He stroked his fat chin, pudgy brow furrowed. "Carstock is a major trading centre, and I must confess that this does have implications for my house. What steps are being undertaken to ensure the rebuilding of the town and prosperity of the realm?"

"I share Lord Bairflute's concern." Said Jundwood. He was a young man, clean limbed with a strong face and yellow hair. "The woods around Carstock are vital for the ships and archers of the realm."

I could see Duke Colsarne biting his tongue in frustration. "With the greatest respects to my Lords Bairflute and Jundwood, while the health of the nation's purse is, of course, a priority, I must point out that the return of eldritch horrors capable of ripping apart reality is a more pressing concern. Carstock was dealt with and its people are safe. Those who were manipulated into the false faith have been shown the error of their ways and punished. The Guilds' Council have been put to death and replaced by those of a less heretical disposition."

Duke Shayne frowned in disapproval. "Those who stray from the true path must be punished. An example to be set to the others. Surely you understand this, my lord? It is well to show mercy, but all those who cleave to the Black Ram should be put to death without mercy. The lands scorched and cleaned. Economics be damned!"

"Fine words, from one with such a fat purse." snarled Duke Witherhide. "The razing of Carstock has harmed Witherhide's business interests enough without your fanatical call for more bloodshed."

"Agreed." said Duke Spechal, pulling on a long, full moustache. He raised his hand. "Anyone else here think House Shayne are a bunch of cunts, or is it just me?"

"Enough!" Queen Karidine shouted. "You are the dukes of this land, and yet your squabble like children." She spat the last word, nails scraping the arm of her throne. "Look at you! With this gaggle of invalids, I am to govern the realm. What would happen should I die?"

The question hung in the air as every man present failed to meet her gaze.

"Before my corpse was cold, you would be divided. I have no heir. Of this I am sure you are all very much aware, each of you thinking your own house fit to take the place of Fairborn. You would cover the land in blood, each of you scrabbling for a crown you have no right or mettle to bear."

She stood up, gazing around the room. "That is the burden of House Fairbourne. We are the ones who must unite the realms. To bring you in line like a pack of hounds before a huntsman. Sellor, explain."

The old man cleared his throat with a sound like rustling parchment. He had aged, but his eyes were the same. He looked right at me and suddenly I became a boy again.

"Brothers." He let the word hang in the air. "We face uncertain times. As the Queen has said, there is no heir. For years she has ruled us with both wisdom and compassion. And so, she shall continue."

Duke Colsarne opened his mouth and closed it. Just for a moment, for the first time, I could see something new, and it scared the shit out of me. Duke Colsarne was afraid.

"What our blessed Patriarch is saying, is that we have found a way to extend my reign to ensure the strength and stability of the land." The Queen chose her words carefully, but I could feel my stomach twisting. Something felt wrong. Very, very wrong.

"My Queen?" Duke Colsarne almost whispered the words, but they echoed around the chamber nonetheless.

"With the correct supervision, the wisdom and guidance of the Order of the Cleansing Flame, and the backing of this council, we will use the enemy's weapon against them."

Sellor interjected. "With the correct wards and binding, a small amount of power may be used to extend the life of the Queen and provide her with the strength and vitality to rule."

Duke Colsarne drummed his fingers. "So. Magic."

"Right. The plan."

Taran stands at the head of the table, his eyes darting over the scrawled map of Craftvale. Windor App Decare pulls at his moustache and frowns. "We were agreed on the overall strategy, were we not, Sir Taran? Break the enemy, utterly and completely."

"Yes, but how are we to go about this? That is the issue."

I gaze over at Ulric, who stands behind his master, arms crossed. He frowns. "Hmmm."

Taran turns to him. "Sir Ulric? Is there something you would like to propose?"

He shrugs. "If I may, Master Taran. I do have some suggestions."

Taran steps back and gestures to the map. "Please. By all means. I would value any input."

Ichabod of Cassioc and Cain Bairflute are nearby, similarly perplexed by the dilemma before us.

"My lords. As you have mentioned, we need to utterly crush the enemy. Drive them out root and stem to set an example for all of Ashenfell."

"Yes! I just said that." Sir Windor snaps. "Get on with it, would you?"

"Yes, lord." He says hurriedly. "With that in mind, we cannot let any escape. Ulf, you mentioned that you and Sir Taran used the wool works to leave the town, by the river?"

I nod.

"Then that is a route we must guard against. I suggest a force of men, mounted on light horses to chase down and slay any that try to flee our judgement." He taps the map. "Here. We send them to the north-western bank of the Grapean. That way, they can hunt down any who escape. Or, if they are needed in the fighting, they can dismount and attack on foot, striking our foes from the flank."

Taran smiles. "A wise plan. Sir Windor, credit where credit is due, you have trained him well. How many warriors will you need?"

Ulric shrugs. "Four score? Maybe a hundred?"

Taran nods in agreement. "One hundred it is. If a job is worth doing, it's worth doing well."

Sir Ichabod scratches at his jaw and sucks his teeth. "What about the rest of our forces? The walls are high and strong. But I see nothing else for it. We have rams and ladders. We smash down the gate and take the walls." He says glumly.

"Men will die, that's for certain." Taran muses.

"Such is the nature of war." says Windor. "Good men will die so that the good in mankind may endure."

Taran sighs. "That's rather poetic of you, Windor, but I'd rather not bleed to death with a spike up my arse just yet if that's all the same to you." He scowls at my brother but goes silent nonetheless.

"This is your Rite of Mettle, Ulf." I look up with a jolt. He sweeps an arm at the table. "Go on. Give us your thoughts."

I stand up and glance over the map, trying to remember the choke points of the streets and the layout of the town. "We need to draw them into the open. We attack on the northern side of the gate, committing about two-thirds of our forces on foot to that point of the wall. There is a big market square behind there so it will be easier to assemble troops once we are over."

"What about the others?"

"The rest will wait in reserve. They will be left with a choice. Either we press and take the walls and then the town or they flood out the gate only to be overwhelmed by the reserve forces. If they do press out the gate, we need the reserve force mounted on heavy horses so that they can engage them swiftly to stop the main army being crushed against the wall."

Taran smiles. "Sir Ulric, you take your one hundred men to the river as agreed. Take men with keen eyes to make sure you can see if you should pursue the enemy or enter the town. Sir Cain, Sir Ichabod, and I will each command a detachment of the wall forces, with Sir Windor in charge of the reserves."

Sir Ichabod and Sir Cain both nod in agreement and I can see Ulric is pleased with the prospect of command. Only Sir Windor is still scowling. "You put a lot of faith in your squire's plan, Sir Taran." he mutters.

Taran smiles. "On the contrary, Sir Windor. Ulf's plan is fine. Rather, I'm putting a lot of faith in you."

Chapter 28:
Butterfingers

Duke Colsarne drummed his fingers. "So. Magic."

The Patriarch fixed him with a stare. "Yes. Magic. Controlled and limited, and under the strictest supervision. The Order will watch like a hawk for any signs of . . . complications from its use."

"Magic." The duke let the word hang in the air. The rest of the council avoided each other's gaze. "Our Queen is to use magic to prolong her life. Blood magic? From the Waystones, is it, Sellor?"

"Duke Colsarne, do not dare to think for a moment that this decision was reached lightly. This has only come about after months of insight and reflection."

"But it has come about, hasn't it?" Duke Colsarne pressed. His knuckles were white, and I could see his left hand shaking. "That is the decision that has been reached, has it not? That the Queen of Ashenfell will use the lifeblood of others to extend her own vitality."

"Criminals, Duke Colsarne." Queen Karidine arched her fingers. "Murderers, rapists. The scum of society. Those whose death benefits us all."

"Really? Because that was not my impression in Carstock." The duke's face set in mock confusion. "Because there it was the adulterers, the petty thieves, and the vagrants who died screaming in agony. The stones in Carstock. That was the crown, was it?"

"Yes, Colsarne, it was." She nodded to her cupbearer and Sellor poured out a goblet of thick, red wine. She took a long draft and exhaled. "Regrettable, but necessary. You have my word that future executions will be performed with more discretion."

Colsarne turned and swallows, taking a deep breath. "My Lord Decare, you have spent your life in the service of the Order, protecting the realm from threats of an esoteric nature. I know you hate me, and I hope you are aware that I hate you right back. But what are your thoughts on this?"

Duke Decare shrugged his shoulders. "The judgement of the Queen is absolute. She has Sellor's wisdom to guide her, and the security of the realm must be preserved."

"I see." Duke Colsarne blinked slowly. "Well. What now, Your Majesty?"

"This has been discussed and debated by both those close to me and the High Council of the Order of the Cleansing Flame. The matter is decided. As the dukes of the land, you have a right to know the changes to the law and to voice your opinions." She looked pointedly at Duke Colsarne. "But my authority comes from the line of kings, and it requires no consent but mine."

She nodded to Sellor, and he removed a parchment from a writing desk. A vast piece of vellum, already bearing the three fishes of the royal seal.

"By this charter, we change the legal code of Ashenfell. Allowing limited magic to be used under controlled circumstances, for the safety and betterment of the realm. The time for suspicion and absolute dogma has come to an end. We move towards enlightened times, and you will each place your seal to mark your assent."

A taper was lit and passed down the table as each lord lit their stick of sealing wax. Decare was first, a vast blood-red blob spilled across the page as the twin swords were added next to the royal seal.

Decroix dropped the wax.

"Oh dear! Bugger it." Duke Colsarne sighed and bent down to pick it up before wincing in pain. "Quentin, would you be kind enough to pass me the wax?"

"Of course, my lord."

Quentin is many things. He is a peacock. A sexual glutton. A fantastic wrestler. And he has a cock like a well-bred donkey. But above all else, he's an actor.

Quentin slipped, stepping on the wax candle and breaking it into pieces.

"You bloody fool!" Decroix slapped him around the back of the head, face like thunder.

"You dropped it in the first place!" he snapped.

"Look! We can scrape the bits together! Sorry Duke Enk, there's just a little bit under your chair. Mind my fingers!"

"Enough!" Duke Colsarne held up his hands in frustration. "Members of this council, I must extend my apologies. I have another stick in my quarters. I will return to you all as soon as I may. If you would excuse me."

He went to rise before the Queen stopped him. "Colsarne. You will return to give your seal upon the charter, won't you?"

The duke spread his palms wide and bows deeply. "Majesty, I will return as soon as I may. And, as I am sure we all agree, to fail to place a seal upon such a charter would be committing a betrayal of the Royal Trust and high treason. And, surely, even Duke Decare doesn't consider me that foolish."

There was a small round of awkward laughter and the Queen gave a thin smile and nodded her consent. We all bowed and left the room, walking briskly.

I looked over to the duke. His face was pale and his hands were shaking badly. I glanced behind us. Ten of the royal guards are following us, keeping pace. Great big bastards in gilded armour, armed with vicious looking bardiches.

We turned a corner then another one sharply. Duke Colsarne led the way, and I felt sure we hadn't been down here before.

The bustle of people and tapestries gave way to bare stone and silence as we moved into a discreet area of the keep. We were in a large, cold chamber, with storage barrels around the edge of the room and cheeses maturing on dusty shelves.

Lady Alexia leaned in and whispered, "Father, what are you doing?"

The guards caught up to us. They stood in formation, ready.

The leader of the group stepped forward. He was a few years older than me, grey-haired with a thick scar across his forehead. "Duke Colsarne. I fear that you have forgotten your way. Please, follow us."

The duke turned, taking his daughter's hand in his. "My dear, I am being foolish enough to commit high treason." He drew his sword in a blinding motion. "NOW!"

Marl charged in first, swinging fast and hard. I backed him up before he got slaughtered, raining down high two-handed blows. I stepped in, sliding the edge of my sword against an exposed neck. His hand flew up to stop the flow and I kicked him backwards, sending him sprawling into a sack of flour. The rest of Colsarne's men joined the fray, stabbing and hacking into the royal guard with reckless fury.

I turned and parried a blow aimed at my chest and riposted with a stab to his face. The grey-haired captain stepped backwards, snarling before sweeping across and snagging my pauldron on the tip of his blade. He pulled me forward and I stumbled, but kept my footing. My vision clouded for a moment as he punched out, a gauntleted fist cracking me between the eyes. I swung wildly, trying to buy time to let my eyes clear and my head to stop ringing. I heard the man scream and saw Duke Colsarne standing over him with a bloody sword. He stabbed his through the eye socket with a neat thrust and went back to the fighting. He darted in like a snake, striking between their armour or feinting to allow Decroix to land a killing blow.

I gripped my blade in a half-sword and shoved against one of them, pushing him into the wall. Simon cut down at his feet in two swift hacks, the fine leather of his boots splitting and filling with blood. He clattered to the ground in a heap so I caved in his skull with my sword pommel.

Marl bellowed like a bull as he forced the last one to the floor, hands throttling each other. His face was a mess of blood and I saw his foe start to shake as the death rattle took over. He flopped around like crippled horse before going still. Marl stood up, breathless and snarling. "Bastards!" He spat.

Quentin shook his head. "They were doing their duty, Marl. Just like you and I were."

"Still a bunch of bastards!" He wiped the gore from his face, then noticed the duke watching him with flat eyes, eyebrow raised. "Oh, apologies, your Grace."

Duke Colsarne sheathed his sword and wiped his hands clean on a handkerchief. "Marl, given the circumstances, I'm sure I can pardon the slightly colourful language."

Three of our own men lay dead and I could see Marl bleeding, but he'd live. Decroix was holding his left hand and gritting his teeth, but he was a tougher bastard than he looked.

We hid the bodies under some sacks and wiped off the blood as best we could. Duke Colsarne led the way, taking us through twisting corridors. He paused occasionally to change the route. We walked in silence, hands on sword hilts with a thousand different thoughts.

"So. It's happening then, father? You're really going through with this?"

The duke sighed. "Alexia, we've just murdered ten of the Queen's own guards, in her own keep. It's a little late to back out now."

She shrugged in acquiescence. "Not an unfair point."

I cleared my throat. "Your Grace, was this all planned? For how long?"

He stopped and turned to all of us. "Let me make this clear. Queen Karidine has forced this. It was her decision that moved my hand. And yes Ulf, I have been prepared for this. For two reasons. Firstly, in case my suspicions of the queen were correct, which sadly they were. And secondly, because I'm not a blithering idiot. I trust you find this satisfactory?"

I nodded.

"Good. This way."

After a few twisting passages, we moved into the bright sunshine. The calm normality around us contradicted the uneasiness we all felt. I noticed a wet patch of blood on my boot as we walked as casually as we could towards Duke Colsarne's hall, and tried to scuff it off in the stable's straw and dust. The horses were saddled and ready to go, held by those who did not come with us to the Council.

"The hall closest to the gates, nearest to the stable." I muttered. "Nice touch."

We saddled up and rode out, the guards waving us through. Behind my shoulder I saw someone running away and coughed pointedly.

"Yes, Ulf?" Colsarne asked.

I nodded toward the running servant.

"LOOK, A HARE!" Duke Colsarne pointed excitedly and lashed at his horse. "FOLLOW ME!"

We charged after him, riding as hard as we could. We pressed ourselves, pushing the horses as much as we dared along the eastern road to Usk, stopping only at nightfall. I practically fell out of the saddle.

Reed's flanks were soaked with sweat. She nuzzled my good cheek, and I held her head tight to my neck, rubbing her ears. I led her to a pond nearby and stooped down beside her, drinking deeply.

We had blankets and all necessities in our saddlebags, but any luxuries, including our tents, had been left behind. We lit a fire and boiled barley and split peas in the one pot we had to share between us.

Marl pulled a face as he chewed on a tasteless mouthful. "Decroix," he grumbled, "would it have been too much to ask to make sure we had a few sausages to go with?"

Decroix dropped his spoon into his bowl, with a little more force than necessary. "Oh, I do apologise, Marl. I'll bear that in mind the next time I organise provisions for a life-or-death flight from the queen's own fortress."

The duke held up his hand and they stopped their bickering. "That's quite enough." he said, voice strained with exhaustion. Wordlessly, he rose and left the fire, finding a place to sleep beneath a tree.

I decided to retire a couple of minutes later. I had no idea what the duke intended to do, or how any of us would survive this. However, we'd still be just as much of a bunch of traitors in the morning after a good night's sleep, so fuck it.

We woke up cold. I knew it wasn't just me, as I heard Marl and Quentin complaining about it bitterly. Decroix winced as he rubbed at his hand. Several fingers were swollen and bent at an awkward angle.

"How did that happen?" I asked.

He looked at his hand and grimaced. "If you must know, I slipped in the fight. The butt of one of those bloody bardiches. Smashed into me."

Decroix had my sympathies. Autumn is a horrible time to break a bone. The cold and the damp sets in and it never heals properly. I stepped forward to help him as he struggled with a boot, but he waved me away, cursing under his breath.

The injury was beyond Quentin's skill to heal, so from Usk we headed northeast to Melpapier, stopping only for food and to find a wise woman to set Decroix's hand, lest it turn crooked. With practised ease, she twisted and turned it back into place. I could hear the horrible scrape of bone on bone, even as Decroix roared in pain. His breath stank of wine, having sensibly made himself good and drunk to dull the pain. Lady Alexia paid her five Wyear for the healing and a full Guilder for her silence.

Within an hour, we were back in the saddle, Decroix's white bandages standing in stark contrast to the stains and grime of travel. We rode along the eastern coast, the cold sea breeze chilling us all as the weather turned bitter. We used all the light we had each day to press onwards.

I glanced over to Duke Colsarne, his shoulders stooped and sleeves pulled down against the cold.

"So where are we headed?"

"Cassioc. It is the only place where we might be safe, and the best place to make a stand."

I ignored the madness of starting a civil war for a moment to indulge the old man. "Right. Because if we continue along the coast, we come to Carstock, or if we go to the southeast through the hills to your manse, we are going to be expected."

He sighed as if explaining things to a very slow child. And I suppose, compared to his vast, scheming mind, I probably was. "Iska."

"I'm sorry?"

He pointed down the coast. If I squinted, I could make out a few ramshackle houses and the smoke of cooking fires. "It's a fishing village. Small. Less generous people would call it a hamlet. They have something I need."

"And what is that, my lord?"

"Boats. We aren't going to ride to Cassioc. We're going to sail there."

It was a clever idea. Buy or steal some boats, sail down the coast, and then up the river Phon to the capital. I had no idea what we would do once we got there, but we could burn that bridge when we came to it.

I nodded. "Yes, lord. I think I understand."

"Good." He threw me a fat purse, clinking pleasantly. "Go with Quentin and make the arrangements."

The others made camp as we both rode down the muddy track to Iska. Quentin was more withdrawn than normal. We rode in quiet for a while until he eventually broke the silence. "Nine years."

I nodded. "Yep."

"Nine of the best years, Ulf. I'm not a young man anymore."

"You look distinguished! Mature."

He snorted. "Hah! That's a load of wank old men like to tell themselves when their hair goes snowy. No offence, Ulf."

I gritted my teeth. "None taken." But I suppose, compared to Quentin and Decroix, I was old. I spent the prime years of my life drinking, fighting, and drinking some more, and it showed. My body aches, and I don't know how to feel normal without either an ale or a blade in my hand. I wasted those years - pissed them away - but at least I still had them.

"And what about Decroix? Ulf, you saw his hand. What's going to happen to him?"

I shrugged. "What happens to everyone when they break a bone? It will set, for better for worse. It will never be as good as it was, and it will hurt like buggery in the cold. I don't know. What else do you want me to say?"

He sighed. "Think about it for a moment. You know why we are going to Cassioc, don't you?"

I nodded. It was pretty obvious what Duke Colsarne had planned.

"We're making a stand. There's going to be a battle, Ulf. It's going to be bloody, and people are going to die."

"That's how battles often go." I shouldn't have been such a sarcastic bastard, but I couldn't help myself. "Quentin, Decroix is cleverer than both of us put together. He's the second most ruthless and devious bastard I've ever met. He'll be fine."

"I hope so. I really do."

We rode into Iska. There were nets spread out on the beach as the gulls glutted themselves on the guts and scales, shimmering like broken glass. A range of craft bobbed on the water, moored to a dock sitting on half-rotten piers. I scanned over a few until I spied the one we needed: a wherry, wide and flat bottomed, with a decent hold. Perfect.

An old man was swearing at some rope, untangling the salt-frazzled strands with gnarled fingers. I could see a few yellowed stubs in his mouth, and as we got closer, I could smell his breath, even over the salt of the sea.

"YES?" he snapped.

I jabbed my thumb at the wherry boat. "Who owns that ship?"

He laughed. "That's Ashab, my fool of a son. Look at her!" He stood up and waved his arm frantically. "Not deep enough to drown a kitten." He grumbled. "I told him, get something deep for the richer waters. Or something small and nippy. But no! Never listens to his father. Always knows best. Married a stupid wife and gave me moon-touched grandchildren and never-"

Quentin cut in. "Where is he at the moment?"

He spat and pointed to a longhouse nearby. The walls and ceiling were covered in turf to keep it warm, but it gave the look of living in a giant, grassy phallus. Two children ran out, screaming to each other and off to the beach. A man stepped out, stooping through the door frame. He was a huge bloke, with bright eyes and a long, shaggy beard that looked like he was eating a badger.

"Hullo? Can I help you, friend?"

"Ashab?" He nodded. "Good. I've got a proposition for you."

Quentin and I laid out the arrangement. Take us and some of the horses in the wherry boat down the coast, then up the river to Cassioc. Don't ask questions. Don't fuck us about.

He furrowed his thick brow and I could hear his quern-stone of a brain grinding together.

"Why does Duke Colsarne want to take horses by the river? Wouldn't you be better riding them?"

"His daughter has woman's troubles." Quentin said quick as a flash. Ashab went bright red and mumbled something. "It's a private matter, so although I'm sure you're thrilled to have someone so important on your boat, we need to employ your professional discretion."

He nodded slowly and Quentin smiled, handing over a handful of thick Guilders. "Do you want to go tomorrow? We could head off tonight, but I'll need to get the nets and things out of the hold if you're bringing horses."

I paused. The sea looked fairly calm and I reckoned that time was of the essence. "We'll make the tide. Ready your boat and we'll see you back here. Quentin, I'm going to help Ashab with the boat, you ride hard back to the duke and get things sorted."

We spent about an hour shifting the bulky fish traps and reeking pots. The whole boat stunk of fish, but that was just something the duke would have to live with.

Ashab brought on some boxes of salted fish, provisions for the journey. "Thanks for the hand, friend."

"Not a problem." I hoped that he was too thick to realise that I just didn't want to leave him on his own because I didn't trust the bastard. He grinned like a loon as he showed his father the golden coins. The old man's jaw fell open and he shook his head with disbelief as he strolled back to the longhouse.

"Where are those buggers? They should be here by now." I muttered, stripping off my armour and storing it safely on board. Heavy metal and seawater are not the best of friends. Ashab introduced me to his son, a gangly youth with a mop of hair who looked like a miniature copy of his father.

More time passed, and I breathed a sigh of relief and frustration as I spotted them further down the coast. Hooves pounding, they rode hard with Quentin in the lead.

"Sorry it took so long, Ulf. We were-"

"I don't care! We need to catch the tide!" I snapped. "Shirts off, now!"

"Pardon?"

"Just do it, and stop pissing about."

Ashab's son laid out the gangplank and I whipped my shirt off, wrapping it gently around Reed's head. "Easy girl." I whispered, rubbing between her ears. I led her gently through the shallow water. She shook her head and whinnied, so I held her around the neck and shushed her for a moment. Hesitantly, she went up the plank and into the hold. The boat tilted slightly, and she blew her lips crossly.

"Come on, hurry up!"

With agonising slowness, we led the horses up and into the hold of the boat. Pressed close together, the horses stamped and chomped, taking nips at the wooden beam holding them in. Eventually, men, weapons, armour, and horses were all loaded. What we couldn't take with us we threw into the sea; no point in leaving clues to our passing.

"Marl, can you kindly hurry the fuck up?" Decroix snapped.

"He's not moving!" Marl pulled down on the reins as his horse stamped about, furious at the whole affair.

"Calm him down!" I yelled. "Let him know that you're there."

He nodded. "LISTEN TO ME, YOU EVIL MINDED BASTARD! IF YOU DON'T GET UP THAT BLOODY PLANK AND ONTO THE CUNTING BOAT, I'LL PULL YOUR BOLLOCKS OFF!" With swearing of sufficient colour and magnitude to make even the fishermen blush, Marl shoved his stallion onto the boat.

"There! See how you like that, you vicious bugger." The horse now on the boat, he noticed his lord's daughter standing nearby, and took on a blush of his own. "Oh! Sorry, Lady Alexia . . ." he muttered.

She smiled. "That's quite all right, Marl. Now, shall we?"

Ashab's son and I hoisted the sail while his father steered at the helm. We just made the tide and after a short while, we sailed down the north coast of Rusia, the hills of Duke Colsarne's lands to our right. I helped with the setting of the sail, making tiny shifts and movements to cope with the fickleness of the wind.

We pulled into a small cove at dusk to spend the night. Simon and I gingerly lead the horses out to graze on a patch of scraggly grass, which clung desperately to the top of the rocks. After a while we tied them up for the night, leaving them tethered to a lonely copse of trees.

Duke Colsarne forbade a fire, and we each took turns at watch. I could hear the water lapping gently, and the cold sea breeze whipped at me. I shifted, with stones pressed into my back, and tried to drift off to sleep.

Chapter 29:
The Honour of The Cleansing Flame

"But we can be there by nightfall if we press hard."

Taran pinches his nose. "Yes. I'm aware of this, Sir Windor. As are the rest of us."

"Then why aren't we pressing forward? We can fight them tonight! The sooner this filth is purged from the land the better, no?"

"I'd rather fight them refreshed, after a good night's sleep, and not knackered from a hard ride."

"It will give them more time to prepare."

"They know we're coming anyway. An extra day is going to make literally no difference at all, except it will mean our troops will be rested and ready for battle, and we can fight them in the daylight to see what the fuck is going on."

He sneers. "It sounds like someone would prefer safety over glory."

I stop fiddling with my belt and look up. I fully expect Taran to whack him in the jaw, but he smiles benignly. "But as Oswald the Fierce said at the Battle of the Silver Shroud, 'Battle at night, monster's delight. Battle in the morning? Safe and boring.'"

"Oswald never said that!" he snaps angrily.

Taran shrugs. "Fine. Well, I'm saying it now, then. By all means, if you don't like it feel free to ride ahead and start the battle without us. See how far you get."

"Sir Taran, can you stop antagonising Sir Windor for just a few minutes? It does get very wearing after a while." Sir Ichabod rubs at his elbow, an old tourney wound that I know plays up for him in cold weather like this.

"Agreed. Sir Windor, I apologise if I was too harsh when critiquing your idiocy and I hope you can forgive me."

Windor snarls and flounces out of the tent, the open flaps showing the fresh morning sunlight. Sir Ichabod puts his head in his hands and sighs deeply. "Taran, for fuck's sake."

"Fine. I take your point, but damn his eyes he's been getting on my bloody nerves lately."

"You think you're the only one? It's not just you. The rest of us also think he's a cunt. The difference is that we can keep our mouths shut and play the fucking game, whereas you seem intent on running yours as often as possible."

"Someone has to tell the truth, Ichabod. People like that spend their whole lives getting by on their family's money. We both know he doesn't deserve his seat on the council. Look how he's shaped poor Ulric over the years! He's not the only one, Ichabod. Dozens more in the Order seem to think that money is the same as virtue and power is the same as strength."

Sir Ichabod sits down and points to a goblet. I get up and fill it for him, stopping when it reaches the brim.

Taran raises his eyebrows. "Little early to be drinking, isn't it? We'll be riding off in just a little while."

He shrugs. "Might as well. Care to join me?"

"I'll pass." Taran says. "But anyway, the point I was making is that a knight needs to be more than just a rich thug with good weapons."

"You're right. He needs a horse as well."

"Very funny." Taran mutters.

"Look, it's all well and good to talk of virtue. Oswald knows you're a better man than the rest of us. A fact you remind us all of constantly by not mentioning it. But without Decare's money, without the support of noble houses and their ilk, the Order would have ceased to be years ago. It's not perfect, but what's the alternative?"

"Right. I take your point. Can we agree on one thing though Sir Ichabod?"

"Depends. What is it?"

"That Windor App Decare is a fucking cunt."

*He laughs. "Taran, I swear the mouth of yours is going to get you killed."
Taran shrugs. "Probably."*

Gulls were screeching and flapping around the boat, drawn to the reek of fish which permeated the timber. I blinked a few times and sat up, instantly regretting it. Too much time with the duke had made me soft, and I'd gotten used to soft beds and not waking up with my arms and legs aching. I rubbed some warmth into my body and my breath steamed in the cold. I gently kicked a few people awake and we got ourselves together.

It was a bitter day. Mist licked at the coast and we all shivered in the heaving boat. The horses weren't happy, either, and I couldn't blame them. We sheltered on stony beaches and in tight coves which warded against some of the biting wind.

On the fifth day, we reached the mouth of the Phon. The boat awkwardly bobbed around, waiting for the tide and the wind to shift before we could sail.

"No point going now." Ashab said. "If we go now, we'll be tacking all the way to the river. Probably run her aground on the banks." I nodded and we waited alongside the other boats. Ashab gave a friendly wave to the other captains, grizzled and salty bastards to a man. In turn, we sailed up the Phon, keeping a sensible distance from the other craft on the river.

We made decent time on the river, with a good wind to our back. It was warmer inland, and although we were still chilled, I felt slightly less grumpy. As we moored on the river bank, the horses seemed happy to have some proper grazing, instead of the salty hay or scraggly grass they had been forced to eat.

Decroix briefed us all on the plan. "We will get to Cassioc tomorrow, in the early evening. Roderick will be at an inn called 'The Broken Barrell.' We'll meet him there, organise the rest of the Colsarne forces in the city, and arrange a conversation with the Steward of Cassioc to see what the situation is."

I looked at Decroix with curiosity. "Situation?"

"We're hoping he will side with us. But if not, then we'll have to kill him and seize control of the city."

"Ah."

"I mean, it will be a violent bloodbath either way, but if we can avoid depleting our forces beforehand and gain an ally, then it's probably for the best."

We paid the mooring fees and bid Ashab farewell, sincerely wishing him a safe journey, a silent mouth, and that we would never have to see his stinking boat ever again. I led Reed down the gangplank and I could tell that she felt happy to have firm ground under her hooves, even if it was the seedy cobbles of Cassioc.

As a duke, Colsarne wasn't subject to the normal prodding and scrutiny, but we still bound our swords and put them on the wrong hip, out of respect for the law of the city.

No inn had space for all of us together, so we split up. After stabling the horses and dumping our gear, Marl and I accompanied Duke Colsarne and Lady Alexia to the Broken Barrell. We left our surcoats behind and tried to move discretely through the streets to avoid attention.

The inn was one of the better ones, near the burned-out husk which had been the Ouroboros. Roderick sat in a corner, squinting over a book and nursing a small cup of wine. He looked up as we approached. "My lord!" he beamed.

"Shh." Duke Colsarne snapped at him.

"Sorry . . ." he murmured. "It is just good to see you alive and well."

I headed to the bar to get food and drink for us all, wincing at the prices. For the same price as some tiny cups of wine and a few slivers of pretentious cheese, I could be blind drunk and stuffed to vomiting in a proper tavern just around the corner. And I'd have probably got a shag or a fight out of it as well. Maybe both.

Roderick smiled at the maid who brought it over. I followed his eyes as she bent over to put down the platter, and I could see why he chose this place.

"Have you enjoyed your stay here, Roderick?" Lady Alexia raised her eyebrow at him in a perfect imitation of her father. He at least had the decency to look sheepish.

Brigandine

"Umm, yes. Thank you." he muttered. "The household troops are nearby. I've got a few of the stable lads from inns across the city on the take. We can get word to everyone and have them readied within a half-hour, at most."

Duke Colsarne nodded his appreciation. "Thank you, Roderick. As always, we are grateful for your service. Where are Rouberte and Johan?"

"Ah." Roderick looked awkward and my heart sank. "The swordsmen are here around the theatre, ready to go, and Rouberte's crossbow unit are stationed around the Eastern Quarter. But as I said, I can get them here easily enough-"

"What about Johan?" Duke Colsarne drummed his finger on the dark oak table and growled. "Seneschal . . ."

Roderick swallowed. "My lord, nothing has been heard from Carstock. No word from Johan, or any of the billmen. Nor from Siffisante or Azrael Bordane."

I snorted. "I just want it to be known that I have said that Azrael Bordane was a complete cunt all along."

Lady Alexia glared at me. "Ulf, how does that help?"

I shrugged. "It made me feel better, my lady."

Duke Colsarne shot me a glare. "As accurate as your character judgment may be, please stay silent. If you can. Roderick, let the others know we will be rallying soon. We will be meeting with the Steward of Cassioc shortly."

For fuck's sake . . .

The houses got bigger and fancier as we moved to the western part of the city. We met with Quentin and Decroix along the route, and Marl led the way, his eyes darting around with suspicion. His hand never strayed far from his sword hilt, and I noticed that the leather bindings near the guard look very frayed indeed.

Eventually, the houses gave way to vast, tended lawn. Huge expanses of manicured grass, dotted with fruit trees and hedges were pruned into intricate shapes of leaping fish. Every leaf and petal was tended, and had been cut to please the eye. But the slow decay of autumn had nearly finished. The trees had lost their leaves, and the roses long since spent their blooms.

Quentin whistled theatrically. "The royal manse. So, this is where the Queen spends winter?"

Duke Colsarne nodded. "It is also where the Steward of the city spends the other nine months of the year. And where we will be meeting him."

An ornate gatehouse ahead led to the entrance. I kicked aside a peacock and got a dirty look from Decroix. The guards at the gate wore the green and blue heraldic colours of Cassioc, rather than the golden fish of House Fairbourne. They were the custodians of the city, devoted to protecting its laws and people rather than any one noble house.

Roderick shuffled forward and after a brief word to the men at the gate, they parted their spears and allowed us free passage.

A servant bowed and escorted us to the lobby outside Steward's private chambers. We were brought bowls of rosewater, laid out on a table with towels and scrubbing cloths. I tidied myself up as best I could, hoping to get rid of the smell of travel. I scraped the grime from my fingernails and wet the cloth, wiping wax from my ears.

A steward coughed discreetly and led us to the High Chamber. As we passed through the halls and corridors, all around us men and women busied themselves for the Queen's arrival. Banners were hung, and the smell of fresh paint lingered in the air. Wooden panels were oiled to shine with a lustre, and bunches of sweet herbs were draped from the walls and rafters.

A large pair of doors swung open and inside a table was spread with fresh bread, along with delicately cut fruit and cheeses. There was a thump and a scrape and an ugly figure with a single milky eye and stump at his elbow limped towards us, leaning heavily on a gold-topped cane.

He nodded at me, and I bowed in respect along with the others. The Maimed Lord, Ichabod of Cassioc.

The mud is oozing into my boots. My calves are splattered with it, and the pouring rain has plastered my hair over my face.

"Fuck me..." I mutter.

Taran sighs. He's standing next to me in the line, his blue tabard filthy like my own. "Ulf, remember what they had last time?"

"Crossbows?"

"And what don't crossbows like?"

I grin back at him. "Rain."

He nods. "Exactly. On the downside, you'll have to spend hours getting my armour clean after this."

"Knights don't clean armour, remember?"

He smiles at me and shrugs. "Fair point. I'll just have to hope I can find some other moon-calf to do it, I suppose. Now, shall we?" He raises his sword high. "FOR THE GLORY OF OSWALD, AND THE HONOUR OF THE CLEANSING FLAME!"

I roar with the others, and we march forward in double time. Looking over my shoulder, I see Sir Windor and the other third of our army, horses ready to spring the trap and put our plan in place.

My trap. My plan. The plan where, if it goes wrong, we could all die.

"RIGHT WHEEL!" The right flank swing round, turning us to the left. Each man moving with hundreds of hours' worth of precision.

"LEFT WHEEL!" Taran barks the command and the left flank moves while the men on the right pivot and with only two dozen yards to go, we strike our target like a dagger. Pathetic bolts fly down, bouncing from armour. I stifle a wince at a horrible scream as a lucky shot finds an eye socket, a flash of crimson gore amid the mud and steel.

"LADDERS!" The ladders are brought forward, spiked into the ground with two stout men holding onto the base. Curses and screams ring out from the walls as the defenders try to shove them away.

"Ulf! Don't look up!" Taran yells.

"What?" I look up and my mouth is filled with sewage, offal, and nameless filth. I retch and gag, desperately trying to wipe the disgusting mess from my eyes. I shake flecks of human shit from my hair and spit hard, the foul taste still clinging to my mouth.

"I did say not to look up." Even with his visor down, I can tell Taran is grinning. "TO THE WALLS!"

We flood towards the ladders, a mad scrum and press of armoured bodies and weapons. I find myself at the bottom rung and I start climbing, heart pounding. My head rings and I fall down into the dirt, a rock rolling off of my helmet. My vision starts to swim back and I can hear a sound like the ringing of steel. Someone's dragging me to my feet.

"My thanks!" I gasp. He grunts and pushes his way up the ladder, shield raised overhead. He climbs slowly but surely, hugging the rungs with his forearms as his muddy sabatons slip on the wood. I follow him quickly, my sword held tight. I can hear myself panting, heart hammering hard against my brigandine.

Some of the men are at the top of the ladders now, desperately hacking away, trying to clear a space. One reaches the top only to be hurled from the walls, landing below with his leg twisted horribly. He screams at the splintered bone before a quarrel takes his throat.

"With me!" The man above me barks. He forces himself over the top, swinging wildly with his arming sword to clear some room. I follow him as quickly as I can, shaking at the top of the ladder. I thrust my blade quickly into a man's side and force him off, sending him falling back into town. I stagger, almost losing my sword and footing. I grab one of our footmen by the scruff of his gambeson and pull him up onto the battlements. There are more of us now, about two dozen. I parry a downward strike from a messer and sweep his blade away, cutting him across the face and neck. He screams and I follow up with a thrust through the heart.

Looking up, I can see the gates opening. The enemy are rushing through, swarms of them pressing into us. Men drop down from the ladders to join the fighting. A savage, swirling melee. They're not climbing anymore and we're up here cut off.

"Down the ladders! DOWN THE LADDERS!" I yell and wave my sword. Some of them hear me, but the rest are overwhelmed. I swing my leg over and skid down the ladder, my bloody sword nearly slipping from my hand. The hilt is slick with gore and I wipe it quickly on my tabard, the golden cup now stained a horrid red.

I glance around, looking for Taran. He's there in the thick of the fighting, a ring of mangled bodies around his feet. There is a deep dent in his pauldron and his mail skirt is torn, but he is fighting like a tiger, each blow fast as a serpent and sure as a hammer strike. "WHERE THE FUCK IS DECARE?"

Brigandine

I see Sir Ichabod swinging a stout poleaxe, the haft painted in bands of green and blue. He is fending off two swordsmen with thrusts from his butt spike and short cuts from the blade. One of them rushes him and cracks a savage blow against the crown of his helmet, denting it wickedly. He staggers back and I try to push forward through the chaos. All around me men are bellowing in rage or screaming in agony. Fallen bodies are trampled to pieces in the crush.

I lean forward and hook the swordsman's ankle with my crossguard. He staggers and I step quickly, cracking him a hard, short blow which caves in his teeth. I turn my sword and strike at him again, the crossguard bursting his eye and caving in the socket.

His fellow thrusts at my chest and I pivot on my left leg, his blade scraping along my armour. My right hand on the hilt and left on the blade, I charge forward, striking down through his collarbone and into his chest. He swings his sword up, catching the brow of my helmet and nicking my forehead. Blood starts pouring into my eyes as I force him down to the mud, pressing my sword blade into his throat. I rake it back and forth as he scrabbles at the blade, cutting the nerves from his fingers before sawing through his throat.

My head is reeling and I'm shaking. I hack down a spear and step down hard on the shaft, sending the splintered pole down into the mud. The fighting is grim and bloody work, and my arms ache and scream at me with each blow I strike. The Order of the Cleansing Flame are the best fighters in the world, but we're backed into a corner, outnumbered, and fighting an enemy that doesn't give a damn if they die.

My vambrace is flapping on my arm, a buckle ripped off by the hook of an axe. Slowly and brutally, they are driving us back. For each one we slay, another two spring forward, trampling their own dead to get to us.

The ground shakes, and fierce cries of bloodlust soar over the din as a tide of horses crash into the rear ranks of the enemy, shattering them like a hammer against glass. I see Decare at the head of the charge, a thrashing footman skewered on his lance. He hurls it to the ground and draws a huge, broad-bladed sword and hacks about him, severing limbs with wild abandon.

Whoops of joy echo around me as the jaws of the trap spring closed. Caught between our blades and the thrashing hooves of our horsemen, the warriors of Craftvale finally break and rout.

I thrust forward, stabbing a man through the back of his neck as he turns to run. I raise my sword to the sky and roar with triumph. I'm young and strong, and the enemy is scattered and fleeing before me.

"Take the gate!" Taran yells, his voice carrying over the din of battle.

We surge onward, the press of bodies driving away any defenders and keeping the gates wide open. The Order starts to march on the main square, and we hear a scream.

I turn, seeing a man clawing at the cobbles as he's dragged into a house, the door slamming behind him. There are shouts of alarm and lumbering, shapeless things lurch from the filthy alleys. An obese, swollen limb lashes out and brains a man before darting back into the shadows.

I gag at a horrible stench and spin around on my heels to see a naked old man stagger towards me, his body hideously warped and distended and his mouth gaping impossibly wide. With a speed that defies his frame, he hurls himself towards me, pinning my wrists to the ground. A vast, barbed tongue lolls from his jaws and I turn my head away, hearing the spikes grate away at my armour. I shift under his grip and throw him back, striking in a fluid movement. Yellow pus floods from the wound, soaking into the street. He lunges at me once more before I take his head from his shoulders.

"MOVE, QUICKLY!" *Taran yanks his sword from one of these shapeless things and we push on. Horrors that once were men strike and claw at us from both sides of the street, tearing warriors limb from limb.*

Decare's horse is pulled from under him, the guts torn out with black talons. His leg is pinned underneath and I rush over, joining the others in protecting him. Dropping my sword, I grab him under the arms and pull him up. He's a giant of a man, and the armour doesn't help.

"Get off!" *he snarls.* "And get moving, NOW!"

Prayers and words of binding are shouted, and with the holy might of Oswald, the things are driven back. We finally find ourselves in the centre of the town, where Taran knew we would find what we were looking for.

Chapter 30:
An Easy Smile

"Ulf." He smiled at me, and I jumped back to reality.

"Sir Ichabod. It is good to see you again."

Duke Colsarne raised an eyebrow at me. "You . . . know the Steward of Cassioc?"

Sir Ichabod's smile faded and the lines on his face blended in with the scars. His voice was warm and welcoming. "Yes. From many years ago, in better times." With the grunts of an old man, he sat down at the table and with a bit of effort broke off a chunk of bread with his one good hand.

"Please, don't stand on ceremony. I can't stand all that 'I'll eat and you can all watch me' nonsense, even if it is apparently good manners." he chuckled. "Plenty of time for etiquette and all that when the Queen arrives, eh?" His thin shoulders shook with laughter and he coughed with the effort. "Excuse me . . ." he murmured.

Lady Alexia gave him a beautiful smile, which he returned. Although, admittedly, with fewer teeth. "Steward-"

He held up his hand to stop her. "Ichabod, please, if you would be so kind, my lady. I would consider it a great favour."

"Ichabod, I will be frank. There is a problem."

He rolled his eyes "There is always a problem of some kind, good lady." Sir Ichabod sighed like a deflating bladder and reached for some cheese, cutting himself a thin slice. "Bandits. Assassins.

Raiders from across the sea." He gestured with the knife at Duke Colsarne. "Edmund, you remember a few years back, don't you? The Vaahl. Snorri Ironhews, wasn't it? Something ridiculous like that."

"I believe so, my lord."

"It's those dozy bastards in Spechal." he moaned. "Always kicking the hornet's nest just to see what comes out. And you know what comes out?"

"Hornets?"

He nodded. "Hornets." he said through a mouth full of cheese. "Anyway, where was I?"

I cleared my throat. "The queen is going to use magic to murder people and use their lives to extend her own. Sellor is supporting her under the premise that together they can control magic and avoid its corruption. They have set up Waystones across Rusia, probably over the rest of Ashenfell. We are starting a rebellion, and we will probably all get killed. We want you to help us."

Sir Ichabod's knife clattered to the table and Duke Colsarne and his daughter looked at me with mouths agape. I shrugged. "What? I thought time was of the essence?"

Ichabod stammered, "But that's . . . impossible! How can you even think of-"

"Sorry about burning down the Ouroboros, by the way. That was my fault. Well, actually, it was the Waystone I destroyed in the basement."

"You . . . had the strength of will to break a Waystone? You had the might and faith to sunder an altar of the arch-enemy?"

"In all fairness, the other three I smashed up in Carstock were a lot harder."

"Wait, so that was-"

"The Black Ram. Yes. And the queen was behind it. They were dropping people onto Waystones and using the spilt blood to saturate and power the Waystones."

Decroix spluttered. "Ulf!"

"And Duke Decare doesn't seem to have a problem with this. Nor, by extension, does the rest of the Order."

"ULF!"

"And we are in open rebellion against the Queen, and we want you to help."

"ULF!" Decroix screamed. "For the love of fuck! Why can't you shut up? Just for a few minutes can't we try some subtle diplomacy without you buggering everything up!"

A silence hung in the air and Decroix went a little red. Sir Ichabod reached out a shaking hand and took a long draft of wine. "Edmund, old friend, you will have to excuse me. Ulf, could you come with me, please?"

He stood up, chair scraping slowly on the floor. I stood and bowed to the others before following. I could feel Duke Colsarne's gaze on the back of my neck, and I felt fairly certain my head was going to explode in a gory shower.

I moved to open the heavy door for us and Sir Ichabod nodded his thanks. "We shan't be long, I should imagine."

He smiled at the others. "Please, do help yourself to lunch. Oh! Make sure you try some of the blue, runny one with the herbs, but please save me some. I know it's picky, but that is my favourite."

I followed after him as he shuffled down the corridor. A frown creased his brow, somehow managing to make him look even older and world-weary. "This way." he murmured.

The servants and denizens of the manse bowed and parted before him and he greeted each one with a nod and a smile. We went on for what seemed like an age. We headed through the kitchens and living quarters, the tapestries and paintings giving way to the utilitarian parts of the house, before finally crossing the courtyard to a large, squat building.

"Are you . . . sure we are going the right way, my lord?"

He frowned. "I've forgotten a lot of things. But it is a poor knight indeed who can't find his way to the armoury."

The guards parted for us without hesitation and pushed open the door. Racks upon racks of swords and halberds, sacks of mail, and barrels stuffed with thousands of arrows fill every space. The air reeked of oil and polish. Each blade sharp and gleaming.

"It's in that box, I think. Behind the quarrels. Would you mind shifting them? I'd help but . . ." He looked sheepishly at his stump.

I hefted the wicker basket full of crossbow bolts, staggering under the weight. There was an old oak chest beneath, worn and stained.

"I told them not to lean on it when they polish." He sighed. "But who listens to me? I'm only the Steward of the damn city."

I opened the box. "You . . . how did-"

"After Craftvale." he said, voice cracking.

"You kept it. For years. Polished and shining."

"I wasn't going to leave it to go rusty, Ulf. I couldn't do that to your brother. I knew him since he was a boy. I saw the man he became."

I swallowed and took a deep breath. I could hear him crying and I blinked my eyes hard. Fucking . . . fuck.

I couldn't think of anything. I could do nothing save stare at it. Every inch of steel. Every rivet. I knew that armour off by heart. I should have, having cleaned the damned thing often enough. I wanted to touch it, to pick it up and hold it as if he was still there. But I simply could not.

"Ulf. What you say about the queen. The Order and the progress of the Black Ram. This is treason, Ulf. Nothing less. If you can do me one thing, I will believe every word you say."

He stepped behind me and took my hand. He forced it downwards, and I was powerless to resist. My fingertips stroked the cold steel of the armour and I held my palm flat against it. Fat tears fell down and slid across the surface.

"Ulf of Banrillar." he said gently. "If what you say is true, then swear it. On your brother's armour."

"I swear." I whispered, choking out the words.

Sir Ichabod released my hand and I looked up, his face streaming with tears and marked with despair. "Then we have no choice. We go to war."

Decroix shook his head. "So, that's it? You say you're telling the truth, and he just believes you?" He drained the tankard and raised his head to the serving maid to bring another.

"Yes."

He clucked with exasperation. "Would you care to elaborate?"

"No."

He threw up his hands. "I give up. I really do." Quentin gave me a wry smile as his brother rubbed his temples. "We've fundamentally signed our own death warrants."

"Yes."

"There's going to be a war. You think the queen is just going to let us squat in her house, mocking her?"

"No." Quentin joined in with me and we shared a grin.

"Oh, bugger off, the pair of you!" he snapped. "Fine. Sir Ichabod's soldiers and men at arms are loyal to him and the city. Through some miracle, they're siding with him instead of simply sodding off like any sensible person would. Duke Colsarne and the Steward are discussing strategy. They'll tell us what they need from us in the morning. What are we going to do now?"

I took a long draft of ale and smack my lips. "Well, let's take a vote on it. All in favour of a few quiet pints then heading to bed at a sensible time? Let's see, that's one vote from Decroix. All in favour of getting piss-drunk and starting a bunch of trouble?"

Quentin and I stuck up our hands up. "Right. That's two votes to one. Drink up, we're going to the dog fights!"

"Ulf, did you not learn a single thing from that time in Missden?"

"Obviously not. Now come on, you're getting the first round in."

"Why do I have to get the first round?" Decroix whined.

"Because I'm the one who persuaded the Steward of Cassioc to side with us in a bloody civil war, and you're not."

Quentin piped up. "Let's bring Simon along!"

Simon sat across the room on a bench, oiling something, his face a picture of concentration. Decroix looked puzzled. "Why?"

I shrugged. "Why not?" I leaned over. "Simon! Get your arse moving. We're going."

He looked up with a start. "Going? Where?"

"On the piss." I finished my ale and gave a fairly decent burp, taking satisfaction at Decroix's wrinkling nose.

The dog fights in Cassioc are great. Really bloody. We got there fairly early, so they hadn't started watering down the beer yet. We checked our swords at the door and waded into the crowd. The reek of beer, sweat, and blood promising a great night ahead.

"It's too noisy. I can't hear what you're saying!" Decroix grumbled.

"Exactly! It means we can spend more time drinking."

The first fight was a long one. Two big buggers with scars all round their jaws and tatty stubs instead of ears. Proper fighting dogs. I stuck down a Wyear on the brown one, just because he was drooling a little, so he reminded me of myself.

Once they slipped the leash, my dog went for the other one and grabbed him by the scruff before he was thrown off. There was a streak of blood against the white fur and they barged into each other, snapping and growling. It went on for a bit until the brown dog sunk his teeth into the other one's bollocks and ripped backwards, tearing out something grey along with a geyser of blood. The white dog went limp and started whining pitifully before his owner snatched him away and called the fight.

Simon winced. "There's no chance he'll survive that, is there?"

I shook my head. "Not a hope. They'll take him into the alley and crack his skull with a hammer. It's the kindest thing to do."

We stayed there for a few hours and I ended up doing fairly well, even if I did drink away my winnings. Simon got into it as well, shouting and screaming along with the crowd. I even talked Decroix into placing a bet, even though it was just a few Ecar.

"Right, so the game is called 'Once Upon a Midnight Dreary'."

I groaned. "What's wrong with just drinking and drinking until you fall over? Why does it have to be a game?"

Brigandine

Quentin tutted at me. "Come on, Ulf! You got to choose the dog fights, and Decroix got to pick this place, so I get to pick the game."

We sat huddled into a hole-in-the-wall tavern, with barely a space to sit between the regulars and the bar; a quiet place full of old men with beards. We were sharing a big plate of sausages and trying to soak up the drink.

I relented. "Fine. How does it work."

"You go 'Once Upon a Midnight Dreary', and then you have to say something you've done. Anyone else who has also done it has to drink. If you're the only one, then you have to down your drink in one. Decroix, come on. Show them how to do it!"

"Fine." Decroix drummed his fingers on the table. "Once Upon a Midnight Dreary . . . I once ate an entire sweetcake for breakfast."

The table groaned and we all drank. "Come on, Decroix! Everyone has done that at some time. Go on, give us something REALLY good." I jeered. I eyed the sausages, picking a fat one and biting into it. The grease rolled down my fingers while I chewed, and I wolfed down the rest.

"Well, why don't you have a go then?" He said sulkily.

"Fine," I replied. "Once Upon a Midnight Dreary, I . . . cut a man's balls off." I looked around the table. "Anyone?" I shrugged and downed my drink.

Decroix tutted. "Well, call me a prude if you like-"

"PRUDE!" Yelled Quentin, and we fell about laughing.

"-but I just think that one should at least *try* to have a certain dignity in combat. Obviously, you kill when and if you need to, but in the bollocks? Come on, Ulf, where's the honour in that?"

I grunted. "He's dead, and I'm not. That's the honour. And believe me, this cunt had it coming to him." I sloshed down more ale. A slug of it poured from the hole in my face and down my collar, but I didn't care. "Anyway, Simon! Come on, play the stupid game."

Simon took a sip of his beer. "Once Upon a Midnight Dreary . . . I . . . umm-"

"PICK SOMETHING DIRTY!" Quentin yelled. Decroix, along with most of the tavern, gave him an angry look. "Go on, what's the dirtiest thing you've ever done with a girl." Just in case he was being too subtle, Quentin backed it up with a few obscene hand gestures, some of which were new even to me.

"W-well. I once, sort of-"

"IT'S AN ARSE THING, ISN'T IT?" Quentin howled. Several old men looked up from their beers to glower, but Quentin seemed oblivious.

Decroix shook his head. "Quentin, not everything HAS to be an arse thing! The arse isn't some joyous beacon of wonder."

"Show's what you know." he muttered. "Anyway, go on Simon! Tell us! Dirtiest thing you've ever done with a girl!"

There was an awkward pause. Simon took a sip and the silence was deafening.

"Right." I smacked my palms on the table and stood up. "Decroix, finish your drink. Quentin, grab the rest of the sausages. We're going to Mary's."

"Mary's?" Simon said.

"Yep. I got the dog fights, Decroix got the boring tavern and Quentin got to play the stupid game. You get to wax your candlestick for the first time. We're going to Mary's."

The landlord sighed in relief as I dragged the rest of them out into the street. I was drunk, but not so drunk that I couldn't hear what people were saying. Nervous whispers and scared gossip bounced around the city. News travels fast, and bad news travels twice as fast as that.

"Here we are." I'd taken a few wrong turns, but I thought the others appreciated the scenic route. The eastern wall looked the same as always. The big man on the door gave me a friendly nod and let us through.

I blinked at the illumination. Scented candles made from good wax sat on every surface, and new rugs and mats sprawled on the floor. I caught Mary's eye as soon as she turned around and her smile made my stomach jump a little bit.

"Ulf! Good to see you again. And who are these handsome men you've brought me?"

Quentin's face went a little soft, and I could seek Decroix's cheeks turn red. Mary gave a bit of a chuckle. "This is Quentin, and his brother Decroix. And this one at the back is Simon."

"Charmed to meet you." Quentin kissed her hand and she smiled.

"Nice to meet a gentleman with manners for a change." she said, looking pointedly at me.

I frowned. "What's wrong with me?"

"Where do I start, my dear?" She kissed me on the cheek.

I could see Quentin picking out a couple, eyeing them up like a veteran merchant might eye a bale of cloth. "Let's see . . ." He stroked his chin. "You, you, and you, if you'd be so kind."

One of the girls ran a finger through Quentin's greying temples. "Are you sure you can manage, darling?" She purred.

"Oh, fuck . . ." Decroix muttered. "Don't provoke him."

He turned to back to us. "Decroix, Ulf. I'm going to be busy for the next couple of hours, proving this lovely young lady very, very wrong. Please don't wait up on my account." With that, he took his harem upstairs and shortly after there followed a delighted scream.

Decroix sighed. "And the trousers are off . . ."

Mary sat us down on some plush couches and brought us each a small glass of wine. She's still a savvy business owner, after all. It was late, so we were the only patrons left by the time she brought out a bevy of beautiful women. They paraded in front of us, and the warmth of the room and the rich wine made everything spin rather wonderfully.

Decroix was grabbed by a pretty brown-haired lass. She was much too skinny for my taste, but he wasn't complaining when she led him upstairs.

"Right, your turn!" I slapped Simon on the shoulder and he glanced around nervously. "What about her? Lovely pair."

Simon shook his head and drank some more wine.

"Fussy. Ah well." Another one of Mary's whores came out. A beauty of a girl with a nice, thick rump. She did a slow little turn which made me feel hungry, like I was looking at a very expensive pie. "Now, she's perfect! You'll have a great time". She moved to take his hand and he snatched it away.

"Sorry." I muttered.

Mary rolled her eyes and went to get some more wine. "What was wrong with her? Come on, it's your first time. How do you know what you like unless you try it?"

"I know what I like," Simon mumbled. "It's just-"

"What?" I snapped. "Come on, hurry up and pick a girl! I want to get my prick wet tonight too."

He blurted out, "I don't like girls! That's the thing."

There was a bit of a pause. Mary set down another glass of wine for us both and then went off to keep busy.

"Oh. Sorry, didn't realise." I hugged him around the shoulders, and he seemed to relax a little. "Nothing wrong with that. Quentin's tugged the odd todger in his time, and he's one of the best men I know. I've known plenty of blokes who plough the muddy field."

"No, it's not that. I like to be . . . you know . . ."

"The field, instead of the plough?"

"Yep . . ."

We both drank some more.

"Quentin would give you one, if you asked him nicely. To be honest, he'd probably give you one if you asked him rudely, but you're better off being polite."

Simon snorted and took another swig of wine. "Hah! Quentin's a good bloke, but he's not the type of . . . I wouldn't go for someone like him."

I furrowed my brow. I'm not good at serious talks at the best of times. And although the wine helped me to speak, it didn't really help in finding the right words. "What do you mean, Simon?"

"I like . . . you know, manly men. Big, strong. Do you remember . . . " he trailed off.

"What?"

"In Scandar. In the hall. When you were washing . . ." His face went the same colour as the wine in his glass.

I suddenly realised what he meant. "Oh. OH! What? REALLY? That's what you go for? Big, ugly scarred bastards?"

"Right, well, you asked!" he said, shuffling on the couch.

I had a flash of inspiration. "Wait here, I've got an idea!" I got to my feet, maybe a little less steadily than normal, and headed over to the door.

"Ulf?"

"Give me a moment!" I called back.

The doorman gave me a friendly nod. "Evening." He looked like a slab of beef. Lots of muscles. Perfect.

"Hello there. Listen, how would you feel about earning five Wyear?"

I was in bed with Mary in her private rooms, away from the rest of the brothel. It was warm there, with thick rugs on the floor and paintings on the wall. Not gaudy, just warm. Like a home.

She was asleep on my chest, snoring a little. The sheets were damp with sweat and the air smelled strongly of sex and wine.

I stared up at the ceiling. She'd been asleep at least an hour, and my right arm was starting to go numb. The back of my head pressed into the hard wooden bed frame, forcing my neck to an awkward angle. I could see the scratches in the wood from my last visit, and it made me crack a smile.

Mary gave a little grunt as I tried to shuffle out from under her, and I gingerly sat up on the edge of the bed. The candle stub burned out a while ago, so there was only the moonlight filtering through the windows. I stared at them for a while. Thick, quality glass, clear as water, with proper lead in the frames. When I first met her, there was no chance she could have afforded glass like that. Or the fine, oaken bed. Or any of the other things she owned.

I sighed. I told myself I wasn't jealous, but I sat there, looking at all she'd managed to do with her life. She had a good place, a place where the girls were treated fairly. Much better than she had been treated, certainly.

She was as old as me, but she didn't look it. She was still beautiful. She could still smile without an effort and her mouth was full of good, strong teeth. I rolled my tongue around my mouth and winced as I poked another dodgy one, same side as the last. "For fuck's sake . . ." I muttered, before sliding back into bed and closing my eyes.

Chapter 31:
An Offer Accepted

Noise. The city was jostled back to life by the rising sun. People buying and selling, cursing and shouting. Just another day. My back felt stiff and I stretched to try and force some feeling into it.

I turned around just in time to see Mary's arse as she slipped into her dress. "Oh. Good morning. Sleep well?"

I nodded, scratching at my chin. "You?"

She smiled and kisses the top of my head. "Always. Now go on, bugger off. I've got a business to run."

I got up and started to dress, tracking down all my crap that lay scattered around the room. "Mary?"

"Hmm?" She'd just put in some earrings and she had a fresh berry in her hand, ready to rub into her lips and cheeks.

"I was thinking-"

She gave a mock gasp of surprise.

"-I was thinking, Mary, that things are going to get pretty hairy soon. I don't know how things will end up, and I don't know if it's all going to-"

"Come on Ulf, spit it out. How many years have we known each other? If you're after another romp then I'm afraid that's not on offer, I can barely walk as it-"

"Marry me?" I blurted it out, spluttering the words.

She sighed and sat down on the bed, and my heart started to sink.

"Ulf, listen, we've known each other for, how long? Years. And as much as someone in my line of work can love someone, I love you. But married?" She chuckled a little and took my hand. "That's not who I am, Ulf. And I don't think it's who you are, either. Yes, I've heard the rumours. Soldiers, war. All that bollocks. I run a brothel. It's a damn good one and I make a lot of money for me and the girls, and I make a lot of people very happy."

I forced a smile. "You made me very happy last night."

She laughed and put her arm around me. "The feeling is mutual. But the point is, I'm not going to give that up to sit around sewing clothes or farting out babies. My life isn't perfect Ulf, but it's mine."

"Can we . . . can we still get blind drunk and fuck each other in alleyways?"

She snorted. "Obviously! Now hurry up and get your kit off!"

"I'm sorry?"

She flung off her dress and gave me a shrug. "I'm not having you leave here looking all mopey. It's bad for business."

I kicked the others awake, and we walked back to the Broken Barrell. Simon was walking slightly more awkwardly than the rest of us, but with a grin on his face that warmed my heart.

"So, did you have a good time, Simon?"

He sighed contentedly. "I had an amazing time. It was-"

"No, no! That's fine-" said Decroix. "I'm happy with 'amazing'. I get enough gory details from Quentin, thank you very much."

"You're pretty prudish for someone who just spent the night in a brothel." I chipped in.

Decroix muttered something, but my attention was drawn to the pair of Colsarne soldiers running towards us. They were part of Rouberte's band; I didn't know their names, and I didn't care.

They scuttled to a halt and panted a little, nearly as red-faced as Marl got from walking up a set of stairs. "Decroix! There's someone at the North Gate. He wants to come in."

He shrugged. "So, let them in? I don't see why I need to be told about some merchant. If they look like a vagrant, tell them to sod off, if not then let them pass."

"Well, it's not that simple . . ."

"Out with it." He snapped.

"The man at the gate. He's Ulric App Decare."

"Shoot the cunt with a crossbow. Strip the corpse and hang it from the battlements." I said flatly. No point sending mixed messages.

Quentin put a hand on my shoulder. "Ulf, maybe someone with a bit less . . . shall we say, rampant bloodlust should deal with this."

"Fuck off." I snarled and stomped toward the northern gate, the others following behind me.

We climbed up to the battlements, and sure enough, there the bastard was. I squinted in the sunshine, but that was him. He held up a sword, point down and bound tightly in its sheath. A sign of peace and a desire to parley.

I couldn't make out his face, but his eyes were clearly better than mine as he spotted me and shouted out a greeting. "Ulf!" He waved his hand frantically, as if there were loads of stupid bastards out there and he needed to get my attention. "We need to talk. I'm sorry for what has happened. It's wrong and it's wicked what the queen is doing. I know it, and so do you!" His horse pawed at the ground and I rolled my eyes.

"Sellor and my father are wrong. No-one can justify the evil of the Black Ram. It's not worth it, not at any price, and no man of honour can stand by while this happens to our country. I will die to protect the people of Ashenfell and fight for this land till my last breath- "

I grabbed a crossbow from a guard and shot the silly bastard.

"ULF!" Quentin shouted, ruining my aim. It thudded into the ground, barely an inch from the horse's hoof and it reared up in surprise, stamping and whinnying about.

"Bugger." I muttered, snatching up another bolt and reloading. Decroix grabbed the crossbow off me and gave me a filthy look. "THAT WAS A WARNING SHOT!" I lied. "NOW FUCK OFF."

He checked the horse, guiding it round in a tight circle to calm the beast down. It snorted angrily before eventually settling. I was a little disappointed it didn't throw him off and snap his neck.

"ULF!" He cried out. "Please! I know you're a good man. We fucked you over, and I'm sorry! How many more ways can I say it? I should have said something, I should have stood up for you, but I didn't, and it was wrong. Your brother was a more honourable man than any of us. He deserved better."

He wasn't moving about. I could have grabbed back the crossbow, steadied it on the wall and taken another shot.

I sighed. "Open the bloody gates."

I pushed past them and descend the stairs, two at a time, determined to be there when the gates opened. He stepped forward and handed over his horse and sword to a Cassioc guard.

He offered a formal bow in greeting and I told the men to bind him. I knew Ulric, he wasn't going to do anything to try and get away, but it made me feel better. We marched him to the palace, the morning crowds all peering at the sight for want of anything better to do. I felt tempted to cry out that he was a donkey-fucker who is being brought to justice, just to get a few bits of shit thrown at him, but I decided not to.

"Ulf?" Quentin asked, a quizzical look on his face. "Why don't you like him again?"

"Because he's a cunt." I snorted.

"Why is he a cunt again?"

"Because he's a wanker."

"And why, exactly, is he a wanker, Ulf?"

"Because he's a cunt."

Having explained myself succinctly, we continued to the palace in silence. The guards waved us through to the central chambers where Duke Colsarne and Sir Ichabod were plotting over the defences. The duke looked up, holding a small wooden block in his hand and smiled thinly. "Ah. Sir Ulric App Decare. What an unexpected delight. To what do we owe the pleasure?"

"The queen is wrong and I won't stand by while she murders innocent people. I want to join you." he said flatly.

Duke Colsarne put down the block and clapped his hands. "Excellent! And how many men have you brought with you, Sir Ulric?"

He shuffled his feet a little. "Well, just one, my lord."

The duke furrowed his brow. "One? Would that include yourself, by any chance?"

". . . yes, lord." he mumbled.

"Ah." Duke Colsarne sat down and drummed his fingers, casting a gaze at Sir Ichabod. "Well, Ulric, that leaves me with a difficult decision. You see, having the son of a man who wants to rape my daughter to death within my camp is obviously a bad thing. If I was able to have, say, several hundred men at arms because of that, then I may consider. But when the risk is so high and the reward is so negligible, I'm inclined to agree with Ulf. Assuming your position on Duke Decare and his protégé hasn't changed?" he asked, turning to me.

I shrugged. "Nope. I say we hang the bastard."

"If I may?" Sir Ichabod interjected. He looked Ulric up and down and regarded him coldly. "You know what a sin it is for a knight to betray his lord, don't you, Sir Ulric? Especially one who has shown you such kindness."

Ulric nodded, and I could see the regret in his eyes. Fucking hells, I could see what was coming like a runaway bull.

"Do you swear what you say is true, Sir Ulric? Do you denounce Queen Karidine of House Fairbourne and relinquish your allegiance to House Decare, now taking up arms in the service of Duke Edmund Colsarne, of the Proud and Fearsome House of Colsarne?"

"I do." He intoned, taking a knee. "For the honour of the Order and the fate of Ashenfell, I pledge my blade."

Oh, for fuck's sake . . .

"I believe him." said Sir Ichabod. "That's that settled, then. Elevenses?" Duke Colsarne gawped at him in disbelief and Sir Ichabod shrugged with his one good arm. "I believed you and Ulf, didn't I?"

Duke Colsarne rubbed his temples and I could see him trying not to yell at the old man. "Sir Ichabod, that is a different matter altogether."

"I don't see how. A knight gives his word. That's good enough for me."

For the first time, the duke was at a loss for words. "But . . . how can you? How can you be so . . . trusting!" He spluttered.

Sir Ichabod looked confused and then smiled. "My dear Edmund, how can you not?"

I counted the coins again, and I swore when they come to the same amount. I didn't know how it had happened, and I didn't care. I waved my hand lazily and she came by again and poured out another one. It slopped down my chin and rolled over my chest.

My hand seemed to be moving around. I spread it on the table and drew my dagger, stabbing it between the thumb and index finger. I levered it out of the wood and took a deep gulp of air, ready to try for the next gap. "Oi! Not on my table, thank you very much!" I didn't bother looking up. I knew it was the fat man behind the bar. So, I got back to drinking. I belched, and the smell rolled out like a cloud.

I could hear a bard playing something in the corner. A long tune. Soft and quiet. I'd heard it before, but I couldn't quite remember. He was singing as well, but I wasn't able to make out the words and the room seemed a little fuzzy around the edges.

"Ulf?"

I looked up and cursed. There he was. Standing there like a prick. He wisely stood just out of fist range, and I managed to focus myself just enough to make out the expression on his face. It was annoying that, even with missing teeth and a crooked nose, he was still better looking than me.

"Ulf?" he said again. "Are you alright?"

Brigandine

I pulled myself up in the chair and spun my dagger on the point, watching it clatter down on the tabletop. "No, Ulric, I'm not all right. Mainly because I'm trying to have a drink and I'm being bothered by a cunt like you."

His expression didn't change, but I could see his hands move into fists.

"You know what, Ulf? Fuck off. I've apologised enough, you've had your fun breaking my nose. We're even. I'm going to do the right thing and I couldn't give a damn if you're still pissy and bitter. I don't know what your problem is, but it's your problem, not mine."

He turned to leave, so I stood up, sending my chair tumbling.

"Fight me! Come on! You and me, outside!" I spat at him and spread my arms, the gobbet landing by his feet.

He shook his head and moves to the door. "No, Ulf. I'm not going to fight you."

I laughed at him, twisting my face into a sneer. "Scared, are we? Fucking coward."

"No, Ulf. I'm not going to fight you because you're a pathetic drunk." He looked me up and down, with a big, sad face. "Taran would be ashamed of you, and we both know it."

There was nothing in my pouch. I don't know where it went. One moment I had a lot of money, the next I didn't have any. I slumped down again the wall, my armour scraping against the brick.

The alley smelled like shit. Probably because that was what it was filled with at the far end. The walls wouldn't stop moving, and I dug my fingertips into the cobbles to hang on.

"Bastard." I mumbled.

I rubbed at the back of my neck. It felt sore, and I couldn't remember what had happened. My knuckles were bloody, with fresh grazes, but I didn't know how they had gotten there.

My breath was steaming, so I knew it was cold. But the beer kept me warm, like a blanket.

I was crying. I'm not sure when it started or what was going on, but I was shaking, and I could feel fat tears rolling down my cheeks into the filth of the gutter.

I could see the stars. They were blurry, but I could see them. Bright lances of silver across the sky.

We keep the ranks tight, refusing to be lured into a skirmish as we march into the central square of the town. The buildings are sagging, their walls crumbling away with rot and decay, and the air has a horrible metallic tinge. My eyes are itching, and I blink hard, feeling them drying out in the miasma squatting around us.

The whole town is there. Men, women, and children, armed with knives, axes, and tools. I can see the hulking gray Waystones jutting from the cobblestones behind them, the twisted symbols writhing with the power flowing through them. I count three of them, arranged in a triangle and protected by the remaining professional soldiers of Craftvale.

Stones and rocks are flung at us, bouncing from our armour and shields as we advance. "Keep it together!" Taran roars. "Don't let them bait you, don't let them draw you out."

I step up to the join front rank, spears and polearms behind us. Like most of the men, I lower my sword into a fool's guard, point facing down. The spears will protect my head and chest, leaving my free to stab at the foe's legs and feet. We step forward in unison, men from the third and fourth ranks splitting round to our flanks as the square widens.

The Waystones are vibrating now, whining and grinding against the flagstones. Over the whoops and jeers, I can hear the low, droning chants of those nearest the stones. There is a flash of red from an arterial spray, and a horrible scream cuts through the air. A bloody corpse is smeared across the stone. They drag it back and forth and the Waystone suckles greedily, sucking the gore into the stone. I then realise with horror that he is still alive, his raw flesh pulled from him in ragged strands. It ends abruptly in a wet gargle, and I can hear the chanting continuing with renewed vigour.

They howl as they rush us. Coming in bands of about a dozen they crash against the line, breaking like waves on a cliff. A woman hurls herself onto my sword, laughing hysterically and clawing at my face with filthy, broken fingers. I stumble back and the blade slides out, slick with dark blood. She grips at my ankle, so I stamp downwards, smashing her face into the cobbles.

The streets are slick with all kinds of filth, and I nearly fall over as we advance. We strike with every step, thrusting forward and pressing straight to the Waystones. Each movement of my limbs is harder now. My arms are burning with every cut and stab and each step is heavy, but still we press on.

Wordlessly, we cut through scores of them. One man, frothing at the mouth, swings at me with a hatchet, only for the spearman to my right to pierce his throat. Another is gutted by a bill, still thrashing with spite as his intestines spill out.

Glancing down the line, I can see Taran. He's fighting hard and hacking through swathes, desperately trying to push them back. They keep up the pressure, hordes of them dying only for more to take their place. We cycle our front rank to prevent exhaustion, but my brother refuses to step back, shaking his head at the man behind. He raises his sword to the sky, crying out "DOUBLE TIME!", *and we force ourselves to press onwards.*

The chanting is louder now. I hear one voice above the others screaming into the sky, the clouds merging and shifting into the colour of an ugly bruise. The sigils on the Waystones are now glowing brighter, with a sickly green light.

"CHILDREN OF THE RAM! COME ONTO ME!"

"FORWARD! KILL THE BASTARDS!" *Taran's voice is hoarse and his helm is streaked with blood. There are hardly any of the townsfolk left by now. The dregs that are left are cut down like dogs. We've lost men, though. I can see patches and gaps in the line and behind us are the moans and shrieks of the dying.*

After we hack through the chaff, we come face to face with the soldiers and guards of Craftvale. Their weapons bristle as they defend their altar, taunting us to approach. Redoubling our efforts, we crash into their lines. They buckle at the impact but fight back with a savage fury. Each blow they strike is like a hammer, and my arms roar with pain as I parry a thunderous strike to my head.

Our swords bind, and he shoves me backwards with fearsome strength. I lunge at his face, a short thrust from the wrists, which he deflects with surprising celerity. He's a big man, with muscles like corded rope. I strike at him from a right ox guard and my blade scrapes down under the collar of his armour. He laughs horribly and strikes downwards, knocking my sword to the ground. I spring forward, drawing my dagger and stabbing him under the arm. The blade shatters the chain links and sinks deep up to the hilt. He grunts and punches me hard, rattling my skull round my helmet.

He swings at me with both hands and I step out the way, jumping in again. I lift his leg and slash open the back of his knee, black blood flooding out. He crashes downwards, and I spring on him, stabbing him again and again. He reaches out and claws at me, dragging me by my armour to his face. He leers at me through a mess of a face before I drive the blade through the side of his head. His fingers go limp and his mouth twitches. I scrabble to my feet, snatching up my sword just in time to block the swing of a battle axe.

Laughter. Maddening, hysterical laughter coming from the rear of us. I risk a glance around and I vomit instantly, the acidic mess spilling down my front.

The shoggoth.

It lurches towards us with echoing farts and hisses. A huge, rolling mound of elephantine legs and twisted, throbbing members. Even above all the filth and gore, I can smell the sickly-sweet reek of decomposing flesh and wet fur, like a long-dead animal.

Oh, fuck . . .

It rolls into our back ranks, pulling and twisting apart men's bodies with contemptuous ease. Some warriors fall to their knees, ripping at their eyes and screaming, while others stand dumb and childlike, even as their comrades are torn limb from bloody limb.

The enemy howls, filled with purpose by their god made flesh. They shrug off blows that should kill a man and return them with phenomenal strength. Our weapon shafts snap and armour is shredded. Despite the fighting, their blades still glisten with razor sharpness and they move like freshly rested men whilst our arms are like wood.

"DECARE, WHERE THE FUCK IS ULRIC?"

"How the fuck should I know!" He bellows, snarling at my brother. Decare lops off a guard's head, grunting with the effort. He's a strong man, but I can see by the dents and tears in his armour that even he is tiring.

They are pushing us back. I can't believe it, but they are. Around me, men are falling back, being forced to the left and backed onto a cluster of houses at the edge of the square.

I follow them, it's either that or die alone. The spearman behind me falls, the top of his head sheared clean off. The billman near to him is downed as well, clutching at a bleeding stump of a leg. I force myself close to Taran and Windor Decare. Both of them fighting desperately to keep the foe at bay.

There is a horrible wail. I can see a flash of bright silver and a shimmer of light. They're here! Ulric and his men plough into the shoggoth. Horses are crushed and sent flying, but with weapons of silver, they are at least harming the monster.

"If Ulric's band can get here, they can relieve us! Hold on!" Taran shouts.

Decare bawls with rage and knocks down another footman. "They'll crush us before they can get here."

Taran grins. He ducks a blow then rises up, cutting his opponent's jaw in half. "SINGLE COMBAT!" He bellows. "WHO HERE WILL DARE FACE ME?"

He throws his helmet to the ground and laughs with contempt. "How many dogs does it take to slay a wolf? Come, there must be one of you who has the balls to stand and fight me man to man!"

I can't believe what I'm hearing. "Taran! Now is not the time for glory! We need to survive."

"Ulf, I need you to trust me." he snaps. "I know what I'm doing. Remember the wrestlers?"

As if by some miracle, the lines part. One of their number steps forward, an old man clutching a twisted metal staff. My brother levels his sword. His chest is rising up and down and I can see he's exhausted. He smiles and winks at me and I understand.

The story of the two wrestlers. One once the greatest fighter in the land, now old and grey. The other, a young upstart. The old wrestler couldn't hope to pin his stronger opponent. So, he insisted they wrestle in a rocky patch. The old one doesn't try to beat him, he just dodges and slaps away the holds, making the young wrester angrier and angrier. He starts stamping on the rocks, drawing out a viper which bites him on the heel, slaying him.

He's buying us time.

"I am Sir Taran of Banrillar. Master of the Order of the Cleansing Flame. Who dares to accept my challenge?"

The old man strikes the ground with his staff, bringing forth a deafening thunderclap. "I am Varnoor. Prophet of the Black Ram and father to these dear, sweet children." He smiles and shows a mouth full of small, jagged teeth. "Even now they speak to me. They cry out to their father demanding vengeance for this desecration! Come, Taran of Banrillar. Come face your doom!"

He snatches a vial from his belt and gulps it down. Varnoor looks up at us with black, soulless eyes and his jaw twists and descends, splitting open. With each step his body twists and flows like molten wax, swelling with awful power. The staff folds into his arm, turning into a wicked spiked protrusion of flesh and steel. Finally, bones crack and stretch and the creature towers above us before hunching down, charging on all four limbs.

Taran spins his sword and grits his teeth. "Bugger."

The sword and staff clash, sending sparks flying. Taran steps to the side to avoid a talon, then blocks from the roof as it moves to crush his skull. He sweeps the longsword round, hacking twice into the massive shoulders. On the second blow, he slides the blade forward, pressing the silver crossguard into its flesh.

Varnoor moans like a slaughtered bull and smashes the blade away, sending Taran stumbling. My brother sweeps round in an arc and the weapons meet again, the weird staff biting a deep chunk into the edge of the sword.

My throat is raw. I'm screaming at him to finish the beast off, yelling his name. I remember the tournament. I think back to the joust, that moment of victory when I knew that nothing could stop us. When I saw his tabard's blue and gold-a tabard now covered with filth and blood.

"OSWALD!" Taran yells, crashing his sword into the staff. He moves to avoid the jaws then slides the blade downwards, cutting deep into the flesh. Despite his exhaustion, he moves like a dancer, stepping out the way of every blow.

"OSWALD!" Again, he screams the name. Holding the blade in a murder-stroke, Taran cracks the monster on the jaw, wrenching the sword down and pulling it off balance. He swings above his head and brings it down with every ounce of strength. The silver hilt shears through the middle of the staff-limb and rips out a chunk of flesh. The behemoth whimpers, crashing into the street, mounds of flesh hissing and bubbling.

The thing twitches and writhes and Taran looks down with disgust before roaring in triumph.

Then, suddenly, I see it.

"TARAN!" He looks at me in confusion before a claw snaps out, ripping his legs from under him. His head cracks into the cobbles and the sword clatters

Brigandine

away. He rolls to grab it before his arm is crushed by a club-like limb. He cries out in agony and I can see the twisted steel of his vambrace, mixed in with the pulped flesh of his sword arm.

Weapon raised, I rush forward, but arms grab me, pulling me back. "STOP HIM!" Decare and some of his men have me, pinning my arms to me side I thrash and scream, desperate to help my brother.

"Ulf! You cannot! It is the honour of single combat! Your brother knows this!" I can feel his breath on my cheek and I'm still screaming. The beast staggers to its feet and grabs my brother around the throat. I lash out with my gauntlets, desperate to be free and they force me down to the ground, a knee pinning my neck.

"Move, and I will cut your fucking throat!" A dagger is against my neck. I twist and thrash and it slips, ripping through the chin-strap of my helmet and cutting open the edge of my mouth. Blood drips across my lips, and from where I am on the ground, I can just see what is happening.

It holds him up, flopping limply like a ragdoll, and the thing's eyes meet mine for a moment. A long tongue flops out from its gaping maw, rasping along Taran's face and ripping open the skin. In one awful movement, it hefts him up and thrusts the jagged metal under the tassets and the mail skirt of his armour. Taran judders horribly and blood pours out underneath him as his guts pour out onto the ground.

His head jerks to the side and I see the skin rip open as the point forces its way through.

As his corpse is thrown to the ground I start screaming. My face rips open with the sound and the cold, fetid air brushes against my teeth. I don't stop. I can't stop, I don't know how to. And I keep screaming and screaming until everything blurs into darkness.

Chapter 32:
Your Majesty

Hands were squeezing my shoulders. I slammed them backwards and lurched up, pinning them against the wall. Quentin stared back at me, his face a mix of surprise and relief. "ULF! Thank fuck I've found you! I've got about half a dozen men looking for you, did you know that?"

"Oh. Sorry." I muttered. "I just got a bit-"

"Do you feel like letting me down? Would that be all right?" I let go of Quentin's collar and he brushed off his shoulders. "Thank you. Now, if you're not too busy?"

I didn't understand. "What?"

Quentin sighed and dragged me out of the alley. Everywhere, people were running and shouting. A woman was lugging a barrel of water, and behind her ran a man with wicker baskets, filled to the brim with arrows. They were going to the western wall.

"Oh."

He rolled his eyes and I followed him, sprinting to the palace. I stopped on the way and dunked my head in a fountain. The cold water woke me up and I took a few gulps to wash my mouth.

We burst into the inner chambers of the palace as servants were finishing armouring Duke Colsarne for battle. He stood and flexed a gauntlet, the joints rolling smoothly at the wrist.

"Quentin, Ulf. It's wonderful that you were able to make it. Not too busy, I trust?" He turned away and fixed his eyes on a large map of the city. "Alexia, if you'd be so kind, please repeat yourself for the latecomers." He moved to leave the chamber. "Oh, and Quentin. There's a hauberk in that chest in the corner. It's a touch better quality than your own. And, if I may make a suggestion, perhaps a war sword. I appreciate your short blade is more stylish, but you may find the extra reach advantageous."

He put a hand on Quentin's shoulder and they exchanged a look. "Good luck, both of you." And with that, he was gone. I turned to Lady Alexia.

"If I may?" she asked, and gestured to the map. "The outriders have reported that the Queen's forces are approaching from the southwest, on the road from Riben."

Quentin frowned. "How many do they have?"

"Well, the bad news is we're hideously outnumbered by the royal guard, the retainers of House Fairbourne, and the Order of the Cleansing Flame. Oh, and Decare's own men, of course. However, that does give us an advantage."

"I'm struggling to see how, my lady." Quite frankly, it seemed like we are pretty fucked. I was rather hoping that pile of wooden blocks was just where they dumped the spare ones, rather than more bastards who wanted to kill me.

"With so many men, we know where they will attack: the southwestern gate. There are far too many of them to try crossing the Phon and attacking the eastern gate. I sent some men to dam the river last night, just to be sure. If they try any sneaky flanking tricks, then they can look forward to men dying in waist-deep mud. The rain last night certainly helped, as well."

I dimly remembered feeling soggy around the third bell, so I nodded in agreement. A thin smile crossed her face, and I saw the same cunning eyes as her father.

"The queen will need a swift victory. We have made her look weak, and she will be looking to punish those who stand against her. Secondly, we hold the royal treasury. She won't have a hope of raising an army for a longer war if she can't pay them."

She drummed her fingers on the map, brimming with excitement. "We've forced her hand, and we hold every advantage!" She said gleefully, clapping her hands together.

She clearly felt she was the cleverest person in the room, but I couldn't quite help but feel that the angry fuckers who outnumbered us five-to-one might disagree with her assessment.

"Right! Decroix is commanding the walls. Rouberte is in position. Father knows what he's doing. Marl is preparing the defences. That just leaves you two. Help Decroix on the battlements. Kill anyone who tries to get over. Clear?"

We nodded.

She beamed. "Splendid. Now, If I'm going to meet the queen, I want to look my best." A lady in waiting rushed over and started clucking and preening. "Oh, and Ulf?"

"Yes?"

"Sir Ichabod wants you in the armoury. You'll need to hurry, it seemed important."

I thanked her and headed off, leaving Lady Alexia to her hairpins.

I knew what he wanted. I knew what was going to happen. I walked as slowly as I could, my mouth dry and stomach light. I deeply wished I'd had time to eat something. Anything to delay what was going to happen. The guards at the armoury waved me through. They'd been expecting me.

"Sabatons." Sir Ichabod grunted a little as he bent down, strapping the metal over the top of my boots. He cursed as he fiddled with the buckle.

"You don't have to-"

He waved me away. He got some help eventually, pulling in the young man who was standing guard outside. Piece by piece they fixed it to me, and I felt the weight building.

I closed my eyes. I didn't want to look at it. Every rivet gleamed; every joint moved like water. The breastplate pinched a little on my hips and the straps on the greaves dug in, but apart from that, it felt horribly perfect. When the last piece was in place, I opened my eyes and reached for my sword belt.

"Not yet!" Sir Ichabod snapped. He turned round and rummaged, before pulling something over my head. I closed my eyes again as the belt was tightened around me. I looked down and I saw the cup, brilliant gold shining on a field of blue. My brother's colours. The heraldry of Sir Taran of Banrillar.

"When did-"

"When you arrived. You'd be surprised what a good seamstress can do for a few Guilder." I looked up, and I saw Sir Ichabod smiling. "Sir Ulric."

Ulric stepped forward, his face expressionless. I wanted to punch him, but then, I always do.

Sir Ichabod placed a hand to my forehead, fingers shaking. "Ulf of Banrillar, as Master at Arms, I charge you with this. Defend this city. This land. These people. Stand for what you know is right, against the Queen's tyranny, and for the ideals that so many have forgotten. Do you accept this charge?"

"I do."

Ulric put his hand on my shoulder, and the urge to punch him rose dramatically.

"Your oath is witnessed, Ulf of Banrillar. I bid you hold to it."

With those words, he turned and left.

Sir Ichabod sighed, sitting back on the now empty chest. "Go on, then. Off you pop."

I went to leave, the armour shifting with every step.

"Oh, and Ulf?"

I froze and turned back. "Yes?"

"Make your brother proud. Be the man he always thought you were. The man I know you can be."

I turned to him and forced a smile. "Let's be realistic for a moment. We both know that's not going to happen."

He shrugged. "Well, if you can't do that, then just kill as many of the bastards as you can."

My smile became genuine. "That I can do."

The sky above the southwest gate was choked with grey clouds, and the air was buggeringly cold. I sent Simon to run off and fetch me some bread before my stomach murdered me, and stood with Quentin and Decroix, watching the sight unfold. I remembered when the brothers and I had first come to Cassioc through the Queen's Gate. They were bubbling with excitement at the Ouroboros, eager to find out the truth. I glanced at Decroix, a shield bound to his injured arm to protect his broken hand. How life had changed.

Soldiers were lining up in ranks, receiving hasty orders and instructions on what to do and when. They'd come to the walls; we all knew that. Some were tasked with pushing away ladders, others charged with hacking down at men. There were runners for more bolts and arrows, and some poor bastards to fetch and carry water. I could see the eagerness in some of their eyes; men who had never seen a proper battle, who had no burrs on their swords. And then there were some men like me, who knew all too fucking well what was going to happen and what it would look like.

The piles of filth outside the painted walls of Cassioc were slick with water. The rain and the deliberate flooding from the Phon had made a sticky quagmire outside the city. The cobbles on the road leading to the gate were slick, barely visible above the mud and grime. It would be hell for men and horses alike, and I wasn't looking forward to it.

Looking up, I could see there were a couple of Colsarne men, whacking away at the statue of Queen Karidine with a hammer. A few weeks ago, an unforgivable act of treason. Now, the defilement of a hated enemy.

"Leave it."

They looked up at me. "Pardon?"

"Leave it. I want to drop it on the bastards as they march up to the gate. Think you can manage that?" They nodded, faces set with grim resolve, and put away their tools.

A rider approached, a herald wearing a tabard bearing the Fairbourne fish. He held a bound sword by the scabbard, pointing down. He stopped a dozen yards from the gate and lowered his hood, licking his lips nervously.

"By the command of Queen Karidine of the Wise and Gracious House of Fairbourne, by right of arms and succession ruler of Ashenfell, I bring a proclamation." His voice echoed, bouncing off the walls. "Her Royal Majesty requests the pleasure of Duke Colsarne's company for a parley, to take place at the royal standard on the plains of Cassioc." His message delivered, he lowered his sword, turned his horse and rode swiftly away.

Runners were sent to Duke Colsarne and he swiftly arrived at the gate, mounted. Our own horses were brought and Decroix, Quentin, and I rode out with Duke Colsarne and his daughter. The gates were opened a meagre sliver, and we rode to the royal standard, the three fish snapping in the cold wind.

The Queen sat on a large, grey stallion, flanked by Decare and Sellor. The horse was draped with a cloth of gold, sewn with pearls in beautiful, swirling patterns. Though there was no chance she would get into anything like a fight, she wore ceremonial armour - bright silver mail, with a gilded plackart and couters shaped like blazing suns. Her horse's shins were splattered with mud, but the rest of her looked resplendent, like something from myth.

Half a dozen men at arms, including the one holding the flag, were standing a discrete distance away. The royal banner was bright and shining, every thread perfectly stitched, delicate silk sewn onto fine, rich wool.

It was hard to look at her. Hard to face down someone with her presence. But we all knew what needed to be done.

"Colsarne." she said, simply.

"Your Majesty." He bowed his head slightly. A delicate gesture, one of courtesy rather than submission.

Decare glared at me. "Where is Sir Ulric?"

I met Decare's icy stare. We both knew how this was going to end. One of us was going to die on the other one's sword. But whatever happened, he knew that his adopted son had left him and his rage brought joy to my cold, bitter heart.

Duke Colsarne smiled thinly. "I'm sure Sir Ulric is well. You have my word that he has been treated according to his rank and station."

"You will, of course, forgive me if I remain skeptical." He snapped.

Colsarne feigned surprise. "Oh? Well, you do of course have every right to be skeptical. I was skeptical, as well, when Sir Ulric approached the gates, asking to ally with us." A smile, subtle as a midnight dagger. He turned his head in thought. "Strange that he would do so. Especially after the kindness shown to him by House Decare. I suppose some men value honour above safety."

The Queen raised her hand, silencing Decare before a brutal outburst. "Sellor, present our terms."

Sellor bowed as deeply as his saddle would allow. "Duke Edmund Colsarne, of The Proud and Fearsome House of Colsarne. You stand accused of treason, to Her Majesty, Queen Karidine and the people and land of Ashenfell. The sentence for this is death."

The words hung in the air. Duke Colsarne blinked slowly and scratched his cheek.

"You will surrender and your men will be spared. The House of Colsarne will be broken, to be discarded from records and its banner hung from the Queen's own hall of conquest. You will have a swift and merciful death. Your daughter will be spared and offered a place of honour and security in the household of Duke Decare-"

"Shove it up your cunt!" I snarled.

"HOW DARE YOU!" Sellor roared. "Any trace of grace or nobility has clearly left the sons of Banrillar."

"ULF!" Duke Colsarne turned to me, face glowering. "This is a parley. A meeting of the nobility to discuss the fate of the realm and the lives of many! You dare to soil it with your coarse language? To speak that way, to your queen?"

He turned and faced the queen, head bowed in contrition. "Please. Shove it up your cunt, *Your Majesty.*"

Duke Colsarne turned and rode back to the city, his daughter and the brothers following him at a swift trot. I shrugged to the three most powerful people in the land, then spun my horse to catch up.

"Well, I think that went well." I said cheerily.

I could feel Decroix's anxiety like a hot oven. "My lord, are you sure that was wise?"

"Oh, absolutely not." The duke said plainly. "But I've been wanting to say it for a very, very long time. I'm just a bit miffed Ulf said it first."

We returned to the city. With a fair bit of protest, Lady Alexia was sent back to the palace under escort, to be guarded by Sir Ichabod. Although exactly what a crippled old man was going to do if a dozen violent soldiers tried and rape and murder her was anyone's guess.

The portcullis was lowered and the gate closed and barred. Huge barrels filled with rocks were placed behind the gates to reinforce them, and other barrels dragged up the battlements to crush the skulls of any bastard unlucky enough to get hit.

Rouberte had a dozen of his crossbowmen aimed in a diagonal killing arc. You can't shoot straight down – the bolt will just fall off the end – but a good shot can fire down and along the walls, picking off men attacking the main gate.

There was also a murder hole at the top of the gate, between the doors and the grate. Quentin suggested we get some oil boiling, but I shook my head. It's nasty stuff, but more dangerous to you than the enemy. It's admittedly more dramatic, but a big pile of rocks does the job just as well, and won't strip the flesh from your arm if you spill a little.

Rouberte took a scrap of bright crimson cloth and tied it to a quarrel. Standing on the wall, he launched it out to three hundred yards, the red fabric fluttering in the wind. "You have your mark." He yelled. The crossbows were winched, wood and metal groaning as the lethal projectiles were loaded. We had a few Wallarmbrust from the armoury - crossbows too big to run around with, but perfect for resting on top of a wall and using to tear a hole through a man.

Decroix whistled slowly. "There's a lot of them, Ulf."

I nodded. "Yep."

They were lined up now. I couldn't see any siege towers or big units of cavalry, but I could see a vast block of shining gold and my heart sank. The queen's own guard. A bunch of brutal, violent bastards to a man. Decroix's eyes were better than mine, and he pointed out bands of skirmishing archers as well as a lot of heavily armoured infantry, backed up by light swordsmen carrying long ladders.

It shouldn't have been a surprise that they were going for the walls, rather than trying for the main gate. It wasn't like the Queen didn't know the layout of the city and where the hardest points would be.

With blasts from war trumpets and echoing horns, the Queen's forces advanced. Hundreds of boots pounded the earth and I could hear the slurred lyrics of battle songs and chants. Men bringing up their fighting courage, that impulse and call to violence that sits hard in the stomach. We launched the first volley of quarrels as soon as they stepped past the mark, roaring with satisfaction as scores of them fall dead or screaming. The line wavered briefly, but they continued, stepping over the bodies or trampling them underfoot.

Crossbows are nasty weapons. Bolts are thick as a man's thumb and most of the time dipped in shit, so you can look forward to a long painful death if the bugger hits you. Archers are thieving cunts - most of them more than happy to slit a few throats for a rusty Ecar - but crossbowmen are vicious little bastards. Trust me.

Muscles strained as they reloaded and shot another wave into the enemy ranks. They were ready this time and fewer fell, most of the bolts finding a shield. They quickened their step and their archers ran forward, each one paired with a pavise bearer, and started to take shots at us. Shooting upwards at a hundred yards at small targets is a big ask of even an experienced marksman, but two of ours staggered back with fletching in their chests.

Rouberte spat and took aim, the stock sitting snugly in his shoulder. It thudded into a shield and I heard a scream as the bolt pierced through the wood to nail the hand behind. He flailed around, opening him and his mate up for just a moment. Enough time to have them each struck with a couple of quarrels and leave them writhing in the mud.

They pushed forward in double time. Some more men on the walls died and arrows clattered against the battlements, cracking off the painted plaster. I heard Quentin curse as one struck the stone behind him, missing him by a hair's breadth.

As they approached, a smell rose up that stung my throat. Not the normal reek of unwashed bodies, but sickly-sweet, like rotting meat. Some of them moved oddly, a shuffling gait that set them apart from the well-disciplined marching of the others. One furiously scratched at his arm, and I glimpsed a mess of pus and buboes before he vanished into the throng.

The ladders were raised, pushed forward by desperate hands as we rained death down upon them. I hefted a rock with all my might and took satisfaction in the meaty crunch as it connected with a steel-clad body.

"MAKE READY!" I bellowed. I drew my sword, grasping it by the blade so I could use the cross guard to hammer skulls as they poked their heads over the top.

We waited for a moment, shooting more bolts into their ranks and killing as many as we could, but the ladders stayed fixed, raised skywards and wobbling slightly in the wind.

Decroix frowned and pointed. "Ulf, what are they doing?"

Oh, fuck.

Chapter 33:
Do You Remember?

There were women at the bases of the ladders. They swayed and staggered, heads lolling drunkenly. Some of them old and haggard, others barely more than children. Their shirts were torn open, and I could see someone smearing a rancid green paste on their exposed breasts.

"Shoot them! Shoot the captives!" I roared.

Quentin looked at me in disbelief. "Ulf! Have you lost your mind?"

"Fucking do it! The foot of the ladders! Shoot them!"

Shields were forming an arrow wall around each ladder, the boards overlapping to the side and above, but I could still see the woman's chest, pale and bare. I snatched a crossbow from a nearby man and aimed, squeezing the tickler. The stock thudded against my armour and even through the plate I felt the recoil. I got her through the neck, but she spun to the ground, dropping out of sight.

"THE CAPTIVES!" I screamed, but it was too late. Daggers plunged into their chests, and even through the shouts and noise I could make out the dreadful chants and droning. My teeth started to ache and my nose poured with blood. Along the wall, men were vomiting and I saw Rouberte clutching his head and screaming. Decroix steadied himself on the battlement, and I heard Quentin splutter and retch.

Brigandine

My feet moved, and looking down I could see the wall buckle and shake. From the earth where the blood was spilt, huge fetid vines and roots sprang forth, covered in barbs which glistened like broken glass. They burrowed under the walls, splitting and shaking the stone as they wrapped themselves over the ladders, shoving them towards us.

I could see those men still aware push and shove at the ladders, but the sorcery held them firm. There were shouts of disquiet from the enemy at the hideous sight, but they were pushed forward, and took some tentative steps up the rungs. They pushed themselves upwards, racing to the top while their comrades took advantage of the chaos. A bronze battering ram was wheeled forward, the head cast in the shape of a gulping carp. The sorcery had weakened and warped the oaken gates, and I could hear the shrieks and cracks from the hinges buckling under the impact.

I pushed forward, desperately trying to avoid shoving men to their deaths as I ran. Decroix was breathing heavily, gulping for air. Quentin had shaken his head free of the fugue, but we were in a slim minority. One of the invaders mounted the walls, hacking a helpless man's head clean from his shoulders in a spray of blood.

Our swords clashed and he cut at me, a short blow from the wrist. I parried with the stark and cut upwards into his groin, bringing the sword up across his belly. His blood soaked through his gambeson, and I tossed him over my hip and into the courtyard below.

I shifted my focus another of the bastards at the top of the ladder, desperately trying to get up and over the wall. He swiped upwards, blocking my thrust but teetering dangerously. I took half a step backwards, out of range of his messer but still able to hack at him. I struck two-handed from the roof, and his foot slipped as he parried. Swearing, he grabbed the rung and scrabbled to regain his footing. I cut down and my sword crashed into his helmet. He yelped with surprise as he came free from the ladder, falling into the chaotic swirl of bodies below.

I hacked at the rungs, cursing breathlessly as the wood cracked and splintered. I smashed the first two rungs, pulling them out of the stiles. An arrow thudded into my vambrace and I jerked myself back away from the ramparts. It wasn't strong enough to pierce the armour, but I could feel a throbbing bruise rising beneath.

Decroix had recovered his wits and was shouting, trying to keep things together. Most of the men were coherent, struggling and fighting along the wall in a press of bodies. Soldiers were falling off both sides of the narrow walkway, either thrown down by their foes or slipping in blood and viscera.

Someone in a Decare tabard crashed into me, our swords pressed against our bodies. He snarled and tried to grab at me, but I broke his hold and drew my dagger, stabbing it deep into his side between a gap in his breastplate. I ripped it out and thrust it under his armpit, splitting the mail links and cutting through tender flesh. My vision blurred as he punched me hard in the face, his gauntlet crashing into my barbute. I dropped my sword and brought my arm up to block his next blow, and then drove the dagger under his jaw. He fell on top of me and blood pooled into my helmet.

I threw off the corpse and forced myself to my feet. We were holding our ground, but by Oswald's cockshaft we were paying dearly for it.

Quentin was wrestling with a swordsman, each snarling and grabbing at the other's wrists. Quentin forced his arm to the edge of the battlement before wrenching away his own sword, smashing the pommel hard into the man's hand. He screamed as Quentin forced the wrist into a lock, cracking his bones before hacking down at his neck. The sword edge bashed against a kettle helm, and it took Quentin two more blows before he cut off the head, leaving a ragged stump.

More of our men were dying. Taran's armour was scratched and dented and my arm ached from the slaughter. Any hope of water or cycling warriors was laughable as they swarmed around each ladder. For each one we killed, more were ready to take his place.

I looked down and ground my teeth. "Decroix!"

"What?"

"The gate!" I bellowed.

Decroix chanced a quick thrust, the point sliding through an eye socket, before following my gaze. "Bugger."

The bar across the gate was flexing with impact, which meant the portcullis had fallen.

I roared and slashed with all my might, the blade shearing through meat and bone of another poor bastard. More of the Cassioc guards climbed up to reinforce us, but we were shoved back. Most of the wall belonged to the queen's forces now.

I saw Marl and a half dozen of his men hacked down. He fought like a bear tearing apart dogs before a short spear brought him to his knees and a knife opened his throat. Marl's head lolled horribly and his corpse was left twitching as the curs moved on with the slaughter.

Quentin and Decroix were behind me at the top of the stairs. I braced myself, pushing back as an axeman swung at me, trying to press me down. I slashed fast from either side, left to right and back again, forcing him to move quickly to parry. Using the momentum, I pushed upward, driving the crossguard into his jaw.

There was more confusion. Shouting. The bloody press and swirl of combat. But amid the chaos, a gap appeared.

Decroix was next to me. He sunk his sword into the axeman's knee and shoved him down, snarling and shouting at the others to follow. "Come on, you bastards!"

Quentin stepped up behind and before we knew it, we were driving them back. No more of them were coming up the ladders, and we could see them scrapping and fighting to get back down, stabbing at each other in desperation.

Fighting our way onwards, we could see the Queen's army was in disarray. Men were fleeing the walls, leaving the ram and ladders and trampling each other in the gore-slicked mud.

The men on the walls were shouting, cheering with ragged tired voices at the sight of their enemy, slain and fleeing before them.

I frowned. "Decroix, what exactly is going on here?"

He pointed with his sword. "Look!"

I squinted as hard as I could, pulling off my helmet to see more clearly. On their left flank, to the north, was a ragged, winding line of men. In the centre sat a big heavy bill block, weapons and armour gleaming.

"It's Johan!" gasped Quentin. "No idea about the rest of them. Archers. Bright white bows. Any ideas?"

I shrugged. "No fucking idea, but they're more than welcome."

Decroix sucked his teeth. "They're not going to be there for much longer, I don't think. Look!"

The Queen's army was peeling away from the city walls. Despite the arrows raining death down on them, they fell into ranks and units with the speed and discipline of professional soldiers. They marched forwarded at a brutal pace before smashing into the billmen. The archers and skirmishers were scattering, grabbing up arrow baskets and falling back, shooting as they went.

I heard a scrape of wood on stone as the gates were pried open. Duke Colsarne sat mounted on a black charger, the vicious stead snorting and stamping with impatience. It was draped in a cloth of blue and silver, links of mail barding rippling beneath. His own armour was exquisite, painted black with gilded edges, and he tapped his saddle pommel impatiently. "Decroix! If you'd be so kind, please get Ulf and your brother down here sharpish. Rather than let Johan be slaughtered, then have them come back to finish us, I would suggest we take advantage of this turn of good fortune."

A page brought Reed over, and I sheathed my sword and mounted her, sliding my sabatons through the iron stirrups. She whinnied at the extra weight and I shushed her gently.

Duke Colsarne drew his bastard sword - a long, vicious weapon, with the pommel shaped into an eagle's grasping claw. Everyone who could still sit on a horse and fight mounted up and the gate was fully opened.

"Ready?" Colsarne's eyes twinkled with vigour, and he gave us a wicked smile. "Good. NOW LET'S KILL THE BASTARDS!"

The ground outside the gate was a swirled mess of mud and viscera, but we roared and charged through, hooves churning the earth to ruin. Reed broke into a gallop, teeth crunching against the bit as we spilled out of the gate like shit through a goat. Men spread out, advancing as quickly as they could, eager to wet their blades in the open field. The wind whipped my face and stung my eyes, and I drew my sword, howling with bloodlust.

Duke Colsarne rode at the head of the army, driving his charger hard enough to bloody its flanks. Decroix was beside him, with Quentin clinging to his gelding for dear life.

Riding swords to the wind, we thundered into the enemy. We were few in number, but the impact sent chaos through their ranks. Men scattered before us and I reared Reed up, her hooves cracking open a man's jaw, sending him sprawling in pain.

Turn. Strike. And, above all: keep moving.

I wheeled Reed round and slashed downwards with the momentum. Squeezing my thighs, she stepped sideways, and I parried a halberd then lunged, leaning in the saddle to stab at the halberdier's face. I righted myself and swept round, using the bulk of the horse to smash footmen aside.

"Keep moving, keep moving . . ." I muttered. There were shouts all around us, and arrows and bolts flew wildly. Our men were in range, and I thanked Oswald that Rouberte had trained them well enough to not shoot us up the arse.

Their horns and banner blazed away, trying to rally and instinctively we went to stop them. "Don't let them have the chance. Don't let them decide what's going to happen. That's you're prerogative."

I cursed under my breath as five spears closed in on me, forcing me back. I blocked a clumsy thrust and the shaft ran against my gorget. Reed cried out, eyes wild, and I spurred her on, riding through the ranks of Decare's infantry and hacking blindly into them.

The air bloomed with wild shouts and the clash of steel. I turned and saw that, after what felt like an age, our men on foot had finally caught up. I fell back to catch my breath and watched Marl's troops carve into them, reaping an act of bloody revenge for their fallen captain.

I caught a glimpse of Simon's face, red with rage and fury. He punched with the edge of his shield and gutted a man from below as he reeled backwards. Simon pushed through, followed by his fellows, and in a handful of heartbeats the enemy's rear ranks were broken into pockets and surrounded, to be torn to pieces like fresh meat to a dog. We kept pushing them, our horsemen routing them any time they tried to organise, as the forces of Cassioc stabbed and slashed at the royal army.

I heard an unintelligible howl of fury behind me and wheeled Reed round to see Duke Decare hacking a swathe through the men around him.

"I AM ALIVE, YOU STUPID BASTARDS!" His red and black tabard was streaked with mud, and there were deep dents across his chest and shoulders. He ripped off his helmet and hurled it to the ground. A cheer rose from the enemy as he severed the head from a Colsarne swordsman, and rode along the line, barking out orders to hold their ground. At last, a proper line was formed; a solid wall of spears and bills to repel attackers and slaughter any assailant who would dare to step in range.

As he turned to ride along the line, our eyes met. Decare's lips twisted into a snarl and he took up a lance, spurring his horse towards me at full tilt. I sheathed my sword and snatched up a spear from the ground, leaning far in the saddle. I urged Reed on, forcing her into a hard gallop.

Couching the spear, we closed the last few yards, horses foaming. I braced myself for the impact, and for just a moment I saw him smile before he lurched to the side, burying his lance deep into Reed's chest.

Reed pitched forward, screaming, and I tried to throw myself from the saddle, but my left sabaton hung in the stirrup and I was dragged to the ground, my leg pinned tightly under her bulk. Her hooves lashed out and she flailed, blind with pain and terror. Reed's blood sprayed hot and wet, pooling down and soaking me through my armour. She looked at me in confusion and thrashed her head from side to side, thumping into the ground. Her mane was matted with mud and the embedded shaft wrenched from side to side in the struggle.

"Easy girl!" I tried to calm her, but she was wild with fear and pain. I pulled my left foot free of the stirrup but the bulk of the horse pinned me into the mud.

"Oh, fuck." I snarled. A hard looking axeman had spotted me and sprinted over, eager to slit my throat and gain some plunder. I drew my sword awkwardly from its sheath and swung it back and forth, forcing him to step back. Reed's hooves stopped anyone coming the other way, but he'd kill me for certain on the ground.

He hacked down at the sword, then followed with his shield to pin my arm to the earth. He quickly chopped down on the breastplate and knocked the wind from me, but the steel was strong and didn't cave in too much. My next breath hurt, a sharp pinch that screamed of at least one broken rib.

He pulled back and aimed his axe at my neck before it tumbled to the earth as a blade pushed through his gut.

"ULF! Are you alright?" I looked up into Simon's warty face.

"Stop asking stupid questions and get me out from here, you dozy bastard!" I shouted.

Simon pushed and grunted with the effort and I shuffled out awkwardly, limping badly from the weight. Reed looked up at me, eyes pleading, and I mercifully cut through her neck with an overhand blow to end her suffering. I stepped back as the ground slickened with blood.

I couldn't see as well then. The fighting all around made it impossible to tell who was gaining the upper hand. In the mud-smeared chaos, only the odd glimpse of red and black or regal gold could tell us who the enemy was.

"Right. With me!" Simon nodded and he followed me towards the rear ranks so I could see what the fuck is going on. His shield was scarred and splintering, so he'd clearly been in his fair share of the fighting but he moved with the energy of a man far younger than me. I snatched up a wineskin, cutting the strap free from a dead soldier and drained it before casting it aside.

I scanned the battle lines, gritting my teeth in annoyance. "Simon! Can you see him?"

"See who?"

I tried not to punch him. "The cunt who killed my brother and my horse!" I yelled.

Simon's eyes darted nervously, looking across the sea of bodies. A stalemate, neither side giving nor gaining ground. "There!" he shouted.

I drew in my breath as much as my bruised chest will allow, ignoring the pain in my ribs. "WINDOR DECARE!" I yelled. "You and I have unfinished business! For the honour of the Cleansing Flame and in the name of Oswald, I command you! Turn and face me!"

Only cunts make speeches in the middle of battle, but it worked. He turned his horse and charged towards me, scattering all before him. I raised my sword to an oxen's horn, ready to guard his blow from above.

Suddenly, a rider barged into his flank, leaping like an acrobat and wrestling the duke from the saddle. Decare rolled with the impact and came up on his feet. We rushed towards them as quickly as we could manage, Simon easily overtaking me.

The stranger pulled out a short sword and darted in with a fencer's thrust. Decare turned it aside with contemptuous ease and pressed the attack with strong blows from above, left to right. The pain in my side stopped me and I bent over, gasping for air. There was a scream of agony and I looked up to see the rider gasping with horror at the bloody stumps where his hands once were.

"QUENTIN!" Simon hurled himself forward, leading with his shield and forcing it under Decare's armpit, binding his sword.

Quentin fell the ground, his face white as a shroud. I sprinted forward, gripping my sword tightly to ward away the pain.

"Ulf! At last!" Decare gave a cruel smile and stamped down hard on Simon's instep, sending him tumbling to the earth. I leapt forward and pushed my sword up, our blades clashing near the hilts.

I circled Decare, getting him away from Simon and drawing him towards me. "Get Quentin to a healer! Now!"

"But-"

Brigandine

"Fuck off, Simon!" I roared. I brought my sword into the plough, point out and upwards. Slowly, Decare smirked and brought his own weapon up to the roof for a downwards strike.

Neither of us said a word. No point. He struck and I barely managed a weak block. He was old, but strong as a bull and he wanted to kill me just as much as I wanted to kill him. He aimed thrusts to my left side, testing and pushing my defences. Blow after blow fell, the steel biting and notching at the impact. The fighting on the wall and the blow from the axeman had weakened me, leaving me sluggish and feeble.

He circled round to the right, forcing me to use my bad leg and he then bound our swords, pushing upwards with the strength in his arms and back. I forced my feet into the dirt but I could feel myself slipping and it wouldn't be long before he had me on the ground and at his mercy. My wrists ached, burning with effort. Between our blades, I saw his face. That smug grin. Those cold eyes.

So, I headbutted him.

I drove my forehead forward with all my might, cracking him on the bridge of the nose. He staggered back, reeling from the impact with blood dripping from his nostrils. I stepped in, and our sword clashed again. His face was swollen with rage and he roared with each strike, our blades biting deeply into each other. I grinned at him and raised my sword high.

It happened slowly. In his anger, he took the bait and lunged forward. I stepped to him and trapped his forearm under my armpit, the metal of our armour clanging together. I smashed my pommel into his face like a hammer, sending shards of teeth down his throat. He swung at me with his off-hand and the blow crashed off my head, my skull ringing. I gripped him tighter, turning my hip to keep him locked before dropping my sword and drawing my dagger, stabbing through his mail under the arm. I stabbed him again in the bicep, and the arm went limp at his side before I swept his legs from under him, tossing him over my hip.

He landed in a pile of tattered cloth, smeared with his own blood. I straddled him and punched him in the face. The first blow shattered his jaw, then another caved in an eye socket, leaving a pulpy mess. Decare tried to ward away the blows, but my gauntleted fist crashed down like a thunderbolt.

I stood up, shaking and panting. He tried to say something, but I couldn't understand him, and didn't care to

After a hard lungful of air, I stooped down for my sword, my torso and leg screaming at me with every movement.

"Windor," I panted, "do you remember . . . do you remember how my brother died?"

Through one good eye, I could see the terror dawn on him. He kicked out with his leg, but I pushed past, forcing the tip of my sword under his faulds and beneath the mail skirt. I felt something soft so I kept pushing, stirring the hilt from side to side. He started screaming. No words, just agony, and I smelt the reek of shit and piss pouring off him and filling my nose.

I pulled out my sword after he stopped moving and gazed for a moment at the mangled corpse before hacking at the neck, the last few tiny strands of flesh and gristle snapping as I wrenched the head free. I stabbed my blade into the earth, and with every last ounce of strength, hurled the gory trophy into the enemy lines, watching it bounce and roll into Decare's own men.

Panic spread like a fire and with a sweeping wave, they started to rout. Decroix rallied our forces, and we cheered ourselves hoarse as the Queen's guard and the surviving men of House Decare broke ranks and fled to the south-west to Riben. I couldn't see the queen or Sellor, and I didn't know what they had planned, but for the moment the field was ours.

"Ulf."

I turned around and see Siffisante smirking at me from the back of a black gelding. She was well dressed in fine furs and wools, but she still looked like an actor. Someone pretending in the role. The problem was, she was very, very good at it.

"Siffisante."

"It wasn't too hard, you know." She simpered as I tried to get my breath back. She gestured at Azrael's men, whooping with joy and already stripping and looting the dead.

I rolled my eyes. "Really? Turning up at the exact right moment to break a siege, commanding hundreds of men, and keeping that C'targian bastard in line? That wasn't too hard?"

She shrugged. "Well, not for me at least. There were hundreds of men in Carstock looking to redeem themselves, all of them trained fighters. I had access to fresh ash as strong as old yew. You decided to shatter their right thumbs, but you don't need a thumb to nock an arrow, so a unit of archers was the obvious choice. Azrael's bandits and Johan's billmen did help as well, though, bless their souls."

"Why?"

"Why what?"

"Why did you come? Why not stay in Carstock or just fuck off somewhere?"

She wrinkled her nose. "Isn't it obvious? Lady Alexia. I'm her lady in waiting. House Fairbourne is dying and so is that bitch Queen Karidine. Lady Alexia is going to take the land of Ashenfell for her own. And I intend to be by her side while she does it."

"How very manipulative of you."

She smiled. "Thank you, Ulf. That's the nicest thing you've ever said to me. But if you'll excuse me, Lord Azrael Bordane has a victory speech to make to his men."

Siffisante rode off to join her lover, and not for the first time I daydreamed about killing her.

I spotted a gelding, it's flanks smeared with mud. "Decroix!" I waved my arms desperately, trying to get his attention until he noticed and rode over.

Decroix looked around, desperately hoping to see his brother walking and well instead of among the managed corpses. "Ulf, I saw Quentin's horse running free, where is he?"

I swallowed hard and fumbled with my gorget, desperate to free myself. The metal felt hot now. Tight and imprisoning. The air was cold on my face and I could feel myself shaking.

"Ulf?" Decroix looked into my eyes and I saw the fear.

"He's with Simon." I said, and Decroix breathed an exhausted sigh of relief.

Then I told him why.

Decroix dismounted and cried and I held him close, the horrid reek of a battlefield melding with the tang of sweat from our bodies.

"Where is Duke Colsarne?" I managed. "He should have been here!"

He told me why.

Chapter 34: What It Means To Be a Knight

"*Wake up. Come on Ulf.*"

My face is on fire. I move my hand to my cheek, but someone gently pushes it down.

"*Don't touch it. Stay still if you can.*"

My mouth is full of blood. "Where . . . what?" *The voice is slurred and I can smell acrid smoke, even beyond the metallic tinge of blood in my throat.*

Sellor is there. He's sitting beside the bed. A cot in a tent. Other things come into focus. Low moans punctuated with screaming. There's another man next to me; dead or unconscious, I cannot tell. "You are fine Ulf. The taint in Craftvale is no more. We are victorious, praise be to Oswald."

"TARAN!" *The stitches in my face send a jolt of agony and I bite down hard against the pain.*

"Shhh! Stop that. Ulf, Sir Taran is dead. He died like a hero and brought enough time for Sir Ulric and his men to drive back the shoggoth and rout the enemy. All that was left of them was put to fire and sword."

I'm not listening. Everything feels numb. Like the bite of midwinter on bare skin.

"You fought bravely, Ulf. I've spoken to the others, and they all agree." *His voice is kind and soft. He holds my hand in his liver-spotted paw and looks into my eyes.* "You saved Sir Ichabod's life. He told me that much. He's injured, badly. After you fainted, there was more fighting and he was gravely wounded. But that was the first thing he told me." He smiles. "Two swordsmen! You did well Ulf. When the dead are buried and mourned, you are to be knighted."

I look at him. His grey eyes bore into me, searching.

"Come Ulf, let us pray togeth-"

"You let him die." I whisper. "We could have saved him, but they didn't let me. They held me down and we watched him die."

The kindly smile vanishes and a pained look spreads across the Patriarch's face. "Ulf, you have to understand. The honour of single combat. You know this. Your brother knew the risks and he accepted them. He lived and died a man of honour."

"He died in agony with a spike up his arse!" I snarl, forcing myself to sit up.

"Ulf." He says slowly. "Do not disparage his memory. Your brother was a great knight and will be missed by us all."

"You were the ones who fucked him over!" My face is bathed in pain as one of the stitches pops free, blood oozing down my neck.

Sellor frowns. "Do you dare to think you were the only one who lost someone today, boy? Sir Cain Bairflute lies dead. Sir Ichabod of Cassioc will never recover from his wounds and will live his life as a cripple. I have known all three men since they were boys, as I have over a hundred others who lie dead. They died with honour, Ulf. For the Order!"

"Fuck you."

"What?"

"Fuck you! Fuck your honour, and fuck the Order!" I shout, forcing myself out of bed. The stitches are loose now, my face flapping horribly. I stagger for a moment but hold my footing. My sword is at the bottom on the bed and I lunge for it, drawing the blade, point to his throat.

He glares at me, the corner of his mouth quivering with anger. "You dare to hold a blade to the Patriarch of this Order? How quickly you have cast aside everything your brother stood for."

I breathe heavily. My arm is shaking.

"PATRIARCH!"

There is a clang and my sword is knocked to the ground. Ulric is there, standing between us, a look of anger and confusion. I didn't notice him enter.

"Ulf! What insanity grips you? I came to see how you were and I find you like this! Sellor, is this sword-madness?"

I shake my head, the gory mess of my face dripping freely. "I meant every word." I slur.

"You have betrayed what we have stood for, Ulf. I am glad your brother is dead and not able to see this. Leave us. Find your place in the world, whatever that may be. But it will never be with the Order. Now, go."

I've been walking for hours now. It's cold. Every step is painful. Every bruise, every rent and tear in my skin stings. The wind whips at my face, now a dull throbbing and the air chills my exposed teeth.

I stop. Half sitting, half falling into a hedgerow. I can still see the plumes of smoke from the ruins of Craftvale, twisting and stabbing up into the sky. I throw down the sack full of armour and take off my sword. The scabbard is filthy, caked with mud and gore. With the hem of my tunic, I scrub at it uselessly before throwing it down, hearing the pommel clatter against the road.

Decroix came out to meet me. His eyes were puffed and bloodshot. He hadn't slept yet, I knew that. If he didn't soon, he'd fall down dead. Decroix closed the door behind me and I walked over to the bed.

He was still pale. There was a half-eaten plate of something on a table and the bandages were fresh, but I could still smell the tang of iron in the room from a pile of bloody dressings.

"How are you?"

Quentin opened his eyes and looked up at me. His face had changed so much. Not just the aging from the magic at Scandar, but from what we had seen and done together. Decroix had made the hard decisions and tidied up the messes, but his brother had felt it every much as him.

"I'll be honest, Ulf. Pretty shit."

I smiled weakly and tried to force my face to stay still.

"Duke Colsarne was right. I should have gone for the war sword. To be fair, at least now I don't have to worry about what type of sword to use ever again."

"Is there anything I can do for you? Anything I can get you?"

"There is actually. I need a book. Can you find it for me?"

"What is it-"

"It's called, 'How To Be a Wrestler With No Hands.'"

He tried to smile but tears started to flow from his eyes and I shuffled backwards.

"Or, if you can't find that one, have a look for 'How To Hold a Woman's Tits With No Hands'. Or 'How To Ride a Horse With No Hands.' Or-"

He broke down in tears. Huge sobs of pain and anger. He brought up his stumps to his face before throwing them back down onto the bed with a howl of grief.

I opened and closed my mouth once before I rushed out of the room.

Simon stood waiting for me downstairs. He escorted me to the palace to speak with Duke Colsarne. My heart sank and churned. I knew this would happen, but it was still horrible.

Lady Alexia was there when we arrived, her eyes just as red as Decroix's. She kissed her father on the forehead and adjusted a pillow before leaving us alone together.

"Good afternoon, Ulf. It is very kind of you to come."

"Yes, my lord."

He shuffled up in the bed, forcing himself to sit up and wincing with the effort. His hand moved to the bandaged wound around his abdomen. I met his gaze and he shook his head in disappointment.

"Honestly. Of all the bloody ways to go." He sighed. "I didn't even get a chance to wet my sword." Duke Colsarne smiled a little. "Not that the ballads will say that, obviously."

I nodded. I'd heard a few lines, and it was good stuff so far. Wasting no time, Lady Alexia had been commissioning the most pretentious bards and poets in the city to come up with something suitably dramatic.

He moaned. "I mean, a crossbow! I mean no disrespect to Rouberte and his lot, but come on. A bloody crossbow." He shook his head and gestured to a goblet and jug. I poured out a measure and held it out to him. He smacked his lips and sighed contentedly.

"How are my sons?"

I frowned and swallowed hard. "Well, my lord. They are both well."

He sighed and slumped his shoulders. "You are an awful liar, Ulf of Banrillar. Remember that."

"Yes, lord."

"Sir Ulf of Banrillar, now." He mused. "Ichabod wants to make it official, obviously. But thank you, Ulf. I do mean that. I have but two dying regrets. The first of which is that I didn't see you kill that bastard Decare, and the second one being hit by that crossbow bolt. Apart from that, I feel like I've had a good life."

He lay there dying. The greatest mind in all of Ashenfell laid low by a piece of wood and metal.

"Is there . . . anything you need, lord? Anything you wish, I will do as you ask."

Duke Colsarne sighed. "And that, Ulf, is precisely why I don't have to ask you to do anything. You know what we face. You know the consequences if we fail. Guard my daughter, Ulf. Offer her protection and council in the wars to come."

He took about a week to die.

The duke asked for me a few more times. Mad and rambling with fever. I stood by his bed and listened to his ravings, nodding along and mopping his brow.

The funeral was nothing short of spectacular. Every man, woman and child in Cassioc stood in the streets to watch the gilded coffin pass by. Most of them wore eagles; small woollen badges stuck to the breast in mourning for a man they did not know, and whose corpse they would have gladly pelted with dog shit if he'd lost the battle.

But he hadn't. He had won, and the money Lady Alexia liberated from the royal treasury was used well. The priest's words at the service even manage to stir a grim bastard like me into shedding a tear.

Every tavern in the city had the bar brought up. From the finest wine bars to the shittiest dives, they have all taken coin from Lady Alexia to drink to her father's memory. Decroix was with Quentin, so Simon and I were alone in the corner of some dingy inn.

Simon raised a tankard. "To the duke." he said softly.

I drained the rest of my ale and wiped my mouth with the back of my hand. "Right. You will fetch. You will carry. You will muck out stables. You will clean the shit out of my armour and keep my weapons as shiny as a whore's twat."

"I'm sorry?"

I rolled my eyes. "I need a squire, Simon. You saved my life. You saved Quentin's life. And you're not a bad fighter. If we work on a few things and give you a bit of a polish, you might be half decent."

"So, I'd be your squire? Training to be a knight?"

I sighed. "Yes, Simon. You'd be a squire. In exchange for putting up with my crap, I will teach you how to ride, how to hunt, and how to recite wanky poetry. I will lecture you on morality until your arse falls off from boredom, and, best of all, I will teach you every single dirty fucking trick I know to help you kill people. So, what do you think?"

Simon nodded eagerly, and I couldn't help but smile. I stood up and gestured for him to do the same.

I placed my hands on his shoulders. "By the name of Oswald the Fierce, I, Sir Ulf of Banrillar, name Simon of Colsarne to be my squire."

"Thank you, Ulf." Simon looked up to me and beamed.

"Right, first lesson."

I raised my knee and cracked him as hard as I could in the balls. He doubled up, retching and gasping for air.

"Remember this: anyone who wears full plate armour is a cunt."

END

Acknowledgement

Thank you for reading Brigandine. Your support and help genuinely means the world to me.

If you have time, I'd really appreciate a review, or let your friends know about the book.

If you'd like to stay updated about my writing and other books, please give me a follow on Facebook or twitter.

facebook.com/JackShannonAuthor

twitter.com/Jack_Shannon

All the best,

-Jack

Printed in Great Britain
by Amazon